it takes a

VILLA

it takes a
VILLA

USA TODAY BESTSELLING AUTHOR
KILBY BLADES

This book is a work of fiction. Names, characters, places, and incidents are the product of the author's imagination or are used fictitiously. Any resemblance to actual events, locales, or persons, living or dead, is coincidental.

Entangled Publishing, LLC
10940 S Parker Road
Suite 327
Parker, CO 80134
Visit our website at www.entangledpublishing.com.

Amara is an imprint of Entangled Publishing, LLC.

Edited by Liz Pelletier and Lydia Sharp
Cover design by Elizabeth Turner Stokes
Cover art by nadtochiy/Shutterstock,
pixel creator, designclub
Interior design by Toni Kerr

Print ISBN 978-1-64937-208-6
ebook ISBN 978-1-64937-221-5

Manufactured in the United States of America

First Edition June 2022

MORE ROMANCE FROM
KILBY BLADES

Looks Good on Paper
The Secret Ingredient
Spooning Leads to Forking
Forrest for the Trees

To my mother, who loved Italy most of all.

AUTHOR'S NOTE

This story is set on Italy's Amalfi Coast, one of my favorite places to travel. The Campania region is vibrant—rich in culture, offering the best of land and sea. Though some of the details in this book are fictionalized (including the names of places—Zavona, Cocenza, and Nanca are fictional towns), I aimed to capture the magic of the region. I hope you enjoy!

At Entangled, we want our readers to be well-informed. If you would like to know if this book contains any elements that might be of concern for you, please check the back of the book for details.

CHAPTER ONE

Natalie Malone had arrived so late the night before, she hadn't really seen the villa. In the dark, she'd strained and craned and blinked to take it in. The headlights of the taxi had flashed over it too quickly as it sped up the gravel driveway. Once she was alone, her phone light hadn't been enough to illuminate all of the villa's hulking form.

Still, she'd stood for minutes in the cool night air, taking in its vague silhouette, searching for recognizable lines based on the photos she'd studied so hard. Anticlimactic as it was, she had traveled all night and day for this, a glimpse of her future against the starry, moonless sky.

Not one to take chances, she'd arrived three hours early for her first flight, Chicago to JFK, then a red-eye to Rome via Amsterdam. The train from Rome to Salerno had taken four and a half hours. Then another two on the express bus from Salerno to Positano. Her final leg was a quick backtrack south in a taxi—Positano to Zavona, on the outskirts of which sat her house.

When she awoke, hours later, to the delighted recollection that she was finally here, her second thought was of the dawning light that would let her see the villa. Her third thought, which ought to have been about how quickly she could get her clothes on, was cut short by—

Is that a chicken?

She rubbed her eyes open and surveyed the rest of the garage, where she would live until the villa was habitable. Beyond an old desk and the lamp that sat on top of the mini fridge next to her cot in the corner, the space was crowded and smelled faintly of gasoline.

And chickens.

Natalie wasn't sure what live chickens smelled like, but the garage didn't smell fresh—not as if animals lived there, but musty from disuse. Worse than the presence of the small beast that strutted importantly near the garage doors was seeing the broken board in the door it had gotten in through, and not knowing how long it had been there watching her sleep.

This one had to be a hen. A rooster would have had the decency to announce himself—to give a courtesy *cock-a-doodle-doo*. But this hen seemed aimless, parading and clucking, regarding Natalie only halfway.

"Shoo!"

The hand that drew her covers to herself in fright emerged long enough to wave the hen away. Impervious, it kept on with its pecking and strutting. Natalie made a mental note of something to look up when she found an internet café. "How to intimidate a chicken" was at the top of her list.

Maybe I should spring for a hotel. Just until I relocate the hen.

But a lack of lodging in Zavona was the very circumstance that gave her plan a shot. This place—*her* place—had been it. The larger towns miles up the coast had honest-to-goodness hotels. But Zavona had only ever had this *pensione*, the Italian equivalent of a B&B.

In its former life, it had been known as Pensione Benone, which translated to "very good inn." She had yet to decide what she would name it, but she liked the idea of quality. Natalie may have been frugal, but she didn't want a mediocre *pensione*, or a mediocre anything. She wanted to restore it to its former glory.

The half of her brain not caught up in trying to stare down the unflappable bird busied itself imagining what it would take to build a chicken coop and recoup her investment in eggs. The hen waddled back through the open hole a minute into Natalie's imaginings.

It was all she needed to get out of bed and begin her morning, to finally relish the moment she'd awaited. The moment she would lay eyes on her villa.

My villa.

Even as she stood on property that belonged to her, that fact was hard to believe. She had never owned much, apart from her art supplies and whatever clothes fit. She was good with money—though most of what she'd earned had gone to her car lease and to rent and student loans and the cheap meals she and Gram had eaten for two years straight. There had been no frills, only saving…for this.

The night before, she'd stripped off her travel clothes—yoga pants and a bulky sweatshirt to combat the cold of planes and trains. Now that she was here, she wouldn't need anything heavy. It would be all balmy temperatures and briny air no matter the time of day. Such was August on the Amalfi Coast.

I'll need a dresser, she mused when she went to unzip the largest of her three bags. She'd only brought the essentials—summer clothes, specialty art supplies, and six bottles of her favorite Kentucky bourbon. Two more cases of the bourbon and the rest of her worldly possessions were on a cargo ship that could take months to arrive.

The garage doors had to be opened manually and pushed out to each side. No remote controls or slider track overhead. It was old-fashioned, but wasn't that part of its charm? Above a built-in worktable were tools that still hung on their pegs. Rusty hedge clippers sat inside a wheelbarrow, and a saw bench had gathered a thick coating of dust. An item draped in canvas had to be a motorbike. In the middle of all the chaos was an old lawn mower, frozen in time and neglected. But it was hers, and she was completely in love.

That's not love. This is love.

She stopped pushing the door, halting to take it in. Not a single one of the twenty-seven preview pictures online had done the villa justice. Even as it looked now, with its walls overgrown, half covered in some leafy vine that crawled up the sides, at three stories high, it stood grand.

The eighteenth-century villa was a classic example of Renaissance style, a fact she knew because of Gram, Urbana's most dedicated architecture geek before she got sick. If Gram were here now, she would go on about the villa's detail—things like the columns in the recessed entryway, the lighter contrast stone on the quoins, and the entablature beneath shallow eaves. Natalie choked up for the third time since she'd left home. Gram should have lived to see this.

She stepped forward at the same time her fingers rose to her neck in search of the chain that held the key she only ever took off to shower. It had been sent by the Economic Development Council, along with her deed. Or rather, her provisional deed. To own it in full, she first had to restore the property.

The garage was on the north end of the house, at the end of a long driveway that ran behind the villa and to a main lot in the front. This private lane delineated the back side of the main building from the gardens and the pool. The easiest way to enter the main building from where she stood at the garage was to cross the side courtyard and enter through the kitchen. But Natalie wanted the full experience of seeing her house for the first time. She wanted to walk through her front door.

Practically skipping down the shaded lane, she ignored the overgrown garden and the loud crunching of driveway gravel beneath her feet. When it came time to round the corner of the building, she cut across the front lawn. She took deliberate steps with high knees to wade through the tall grasses and get to the steps. Breathless with anticipation, she finally reached the stone archway that encased the double-knobbed, blue-painted front door.

After turning her key in the tight, ancient lock, Natalie gave a firm shoulder push. The door creaked open, giving her the first glimpse of the entryway she had longed to see. The two-story ceiling was grander than it had seemed through a camera lens. A staircase in the middle was a curved beauty of rare white marble, with wrought-iron railings that flared artistically at the base. It had an elegance that commanded the rest of the space to rise to the occasion—or, at least it would after it underwent some repairs. A chandelier had fallen from the vaulted ceiling of the second story, ruining two of the steps and part of the entryway floor.

Natalie strolled left, toward rooms that were western-facing—a spacious sitting room, a cozy library, and a rustic dining room all in a row. Each had arched glass doors to the outside that stretched much higher than her head. When opened outward, these would flow elegantly to the loggia, which led to expansive patios that would be perfect for taking in the sun and the seascape—the Gulf of Salerno, the Tyrrhenian Sea, and the Mediterranean beyond.

These would be the preferred common areas—the spaces where guests would want to spend their time. No matter how beautiful her restoration of the interior promised to be, it was hard to beat the outdoor views. The villa had been built in a way that made all the second-floor guest rooms ocean-facing. Natalie stood on the western lawn, using her hand as a sun visor as she looked up at the wrought-iron guest-room balconies from outside, when a masculine voice cut through her thoughts.

"Hello?"

The owner of the voice sounded American. She turned in the direction from which it had come. The shorter of the two approaching men seemed to corroborate this suspicion. He was beefy, wearing jeans and a baseball cap and a faded T-shirt that read: *You might be a farm boy if…*

"Hello— *Ciao*." She remembered to use the standard Italian greeting at the last instant.

The farm boy's thumbs were hooked in his pockets, and he walked with a sort of ease. He had light—nearly clear—blue eyes. It was harder to guess at the nationality of his companion. Smart blue glasses framed dark-brown eyes that went with coiffed hair of a similar hue. He wore a button-down shirt and leather sandals with white jeans. His arms held a wide wicker basket that was full of something she couldn't quite see.

"I am Jorge from Argentina," the one wearing glasses said.

"And I'm Chris from Texas." The farm boy gave a little wave.

"And we are your welcoming committee!" Jorge practically trembled with glee as they came near.

Natalie startled at his exuberance. She hadn't had her coffee yet, and Jorge seemed to be at least five cups in.

"We brought you a basket," Chris said as Jorge held it out to her. "We heard you were coming in last night. Thought you might like to settle in."

"Thank you. I'm Natalie, nice to meet you both."

Chris jutted his chin toward the villa. "Looks like a beauty of a beast."

No sooner did she accept the basket than Jorge stepped past her, his chin tipped upward in appraisal. "This is much bigger than Ellie's place…"

"What's the square footage on this thing?" Chris slid all of his fingers into his pockets.

"Sixteen thousand square feet inside and just over three acres of land."

Jorge let out a whistle. "And all of this is just for you?"

"No." She didn't mention Gram. "The villa will be my business. I'll open it as a *pensione* in six months' time."

Chris and Jorge shared a knowing look, each raising their eyebrows at the same time. It was so in sync, Natalie wondered if they were a couple.

"Six months isn't enough," Chris said with a note of apology.

Natalie lifted her chin. "It is if I work on it full-time."

Chris and Jorge shared another concerned look but said nothing.

"Six months is all they give us," she said.

Chris and Jorge looked at each other again, then looked at her. "We know."

"That's why we do our own welcome basket," Chris continued. "To help people with their time."

Natalie had questions—lots of questions—but the basket was enormous and it was starting to feel heavy in her arms.

"Do you mind if we…" She motioned as best as she could to the garage. "All I have right now is a mini fridge. I can't imagine how I'll keep all of this cold."

Jorge abandoned his villa-gazing to throw her a pointed look. "Refrigeration is a lie."

Natalie was too baffled for intelligent speech.

"This is propaganda from the United States," Jorge continued. "Everything in this basket can be left out."

"But the eggs…" she stammered.

Jorge slung a casual arm around her and kept them going toward her garage. There were at least half a dozen eggs—a mix of brown and white—in a tiny wire basket. There were also two loaves of bread, an array of fruits, several small packages of cheese, and three small, uncut logs of cured meat.

"These are not commercially produced eggs." Jorge looked disgusted by the notion. "They do not come from a factory. They come from a local farm. You can leave these eggs out. Yes?"

Natalie swung an alarmed gaze to Chris, who only offered a shrug. "Welcome to Italy. We do things different here."

She blinked, fully resolved that she was going to refrigerate the eggs and the cheese and the meat and every last item that the US FDA recommended, even if it took up every inch of real estate in her tiny fridge.

"I take it the EDC already gave you your list of recommended vendors?" Chris's gaze was on Natalie as he waited for her to lead them. Jorge's gaze was already taking stock of the garage.

"It was sitting on my bed when I got here."

"Do you have a pen?"

"Somewhere," she murmured, trying to see past the basket in her arms. Finding something to write with would require digging deep into her backpack.

Jorge located the photocopied list that had been printed on green paper and left by the EDC. He took the pen that Chris had spontaneously produced from somewhere and began crossing off names.

"Not all the vendors they recommend are good," Chris explained. "There's what they tell you, and then there's the truth."

"Trust me," Jorge insisted. "I am saving you twenty thousand dollars and many tears."

Natalie craned her neck to see what he was crossing out. She didn't like the idea of obscuring information but kept quiet. Natalie did not like confrontation. And besides, Jorge had brought her cheese.

"There's other things you ought to know about. Things they won't tell you in that packet." Chris jutted his chin toward Jorge as he worked. "Like that we get together and talk."

"Who is we?"

"Some of the folks in the program. I know you're still settling in, but it'd be good for you to meet some people. To find out the real deal."

As opposed to the fake deal?

This was a lot to take in. Chris and Jorge made program infrastructure sound grave.

"When's the next time you all are getting together?"

Jorge put a cap on his pen and handed me the paper. "We meet at Café Ludo on Wednesdays at eleven a.m."

CHAPTER TWO

"I cannot believe it. You've saved my life!" Signora Sanguigna said after Pietro handed her the paper. The legal authorization she held was a grand affair. It was printed on the official letterhead of the republic. The national emblem was drawn in vivid color, the green of its branches bright, the rich reds forming the ribbon and the border of the star.

"Let's hope your life didn't depend on the town's recertification," Pietro said. Zavona had to be reconfirmed as an official municipality each year. Not having the certification letter on file by August first meant a potential freeze on the town's bank accounts, which would mean a huge headache for Signora Sanguigna.

Pietro put down his leather satchel, then settled into a nearby chair. They had both arrived in the same conference room to attend an Economic Development Council meeting. Signora Sanguigna tore her eyes off the letter and finally looked his way.

"You don't know how desperate I was becoming. I had plans to go to Naples, to personally knock on the regional controller's door. Seriously, Pietro. How did you do this? It's signed by the finance minister himself."

Pietro didn't mention the frank conversation he'd had with the man about certain people in his agency and the egregious dragging of feet depending on who was doing the asking. Getting things done quickly in Campania relied on favors and bribes. Signora Sanguigna may have been the best controller Zavona had ever seen, but the bureaucracy wasn't easy on women, so Pietro didn't mind cutting a little red tape.

"I do what I can," he responded simply. "It'll be easier to deal with Naples from here on out."

"Don't be surprised if my husband calls to thank you." Signora Sanguigna laughed. "The regional controller is all I complain about these days. Carlo has been cursing that asshole for weeks."

"Who is cursing me this time?"

The booming words were spoken by Alfonso Indelicato, who stepped through the door with a wide smile on his face, followed by his minions. Pietro's back stiffened, his face dropped, and his casual chatter with Signora Sanguigna went quiet. She nodded in greeting to the man who was well-liked but tricky to deal with when it came to the business of the town—the mayor...and Pietro's father.

"Are you starting in on me already, son?"

Signor Schivo and Signor Razzo smirked as they sat down at the table along with Alfonso. Everyone on the council knew how often Pietro and Alfonso were at odds. Pietro resented when his father treated their differences like a joke, patronizing him in front of the others. The things they disagreed on weren't petty. People's livelihoods were at stake.

"This meeting of the Zavona Economic Development Council will now come to order," Signor Schivo called as he passed out copies of a spiral-bound report. The cover read *Sognatori*, the name of the council's special program. Alfonso had led them into the business of selling dilapidated properties in town to foreigners for the reasonable price of a single euro. More than thirty properties had been included in the initial pool.

It had been eighteen months since the first group of *sognatori* had arrived and started renovations, and no one apart from Pietro wanted to admit that things weren't going well. The schedules the *sognatori* had to adhere to were too stringent. The funding requirement was too low. And there were too many incentives to cut the wrong corners.

"I see we have two new arrivals this month." Alfonso paged through the report.

"One residential, one commercial," Signor Schivo confirmed. "That brings our active projects to fifteen. We expect a short lull for the rest of the summer, with another five arriving at the end of fall. I don't think we'll see a problem getting to twenty. The program is very healthy at this point."

Sure, if "healthy" meant "terminally ill."

"Good." Alfonso gave a brief nod. "Then we can move on to the financials. Signora Sanguigna?"

"Wait." Pietro held up a hand. There was something Signor Schivo hadn't mentioned. Something big. "I disagree with this report."

Alfonso's eyes—the same green as his—narrowed in suspicion. "Disagree with what part?"

Pietro's gaze remained on Alfonso. "The report says that our numbers are up by two *sognatori*. But three *sognatori* left the program in July, which means that we're actually down by one."

Alfonso's eyes narrowed further. Signor Schivo

threw Pietro an equally hostile look.

But he couldn't just let this go.

"I've done my own calculations," Pietro continued. "Our attrition rate is thirty-five percent. More than one third of people who came here are leaving Italy, penniless and shattered."

"Say what you mean to say, Pitruzzu."

Pietro didn't like it when his father called him that—the diminutive version of his name. It reminded everyone in the room that Alfonso was the elder in a place where seniority mattered. And Pietro was merely the idealistic boy of yesteryear, who all the others had known as a child and still viewed as one.

"What I mean to say is that we can't solve problems if we refuse to admit they exist. We can say what we must to the regional council, to the national preservation society, and anybody else outside of here. But, at least to ourselves, to the ones who care most about Zavona, can we not openly admit that the program is failing?"

The room fell silent, without so much as the tap of a pen or the shuffle of a foot.

"Why are we so afraid to say it?" Pietro said.

No surprise, the first person to defend the opposite position was his father.

"We knew when we started that not every buyer would be a fit," Alfonso retorted. "We knew we would not see a perfect success rate from our pool of opportunities."

Pietro squeezed his pencil with a death grip. "Stop calling it an opportunity. Call it what it is—a revolving door."

A look from Signora Sanguigna told Pietro she half agreed. Signor Schivo and Signor Razzo, as usual, seemed to side with Alfonso.

"And what is our alternative?" his father asked in the same manner he did every time they had this argument.

"Private financing to restore the homes. We need an investor so the renovations can be done right."

Alfonso smiled with something that looked like pity.

"Pietro. My preservationist son…it is not only about the buildings. Your wealthy friends cannot engineer the restoration of the town."

Signor Razzo, who had been quiet until then, turned toward Pietro with gentle defiance. "Your father is right about this. It is not only a matter of restoring Zavona's beauty. It is a matter of rehabilitating the economy of the town. Even if every home were restored, it would not solve the problem of our commerce. With the program, the *sognatori* are required to start a business."

"Yes, we must think of commerce," Signor Schivo chimed in. "The buildings have been here for hundreds of years. They can wait a few hundred more."

Pietro clenched his jaw at the faulty logic he'd heard too many times. His father and his cronies believed too much in their own rhetoric. Among the 65 percent of *sognatori* who had "succeeded," some of those projects were barely scraping by.

"I remember the advertising brochure," Pietro said to the room. "I helped write it, back when I believed in what we were doing. But now, who are you trying to convince?"

"It is you who needs to do the convincing, Pietro. You are an architect, not a business person like all of us. If you want to convince us, then bring an investor. Until you have one, you will not speak of this again."

• • •

Unenthused by the idea of sharing a small metal box with people who had started to feel like rivals, Pietro opted out of taking the elevator in favor of the stairs. He had personally supervised the *municipio*'s restoration and maintenance. As he descended the marble staircase, Pietro thought of the bustle this city hall building had seen once upon a time.

A very long time ago, Pietro thought, pondering how many years it had been since the town had really thrived—since businesses were healthy because they were passed down through generations. Zavona's dilemma was a consequence of flight, the result of children who had left to seek their fortunes elsewhere in Italy or abroad. Parents were left with businesses and nobody to leave them to. In order to live closer to sons and daughters and grandchildren, some of the parents and grandparents had fled as well.

Zavona was still the best place that Pietro had ever known—uniquely beautiful, even if it had become a bit sleepy. Nowhere else in Italy could you find black-sand beaches, perfectly preserved *piazetta*, and hidden coves between the cliffs. Nowhere else could you find ancient villas and palazzos—some in poor repair, yes, but with such great potential. Nowhere else could you find seafood that was so flavorful, produce that was so fresh, and cheeses that weren't produced anywhere else in the world. Pietro wanted to see it vibrant again.

If only he could get the others to accept that this was not the path—that their plan needed adjustments if they expected it to work. That building businesses and attracting new residents would be easier if the town were restored. That historic-landmark status for more of their buildings—a virtual guarantee of renewed tourism—was within reach if they played their cards right with the restorations. If only his father weren't so stubborn, weren't so dismissive of Pietro's expertise. Arguing with his father made him feel like a child.

Pietro was twenty seconds from freedom when he stalked by the freestanding sign that read ADMINISTRATIVE OFFICE. The sign was double-sided with a heavy iron base. What he wanted to do was to keep walking—to hop on the back of his Vespa and clear his head with a long drive up the coast. But if he left without turning in the final piece of paperwork he needed to take possession of his latest restoration, he would only have to come back before the weekend.

Five minutes, he promised himself.

It would only take him five minutes to drop by the office, sign the paperwork, and leave with his deed. Five minutes closer to fully owning another dilapidated property. Five minutes closer to spending the entirety of his last big paycheck from a client restoration as easily as it had come. Five minutes from the only thing that made him feel better about the disaster that had been made of the program.

That he could guarantee at least a few gorgeous restorations by doing them himself.

Cutting a sharp right, Pietro made his way toward the north side of the building and trotted toward a side hall. The administrative offices were on the ground floor. A working office with bullpen-style desks was situated behind a high counter where applicants could stand. It was rare nowadays to encounter a line. Still, two rows of waiting benches stood in the middle of the floor where they always had. Pietro wasn't surprised to find them empty when he arrived.

The counter, however, was occupied. A woman stood straight, her back to him, as she spoke animatedly to the clerk. He had arrived a second too late to hear what the woman had said, but he saw the clerk's—Maria's—face.

"È *chiuso*." Maria spoke in very slow Italian, exasperation clear on her face. This was likely not the first time she had said these words. When the woman at the counter said nothing in response, Maria translated her own words into English. "It is closed."

"But—" The woman began to speak in English, then stopped short, tipping her head downward. Pietro quickly surmised from her frenzied tapping that she was on her phone. When she looked back up, she spoke in stilted Italian, and her accent gave her away as American.

"*Questa è l'agenzia dei permessi*?"

She was asking if this was the permit agency, then she pointed at a paper that sat between them on the counter. Maria looked more exasperated than ever when she pointed to a wall calendar, then turned back to the woman, the fingertips on each hand brought together in a purse.

"*Chiuso ad agosto.*" Maria had said it more slowly and more loudly this time.

She was telling the woman the permit office was closed in August.

"May I see?" Maria asked in English, pointing to the woman's phone.

The woman only shook her head and pointed to her paper again. "*Aperto*," she replied with just as much emphasis. "Open. It says so right here."

"Excuse me." Pietro took a step forward, casting an understanding look to Maria. He saw her frequently these days. He, too, had to get all the permits and clearances required to carry out his own restorations.

"May I help you?" He turned his attention to the woman, whose face he still hadn't seen, though he wanted to. She had dark hair and a plump bottom that filled out her jeans and flattered her curvy figure.

"Pietro, thank heavens," Maria finally said in Italian, seeming relieved. He took it as his cue to approach. As he did, he caught sight of the paper that sat on the counter between the women. It bore the insignia of the council.

"What's the problem?" he asked Maria in Italian. He had gathered that the woman was an owner in the *sognatori* program from her line of questioning and her general naivete. To be faced with such a person after having spent the past hour bickering with his father over the hopelessness of the program was the irony of ironies.

"This woman arrived yesterday," Maria explained, "and she's seeking her permit to begin construction. I have tried to tell her that the permit office is closed for the rest of August. She doesn't understand that I'm not the permit clerk but the zoning clerk. I tried to explain it to her, but she doesn't speak Italian."

"Madam." Pietro finally neared the counter and turned to face the woman. Whatever smooth words had been on the tip of his tongue stopped themselves short. He'd seen many men and women from all nationalities who had arrived in Zavona to be part of this program. But this woman didn't look like the others.

For starters, she was young—younger than a person should have been in order to afford the program buy-in of $75,000. It was likely that the woman in front of him was wealthy. She didn't dress expensively, but her skin was fresh and smooth; her hair was shiny and thick, a crown of curls tied up in a scarf and springing forth in such a way as he had never seen; this sort of effortless beauty was not surprising among the rich.

"Madam," he repeated, realizing he'd faltered. "You are here to acquire a building permit, no?"

Her brown eyes widened and became a bit brighter upon her response. "You speak English?"

Something about the hope in her voice—and her surprise at his capability—kept Pietro on the streak he'd started that morning with the council. He narrowed his eyes.

"You sound very surprised by this. I am now mildly insulted."

"I'm sorry. I didn't…"

"The Italians are a learned people, madam. We are more than the Tony Soprano and Don Corleone you see on American television. Trust me. You do not want to think about how bleak the world would be without the inventions of the Holy Roman Empire and the Renaissance."

Pietro made to turn back to Maria, to begin to bring resolution to things, when the woman finally spoke.

"I didn't mean to insult you," she said, her tone sounding genuinely apologetic, "or to insult the Italian people, and especially not anybody from Campania. You gave the world pizza and Sophia Loren. And Renato Caccioppoli."

Pietro blinked in disbelief. Most Italians—let alone Americans who barely spoke the language—had never even heard of Renato Caccioppoli, one of the most important mathematical thinkers of modern times. His work on differential equations had influenced understanding of structural engineering and architecture. Who was this woman?

"Pietro…" Maria trailed off, and her voice brought him back to task.

"The clerk has read your paper and understands that which you seek," he said. "She is telling you the permit office is closed. It is closed until the end of August."

"But this is the right address. I'm in the right building on the right floor. If the office is closed, how are all three of us standing right here?"

Pietro shook his head, taking a moment to think on how to explain something that was so basic to those who lived here. "The office is open for essential services. Behind her, these are empty desks." He motioned past Maria to the scattering of abandoned workstations behind the counter. "The person who you should talk to is on vacation."

The woman blinked in disbelief, shifting her eyes to the space behind the counter, then to Pietro, then back to Maria, as if to test the truth of the claim.

"*Vacanza*," Maria confirmed.

"Until the end of August?" the woman asked with alarm.

"*Sì*." Maria nodded again at the same time as Pietro said, "Yes."

"But this is a *government* building." The woman seemed truly perplexed. "Shouldn't government offices be open all year?"

"Yes," Pietro repeated. "For essential services."

"But building permits are an essential service."

Pietro gritted his teeth and reminded himself not to take out his irritation with his father on this innocent woman. "In Europe, many people go on vacation. This is very true in August. Many things are closed."

The tops of the woman's cheeks had begun to turn pink, a flush that accompanied the narrowing of eyes that cast downward to her bag. Frantically, she rifled through it and then pulled out a different paper bearing the insignia of the council.

"I am a member of the redevelopment program," she proclaimed, shoving the paper into Pietro's hands, as if he—and not Maria—were the official. "The letter told me to show up within sixty days. But now that I've arrived, don't I have a right to work on my house?"

Pietro held his tongue. Was there anything more American than entitlement? He wanted to say that she also had a right to do her research and even an obligation to know a little bit about the country where she had bought a house. The custom of summer vacationing wasn't exactly obscure knowledge.

"This clerk cannot help you," Pietro replied evenly. He motioned to Maria. "This is not the right person. Even if she wants to, she cannot give you what you need."

The woman, who only moments earlier had been filled with fervor as she waved her official paper, went from petulant to resigned. The shine of tears in her eyes gave him a sting of pity.

"But I only have six months to finish. If I can't start now, I'll only have five. I don't even have running water."

The woman looked between him and Maria with pleading eyes. His pity doubled as her voice came out hoarse and a bit choked. "What am I supposed to do until then?"

Pietro's jaw clenched—his senseless father and these senseless messes. Something inside him softened toward her as hope drained from her expression. He delivered the truth with what compassion he could muster. "Come back in September."

CHAPTER THREE

Plucking her new electric kettle out of its box wasn't as exciting as plucking it off the store shelf had been. Natalie had tried to be excited about the first purchase for her new house. In truth, she was more excited about her second purchase—the bottle of wine she'd lugged back up the ancient steps that served as the quickest route between her villa and the town center. She was ready to crack it open now—more like ready to down half of it—and it was barely even noon on her first day.

Looking at the electric kettle now, with its white plastic body and dangling cord, she wondered where to plug it in. The lamp by her bed was a testament to functioning electricity. Though, as a walk-through of the house had proven, it worked only in the garage. A five-minute perusal of the rest of the space drew her to the conclusion that the plug used by the lamp and mini fridge was the only one.

Power strip.

She wrote down the next item on her shopping list in the memo app on her phone, right below where she'd noted the need for a *heavy-duty flashlight* and *second power converter* that morning. Tomorrow, she would find the hardware store, but hitting the kitchenware store first had been the way to go. She'd needed dishes to eat from, a glass for wine, and a hot plate and pan to cook. Plus, hot water from the kettle meant she could shower.

You mean take a sponge bath.

Technically, the plumbing inside the villa worked. It would come in handy for the toilets. But no electricity meant no hot water. Ten minutes running the main faucet in the kitchen, and the cold water still ran brown. Even if it had run clear, Natalie would have remained cautious to use it. Better to have it tested first by a lab.

Among the range of odd items left in the garage, a wide-bottomed steel bucket would serve well as a basin. She would use bottled water to get the bucket—then her body—clean. After heating her water and scanning for hens, Natalie slipped her clothes off and washed up. It wasn't luxurious, but it was more hygiene than she'd had in the last thirty-six hours. She dried off with a pink towel from her suitcase that still smelled like fabric softener from home. Then she resolved to get to work.

Unofficially, of course.

She thought it with no small measure of anxiety. She'd gone directly to the permit office that morning because she liked to do things by the book, and because it always made sense to do the heavy construction first. She didn't want to discover a crooked foundation or an infrastructure problem at the tail end of a job. If there was one thing Natalie had learned from thousands of hours spent watching HGTV, you had to renovate from the inside out.

She wondered how she could do that without a work permit. Today being August fifth meant another twenty-six days of the permit office being closed. It was bad news—no, *devastating*—to already be experiencing a major setback, devastating no matter how beautiful the package the message had been delivered in.

The man who'd translated for her in the municipal office had been beautiful in a surprising sort of way. Surprising, because he didn't look the way Italian men looked on American TV. He wasn't dark-eyed, or dark-haired, or particularly olive-skinned. He was, however, quite sexy. That part of the stereotype, American television had gotten right.

"Sexy" might have been an understatement. The man—whose name she had never caught—carried an extraordinary and unique beauty. Everything about him was an exquisite light brown, as if every part of him had been kissed by the sun. His hair was lighter at the ends than at the roots, making Natalie wonder how dark it appeared in the winter season. His skin, which was smooth and tanned, had a light sprinkling of freckles on his nose and underscored the notion that he spent a good amount of time outdoors. The light stubble on his jaw matched the hair on top of his head but appeared a bit more golden.

And his face...

Natalie couldn't stop thinking of his face, which was somehow heart-shaped and angular at once. It had been a sight to behold. She might try her hand at drawing it all day and never be able to re-create the definition of his jaw. It might take her hours of intermittently staring into them and trying to mix her paints and get the blends just right without her ever capturing the exact hue of his dark, green eyes.

But I didn't like the way he looked at me.

Just thinking about it made her heart drop a

second time. She could have done without the way their brief interaction had made her feel—as if Natalie had arrived unprepared instead of operating from incomplete guidance. If there was one thing Natalie prided herself on, it was her ability to think through contingencies and risks. She was an actuary, for cripes' sake.

Used to be an actuary, she thought with satisfaction as she pulled on a pair of camo TOMS. She had given away her Rothys—no more washable business casual for her. No more gaping button-up blouses or stuffing herself into Spanx or dress pants pockets waging war against her curves. From here on out, it would be all wrap dresses and V-necks and comfy, stretchy fabrics that both forgave and accentuated her figure.

When she'd gone through the villa for the first time, after Chris and Jorge left, she'd given herself a single, glorious hour to revel in sheer pleasure, to walk through slowly without even her clipboard. It had been a moment for her heart—to congratulate herself on the accomplishment that had been two years in the making, and to shed a tear or two over not being able to do this with Gram.

It had also been a moment to say a prayer for the mysterious Franco Pelagatti, the man who hadn't forgotten Gram in his will, never mind that Gram hadn't mentioned him once when she'd been alive.

Natalie and Gram had raised nearly all of the money—the $75,000 they needed to prove they had funds to carry out the renovation—before Gram's medical bills had cleaned them out. Then...a surprise windfall had revealed itself as the probate courts were clearing Gram's estate. Unclaimed funds willed to her years earlier by one Franco Pelagatti totaled more than $50,000, appearing at the very last moment to salvage their Italian villa dreams.

"Okay," Natalie said to herself, ready to do a walk-through of the villa with different eyes—not the eyes of a proud new owner but the eyes of a restorationist—as someone ready to reconcile what could be with what actually was. The place had beautiful bones, but it was horribly neglected—covered in a layer of dirt and damaged from overexposure to the elements, with some significant issue in nearly every room.

Writing the word "entryway" on the first page of her notebook, Natalie stood at the base of the broken staircase, methodically noting everything that needed work, from simple cleaning to major and minor repairs.

Ten minutes into her walk-through, her first page was completely full. There was crumbling plaster in every room, water damage in the library, and abandoned bird's nests in the sitting room. And nests meant there was some way the birds were getting in. No obvious clues from inside could mean a problem with the roof.

Out on the terrace, some of the exterior walls were missing stones, as were the steps that allowed guests to descend to the western lawn. The benches on the eastern lawn looked unstable and might have to be replaced. The three-tiered fountain in the center of the gardens that had looked so lovely in old photos of the *pensione* looked like it hadn't run in a very long time. It was alive with a bright-green moss that was oddly beautiful but which Natalie doubted was what her guests would have in mind.

An hour into her walk-through and four notebook pages were filled on front and back—one big, disorganized list. More evidence of water damage in the second-floor guest rooms and even in the owner's apartment suite on the third floor caused her to flip back to page one and circle an earlier item: *roofing consultation.*

Surely I don't need a permit for that, Natalie thought bitterly. Having someone conduct an inspection and giving an estimate didn't constitute starting work. Maybe that was Natalie's best play—her *only* play for the month of August. She would call in all the vendors she needed to inspect the hell out of everything that needed inspection, then she would book the ones she liked to be back on-site beginning in September. Grumpy hot guy or no grumpy hot guy—permit or no permit—Natalie fully planned to get to work.

• • •

Find out about trash service.

Day three of cleaning—it was barely past noon and today's list already had a page two. Slow progress on the contractor front meant she had plenty of time to clean. She'd called nearly every vendor who had made Jorge's cut. At this rate, she was getting desperate enough to start calling the ones who hadn't.

In an hour, she would descend to town and pay a personal visit to the roofing outfit on Via della

Republica, which she had already called five times. The answering machine message clearly stated their open-for-business hours, but they had yet to pick up their phone.

In the meantime, Natalie would have to find a place for the eighteen heavy-duty trash bags she'd filled with used paper towels and cloth rags. The latter had turned out to be not so reusable without functioning electricity and a washing machine. Some of the grime on the windows and the shelves had been so thick, she doubted it would come out with a good wash.

What few books remained in the library had been musty, the pages stiff and wavy, none in good enough condition to keep. She'd thrown away old candles, slumped over and warped and tucked inside a sideboard. She'd spent the past thirty minutes with a ladder and a broom, batting down and sweeping up old bird's nests in the sitting room. She worked with the windows open to let out all the dust.

Walking yet another filled trash bag from the front to the back of the house, Natalie got a good workout in both of her arms. If these first three days were any indication, rehabbing the villa would let her eat as many plates of pasta as she wanted. She'd been surviving solely on the contents of her welcome basket and the coffee she drank every morning at a cart on the square on her short jaunts into town. She would try restaurants eventually, but the frugal part of her couldn't bring herself to waste food. Wastefulness felt like an insult to Gram.

After moving through the kitchen and all the way to the back door, Natalie stopped short when she smelled something she didn't expect. Something she shouldn't have smelled at all.

Is that smoke?

Not smoke, as in fire. Smoke, as in cigarettes.

She wasn't alone.

All she had to do was turn the corner to identify the source of the smell—a balding man whose remainder of hair was peppered with gray. He looked to be a bit taller than Natalie, which wasn't saying much, considering that she was only five foot seven. The man wore a short-sleeve button-down shirt and, like many older men she had noticed since arriving, pants and shoes that seemed dressy for everyday wear.

"*Bongiorno*," she said, not nearly as loudly or imposingly as she had sounded in her own head. She'd meant for it to sound suspicious and foreboding—not like a friendly "good morning."

The man spun to face her.

"*Ciao*," he returned jovially. "Miss Natalie?" He switched to English, then motioned to himself. "I am Aldo Fumigalli. The electrician."

He pronounced his title with a heavy accent, which Natalie supposed she must have, too, when she had called him two days earlier and asked in patchy Italian whether he was Aldo the *elettricista*. Her language skills were coming along.

Gram had always taught her that when you visited a different country, it was your responsibility to communicate. Though she'd studied for a year, Natalie still found herself dependent on her phone translation app. She understood pretty well, but when she had to string together actual sentences in

Italian, she just…froze.

"I expected you yesterday." Natalie remembered the word for yesterday, *ieri*, but defaulted to English. She didn't know how to ask him in a full sentence what had happened to their appointment time.

Aldo waved a hand. "Yesterday, it was no good."

Natalie narrowed her eyes. "You were supposed to be here at two o'clock."

He shrugged. "I am sorry. I did not remember."

Looking past him, she spotted his car, a simple little Fiat, not an outfitted van or utility truck. He had ignored convention, parking halfway on the driveway, halfway on the lawn. The grass was in sad shape, but still, the driveway would have been a fine place to stop. It also would have been fine to park in the gravel parking lot in the front and knock on her actual door.

He motioned toward the villa and took a drag of his cigarette. "Do you have time now? I can look at your house."

The beacon of professionalism Natalie had been hoping for based on Jorge's curated list had yet to shine in her favor. But beggars couldn't be choosers. The other contractors she had called were either on vacation or booked out for months.

"Okay." She motioned him inside.

With not even close to a level of language proficiency that would allow her to carry on small talk, she silently allowed Aldo to peruse the kitchen. He walked slowly, his hands behind his back, looking toward the two rustic, wrought-iron fixtures that should have lit the room from overhead. His eyes scanned laterally, possibly looking for the switches that were next to each door. When he strode toward the appliance wall, he bent to unplug the refrigerator, then plugged it in again, pausing for long seconds, as if waiting to hear it buzz to life. When it didn't, he put his hands behind his back and resumed his perusing stroll.

Reaching the doorway that led to the hall, he flipped the switch on the panel, glancing upward and waiting long seconds for the bulbs in the fixture to light. When they didn't, he meandered to the darkened hall, where he tried more switches and waited more long seconds for the power to flicker on.

By the time they had been through each and every room, Natalie seethed silently, resentful of the way he raised his eyebrows in hopeful expectation with the flipping of each switch. He had shown up on the wrong day. He was using what even an amateur could see was a bad approach. And he was slower than molasses.

Natalie didn't like to back seat drive—didn't like to openly challenge people. If her Italian were better, she would have made an exception. None of her language apps covered construction terms or curses. Knowing how to say things like, "Can we move this along? I don't have all damned day," would come in handy right about then.

They walked up the stairs to the second floor. More switches and panels. More raising of eyebrows in anticipation of lights that never came on. At one point, he disassembled a sconce fixture and rescrewed the bulb in before trying the wall switch again.

Natalie was just about ready to lay into him in

English when they finally got to the end of the top-floor hall. Then he turned to her and spoke a single phrase that even Natalie could comprehend in her intermediate-at-best Italian.

"*L'elettricità…non funziona.*"

The electricity doesn't work.

CHAPTER FOUR

"Nonna?"

Pietro called for his grandmother the moment he entered the store. He didn't need to call too loudly. The store itself was always very quiet. No matter how often he came inside, he couldn't get used to how small it felt to weave in between the displays and how low the ceilings were that forced him to duck to avoid the chandeliers. But it still looked and smelled the same, still transported him, somehow, to twenty-five years earlier when he'd spent his afternoons there as a child.

"Coming, *piccolo*!" His nonna's voice sounded from the back room, where she was likely stowing her broom, taking off her apron, and putting on her shawl. She moved more slowly these days, which led Pietro to thoughts he didn't enjoy. His nonna was the only person in his family who called him *piccolo*. It meant *little*. She'd taken care of him since he was a little boy.

The elementary school was close to the center of town, right off the Piazza della Republica, walking distance to Nonna's store. Landing there after school had begun as purely logistic. His sisters—much older—had attended the middle school, which was located away from the town center. Too small to fend for himself or walk home alone, he was picked up every day by Nonna and brought back to the store.

When he was very young, she had indulged his

every whim, playing hide-and-seek and other games with him inside and assigning him little jobs, letting him try on responsibility by sending him on errands to other shops in town. Even when he was older, in middle school himself, he would make the long walk down the hill from school to see his nonna. Her store was his home base for venturing around town, exploring all the old buildings there, and drawing.

Best of all, he and his grandmother talked and talked. Only as an adult did he realize how much this had helped. To be the youngest in a large family and to be the only boy left him feeling ignored, especially with how things were between him and his father. His friends' fathers were different—not so busy, not so serious, not so complex. Politicians were tricky animals.

"I'm ready." Nonna came shuffling out from the room in the back, purse in one hand and prayer bag in another.

He was fairly certain that the latter was just for show. Nonna went to church three times a week, but Pietro had always suspected it wasn't purely out of dedication to her faith. Nonna herself would readily admit that Tuesday nights at church were when the devout could expect the very best gossip.

This was why, every Tuesday, whenever Pietro was in town, he met his nonna at the store, helped her close up early, and walked her to church. It was a tradition they'd enjoyed for years.

For a town the size of Zavona, the church was rather grand. It had bronze Byzantine-style doors that had been traced back to Constantinople. The Arabic-Norman bell tower dated back to the twelfth century. It had been built at a time when Zavona was at the peak of its potential, when it was planned to be a much larger town. As a result, some of the most beautiful buildings in Campania found their homes in Zavona. The town was an architectural gem.

"You are better company than Giovanna," Nonna informed him the moment they took to the street. "The girl likes to talk and talk. But she does not say much. You know?"

Pietro smiled at the blunt but accurate description of his cousin.

"Giovanna is a curious girl," he commented mildly, not wanting to speak ill of his cousin.

"Curious, yes. But her thoughts do not run deep. You, Pietro. You have always been my thinker. Sometimes you think too much."

Pietro wondered for a fleeting moment whether his nonna would bring up his father. It wasn't worth wondering for long. Nonna always said what she thought he needed to hear. To her credit, she was the only person who said things in a way that he would listen. He could trust her not to try to persuade him of whatever his father or anyone else might want of him. Nonna's wisdom stood alone.

"You don't like the way things are now, between Papa and me."

"Do I like my son and my grandson fighting?" She took three more steps before shaking her head. "Of course I don't. But I'm not worried about your papa. I'm worried about you."

"Nonna…I can take care of myself. Papa doesn't intimidate me."

She chuckled. "That much is clear. I think it is you who intimidate him. You have never been the son he expected."

Pietro had always known this fact, but it still injured him to hear it said out loud.

She's right. You're not the boy Papa wanted.

Alfonso Indelicato had always wanted Pietro to be some smaller version of himself. The pressure had been there since he was a child. Where Alfonso was cerebral, Pietro was artistic. Where Alfonso was showy, Pietro was subdued. The only thing the two men shared in common was stubborn resolve.

"What worries you?" he asked Nonna. Her days spent in the shop downtown, chatting with her gossipy friends, ensured that she always knew what was happening in Zavona, and anything being said about the family in town.

"You will have your reckoning with your papa. There is no doubt that such an occasion will occur. Yet, in the meantime, it eats you up. It has changed the way you talk to people. This anger at your father is turning you into a bitter man. It is getting in the way of you and other people—it is taking too much of your heart, Pietro."

He said nothing to this proclamation. Nothing about his nonna's claim was wrong. Pietro *had* felt angry, and less in control. In bad moments, he had struggled to keep his patience. He had said and done things in ways he wished he could take back.

"This is true," he admitted with no small measure of shame. "I am not myself."

"Then you must choose to be yourself again, Pietro. This means letting go. Nonnuccio and I were married for thirty-three years before he died. Believe me when I tell you, you cannot change a stubborn man."

"I think you and Nonno were equal parts stubborn," Pietro ribbed. "I still haven't forgotten the time you made him sleep in the cottage. For a month."

Pietro was gratified by the way her face lit at the recollection, and at the sound of her chuckle. Whenever he could, he loved to make his grandmother laugh.

"You would be surprised," she said.

Even as their elbows were linked, she patted Pietro's arm. She settled into silence and they continued to walk slowly, making their way up to the church. Pietro knew her well enough to know that her lecture was over. Still, he needed her, would always need her advice.

"I don't know how to stop caring what he thinks."

He said it a full minute later. It took him time to formulate the words—to articulate the full extent of what he was feeling.

"Papa wants me to abandon my life's work and the philosophy that drives it. He wants me to stop being who I am."

She tutted at him. "Pietro. You know that your father does not want this."

Pietro replayed the sentence back to himself.

"He makes no room for my opinion." Hopefully Nonna could concede at least that. "He fights me on things I can prove on paper, in black and white. He has never believed—will never believe—in doing things my way."

Usually, when Pietro expressed such opinions to other members of his family, he was met with excuse after excuse. His father was an elected official. He had responsibilities outside himself. Pietro had heard every narrative imaginable about what consideration he ought to show to Alfonso.

"You cannot let this steal your joy, *piccolo*. You must be careful that too many parts of you do not become sour. You must not forget that life is sweet. That your purpose in preserving the buildings you love is for their beauty. You cannot be who you are if you do not keep that outlook for yourself. Do not let your father—or any other person—take this from you."

• • •

"Ciao, Pietro."

Pietro pocketed his phone and turned in anticipation of the man he'd been waiting to meet. Roman Kissinger was a client. He shared Pietro's love for classic Italian architecture and was a patron of the arts. He'd made his fortune in the hospitality industry and liked to spend money on beautiful things. He was also richer than Copia, the Italian goddess of wealth.

"Roman," Pietro greeted with a warm smile and cheek kisses. Roman hailed from Austria, from just across the northeastern Italian border. He was shorter than Pietro and fine-featured, with dark hair. He was a perfectionist and could be intense when they were working on a restoration. But everyday Roman was soft-spoken, with a certain sentimentality. No one who could appreciate the domes of Brunelleschi or Carolingian cross vaults had a cold, dead heart.

"It's been a while since you've been out my way." Roman motioned for Pietro to sit.

The cupola booth had high backs and fine slate-gray upholstery. Pietro was accustomed to seeing Roman in the private homes he'd hired Pietro to help reconstruct. Today, Pietro had flown to Alto Adige to meet Roman in the bar of one of the dozen hotels he owned.

"What are you working on these days?" Roman asked once they were both settled.

Roman was a sophisticated architecture buff. Pietro had worked on three of his restorations. A full-out castle, a small hotel, and a villa that was quite large. The first had been a particularly tricky project that two earlier architects had messed up. When Pietro had delivered a gorgeous restoration on time and on budget, he'd earned Roman's business—and his loyalty—for life.

"What am I working on?" Pietro repeated with a playful smile. "Nothing that's for sale."

The two men liked to joke with each other.

"Anything I'd be interested in?" Roman prodded.

"A bit beneath you, to be honest," he admitted. "But very old and very beautiful and possessing of its own charm."

Not wanting to force the man to beg, Pietro pulled his tablet out, navigating to the photos. It was a little church in a tiny town that had done a beautiful job maintaining the church's facade. But inside, it was falling apart. Pietro's job was to oversee the reinforcement of its structure and to co-sign on the historically relevant details.

Roman nodded approvingly as he began to look

through, as if seeing the images alone let him smell the plaster and dust. Pietro understood that it was like an addiction. Some clients—the kind Pietro didn't take—wanted no more than a team of elves to work quickly, to make demands without understanding the history or context for what should be preserved. Roman was different. He liked to get dirty. In an age of modernizing and flipping for profit and vanity real-estate buying, Roman was a true restorationist, dedicated to preserving history.

"Very nice." Roman's compliment sounded sincere. "Interesting mixture of Roman and Byzantine. Eighth century?"

Pietro looked on with shared admiration. "Seventh."

Roman let out a low whistle. "Not in bad condition, considering the circumstances. When will you finish it?"

That was Roman's code for asking what Pietro would work on next. It was also the perfect segue.

"That depends on you."

Roman sat up a little in his seat. "You have something for me?"

He thought Pietro had the drop on some shiny gem that was about to go up for sale. Sometimes when very old, very valuable properties were about to go onto the market, Pietro was called in for inspections.

"I do have a project you might be interested in. But not for the reasons you think." He took his tablet back from Roman and went into a different folder this time.

"I'll be honest with you. This is personal. Zavona is where I grew up. My family still lives there." He handed the tablet over once again. "I should also disclose that I'm part of the development council, and there may be a conflict of interest for me to even propose this, but I feel that I have no choice."

Roman thumbed through the photos. "What are these?"

"Residences, mostly. Modest in size. Not at all something that you would be interested in for yourself."

"Then why did you want me to see these?" Roman's tone was one of intrigue.

"The properties that you restore are beautiful, yes. And you do a service by bringing them back to their former glory. But I'm guessing, it is not only your homes and your properties that you love?"

Roman likely didn't know what Pietro was getting at but humored him anyway. "Yes. I love everything about Italy. Not just the properties I own."

"Good." He paused for effect. "Then I hope you'll consider helping to finance the private restoration of historically significant homes in Zavona and on the Amalfi Coast."

Roman picked up the glass of wine in front of him and narrowed his eyes, thinking. "You know how I run restorations. I spare no expense. It is all for the sake of the history of the building. My projects are not profitable. Why would you want me to finance the restoration of properties that I cannot sell at a profit?"

"I do know how you run your projects," Pietro agreed. "Caring more about the integrity of the work and the preservation is why I thought of you for this. I don't know who these houses will go to, ultimately, or how the fair ownership pieces will work out. All I know is, we need a benefactor in order for them to be done right."

Pietro dove into the bigger picture then, about the development committee, about the foreign investment program that allowed virtual amateurs to come in and do restorations. He talked about the screening process and their attempts at checks and balances but was candid about the fact that their efforts were not enough. He talked about the turnover rate and how many people had abandoned the program, in some cases leaving the houses worse for wear.

"These may be modest properties," Pietro concluded, "but they are vital to the history of the region. If somebody does not restore them well, they will be lost. If I had the money, I would buy all of them. I am already restoring four, which is all I can afford. Now I need someone who will do it well to buy the rest."

Roman looked thoughtful again. Pietro didn't expect an answer, not then, maybe not for a while. The important thing was that Roman was considering it. And even if Roman didn't bite on his own behalf, he might know somebody who would.

"The region..." Roman mused. Pietro's wording had been deliberate. For most men as wealthy as Roman, thoughts of legacy came into play.

"I don't need an answer now." Pietro let him off the hook. "But promise me you'll think about it. Either that, or introduce me to some of your wealthy friends."

CHAPTER FIVE

Café Ludo was far down the hill, below the central area where Natalie ran her errands, closer to the water than she'd been yet. It seemed like a magnet for foreign visitors compared to the rest of town. A sign out front advertised FREE HIGH-SPEED INTERNET written in English, right above a stacked greeting in four languages: WELCOME, WILKOMMEN, BIENVIENUE, and *BIENVENIDOS* next to corresponding European flags.

Like most eateries in Zavona, Café Ludo had seating outside. Natalie arrived early and scanned for Jorge and Chris. After a week spent mostly alone in her palatial villa, she was eager to see a friendly face. She didn't spot them, but she did see a group of four people who looked too comfortable to be tourists, sitting at a table, speaking English.

A woman with hair dyed purple over blonde sounded as if she came from England. A bearded and mustachioed man with glasses sounded German or Dutch. A man next to him spoke with an accent Natalie couldn't place and another woman had yet to speak. She could have simply waited for Jorge and Chris, though the longer she tried not to stare, the more certain she was that this was her group.

Three of the four had on what could have been work clothes—practical pants and sensible shoes. The two holding hands wore boots that were flecked with something that looked like paint. Only the Brit was dressed stylishly, in a sundress and sunglasses that made her look like she might be on a permanent vacation.

"Excuse me?" Natalie said.

Approaching strangers was one of her least favorite things, right next to not knowing anybody in a social situation. The fact that she had approached these four at all was a testament to how starved she was for companionship. They all turned around and looked, some with polite smiles and others with curiosity.

"Sorry to interrupt you. Do you happen to know Jorge and Chris?"

"You mean the farmers?" the Brit replied.

"I think so?" Natalie cringed a little as she spoke. "I only met them once, last week. They came by my house. They were sort of, like, the welcoming committee. I'm a member of this local housing program?"

That was the other thing she did when she was nervous. She spoke in a way that her statements sounded like questions—as if she were asking the other person to validate everything she said. Awkward Natalie was the part of herself she liked the least. She was going to have to get that under control. She hadn't come to Italy to be American Natalie. Expat Natalie had to be a much better, much cooler version of herself.

"You must be the one who bought the hotel," said the man with the accent she couldn't recognize. He looked to be older than her, probably late twenties. Natalie was still a "mid." He had blond hair that fell nearly to his shoulders, or at least the back part did. The front was pulled into a sort of man bun. The woman who held his hand—the one who hadn't spoken yet—had almost the same style.

The Brit pulled out the chair next to her, inviting Natalie to sit. They seemed welcoming, judging from their smiles.

"Oh, good," she said, "I'm in the right place."

It didn't take long for her to learn their names. She was good at mental cataloging. The couple from Sweden—Greg and Soni—had only arrived the previous month and were renovating a property in the center of town, close to the Piazza della Republica. The man who Natalie had thought was from Germany was really from Switzerland. His name was Helmut but liked to be called "Helle." He had already finished the rehab of his house, which was somewhere up in the hills. His pregnant wife, Julia, was manning the offices of the business they were building, a game development company.

Ellie was the Brit in the sundress, who had been there for two months and was rehabbing a cottage that had once been part of a larger estate. She smiled and laughed a lot and had a vivacious way of talking about things. She was animated, the social lubricator of the group, and she was the only one in the program doing her rehab alone. Everyone else—except Natalie now—was paired up.

"So how is your rehab coming? Made any progress this week?" Ellie asked just as Natalie's drink came. *Caffè con panna* was a double shot of espresso with whipped cream. It felt luscious to drink, a large improvement from the plain tea and bottled water she drank for most of the day at the villa. Her stomach practically growled at the prospect of a hot lunch.

"Slow going. I'm having trouble finding a reliable electrician. The one I met with yesterday..." Natalie shook her head and gave a little eye roll. "He's not going to work out."

"Who did you call?" Soni finally spoke. She had an ovular face, a soft voice, and feline gray eyes. Her accent was heavier than Greg's, and it was clear she had less facility with English.

"A guy named Aldo Fumigalli?" Again, it came out like a question.

Everyone at the table looked at one another. It occurred too late to Natalie that her clear disdain for Aldo might have offended somebody—that maybe one or all of them were working with Aldo already. How had she already alienated a group of people who she desperately needed to be her friends?

Ellie was the first to burst into laughter, and the rest soon followed, though not to Natalie's immediate relief. She would feel much better once she was certain of what they were laughing about.

"Have you heard of him?" Natalie finally asked.

Helle explained. "Unfortunately, all of us have. Some of us hired him before we knew. He is the worst electrician in Zavona."

It felt good to laugh with people who could commiserate, but there were other reasons why Natalie wouldn't be hiring Aldo. Bullshitters were the one type of person she couldn't endure. The flimsy excuses for why he'd missed their original appointment and why he hadn't shown up with real equipment or a real truck were dead giveaways. The stench of low integrity had rolled off him in waves.

Natalie had learned the hard way to beware the smallest, simplest lies, to steer clear of people who lied about things they didn't need to. It masked other dark psychology of which she wanted no part. It was the mark of a player—using small manipulations to influence the outcomes of situations. But her life and restoring this villa were not a game.

"Jorge," Ellie scolded, prompting Natalie to look behind her. He and Chris were on the approach. The two arriving together—again—and being referred to as "the farmers" seemed to confirm that they were a couple.

"What did I do?" Jorge asked at the same moment Ellie rose, and they did the cheek-kiss thing. Natalie had looked up the etiquette of this. It seemed complicated.

"You were supposed to tell her which contractors to avoid. She called Aldo."

Jorge looked down at Natalie, clearly scandalized. "I did not cross him out?"

Natalie shook her head.

"*Ay, mi dispacie,*" Jorge apologized in a mixture of Spanish and Italian.

Ellie had too much fun laughing her head off at Natalie's story about her run-in with Aldo the day before. Not just a little chuckle—gasping laughter that sent her chin up and her head back.

"Do people really pay him to fix their electricity?" Natalie asked when her story was done. "He didn't even come in a truck. Does that guy even have a crew? Or a license?"

Chris, who had pulled up a seat next to Natalie, leaned forward on his elbows. "Oh, they all have licenses. That's why we try to warn folks who to avoid. If a contractor messes up, it's the homeowner who gets fined."

Her stomach dropped. "They fine people over renovations?" Natalie hadn't heard of anything like this in all of her research.

"They can, and sometimes they do," Chris replied. "We're protected for now, since we're in the program. But keep that in mind for whatever renovations you do after."

"Why don't you call the Fiorello brothers?" Ellie chimed in.

"I did. They told me they were booked."

Ellie gave Natalie a sidelong glance that told her she knew something about this.

"Not anymore..." Ellie trailed off. "Kevin and Lisa threw in the towel. They're abandoning their projects. They went to the *municipio* to relinquish their deeds this morning."

"What happened?" Why would anyone abandon their project after all that work?

"The same thing that happens to a lot of people," Jorge responded with a tinge of bitterness.

"That's why I'm holding on to my farm in Texas," Chris interjected. "I almost had my brother sell it for me... Now I'm keeping it as a plan B."

At this, all the others went quiet. Natalie realized neither of them actually answered her question, and she was afraid to ask again what had happened. Now that she was here, now that she was in it, now that even simple things weren't going right, the idea that anyone had reached the point of giving up was terrifying.

"So what happens to the property now?" she asked.

Chris spoke again. "The development committee will reassess, find out what condition the house is in, then determine whether to put it back in the pool."

That didn't make her feel any better. The notion that any of them were dispensable made this whole thing sound like a scam. And, unlike Chris, she didn't have a plan B.

"Anyway," Ellie continued, spreading a mysterious smile. "The Fiorello brothers are newly available. Give them a call. I can personally vouch for their work."

• • •

The Fiorello brothers came on the right day, arrived in a truck bearing their name, and seemed like actual electricians. They started in the garage, where the electricity was working, to test the switches and plugs. Like Aldo, they flipped switches, but they also used small devices and instruments she didn't recognize to test she-couldn't-imagine-what. She liked that they wrote down their findings and used a clipboard, just like she did.

When she told them the main house was completely dark, they returned to their truck and hefted out a serious-looking generator. Natalie lit their way to the basement, where they hunted down a circuit breaker that she hadn't thought to look for and that Aldo had ignored. They used one of their instruments to test something on every switch on the panel. They stopped to ask her questions and made her feel included in the process.

The brothers, who were identical twins and easy on the eyes, had been chattering the entire time, in a quiet but animated back-and-forth. They volleyed so quickly that Natalie made no attempt to understand what they were saying. But she didn't need to understand them to enjoy the lifting and lowering of their intonations, the quickening and slowing of their staccato speech.

Nico had been the more vocal of the two in conversation with his brother and had said the most to Natalie. It was hard to tell whether he was just a talker or whether he spoke better English. Nero had a more serious look about him, and he'd nodded in agreement with Nico when he spoke to Natalie. But he had yet to say a word directly to her.

"The power line that goes to the garage is a different line than the one that runs into the house. To fix power to this house, you must call Enel," Nico was saying.

Enel was the gas and electric company. Telecom Italia would be for internet and phone, neither of which she could get until she had power.

"We will use this generator to test what lights are working inside the house. We will detect wiring problems. Please open the windows to help the generator be safe."

What happened next was the most joyous occurrence since she'd arrived. From the doorway at the top of the stairs came a warm glow of artificial light.

My lights work!

She didn't realize she had said it out loud until Nico turned around and gave her a small smile. "*Sì, Signorina.* Your lights work."

As soon as the brothers reached the top of the stairs and fanned out to the left, back toward the kitchen, Natalie went right, walked to the center of the dining room, and spun around.

In better light, it was still beautiful, but with more details she hadn't been able to see before. Her front hall discovery was even better. What she had believed to be a plain ceiling in this room turned out to be some sort of fresco. It wasn't Michelangelo, but it held some subtle design that had merely been obscured by cobwebs, dark, and dirt. The voices of the brothers, still at it with their back-and-forth, faded away as they took one route and Natalie took another.

Leaving the downstairs to the brothers, she climbed the back steps, flipping a hallway switch only to find that this one didn't light up. She was taken down another peg when the first switch she tried on the second floor failed, too. Further inspection of the lights on that floor revealed more outages.

It's better than nothing, she reminded herself. *It's more than you had yesterday.*

More importantly, it was enough for her to begin serious work. Zero electricity meant a lot of wasted time. Without an illuminated assessment, how could she create a proper plan? She couldn't even clean properly in bad light. She wondered how much the Fiorello brothers would charge her to rent their generator.

Forty-five minutes later, all three of them sat at the back table as Nero read from a list of repairs. He had just told Natalie that 70 percent of her electrical infrastructure functioned well. A nervous flutter rose in her throat, though she managed a smile. She had finally tracked down electricians who seemed competent and professional. But what would they charge? Her entire plan hinged on her budget.

"Can you fix the broken ones?" she asked.

The brothers nodded in tandem.

"We must repair the wires," Nico said. "Your broken wires are because of…" He looked toward his brother for help. "*…roditori.*"

But Nero didn't reply. Still, a second later, Nico popped up with the correct word. His eyes were on Natalie again when he said, "Rodents."

"Mice?" Natalie repeated.

Both brothers nodded and seemed pleased that she understood.

"But nobody lives here," she protested. "No people, no food. No food, no mice."

"It is possible that they are gone now, but we found much evidence inside your walls. You should call the man who comes to close the mouse holes."

Nico looked at his brother again for a long second before turning back to Natalie with the correct word at the ready. "Exterminator," Nico supplied.

A bolt of cold fear rushed up her spine at the thought of tiny creatures burrowing tunnels and roaming freely inside her walls. "You know a good one?"

Nero nodded, but it was Nico who said yes.

Nero then pulled out his phone, navigated to a

number, then showed the screen to Nico, who began copying it down. Watching the two of them together was like watching a show.

"How much will you charge for your repairs?" She held her breath, awaiting the answer. Natalie had some cushion, but she couldn't afford to pay an arm and a leg.

Nico ripped the top sheet off the estimate he'd been writing in triplicate. "Forty-seven hundred dollars?"

It could have been worse, especially given the size of the villa. Still, it was more than she had budgeted. The house had been listed in good condition when she'd signed. A $4,700 fix to get to basic functionality seemed to indicate otherwise.

While she was still reviewing the estimate, Nero silently pulled the paper from her hand, plucked the pen from his brother, and wrote a single character on the page, applying pressure to the pen as he did.

He handed it back to Natalie at the same time as Nico clarified, "Not dollars. Euros."

Crap.

$4,700 would have been bad enough. But with the currency difference, the amount would be $1,000 more.

This time, she cringed openly. Then she thought about fire hazards, and Aldo Fumigalli, and the fact that Ellie had given a glowing personal recommendation. She thought about the litany of reasons to do your electrical work right, and she made her decision.

"Do you think you can start in September?"

Nico nodded, but Nero spoke in rapid-fire Italian,

uncrossing his arms long enough to motion here and there around the room. Whatever point Nero was making, Nico seemed to agree.

Nico finally translated. "Because of the questions you asked earlier about construction in the basement and near the staircase, we recommend you seek consultation before we begin. My brother recommends hiring an architect."

"Oh." Natalie wrinkled her nose. "I've been calling general contractors. Isn't that who I need?"

Nero shook his head and Nico spoke. "The architects in Italy are not like the architects in the United States. They help you understand the entire project. They see big things you do not know. They help you to have a good plan."

Natalie didn't like the idea of an extra expense, especially if she would still need a contractor later to do the work, but she loved the idea of impartial consultation. The truth was, her questions were piling up. And she saw the wisdom in seeking expertise in order to avoid costly mistakes.

"Do you know a good architect?" she asked politely instead of grumbling.

"Pietro, *claro*," Nero said to his brother at the same time Nico nodded.

Nico put pen to paper once again, writing down a name and a number on Natalie's estimate. "Pietro Indelicato," he said. "The best."

CHAPTER SIX

Pietro's first thought upon waking up that day was of his afternoon appointment with the American woman. He'd known whom he was speaking to the second he'd heard her voice—the beautiful, naive woman he had seen that day at the *municipio*. The one who he had been impatient with.

Natalie Malone.

On the phone the day before, he had repeated her name and the address of her villa in his best American English accent so that she would know he heard her clearly. Affecting an American accent was as easy as pretending you had marbles in your mouth. Pietro owed his fluency to a year spent studying in England.

He'd repeated her telephone number, which he didn't strictly need to do, given caller ID, and saved it in his own phone. But her call had been more than just transactional. She'd been circumspect in her questions and sounded knowledgeable and prepared. It also said something that the Fiorello brothers had even given her his number. They knew how busy he was and that he rarely worked with amateurs. They had to see something special in her renovation—something redeeming. All of it was evidence that he had given her a bad rap.

More like been in a bad mood.

He didn't like how often he was having to admit to his share of those. His father had set him off again the day before. Pietro had recommended against two program applicants he didn't believe were ready for the demands of the restorations. He'd invoked a veto vote of serious concern in the council meeting. His father had him overruled.

But his nonna was right. The vicious cycle of him feeling triggered and taking it out on everyone else would have to stop. He would go to his family's Sunday dinner this week. It was time to make amends.

• • •

Pietro hadn't been to the old villa in many months. Now that he thought about it…just under two years. Not since he had performed an initial inspection assessing its viability for the program. He had always thought it to be a beautiful property—if not beautiful now, formerly so and holding the potential to be once more.

Pensione Benone had always been a romantic place owned by a series of epic lovers, even back in its day as a family home. In Pietro's lifetime, it had only ever been owned by Rosalinda LaRue, who had married Alberto Benone and jointly procured the villa by happenstance. They had run it together for more than forty years. She had died first—some six years earlier—and he not long after. When people had asked them, as local families would, why they never had children, they always gave the same answer—their biggest joy had been taking care of their guests.

As Pietro approached the back of the property

past the front lot where guests had once parked their cars, he scanned the main building with a trained eye, making a casual assessment of the exterior. From the outside, the structure looked aligned, and the roof was in good shape, though parts on the south side had begun to show signs of wear. He wondered how much weather was getting in.

"Hello?" he called lightly, having already peered through the open door to the kitchen and, seeing nobody, made his way inside. Passing all the way through, he looked left to find a thick cable emerging from a door that was open only wide enough to accommodate it. The faint sound of a motor running came from the other side. The wire stretched away from said door, followed along the wall side of the hallway, and disappeared around a corner through a second open door in the other direction. If he found the wire, he would find the woman.

"Hello?" he called again in English, seeing neither hide nor hair of Natalie yet, though he was certain he'd arrived on time. He strode in farther, following the endless cable. He was halfway to calling a third time, louder, when, upon finally finding Natalie, the sight of her stopped his breath in his throat.

Ostia.

This wasn't the same frazzled Natalie he'd seen that first day at the *municipio*. This Natalie seemed confident and at ease. She stood on a good-size ladder, perched on the third rung from the top, broom in hand. She appeared to be clearing away cobwebs and brushing a thick layer of dust off the ceiling.

"What day is today?" she asked in Italian, then

paused. Her words were slow and deliberate, and her pronunciation wasn't bad. For a moment, he thought she was on the phone. Wireless earbuds stuck out of her ears, and he could see the imprint of a phone in the back pocket of jeans that fit snugly against her curves.

"Today is the twenty-second of September," was the phrase she said next.

Only, today was not the twenty-second of September. It was August sixteenth. Pietro frowned, not making himself known. He wanted to hear more of her strange conversation.

"Tomorrow we will visit the Vatican City," she said just seconds later, though she tripped over the word "city." Only when she repeated the word in better pronunciation, then a second time, did he realize what he had walked in on. Natalie was practicing her Italian, repeating phrases that she heard as part of an audio course. This version of Natalie was a far cry from the frazzled woman he had seen on that first day. She was beautiful like this.

"Vatican City." She said the final phrase once more, lowering her hand that held the broom while wiping her brow with the back of the other. Pietro had cleaned enough ceilings himself to know that it was hard work, more physical than it looked. Now, she reached with her free hand toward her back pocket to pull out her phone, clearly set to rewind the lesson. If Pietro's theory was right, stopping to repeat had placed her half a minute past the part about the Vatican City. It wasn't until she had stuck her phone back in her pocket that she turned her head slightly to the side, wiping the top of her nose this time with the back of her hand. That was when she caught a glimpse of Pietro.

He was already on his way to her before she let out a small scream. She had begun to teeter, the surprise at discovering his presence causing her to jump. Since startling and ladders didn't mix well, she was barely hanging on to her footing. Pietro arrived just in time to grab her before she could fall.

Three things happened then—the broom fell from her hand, cast off toward the window as the ladder fell off to the other side, a casualty of her shifting weight as she failed to catch her balance. Before either one of those hit the ground, something else landed with a distinct slap—her phone.

Pietro had moved too quickly to drop anything. As he cinched his arms around her, his messenger bag was still on his hip, though the angle at which he caught her pushed it farther off to the side. He had caught her mid-fall in an iron grip, one forearm across her stomach, the other across her hips. Their bodies were flush, her back to his front. The way he had her suspended, her feet hovered by his knees and his chin was just above her plump backside.

"Omigosh."

She said something quickly in English that Pietro could only guess was some sort of gratitude word. The word was whispery, as if she were out of breath. It registered in this same moment that she smelled very nice. Not nice in a perfume-y sort of way—fresh and fragrant and natural, as if she'd been walking among the wild jasmine at the edge of his family's lemon groves. Without dropping her too quickly, he released her to the ground.

"I apologize," he said. "It was not my intention to surprise you."

He set his hands on her hips to steady her. She wobbled a bit on her feet, then began to turn around. Even after she faced him, he kept his hands on her waist long enough to give her a once-over. It was clear the last fifteen seconds had left her disoriented. Pietro didn't want her to fall.

She blinked, and he saw the instant that the last of her haze cleared away and a new realization set in. Her eyes widened in recognition of the day that Pietro would rather forget. Natalie took a step back, hastening to extricate herself from his arms.

"You're—"

Creating the compulsion to retreat abruptly wasn't the effect he usually had on women. Her withdrawal stung.

"Pietro Indelicato. The architect. I'm here for your inspection. I am sorry. I should have more loudly announced myself."

When she ripped the two tiny buds out of her ears, Pietro wondered whether he would have to apologize a third time. Before he could decide whether to repeat himself, her eyes darted to the floor, her gaze scanning the dusty tile until they located her phone. He bent over to set the ladder upright at the same moment she picked up her device.

"It's okay," she insisted, stuffing both her phone and her earbuds into her pocket. "I was just..." She motioned to the ladder and blushed furiously. "Practicing my Italian."

Pietro thought of paying her a compliment—of

telling her that her accent sounded good. It wouldn't even be a lie. But he had enough sisters to know not to pay a woman a compliment when she was out of sorts. Instead, he leaned over to pick up her broom, then walked it to the wall next to the window where it could be leaned securely against a shutter.

"If it is okay with you," he said, "may we begin?"

She nodded and motioned in front of herself, as if to invite him to walk farther into the house, or at least to walk away from the disaster that had been their encounter.

"What sort of changes would you like to make?" Pietro slipped into professional mode, shaking off the way she smelled and how she had felt sliding down his body.

"Changes?"

He took a mental note of a few damaged stones in the wall of the room they had just walked into, which had served as a guest dining room in years past.

"This is why you called me, no? To make changes?"

Pietro had worked with enough rehabbers to anticipate current preferences and styles. If he had a euro for every time somebody told him they wanted to "open up" a room, he would be a wealthy man. Americans especially loved to knock down walls.

"No. I don't want to make any changes." Her voice was softer now. "The villa is perfect as it is."

Pietro stopped just short of the wall, turning away from the missing stone he had been set to inspect. A glance back at her found her expression much changed. Her smile was dreamy and her eyes were bright and enchanted as she looked toward the double-arched doorways and up at the ceilings with their exposed beams. She looked more than a little in love.

"Then why did you call me?" Pietro's question sounded brusque to his own ears. The dreaminess in her eyes disappeared, and she began to look more like she had on that first day.

"I told the Fiorello brothers I wanted to restore the staircase. And to learn about earthquake proofing. They said you could help me with both."

"You will not destroy these walls?"

When she gritted her teeth, he realized he might have used the wrong wording.

"Why would I destroy these walls?"

"My apologies. I did not mean to offend. I was merely surprised."

"Are you able to perform an inspection?" She was a bit impatient now. "It won't do me much good to have a pretty house if it might fall down."

It was the most logical sentiment in the world. Still, it was not one that Pietro heard often. He made certain to give her his most earnest look before he spoke again. "I could not agree with you more."

She narrowed her eyes a bit and crossed her arms.

"The basement is this way, no?" Pietro started walking in the direction his memory took him.

"You've been in this house before?"

"I've been in most houses in Zavona, if not as a guest, then as a council official."

"You're on the Economic Development Council?"

"Yes," Pietro said plainly. "I inspected this house two years ago. I approved this house to be part of the program. This is why I asked you what changes you wanted to make. All of the houses in the program are structurally sound in their original configurations. Most people who call an architect want to make changes to the layout."

She scrunched her nose up a little. "No one else wants to earthquake-proof their house? This is one of the most seismically active areas of Italy."

"It is very smart to do so, but it is not required. Most *sognatori* do only what they must to satisfy the contract."

"*Sognatori*?"

"The name we call people in the program. It means, *those who dream*."

Pietro didn't know why the simple translation made her blush again, but he was transfixed by her reactions, her subtle frowns as she stopped to think. He even liked the tiny annoyances that showed on her face. It had been a long time since Pietro had enjoyed a woman, and he didn't mind a woman with a temper.

"Dreamers..." she repeated. Pietro couldn't tell whether she liked the name. "I think I understand."

He could have kept standing there, drinking in her face, deciphering her every reaction. Though something fiery lay beneath, she was shy.

"I will begin in the cellar," he announced. "The only way to truly understand a home is to get beneath her. I will start from the bottom and go up."

CHAPTER SEVEN

Natalie was grateful for the darkness of the basement and for the quiet concentration of Pietro, who seemed wholly and completely focused on his task. Pietro training his gaze and his instruments on her walls and her beams and keying notes into his tablet meant he couldn't see her traitorous face.

Pietro.

Even repeating his name in her mind made her blush. He was the man from city hall. The man who had all but told her to give up. The man who had looked upon her with certain, unmistakable pity. The man who had witnessed her speaking bad Italian and falling off a ladder. The man who had caught her in midair.

That makes twice with Pietro to the rescue.

But was rescuing her what he had done? It had certainly felt like rescuing. Not that Natalie had experience with that sort of thing. Only, every time she'd imagined it, it had involved a tall man and good, solid arms.

Don't forget his voice.

Natalie wasn't sure that any of her earlier rescue fantasies had actually involved voices. But since she'd met him, she couldn't *not* recall his. His voice was a double threat. The hoarse, husky timbre of his baritone was sexy enough. But what got her in her nethers was his accent.

Focus, Natalie.

She needed to…because this wasn't like any rehab Natalie had seen on HGTV—the ones that had made her confident she could renovate a house. Even the houses that were in total shambles—the ones that had to be stripped down to their frames—had architecture she'd understood. The houses in Zavona were different. They weren't all sloped roofs and load-bearing walls made from measured materials like stone or brick. They were dug out and cobbled together, indistinguishable from the wet earth from which they'd sprung forth.

Staring down at her own cellar floor, which seemed solid and even but unfinished, lacking in poured concrete or a utility room or anything else a proper basement ought to have, Natalie couldn't quell the unease. On some level, it all just looked like rubble.

"Does my foundation seem okay?" She had no idea whether inspecting conditions in the basement was the same as assessing the foundation. But she did know that she wanted to break the silence. Too much time with her own thoughts, watching the shadow of his silhouette and breathing in the scent that trailed behind him—the fresh scent that cut through the musty smell of the basement—was doing her no good.

"The walls are in good condition, and the foundation looks secure. They meet the standard requirements for structural integrity."

"But?"

Even in the light, she could see that he looked apologetic.

"But to be safe against earthquakes, they will

need reinforcements."

Natalie nodded, having suspected this, tamping down the urge to wring her hands and ask how much a job like that might cost.

He led them back up the stairs. Natalie followed silently, feeling differently than she had with the contractors who had been there before. Whereas Aldo had been no-business and the Fiorello brothers had been all-business, something about Pietro was reverent. He walked carefully, spoke quietly, and observed with admiration.

As they walked through halls and poked into rooms, he shared little insights about this or that. They were random facts about the architecture—things that had nothing to do with earthquake proofing or structural soundness. Gram would have loved it. Listening to Pietro was like receiving an architectural tour of her own house.

"I remember this staircase," Pietro murmured as they approached the front of the house, past the dining room and the library, right into the front hall. He walked far past it, all the way to the front door, then turned to take in the full effect. "This was once very beautiful."

She fell into step next to him, wanting the same view. The staircase always gave her pause.

"I want it to be again." She sounded insecure, like she didn't know whether she could pull it off, because she didn't.

"This is a very rare marble." Pietro stepped closer and turned on his flashlight, getting a closer look at the detail, even though buttery afternoon light filtered through the glass above the door.

"Calacatta," she said.

Pietro blinked over at her in surprise. "You know this marble?"

Yes, she knew a lot about marble—she and Gram had been over every detail of what they would do if they got the house.

She nodded. "The steps that aren't damaged are in pretty good condition. I'm hoping that I can find a good match."

Pietro turned back around to look at her. "You will restore these steps?"

"I want to get this right." Natalie was starting to feel like a broken record.

"And you have budgeted enough money for this?"

She frowned a little. "I tried. I was hoping to hear your opinion on what a fair price would be for some of these fixes."

She motioned to his tablet, a not-so-subtle suggestion that he finally share some of his findings.

"Is there somewhere we can sit?" He looked back toward the front door, but she tipped her head in the opposite direction.

"The only table right now is in the back, outside."

He nodded and she led the way. She hadn't been self-conscious about her outfit when she'd gotten dressed that morning, a soft gray V-neck and snug jeans that fell to mid-calf. But as she walked, she could feel the heat of Pietro's eyes.

Once outside, they sat together at the table that had become her eating space, her conference table, and her desk. It sat left of the garage, next to an olive tree that shaded the table from the sun at certain hours of day. Pietro sat next to her rather than across from her and pulled something up on his tablet, moving close enough that she could see. The document was in English and the header read *Project Plan*.

"I am very impressed by your dedication to restore your villa to a very high standard. The improvements you are thinking about are the same ones that I would do myself. They are the right things but expensive."

She didn't know why her heartbeat sped up the way it did. He hadn't told her anything she didn't already know.

"Some of the areas that you asked about are in very good condition and will not require additional work. I can confirm that the architecture of this building is the original construction. This is very good. It means that no one tore down walls. And there was no additional subdivision of existing rooms."

That wasn't just good news—it was great news. It meant she didn't have to worry about fixing odd or lazy choices made by a previous owner. All she had to do was restore what was already here.

"So how much for the earthquake proofing?"

"Sixty-five hundred euros to do it correctly. You could achieve some protection with less money, but it would not be ideal."

Natalie had budgeted €5,000, already an exorbitant sum, but going €1,500 over budget would cut substantially into her €10,000 cushion. Between the Fiorello brothers' estimate and this one, she was nearly halfway through her safety budget and it was only her second week.

"What about the staircase?"

She managed to keep her voice even, though she suspected that a bit of despair showed on her face. The pity in his own expression doubled.

"Calacatta marble can cost at least a thousand euros per square meter. To reconstruct this staircase would require at least two days of labor by an artisan and a very specialized cut. I do not recommend entrusting this job to a standard stonemason."

But that was exactly what Natalie had planned to do. She had also planned on a single day of labor. At least her research about €1,000 per square meter for Calacatta marble had been correct. She sighed.

"What do you think the whole job could cost?"

"Just under four thousand euros to restore it completely."

Natalie didn't realize her eyes had fallen shut, that she had swayed a little in her seat, until she opened her eyes, feeling a bit dizzy. She blinked quickly to get her bearings again. To her credit, she didn't cry. It wasn't because she didn't want to. In one swift slice, he'd lopped off another 10 percent from her reserve budget.

"Is there any way to save money? To do part of it myself?"

The smart thing to do would be to get a second opinion. But there was something right about him, some way that he understood her and his profession and this house.

"Unlike other kinds of repairs, these must be done by experts." His voice held an insistence she didn't like. It wasn't quite chastisement, but close. "If you must save money on your restoration, do not save money on this."

Natalie frowned a little and thought quickly to the sorts of tasks she'd always imagined being able to chip in and do herself. "The experts can do all the heavy lifting on the stone repairs. But I can always come in behind them and plaster the walls."

Pietro's eyes narrowed in a way that foreshadowed a comment she wouldn't like. "Have you ever worked with Venetian plaster?"

She lifted her chin. "I've researched some techniques."

"Which one do you prefer? *Marmorino*? *Sgraffito*?"

Natalie vaguely remembered the terms, but she couldn't explain the difference, a testament to how shallow her knowledge was, which she was certain had been exactly Pietro's point.

"I'd have to think about that," she answered, crossing her arms.

"Have you ever mixed plaster?" he asked in quick succession.

"No." Natalie knew she sounded defensive. "But I'm damned good when it comes to paint."

"I see," Pietro remarked. "Because you can paint, you believe you can plaster as well, even though plastering is an artisan trade?"

"Yes." At least her voice sounded confident, even as her insides quivered.

"Then I wish you luck, Natalie Malone." Pietro returned his tablet to his bag. "I think that you will need it."

• • •

Crap. I think I missed them.

Natalie was halfway out of breath as she fast-walked up Via della Republica, where she clearly saw shuttered doors at number thirty-five. It had been her plan to stop there well before closing. The unexpectedly long and thorough visit from Pietro Indelicato had not only taken two hours—it had addled Natalie's brain and made her lose track of time.

Thirty-five Via della Republica was the office location of a respectable roofing outfit that hadn't been crossed out by Jorge. It was the only un-crossed-out roofer who might still be in town. After calling around to so many contractors, Natalie didn't mind paying a personal visit. Understanding Italian over the phone was about ten times harder than comprehending it in-person.

When she reached number thirty-five, she stopped to catch her breath, craning her neck to see whether anybody was visible through the windows – anyone who might take pity on her. Maybe people were still in there. Though, the closer she got, the more she was able to see that the window was shuttered from inside.

"*Sono andati in vacanza*," came a voice from across the street, a voice Natalie had to look around to see. It was a sunny afternoon, and she placed her hand above her brow to block the sun. The owner of the voice was an older woman, though something about her was spry. Natalie hadn't quite caught what the woman said.

"*Sto cercando lo scalpellino*," Natalie called up to the woman. *Sto cercando* was one of her most confident phrases. It meant, "I am looking for..." In the past forty-eight hours alone, she had explained to shopkeepers that she was looking for drop cloths, and a hand broom, and lots of cleaning products.

"*Sono andati in vacanza*," the woman repeated, more slowly and louder this time.

Natalie's accent had clearly given her away. Recognizing part of the response should have made her happy. Only, it didn't. It couldn't, because the word she recognized was the last word she wanted to hear again—"vacation."

"*Vacanza*?" Natalie repeated, her disappointment multiplying.

"*Sì, tornano a Settembre*." The woman nodded and smiled.

Natalie tried to smile back, but she didn't succeed, because she recognized another dreaded word—September. It would be two more weeks before the roofing contractor returned.

"*Grazie, Signora*." Natalie readjusted her messenger bag, which had become a bit jostled on her hurry into town.

"*Prego*."

Natalie saw now that the woman was sweeping up in front of a shop—Natalie's kind of shop, from the looks of it. Through the window, she spied furnishings and decor. Trinkets and antiquities and treasures.

But the woman, too, looked as if she were preparing to close up, and Natalie was in a grim mood. What she really wanted was something decadent, like cake, to finally sample the wares at the local *pasticceria*. If it had Wi-Fi, she could get in a solid hour of research. Wrapping up her life in America had consumed the better part of the last two months. Now that she was in Italy, it was time to find the story of Franco.

Beginning her walk to the *pasticceria*, Natalie tried once more to place him—to place why and how an Italian man she had never heard of had fit into Gram's life. The where and when seemed obvious. Gram had lived in Campania—the region of Italy where Zavona was located—during her teenage years. She was an army brat whose father had been stationed at the base in Cocenza for a time, to help decommission a World War II–era American base.

Natalie had grown up hearing idyllic descriptions and fond memories—countless stories of how Gram had fallen in love with the region and how she had also fallen in love with Gramps. Natalie's very American and much beloved late grandfather had been an army kid in Italy at the same time. Wanting to return to the region, to retire here and live out her final days, had nudged them toward this path—the adventure Gram wanted to relive and the adventure Natalie had always longed for but was ill-equipped to have.

But what had Gram wanted to relive?

Maybe not memories of Gramps, as Natalie had assumed, nor the old haunts of their youth. Though, whenever Gram had talked of Italy, it had included thoughts of him. But Gram had never once mentioned Franco Pelagatti, whose bequest letter mentioned Nanca, another town in Campania. And no one left five-figure sums to casual friends.

Natalie forgot her questions for a minute as she walked down cobblestone streets, still learning and delighting in their labyrinthine halls. Like most towns on the Amalfi Coast, it stretched vertically, its lower parts kissing the water and its upper parts high in the hills. Complex topography meant that this and other coastal towns were essentially built into the side of mountains. It made getting anywhere in town either a descent or a climb.

Character-wise, Zavona was everything Urbana wasn't. Its shops were distinctive and quaint—no chain stores or mega-retailers. There was something refreshing about not coming across a Starbucks every half a mile. And the coffee she'd indulged in every morning from the kiosk on the piazza was the best she'd ever tried.

The photos on the town website hadn't done Zavona justice. It was attended to, with people taking care. Flower boxes potted with geraniums, or dahlias, or begonias were outside every window. Those who lived in the center of town kept up daily tidying rituals, like washing front windows and steps. It was easy to see the pride people felt for their town.

It was also easy to see their contentment. Natalie had hoped that seaside living would come with a tranquility she had craved. At twenty-seven, Natalie had been working for most of her life. She had no illusions that she would be working just as hard—if not harder—at the *pensione*. But at least she would get to do it in a beautiful place.

She understood now what Gram had missed about this place. The history of it all was astounding—the charged energy of walking among stone buildings that were seven hundred years old. The streets were rarely crowded. And even when Natalie found herself strolling down a lane by herself, there was a hum to this place that resonated to the tips of her toes.

"*Buona sera, signorina.*"

"*Buona sera.*" Natalie echoed *good evening*, then pointed to one of the marble-topped rounds that veered off from the area with the register and the displays. The pastry shop seemed to do a good business from cash and carry, but there was also a small gathering of tables for anyone who wanted to sit.

"*Siediti, per favore,*" the woman implored, encouraging her to sit down.

Natalie set her bag on a chair and circled back to the display case to choose something decadent.

The array of pastries did not disappoint, though she couldn't name any. A half sphere that was smooth and white and the size of a tennis ball looked interesting. It had some small garnish—maybe lemon zest—sprinkled right in the middle on top. One tray held small glasses, half of them full of something that looked like chocolate pudding, the other half filled with a yellowish pudding that wasn't pale enough to pass for vanilla. A tray of larger glasses next to those were filled with something creamy and cakey in alternating layers. It seemed that half the confections in the case were covered in powdered sugar, though the cakes and cookies and puff pastries covered an astounding range.

"Which one would you like?" the woman asked in English.

Natalie hated herself a little for feeling relief at

the woman's linguistic choice. "This one, please," Natalie replied in English, pointing to the tennis ball.

"*Delizia al limone.*" The woman smiled.

So it does have lemon. Though she didn't know what a *delizia* was. She would look up the word later. At the moment, she had other things on her mind, like opening her laptop, navigating to Google Italy, and doing a location-based search. Browsing from here in Italy would spawn different results than she had gotten when she'd attempted searches from the US. The law firm named in the inheritance letter was in Nanca, a town just down the coast. She typed in her first search term as she awaited her *delizia*.

Franco Pelagatti Nanca.

CHAPTER EIGHT

"Pietro. Just in time."

His sister Lucia greeted him with a quick kiss to his cheek, an impressive feat considering that both of her hands were full. One hand held a teeming platter of clams steeped in broth; another held a long, ovular platter full of *aqua pazza*, poached fish with tomato and olive oil.

"Just in time for what?" he said.

Pietro eyed both dishes hungrily, hoping they would sit down to eat soon. It was a good sign that Lucia looked to be on her way to the table. He had entered the kitchen through the inner door that connected to the rest of the house. Lucia was set to walk out the open side doors and down the steps to the family table in the garden.

"Just in time to get the wine," she said. "No one has brought it up."

By "no one," she had to mean that none of the twenty or more family members currently on the property had taken care of it yet. To be fair, half of said family members were children. He had already greeted the smaller Indelicatos on his way into the house. He'd joined in briefly with their soccer game in the yard. Growing up with three sisters—all older and all married—meant that Pietro had nieces and nephews in spades.

"I'll bring it up," Pietro promised her retreating form, striding to the sink to wash his hands. No more adults in the kitchen had to mean the others had begun to sit. He raked his eyes over the few steaming dishes that remained on the island countertop and resisted the urge to steal a taste. Between traveling earlier in the week and eating the simple packed lunches he settled for while he worked on his restorations, he was looking forward to cooking from home.

Riffling around in a gadget drawer, he located a wine opener, stuck it in his pocket, and made his way back toward the inner door, meaning to take the hall to the cellar. Turning the corner, he promptly ran into his nonna. He caught her shoulders before they could knock each other over, then grinned at seeing his grandmother. He'd wondered where she'd been lurking.

"Quiet as a church mouse, as usual, Nonna." He bent to kiss her cheek.

She angled her face upward to receive it and grasped his forearm all at once. "I'm as loud as an elephant. You need to eat more chocolate. You have very bad ears."

Pietro bit back a smile. There was nothing wrong with his hearing. According to Nonna, a variety of ailments and deficiencies could be remedied by some exact food. Sardines for viruses. Black licorice for digestive problems. Lemons for just about everything else.

Folk medical advice notwithstanding, Nonna did seem to have bionic hearing. Even at seventy-three years old, she knew everything that happened in their family and in this house. Even in her younger years, when she had been occupied by the day-to-day duties of managing the groves and the family, there had been no getting anything past her.

"Come, Nonna. Let me walk you to the table." He faced the direction she was walking and held out his elbow for her.

She swatted his arm away. "Lucia told you to get the wine."

See? Bionic hearing. She could hear around corners and down halls.

"Nonna, I can walk you to the table and still have plenty of time to bring the wine."

But she had already resumed her shuffling walk away from him. A second before disappearing into the kitchen, she issued a smiling command.

"Put the good stuff by me."

• • •

In the summer, Sunday dinner was eaten outdoors below an oak wood pergola that was three times as long as it was wide. It had been built specifically to accommodate the long table. Though light shone through its slatted top in spots and dapples when there was sunlight, climbing bougainvillea the color of fuchsia twined around the wood, affording even better shade.

At six p.m., it was far from dusk, but the sun had begun its descent. Before the meal was finished, they would see it set, an orange ball dipping into the ocean, light fading lazily and giving way to night stars. Its western-facing orientation made sunsets in Zavona a sight to behold. Most days, if Pietro caught a hint of sunset from the corner of his eye, he paused for a moment of peace, stopping what he was doing to take it in.

Not today.

Wherever his father was present these days, moments of peace were few. Even Sunday dinner had become an exception. Week by week, the seats that Pietro and Alfonso took at the table had become farther apart. Soon, it might be as it was at EDC meetings, with Pietro at one end and Alfonso at the other.

Tonight, however, it seemed that Pietro had taken too long to scout out the good wine. When he returned from his task, the only remaining seat was practically right across from his father.

"I had interest in the hilltop villa today," Pietro's sister Caterina mentioned from a few seats down the table. Pietro had tucked in to his food as soon as his mother had led them in saying grace. On any other day of the week, other members of the family might lead, with some of the more entertaining gratitude coming from the youngest Indelicatos, but on Sundays, the blessing belonged to her.

"What kind of people are they?" Pietro asked after he swallowed his bite. He'd started with the squid and potatoes, though the *acqua pazza* was his favorite. With his growing teenage nephew—Caterina's son Carlo—at his side, it seemed wise to help himself before it was gone.

"The kind of people who can afford to buy it in cash for fifteen percent above the listed price," Caterina returned with a pointed look.

Approving murmurs sounded from all around. The hilltop villa Caterina spoke of was Pietro's property.

"But where are they from? What is their situation?" he asked between sumptuous bites. He liked when it was Lucia's turn to cook. She was the best at preparing anything that came from the sea. And she was a better chef than Caterina. Judging from how well Caterina's sons ate on days when Lucia cooked, they had reached the same conclusion.

"They are buyers. Their situation is they have money and your house is up for sale," Rodrigo piped in. Rodrigo was Caterina's husband. He was also the manager of the local bank—supremely logical and calculated in everything he did.

Pietro ignored Rodrigo and continued to question his sister. "But why do they want to buy the house?"

"It's a couple from London," Caterina replied. "They want to spend their summers here."

"What do they do for a living?"

"They earn enough money to buy houses in Italy," Rodrigo cut in again.

Pietro set his fork down and pinned Rodrigo with a stern look. "Caterina can answer for herself."

"The husband works in business," his sister answered curtly. "The wife works in government—something related to Parliament."

"So they would only come a few times a year?"

He and Caterina had had this conversation before. Pietro's plan was to sell all of his rehabilitated properties, but only to people who would maintain each house—all year round.

"Yes, though they would spend most of their time here once they retire."

The lightness in her tone from earlier was all but

gone. Pietro resented the way her disappointment stabbed him with guilt. His requirements, he knew, were stringent, but he had made his preferences clear. It had always seemed to him that Caterina herself was partially responsible for so many willing buyers they had to decline.

"They are not the right buyers, Rina." He heard the edge in his own voice. "You know I only want buyers who will stay all year. But thank you for trying."

"She's doing more than trying." Rodrigo's annoyance showed through. "The hilltop villa has had three offers in two months. It seems to me that you don't really want to sell."

Pietro set down his fork, picked up his napkin, and wiped his hands, slowing his chewing in preparation for what he would say. Rodrigo had no hair on his tongue when it came to his opinions.

"My restorations are a waste of time if I sell them to buyers who won't maintain them. I want buyers who will treat them as their homes."

"Pietro," interjected Matteo, the husband of Lucia. "The villa was abandoned for ten years. Four months out of the year is better than none."

"Matteo…" It took effort not to snap. "Many of my client rehabilitations are vacation properties in disrepair. You would be surprised how quickly a house can decline."

"What your brothers are saying," his father finally cut in, "is that it is not fair for you to waste Caterina's time showing a property you refuse to sell. She has a family. It is only fair that she has an opportunity to earn a commission."

Pietro didn't like that his father was butting in. He also didn't like that his father may have been right. And he absolutely refused to answer Alfonso directly.

"Caterina is a big girl," Pietro said. "If she would like to change our fee structure, she can speak to me, in her office, instead of here, considering that this is our business."

"Business and family go together," Alfonso argued. "We all must do good business so that all of us in the family can thrive. You must stop looking for hairs in the egg."

Pietro dropped his fork and considered rising from the table. It was not something that he—something that anybody—had ever done. Which would be worse? Taking heat for such rudeness or losing his temper with his father?

"Enough."

Pietro silenced—everyone did—upon hearing the voice of Carlota Indelicato. When Nonna said something, everybody listened.

Nonna regarded Alfonso with a gimlet eye, chastising him with a look, her very own son and her firstborn. "Pietro runs his business the way that I run mine. There is nothing wrong with this. Do you think that I sell my treasures to just anybody?"

Alfonso had the decency to soften his tone, to sound more deferential. "Of course not, Mama. But this is not the same. Your shop is not profitable, but you don't need it to be. Pietro must earn back his money on these restorations. He must think about his future children and their stability. To one day support a family of his own."

Nonna leaned forward in her chair, her intense gaze still laser-focused on her son. "The houses belong to him just as my treasures belong to me. What he does with them is for nobody but Pietro to decide."

• • •

"You must begin speaking to your father again."

Pietro hadn't heard his mother's approach. His thoughts were as swirling and swept up as the tide. He'd wandered down and across the terraced hillside until he reached what had always been *his* perch—the far corner of the southern grove.

His family was in the business of lemons—and not just any lemons—sweet *sfusato* lemons that only grew on this stretch of the Amalfi Coast. They were given this name—*sfusato*—because of their oblong shape and how they tapered at the end.

It wasn't just their shape and their sweetness that were distinct—it was the way that people ate them, like apples or pears. You could eat a *sfusato* lemon by biting right through its skin. They were sold in markets locally, shipped to fine establishments around the world, and used in all manner of dishes, sweet or savory, up and down the coast.

The ones that Pietro's family grew went to another of the region's—and the lemons'—highest purposes. For generations, they had used their lemons to produce a fine limoncello.

The spot was close enough to the water and far enough on the edge of the trees that briny air sailed in, melding with the grove's astringent zest. It was

Pietro's most beloved aroma. Adding to his respite was the distinct scent at this time of year, the warmth of the summer air somehow softening the sweetness of the lemons. His mother's voice was calm and low, steady as it had always been—powerful, somehow, in its quiet.

"I have never stopped speaking to Papa," he said.

Pietro shifted from the middle of the bench that had been built between two pillars of the trellis, making room for his mother to sit. Her hands drew together to hold her familiar evening shawl in place.

"At dinner, you barely spared him a glance," she said. "This was worse than last week and the week before. You will not overcome your differences if you do not speak."

He wouldn't say to his mother that all attempts to talk sense into his father had been as fruitless as their groves in a bad winter or that—perhaps for everybody's sake—it was better that they didn't speak. Grudging silence had to be better than inviting all the others into the fight.

"I see Papa in town frequently. He and I have shared many words. We spoke at length just last week."

His mother scoffed. "More like, you yelled at each other so loudly in Piazza della Republica that Signora Mariaelena had to close her shutters just to drown out the noise."

"Mama..." He threw her a disbelieving look. "Signora Mariaelena has never closed her shutters on any conversation in the piazza. No woman her age should be eavesdropping so diligently from the second-floor window. I once saw her lean so far out, she fell. Only her flower box saved her from certain death."

When his mother chuckled, Pietro smiled. He much preferred this version of her—the one who showed her dimples. It wasn't lost on him how things between him and his father caused her distress.

"No matter what happens with the program, or even with the town, he will always be your father. What he will not always be is the mayor. This conflict is temporary, Pitruzzu, no matter how it may seem."

Pietro's back stiffened at his mother's sentiment. A logical one, yes. But Pietro's position was logical, too. This constant rehashing of their conflict might find its natural end at the close of his father's tenure. But there was nothing temporary about the consequences of decisions made now, decisions that would have ripple effects for generations.

"Mama. I have my reasons."

"Men always do. But whether they are good reasons is always the thing to be seen."

CHAPTER NINE

"Oh, this is gorgeous."

Ellie drew out the "o" in gorgeous long enough that it seemed to take on an extra syllable. Her face held an extra bit of awe. She'd promised to drop by with trowels and spackle knives and all manner of tools her own rehab no longer needed. She'd found her way into the villa and now strolled out toward Natalie through the open doors in the library, looking like a diva with a utility bucket in hand.

"I'm glad you have an eye for potential," Natalie quipped. "That makes exactly two of us."

"What do you mean?"

Natalie took off her rubber cleaning gloves and stood up from where she'd been crouched down, a scrub brush in her hand the size of a brick. It had taken all morning to clean the neglect off the walls of the western patio. Now she was on to the large stone planters, her solution of baking soda, dish soap, and water nearly gone.

Ellie set down her bucket and used her newly freed hands to remove her wide-brimmed hat and run her fingers through her pastel-colored hair, shaking it out as if to enjoy the breeze. A smile bloomed on her face and she took in the view. Even when she ought to have been cleaning straight through since breakfast, Natalie had been transfixed a few times herself.

Ellie waved a hand in front of her face. "Don't

pay attention to me. I'm sulking. I got doom and gloom from the roofer last night. And the architect I met with the day before yesterday wasn't optimistic. At the rate I need to pay for repairs just to keep this place from falling apart, my guests will have to sleep on the floor."

She walked down the patio steps, toward the stone benches at the edge of the lawn that overlooked the water. "People would sleep on a bed of nails if they got to wake up to this view. You're going to make an absolute killing."

Natalie set down her gloves on the wall and followed Ellie, wiping her brow with the back of her wrist. "Let's hope the rehab doesn't kill me first."

Ellie smirked at that, then said, "Take my photo? This will make a great shot for my Insta. I like to keep the ex on his toes."

Natalie took her outstretched phone and Ellie sat on the bench.

"You let him follow you on social media? Is he some kind of glutton for punishment?"

Ellie smiled wickedly as she put her wide-brimmed hat back on her head. "No. But my mum is."

She stopped talking then, long enough to pose like a model, giving Natalie several shots with every new angling of her face. A nod of thanks and a hand reaching out to take her phone back was Natalie's signal that the photo shoot was over.

"Now I'm intrigued." Natalie settled down next to Ellie on the bench and pinned her with a "do tell" kind of look.

She hadn't needed to know Ellie long to be

convinced of how much she liked her. Ellie was candid, and fun, and free somehow. She couldn't have been more than five years Natalie's senior—in her early thirties at most. Still, Ellie was who Natalie wanted to be when she grew up.

"It's quite simple, actually," Ellie said with blunt nonchalance. "My husband was shagging my sister. I told them they could have each other and tossed both of them out of my life. But not before the judge who presided over the case sided with me about him being a lowlife piece of shite and awarded me seventy percent of the marital estate."

Natalie raised an impressed eyebrow. "Money can't buy happiness, but I'd imagine it got you off to a good start."

"An hour after the judge made her ruling, I texted him a photo of me wiping my tears with a £100 note."

Natalie had to giggle at that.

"Not just that," Ellie went on, "but both of them worked for me in a real-estate agency that I'd started. Naturally, I fired them. They've been forced to move in with my mum who—let me tell you—is not a subtle woman. It seems they hear from her what I'm up to at dinner every night."

Natalie shook her head, not in disapproval but admiration. "I'm calling you next time I need revenge on my ex."

"You know what they say, darling. It's best served cold. I take it you've left some sad sack behind back in the States?"

"Well..." Natalie tried to keep a light tone, even as mention of Reggie took her to dark thoughts she'd rather forget. Tones of self-deprecation were clear in her voice. "It's been a while since I've dated a guy. It turns out I'm not an excellent judge of character."

"Uh-oh…" Ellie returned. "What was his transgression?"

"He was just…controlling. And he left me hanging one too many times. He wanted to be the big man in the relationship. Talked a big game about how he wanted to take care of me and manage all the money and the bills."

What Natalie didn't say was how easy she'd made it for him to seduce her with lofty promises. Having someone take care of her—truly take care of her so she didn't have to worry about anything—was the one thing she'd always wanted but never had.

"Please don't tell me he stole from you." Ellie looked preemptively disgusted.

"No, nothing like that. He was honest with the money that came in. But he lied about a lot of little things. Lies designed to convince me everything was under control. Meanwhile, he was busy dropping a lot of balls. It took a year before I realized how sporadically he was paying our bills. Whenever they piled up too much—which was usually after a month or three—he'd just pay everything at once."

"Bloody hell." Ellie shook her head in disapproval.

Natalie nodded in confirmation. "I started getting alerts from my bank about my credit score going down. And that's not even the worst part. Taking Gram to a dentist appointment and being told they wouldn't see her until the past-due amount was paid? That was the last straw."

Ellie scoffed. "Good riddance."

Natalie didn't expand on all the hell that had ensued. Gram had taken her back in, rent-free, but it had taken two years for Natalie's credit to go back to green. Hours on the phone with customer service trying to sort out her student loans. Thousands of dollars in late fees and penalties, not only for her but for Gram, all because Natalie had been too eager to trust the wrong guy.

"Maybe you ought to start an Instagram account for the villa," Ellie suggested next. "Invite him to follow the account. Make sure he sees everything he's missing in HD."

"Honestly?" Natalie returned. "I don't care anymore what happens to Reggie, as long as another Reggie never happens to me."

• • •

Why don't they make these glasses bigger?

Natalie poured her third serving of wine, a Campanian red called Aglianico. It was the last of the initial supply she had bought from the wine merchant in town. The woman at the kitchenware store had insisted the stemless glass, which was more trumpet than globe, was a typical vessel used locally, though it didn't hold that much liquid.

Big, fat American wineglass, she added to her mental list, picturing the oversize ones they sold at Cost Plus. If there was one thing she hadn't thought she'd run into problems getting enough of in Italy, it was wine. As it turned out, there were many things she'd thought wrong, like that €10,000 was enough of a contingency fund and that YouTube videos didn't lie. As she'd spent the past hour discovering, the DIY grease-cutting tile cleaner made out of vinegar, baking soda, and dish soap needed more than the "little bit of elbow grease" to make her kitchen backsplash shine.

Deciding that one more viewing of the video would not improve her results, Natalie turned off roaming on her cell, flipped on her Bluetooth speaker, and navigated to a song. The thought of her data bill already made her cringe. Home Wi-Fi couldn't come soon enough. In the meantime, she would settle for music and wine.

Tonight seemed like a Beyoncé kind of night. If she listened to her whole playlist—which included some Destiny's Child—she'd get the right mix of wallowing and [illegible] you. Given her week, she could use a bit of both.

"Hello?"

Seconds after she had turned her speaker up on "Independent Women," the sound of a voice broke through her groove. Who would be dropping in on her unannounced on a Friday night?

"Natalie?"

Oh no.

It couldn't be. Only, when his head peeked through the door, it was. His brows rose a little as he took in the scene. The music was loud, the counter was full of filthy rags, and Natalie might have been quite sweaty, and not in a flattering, glisten-y way. In a way that screamed, "I scrubbed so hard, I broke a sweat." She turned the music way down, then inched toward the door. Why hadn't he come in?

"Pietro? What are you doing here?"

And then, a double surprise. For one long, puzzling moment, Pietro didn't look as if he knew the answer himself, even though it was he who had come, he who stood in the light of the setting sun between the kitchen door and her garage. He didn't wear the more formal clothes she had seen him in both times before—no button-downs or slacks or fine leather shoes. This Pietro was dressed in casual clothes, worn jeans, and a T-shirt that revealed tanned arms and chiseled muscles at the cuff. A pair of leather work gloves was grasped in one of his hands.

"Did you forget something when you were here this week?"

Natalie racked her brain to think of the equipment he'd had with him and tried to remember whether any of the handheld devices she'd seen him with had caught her eye that day. The lighting situation inside still wasn't perfect. Her mind raced to what it might be like to have to go back through her house with Pietro, just the two of them, by flashlight again.

"Have you ever actually worked with plaster before?" he said.

The question caught Natalie off guard. It was a non sequitur and she couldn't imagine why he would ask. Though the simple truth seemed like the best of responses, regardless of his reasons.

"No," she admitted.

"But you said you have time, and you want to do things as inexpensively as possible."

His question came out as a statement, albeit an accurate one. Natalie didn't know why they were talking about this.

"Yes," she confirmed. "I do want to do this as inexpensively as possible. But I also want to do it right. You were right earlier. I have no experience with the pieces we talked about. I need to hire someone to do it. Someone who is an expert at this sort of thing."

From there, Natalie half expected a lecture about what an enormous expense it would be with so many hundred square meters of wall. But she didn't need a lecture about how far off the reality would be compared to her estimations. She guessed he had the right.

"What if you could become an expert?" Pietro asked then.

Natalie blinked, not knowing what he was getting at. He seemed to be implying that *she* could somehow get up to speed. She thought to remind him that, just twenty hours before, she hadn't known the difference between *Marmorino* and *Sgraffito.*

"I'm pretty sure I'm in no danger of that." Natalie's voice wasn't bitter, it was flat, as if the past day had taken the rest of the fight out of her body.

"This is the activity that you would do very much of, no? The activity where you would spend the majority of your budget if you had to hire a contractor for the work. But if you learned to do it as well as a professional, you really could do it yourself."

Natalie didn't ask the question that she knew was in her eyes—the question that anyone in her position would ask. How did he presume to get her the training of a professional?

"Plasterers go through training for at least three years." She'd read up on it the night before, after she had been thoroughly shown up by Pietro. "Two in direct training and another year in practical apprenticeship."

She felt a bit awkward spouting off facts, but it seemed fitting to remind him that he himself had alerted her to what a specialized function it was. What could have happened to cause him to change his mind?

He took another step forward. Natalie couldn't say whether she loved it or hated it. On the one hand, he got a bit close for somebody who barely knew her. On the other hand, he smelled really, really good.

His voice lowered and softened at the same time, yet it also held authority, a strange hypnosis that both commanded her of what to do at the same time as it reeled her in.

"If you wish to learn the correct method, I can teach you how. I can help, if you would allow me to."

Upon hearing his words, she closed her mouth. Pietro had shown up on her doorstep, on a Friday night, to ask about helping her. Her confusion must have shown on her face, because his mildly pleading look was clear evidence that he would try to persuade her but knew he had a lot to explain.

"There is much to do and you are alone. As I said, I have some experience with this."

Natalie thought for a minute. Was this logical? Yes, she was alone and would benefit from help. Yes, Pietro would know what he was doing. Yes, it seemed less and less likely every day—with every new challenge—that she could do this alone. But there were other pieces that weren't logical, like why a guy like Pietro didn't have anything better to do on a Friday night and what could possibly be in it for him.

"Why would you help me?" She hadn't meant for it to come out the way it did—so blunt and accusatory. She corrected herself. "I mean...I'm not the only one in town who's in over my head. You could be helping them."

Natalie had said that last part with a self-deprecating smile. Pietro gave a little smile back but didn't say anything in return. That was when Natalie understood—she may not have been the only *sognatori* who felt in over her head, but she was clearly the one who was furthest under. Pietro had chosen to help because he pitied her.

The proud part of her lifted its chin in indignation, insisting that she refuse his help, reminding her that so much of what she'd achieved in her life, she had done alone. Growing up in Urbana had meant watching most of the kids around her enjoy privilege that was out of her reach. Yet she had already achieved—and truly earned—a lot more than kids who had started with more.

But a bigger part of her—the part that remembered sitting in the small living room in the house she had shared with Gram, talking about who would do what if they were accepted into the program—remembered that this entire experience was meant to be shared. That Gram had always looked forward to doing the gardening and the fixing while Natalie had always talked about decorating and painting. Natalie was still letting go of the fact that part of that could never be salvaged—that she could never do this with Gram. Sooner or later, she did need to fully redefine what it meant to receive help.

"I would like to help you, Natalia." Pietro spoke again when she didn't respond, his voice deeper and lower somehow. All pontifications about accepting help or not flew right out of Natalie's head as Pietro stepped closer.

"Natalia?" she repeated. She had already enjoyed her name on his lips more than she should. But this small change—one single letter—it made a difference.

"You plan to stay here in Italy, yes?"

She nodded.

"To live here for a very long time?"

She nodded again.

"Do you prefer that I use the English pronunciation of your name?"

It took her long seconds to find her voice, but she shook her head in the meantime. Finally, she uttered a soft, "No."

He nodded a bit, as if in understanding, then gazed down at her for another long moment in a way that no one had gazed at her before. Every moment she had ever shared with Pietro felt new. She couldn't tell whether it was a fact of time or simply a feeling she had when she was around him—when Pietro was near, things slowed down.

"Natalia," he repeated. "I am here to help you with your restoration. I offer you this help freely and with no expectation that you reciprocate for this help or compensate me in any way. Natalia…do you accept?"

CHAPTER TEN

"*Piccolo*!"

Pietro would never tire of that smile on his nonna's face—the one she beamed when his visit was a surprise. Living on the family farm meant that he saw her almost daily. Still, she treasured his drop-ins, more so when they were unannounced.

"*Piccolo*," she repeated. "I had a good feeling that I would see you today."

"Ciao, Nonna." He was certain that his own smile was just as wide. Careful not to bump or rattle any of the delicate items on display around her shop, he took the widest route toward the back, coming up to the chair where she liked to sit.

It occurred to him, not for the first time, how lonely it must be for her in the store. It was only open in the afternoons. Those of her friends who were still able-bodied dropped in from time to time, to gossip and talk. But Nonna was one of a small group of septuagenarians living in Zavona. And her friends were dwindling in number.

"Did you have lunch in town today?" she asked.

"Come, Nonna." He threw her a charming smile. "If I had planned for lunch in town, I would surely have invited you."

She tutted out a dismissive little laugh and pointed at him in accusation. "Such a flirt. You should save your flirting for your women."

"I have more than one?" he quipped.

"You have less than zero, Pietro. Patrizia tells me that her grandniece is very interested in you. Beautiful girl. I have seen her. What is wrong? Do you have another girl in another town?"

Pietro had forgotten to anticipate this line of questioning. Tonia Lupone was the grandniece of the Patrizia of which his nonna spoke. He and Tonia had run into each other two weeks earlier on a train from Salerno to Naples.

His nonna was right—she was a good-looking woman, if not a bit young. They had parted ways at the taxi stand in Naples, but not before Tonia had asked him whether they could see each other again. As kindly as he could, Pietro had declined.

"Nonna, please…" He didn't immediately know what he was pleading for her to do. "I can choose my own dates."

Pietro was considered to be a very eligible bachelor and Zavona was a small town. Knowing everybody meant there was no such thing as a casual relationship or even casual sex. Things would not have been so bad if so many young people—so many young men—hadn't left.

He couldn't tell his nonna how badly he wished things were different. Men in the prime of their lives had needs. He got most of his fulfilled when he traveled. Never the same woman, and it was never planned, but he got pieces here and there on the rare occasion he met a woman and felt a tiny spark.

Or a big spark.

It had taken only half an evening with Natalie for Pietro to realize his mistake. Or, if not his mistake, a complication. He had offered his help—one-on-one help—to a beautiful, complex woman. Shallow beauty, he could ignore—predictable beauty that bottomed out too soon after you breached the surface. But with Natalie, each encounter revealed new depth.

It didn't help that every time he'd seen her, she had on less and less clothing, revealing more curves and smooth, fragrant skin. Being around her awakened the part of him he'd neglected for too long. The part of him that liked sex—incendiary sex—not just sex of the hotel-bar-encounter variety. Sex with someone he'd nursed an attraction to. Someone he couldn't get off his mind.

Nonna regarded him with a sharp eye. For a moment, he was certain she could hear his thoughts. "You did not answer my question. What is wrong with Tonia?"

"Yes, Tonia is a lovely girl. No, I do not have another woman in another town. Don't worry about me, Nonna. Nothing is wrong."

He waited for her look of disapproval. At this point in the conversation, he typically got a scowl, though his grandmother's scowls didn't have teeth when they were cast upon him. Instead, a look of worry—of genuine concern—crossed her face.

"You can tell Nonna the truth, Pietro. I will not like it, but I have prayed on this question. I will accept it if it is true. Tell Nonna. Do you like boys?"

Pietro blinked rapidly, barely believing his own ears but completely believing the worried look on his nonna's face. It was wrong of him, but he was so shocked by the question that he could not stop his booming laugh. He had spent the previous night helping a woman he barely knew, scolding himself all the while not to let his eyes linger on her body, and chided himself just seconds earlier to cleanse his thoughts of her.

"Nonna..." Pietro gasped once, an attempt to bring his laughter under control. He doubted his reaction would have been so immediate had he actually slept enough the night before. "I like women. I like women very much."

She narrowed her eyes, as if she wasn't sure she believed him.

"Please, Nonna. Don't worry. I'm very happy alone. And very busy with my work."

He let out his last few chuckles, but her expression forced his laughter to fade. Behind her persistent questioning hid real worry.

"Nonna, not everyone gets married these days. Maybe I will, maybe I won't. But I can be happy either way."

She remained quiet, and he wondered whether this part of the conversation was over—whether he could finally ask her the question he'd come here for. He wanted to borrow a few floor pieces for photographing one of the projects he owned. He and Caterina had come to an understanding.

When it seemed that Nonna wouldn't speak again, he got set to broach the subject. Then, at the very last minute, a bomb.

"Once upon a time, a family was all you wanted. When she left, you allowed her to take your dreams with her. Now you pretend you never wanted a family at all."

"Nonna..."

If he had barely known what to say a minute before, he certainly didn't now. How had it come to this?

"I didn't say that I didn't want a family. I said I could be happy without one. Maybe I don't have a wife or children of my own—but I have all of you. And I'm ready for the right woman if she comes along."

"Then why haven't you sold that house?"

Nonna didn't need to specify which one. It was the house he'd bought for himself and Vittoria. Vittoria, who had left and never looked back. Once upon a time, he *had* thought they would live there together, would raise children and build their own lives. Once upon a time, it *had* been his favorite house in Zavona.

"The house is not finished. It will be complete this year—before Christmas. And it is as I told Caterina. I'm waiting for the right person to buy. This house is no different from all the others."

Once again, his nonna didn't look as if she believed him. "I'm glad to hear you say that, *piccolo*. If you intend to move on, you must let Vittoria go."

CHAPTER ELEVEN

"Praise the Lord."

Natalie sent up silent thanks to the Fiorello brothers, one of whom had come by several hours earlier to drop off a second generator and two construction lights on stands. Whichever Fiorello it was—Natalie couldn't tell—had also come carrying long coils of orange and black extension cords—some of the longest, heaviest-duty variety Natalie had ever seen. With three floors and so many rooms, things were getting complicated. The Fiorellos had offered both generators for the rest of the month of August, then for after they officially started in September—however long it would take them to complete their work.

Construction lights were helpful to the work she was doing with Pietro. It seemed that evenings were the time he could often come, though he'd only been by twice and she had no idea whether to expect a pattern. Normally, she might have liked a regular schedule, rather than him just dropping by, or a head's up text letting her know that he was coming. As she was quickly learning, Italy wasn't a stick-to-the-schedule kind of place.

They had accomplished quite a bit the first night he'd come over. No hands-on work but a concrete plan. He'd walked through the villa and helped her do the math on her budget for wall repairs, with Pietro dispensing insider advice. He'd suggested removing the plaster in certain rooms and reverting to the exposed stone for a more rustic look in others, restoring the original aesthetic of the home. He'd shown her which rooms had walls that simply needed a good cleaning versus walls that could be plastered soon versus walls that shouldn't be touched pending an assessment of water damage.

On his second visit, he'd brought over samples of the full set of products they would need, previewing the end-to-end process and explaining the purpose of each one. He'd told her where she could buy in bulk and advised her to get a business license for the *pensione* in order to set up discount-eligible commercial accounts. He told her which suppliers to buy from and which to avoid. She had listened gratefully and eagerly taken notes. He'd saved her thousands of euros based on that advice alone.

Tonight, on his third visit, they were still days away from doing any actual plastering. It turned out this plastering technique involved a lot of prep. The parts that required trowels and technique wouldn't come in until later. For now, it was cleaning the walls and repairing some of the stonework flaws beneath with a filling agent, which found them side by side and finally at work, brushing and scrubbing as they stood upon ladders in the sitting room, just feet apart.

"This is better, no?" Pietro asked as he brushed. The space was quite transformed. He had brought over yet another truckload of supplies—drop cloths and troughs and specialized brushes. He'd brought over a jug of the mild, professional-grade detergent he'd shown her the time before, hundreds of dollars of equipment he'd insisted he'd just had lying around.

"It's amazing. Thank you."

She managed not to fall off the ladder as she sent over a grateful smile, though she did wobble a little. She steadied herself before it could go farther than that. Her balance was generally good, which meant that Pietro was the problem. Like this, he was utterly distracting. Surely Natalie couldn't be blamed for that.

Today, he had on work pants—a common brand that shouldn't have looked like couture. But they fit him in the most flattering way, with enough give to let him move but enough fit to show his lines. He had a swimmer's build, tall and lean with cut muscles on every plane of his body that were hard to un-notice once you'd gotten a good look.

A good look was exactly what had caused Natalie to wobble. As he scrubbed at the higher areas of the wall, his shirt was riding up. Given his height, he had insisted upon working closer to the top. Not that she had meant to stare, but watching Pietro with the cleaning brush was like watching soft porn. His corded forearms, the flex of his triceps where chiseled muscle met the cuff of his short-sleeve tee, the peek of his V-shaped abs as he stretched his body to extend his reach were all divine.

"So…you are from California?" Pietro asked after a minute or two. Music playing from her phone through her speakers, at normal volume this time, was the only thing saving them from silence. She couldn't imagine what sort of music sexy Italian men might like, so she'd gone with Queen. Everyone liked Queen, regardless of where you were from.

"Wow, I'm surprised," Natalie admitted, smiling as she continued her brushing. "Most people think California girls have blonde hair and blue eyes."

"Just like most people think Italian men are very dark."

Kind of like I thought.

"You are afraid of earthquakes." Pietro continued his logic. "California is where these are in the States, no?"

"I'm afraid of earthquakes because you get them here. In Illinois, we get tornadoes."

"You are from Chicago?"

She shook her head. "Downstate. Like, two hours away, in a place called Urbana."

"A big city, then?"

Natalie nearly laughed. "Uh, no. A small city, more like a big town."

"But *Urbana* means urban." The name of her town had never sounded so sexy on anybody's lips.

"Honestly? I have no idea who came up with that name."

Pietro kept brushing. "What did you do for work in Illinois?"

She was enjoying his hypotheses. "Guess."

"A painter," he came back with a playful smile. It was the one thing she'd indignantly insisted she knew how to do.

"Guess again," she deadpanned and he chuckled.

"I think you were a student. You are very young."

She couldn't tell whether he was complimenting her. The notion that he might be gave her a thrill.

"I did go to college. I studied art history."

She surprised herself by leading with this. Mentioning this was revealing the most important part of her.

"This explains your appreciation for art and architecture."

"Art history was my minor," she clarified, realizing she still hadn't answered his original question. "I double-majored in statistics and math."

"You were a teacher?" he asked next. It wasn't a bad guess.

"I was an *attuaria*," Natalie translated for his benefit. She had taken the time to learn the specific word for her profession. Actuarial work was obscure enough, and her Italian skills were weak enough that she didn't want to have to explain it if she didn't have to.

Pietro nodded. "Ah, *attuaria*..." he repeated. "How do you say this in English?"

He spoke beautiful English, flowing English, English that was adorably flawed in some moments but impressively correct in others. Some of Pietro's grammar, and the formal respect of his speech, could put your average American speaker to shame. Add in his accent on top of it—where he placed weight on his consonants and how he pronounced his vowels—and it made Natalie want to listen to him all day long.

"Actuary," she translated.

When Pietro repeated it again, it sounded a bit more like the word "ashuerry" with the emphasis on the "erry" rather than on the "ash." Natalie doubted she sounded remotely as sexy pronouncing anything in Italian. She doubted her Italian was even cute.

"This is like a financial adviser, no?" Pietro asked for clarification.

Natalie was a little impressed that he knew anything about actuaries at all. Most people didn't. It was an obscure profession.

"Close," she praised. "I don't advise people. I advise corporations. It's an actuary's job to assess risk."

Pietro actually stopped brushing and looked over at her, narrowing his eyes in comprehension. "This explains your desire for earthquake protection."

She shrugged, owning it. "I don't like taking risks."

"Yet you decided to move to Italy, alone. A place where you have never been. To do something that you have never done."

He didn't seem to be making fun of her exactly, though he did have humor in his eyes. Still, she got the sense that he was genuinely asking the question.

"I didn't jump into this without thinking. I researched. I put together detailed financial projections. Before I even got here, I'd thought all the way through the job."

"Your Calacatta marble," he interjected with a little smile, and she nodded.

"When you think through something ahead of time—end to end—that's what stops it from being scary. I don't mind taking calculated risks."

Pietro seemed to accept this answer. "Still, you are very bold to take this on. Not just a cottage home but a villa."

Natalie had been there for two and a half weeks and still hadn't told anybody about Gram. Her decision to abandon her life in Illinois to move permanently to the Amalfi Coast was a convoluted story. But the more time passed that she didn't mention Gram, the more wrong it seemed to erase her, as if Gram hadn't seeded this dream, wasn't the reason why Natalie was there in the first place.

"I wasn't supposed to do it alone."

"Ex-husband?" Pietro asked with an eyebrow raise. "Most people in the program are couples."

"I had planned on coming with my grandmother."

He stopped brushing. There must have been something to her tone. His smile fell, and she hoped he wouldn't ask her to say it, but the truth must have shown on her face.

"I'm sorry," he said simply, only it didn't feel like the same platitude as she'd heard from others. From Pietro, it sounded heartfelt, sincere. She wondered whether he had lost his own.

Natalie nodded her thanks, then went back to her own brushing, knowing that if she let him look at her like that for much longer, she might actually cry.

Scanning her memory for what they had been talking about before that revelation, a recollection emerged, one that brought a smile to her face. She could hear Gram's voice in her head as she remembered.

"Anyway, I'm not so much a risk-taker as I am a planner. My gram always used to say, 'A goal is just a wish without a plan.'"

The scratch of tandem scrubbing confirmed that Pietro had gone back to using his brush as well.

"I like this saying," he declared. "But there is much that cannot be achieved with a plan. Here, we say, '*non tutte le ciambelle riescono col buco*.'"

Natalie only recognized the first three words. They meant "not all of" something. But not all of what? She shook her head, silently asking Pietro to translate. A small smile came over his lips.

"It means, 'not all doughnuts come out with holes.'"

Natalie just blinked. Pietro gave a little chuckle, a low one that made her forget to care whether the saying made any sense. Even kind of, sort of laughing at her, Pietro was ridiculously gorgeous.

"Things do not always happen as we plan them," he said by way of explanation. "Sometimes we must be flexible to change."

Natalie doubted that Pietro was calling her inflexible, though she'd certainly been called that before.

"Believe me, Natalia. I wish that every *sognatori* thought about risk as much as you. But in Italy, with buildings this old and unpredictable, restorations rarely go as planned."

• • •

September would arrive in just over a week, not that she'd been counting the days. Except, it was eight days away and she totally had. To her delight, the prediction that contractors would return in September wasn't literal. She'd already begun receiving callbacks from messages she'd left with them weeks before.

She had finally managed to book a consultation with a guy who could test her water. Pietro had given her an inside track, and the contractor had been out the day before. The heavy-lidded concrete stump behind her garage was not some utility access point, as she had assumed. It turned out to be the cover to a working well, which, according to a series of tests, turned out to be drinkable.

After multiple faucet runs and toilet flushes, the water inside the house still ran brownish, prompting a test of the spigot water. The results were refreshingly precise. It was contaminated with metal particulates and soil. Somewhere down the line, pipes had been breached and the lines exposed to air.

But that's all for tomorrow.

Natalie smiled to herself, very much liking the idea of an afternoon spent playing hooky. She had worked hard these past weeks, cleaning away things that had been left that she couldn't use, scrubbing and prepping and priming her many walls. Apart from the physical work was the mental work, massaging numbers and finessing budgets, suffering minor heart attacks with every new estimate that came in.

Today, she would treat herself to a few luxurious hours in town, exploring unventured streets and popping into unvisited shops. Most places she'd been to so far were for practicality's sake, for getting food in her belly or buying things she needed to repair the house. Today, she would visit the places that had charmed her, the tiny experiences she had been aching to try.

After visiting the coffee kiosk she liked on Piazza della Republica, she debated where to go first. Art shops had to be a focus. Even if she wanted to paint, she was spotty on basic supplies. She'd seen a paper store that appeared to sell easels and canvases and knew of two galleries in town. The former she would visit to outfit herself. The latter, to start to develop a sense for where she could find large-format art.

Both galleries were up a side street that she knew of but had never taken. It would be a bit of a walk. The paper store was down, below Café Ludo, and closer to the water. She also wouldn't mind heading to the *pasticceria* at some point. She wanted to treat herself to something sweet, something she had yet to try. And she still hadn't gone into that antiques store.

The antiques store is closest, Natalie mused. She was getting better about knowing her way around, no small accomplishment given a mazework of streets that lacked rhyme or reason. She would go in a minute, after she savored the last of her *espressino*. The woman who worked at the coffee kiosk had been expanding her horizons. Her current favorite was this—espresso brewed on a base of cocoa powder and mixed with steamed milk.

By the time she made her way up Via della Republica, she was enjoying the buzz of caffeine and the brine of the afternoon air. Even this high up, you got a bit of a sea breeze. A smile played on Natalie's lips as she approached the store. It had an elegant blue awning that showed no name but was accented in gold, which drew out in front and provided shade over items that had been placed on the sidewalk. A rolling drink cart with glass on top and crystal carafes caught her eye from where it sat on display. Through the window, she spied gorgeous lamps and clocks and statuettes. But when she walked in, she was transformed.

I could spend hours here.

Natalie walked in slowly, her eyes already feasting over every standing, hanging, and set-down item in the store. Furniture pieces—beautiful in their own right—displayed fabulous trinkets on top, understandable items like tea sets and statues as well as random, pretty items that did she-didn't-know-what.

From the ceiling hung an impressive mishmash of chandeliers. The walls were lined with paintings and sconces and mounted art pieces that fit somewhere in between. It was the best kind of visual explosion, a collection in which nothing—and therefore everything—made sense. It was one treasure on top of another.

"Ciao, Signorina." A jovial voice came from somewhere deep inside the store.

The person must have had a line of sight to Natalie. Her greeting had identified Natalie as a woman, and a young one at that. But the store was so full—so visually engaging—she imagined that finding the woman would be harder than finding Waldo.

"Ciao," Natalie called back, expecting to see the woman she had seen two weeks before, the woman who had been outside sweeping.

Venturing deeper into the store, which was a lot larger than it looked from the outside, Natalie finally found her close to the back. She sat knitting on an antique chair upholstered in a pristine chartreuse in Rococo style. A propped-up iPad stood on a small table situated between the antique chair and its twin. A plate of cookies sat next to her, as did a glass of something that didn't look like water. Judging from the dramatic music, she had been watching some sort of soap opera.

How did she even hear me from all the way back here?

"*Benvenutto*," the woman welcomed her. She had dark-blue eyes and a kind smile and looked to be in her early sixties. Her gray hair was short and cut stylishly, and the red plastic frames of her half-eye glasses gave her a bit of pizzazz.

"*Grazie*," Natalie said, then waited for the familiar question—*is there something I can help you find?* She'd been asked that in the hardware store, the kitchen store, the wine store…nearly everywhere she went.

But the woman didn't ask her. She didn't even get up out of her chair. She unbusied one of her hands instead, motioned around the store, and said in Italian, "Please look. Enjoy."

It was all the permission Natalie needed to take her time. For nearly thirty minutes, Natalie did look, and she certainly did enjoy. She began her mental list of the items she would love to have for the villa, began to hope they would still be there in a few months' time. The items didn't have price tags. For the moment, she was too afraid to ask.

She could have stayed for much longer but forced herself away. Exploring only part of the store now would give her a good reason to come back.

"Thank you," she told the woman in Italian. "You have a beautiful store."

"Did you see something you liked?"

Natalie smiled and looked around. "Everything."

The woman's face opened up with a smile that gave Natalie a glimpse of what she might have looked like as a younger woman, though she was very beautiful in her advanced age.

"I am Carlota," the woman said.

"Natalia." She spoke her own name in the Italian pronunciation for the first time, and it filled her with a sense of delight.

"Signorina Natalia, you may return whenever you would like."

CHAPTER TWELVE

"Natalia!"

Pietro frowned at Natalie's open front door, a door he would tell her again should be closed. He was alarmed by the number of times he'd arrived to her villa to find the place wide open. The more he thought about it, the less he liked the idea of her up in this palatial house all alone.

But there was another reason why Pietro had called her name. He hadn't forgotten the first day he'd come there—the day he'd caught Natalie by surprise, the day that she'd practically landed on him after falling off her ladder. However many times he'd recalled that moment—of how decadent the sensation of Natalie sliding down his body had been—he also worried that she was clumsy. That, but for his fast reflexes, a tumble from her ladder might have ended much worse.

"Natalia!" he repeated, dropping the bag of dried plaster he'd hauled in on his shoulder. He had more in his truck. Also in his truck was a better-quality ladder, a steadier one that would make it difficult for Natalie to fall. He would remove, and take with him, the one she'd been using until now.

But first, he wanted to find her. Brushing dust from his hands, he wandered past the front hall, through the courtyard, and toward the kitchens. It could be that she was listening to music or to an Italian lesson on her earbuds again. Being cut off from awareness of her surroundings was another notion he didn't like if she was up here alone.

Or not alone, Pietro realized as he turned into the hallway near the kitchen and nearly ran into Nico Fiorello, who, apart from startling a little at nearly bumping into him, seemed unfazed.

"Ciao, Pietro. Natalie is outside near the garage."

Pietro relaxed a little.

"Ciao, Nico." He gave his friend a pat on the back and paused to talk. "Is Nero here, too?"

"Not today." Nico jutted his chin toward the kitchen. "Fabio is with me. We're fixing some wiring damage in the kitchen. Now that she has her permits, we have started work."

The prospect of walking through the kitchen en route to Natalie dampened a bit at the mention of the braggadocious younger cousin of the twins. Pietro bumped into Fabio from time to time on one job or another. He spent more time talking than working, had never met a mirror he didn't like, and was known throughout Zavona as a notorious flirt.

Pietro gave a brief nod and proceeded toward the kitchen, more eager to get to Natalie now, despite having confirmed that she was, in fact, not all alone in an unlocked house. He would report that he had delivered the plaster and would confirm a time when he might come over next. When he arrived at the back door, Pietro found Natalie and Fabio outside, poring over a folded paper as they stood next to her table.

"This is a very far ride," Fabio was saying

They were too close for Pietro's liking. The paper was much larger than standard and creased with evidence of numerous folds, even though it was extended now. Fabio was speaking to Natalie and tracing lines with his finger on the paper. It seemed they were looking at a map.

"A woman like you who does not speak much Italian should not ride the bus. The map is very confusing. Please. Allow me to give you a ride. The bus station in Nanca is very far away from the Hall of Records."

Pietro frowned at Fabio's obvious flirting. He was still standing inside the kitchen door and able to see their entire interaction perfectly. Neither Natalie nor Fabio had noticed his arrival.

"Oh, I can't ask you to do that," she replied. "I don't know how long it might take me at that office or whether they'll tell me there's some other place I need to go while I'm there. Besides, I live here now. I've got to learn how to get around."

"Then please allow me to help you with translation."

Natalie chewed her lip, clearly swayed by this notion, predictably so after the way things had gone in the permitting office weeks earlier.

"Come. We will make a day out of it. After the Hall of Records, I will show you a café I like on the water. We will have lunch."

The moment Pietro comprehended the suggestion, his feet began to move, making their way down the steps that led to the backyard with more than a little urgency.

"Ciao, Natalia. Ciao, Fabio." Pietro was careful to sound casual. He was also careful to turn to Natalie, to speak directly to her. He didn't want to make what he would suggest in due time to sound like a negotiation. "Your plaster is in the front. Next time, I hope to show you a mixing technique. There are tricks one can employ, for consistency and color."

As Natalie's eyes were on Pietro, Fabio's eyes were on Natalie's breasts, with such concentrated attention that Pietro saw it clearly from a quick glance out of the corner of his eye.

"Thank you, Pietro." Natalie sounded grateful and kept her warm, shy gaze on him for a moment. Her look made something inside him melt.

"I will be finished in less than an hour," Fabio cut in, or at least it felt like that, even though no one was speaking. Pietro frowned at the interruption of the look, Natalie's look, that had been just for him.

"I don't know..." Natalie turned her attention back to Fabio and began to fold up the map. Pietro had never met anyone so reticent to accept help. He would not mention this now, as Fabio was certainly not the person who Pietro thought ought to be giving it to her. He would mention it later that day, when he took her to lunch in Nanca himself.

"Did I hear you say that you were going to Nanca today?" Pietro was all curiosity and innocence.

"Yes. I will give Natalie a ride." Fabio swooped right in. "I was just explaining to her that a young woman such as herself should not take the bus alone."

Pietro's gaze had remained on Natalie as Fabio spouted off. Pietro was glad that it did. If he hadn't been looking at Natalie, he wouldn't have seen the hint of a cringe that passed over her face when

Fabio referenced "a young woman such as herself." Pietro wasn't certain why this should bother Natalie. Her reaction only proved that she was a very complex woman.

"Pietro, please tell Natalie. She should allow me to take her to Nanca myself when Nico and I are finished. I have my moped today. I did not come with Nico in his truck."

Natalie's eyes widened in mild fear as she laid eyes on the black moped Fabio motioned to offhandedly.

"Tell her, Pietro. This will be much better for her."

If Fabio thought that Pietro was going to help his cause, he was in for a rude awakening. Pietro fully planned to persuade Natalie to come to Nanca with him. Only, he had enough sisters that he knew better than to try to tell a woman what to do. He also remembered that Natalie was risk-averse and had said once that "motorcycles were death traps on wheels." Now was not the time to bring up the fact that motorcycles and mopeds were not the same thing. Now was the time to use what he could offer in the moment to his advantage.

Pietro turned back to Natalie. "I am going to Nanca this afternoon. There is somewhere I need to visit. I can give you a ride. Since I was already planning to go, driving you would not be an imposition."

"Truly, Natalie…I would not mind—" Fabio interrupted.

But Pietro cut him off, knowing exactly what Fabio would not mind doing. Pietro wouldn't mind doing the same thing, but that was hardly the point.

Fabio was young. Immature. Already demonstrating that he could not read her signals and was therefore unworthy of a woman like Natalie. Pietro could not be sure that Fabio would know to be careful with Natalie. He doubted that Fabio knew what she had been through recently, how she had abandoned the only life she had ever known at the same time as she mourned her grandmother's death. Only Pietro knew how fragile she was.

"I brought my truck," he said, throwing down the final card in his favor. He motioned back to the building. "It's right out front. If you're not ready to go now, I could pick you up after I run a different errand here in town."

All errands that Pietro had mentioned so far were of the entirely made-up variety.

When Natalie turned to Fabio, Pietro held his breath, unsure of what she would decide and not liking the feeling one bit.

"Thank you for your offer, Fabio," Natalie began. "But it sounds like Pietro was already planning on going to Nanca today. It makes the most sense if I go with him."

• • •

Pietro enjoyed the way Natalie angled her body to get a better look out the truck window—how the hand that didn't secure her bag on top of her lap gripped at his passenger side door. It was as if some part of her wanted to climb outside. The window was cracked and her nose tipped upward as if she were eager to breathe in the sunshine of the warming afternoon and the briny air. Her curls, now free from the kerchief she liked to wear when she was working, were loose and wild as they blew in the wind.

There was more that Pietro enjoyed about having Natalie in his front seat. His car smelled distinctly of her—of coffee, and sugar, and jasmine, and something else that he hoped would linger. With her attention on the scenery and on the sea below, Pietro was free to take her in.

"It's so beautiful," she breathed in such a reverent whisper, Pietro wasn't certain she knew she'd said it out loud.

"Have you had a chance to go down to the water?"

Pietro's voice was soft to his own ears, some involuntary response to the way she disarmed him. It was quiet and low and as relaxed as the breeze. Like most towns on the coast, Zavona could be navigated as a meandering hill. Practical elements of daily life happened up top—shops and homes and commerce—but the best that leisure had to offer happened on the water.

Natalie took a deep, stuttering breath, as if waking herself from a trance, before bringing her gaze toward him. "Not really," she admitted on a long sigh.

"You cannot work every day," Pietro pointed out.

"I'm not working today," she replied in her own defense.

"Then what *are* you doing?" he finally asked. "What business do you have in the Hall of Records?"

Natalie smiled that half-open, half-mysterious

smile that he had come to crave. "It's a very long, very convoluted story."

"We have plenty of time," Pietro lied. In truth, they could arrive in as few as fifteen minutes if he took the best route. Nanca really wasn't a far drive.

"So I already told you how, earlier this year, my gram passed away…"

Pietro nodded, regretting having prodded her to talk. It occurred to him only then that her reason for going to the Hall of Records might lead to some painful memory, though he couldn't imagine what such a memory might be. Pietro had assumed Natalie's grandmother had been American. He'd drunk in Natalie's features every chance he'd gotten. As he glanced at her now, it seemed entirely possible that she might be part Italian.

"A man named Franco Pelagatti left her some money," she said. "Franco Pelagatti from Nanca. He died more than twenty years ago, but since he left the money under her maiden name, she never knew about it when she was alive."

"You did not tell me…your grandmother was from Campania?"

Natalie shook her head. "She lived here when she was younger. On the army base in Cocenza."

Pietro nodded. "And this Franco Pelagatti. He was her first love?"

Natalie looked over at him, seeming troubled now. "That's the problem. I don't know who he was. My gram married my gramps when she was eighteen. She never mentioned Franco once or anyone whose last name was Pelagatti. And she talked about her life in Italy. She talked about it a lot."

Pietro considered this for a moment. Just because Natalie's grandmother had married young didn't mean she hadn't had a great love before that age. Pietro himself had fallen hard in love with Vittoria at the age of five.

"How did you find out only recently about the money if he died so many years ago?"

Natalie launched into a story that Pietro didn't completely understand. It sounded every bit as convoluted as Natalie had indicated it would. Though Franco had willed her grandmother the money, the executors of his estate had been unable to locate her years earlier, when Franco had died. Franco's will had named an old address for her grandmother. As a result, the funds had remained with the state of Illinois for twenty years, listed under her grandmother's maiden name as unclaimed property.

It had only been discovered after Natalie's grandmother died, something to do with her estate needing to be cleared by a special probate court and the state finally matching up all former names and addresses. It was part of a process of making sure the deceased had no liens or debts. It was, indeed, turning out to be a very long story. But Pietro enjoyed hearing her tell it and took a very long way around, past the town itself on the coastal highway, then on a far road that tracked them back toward central Nanca. It was barely midmorning and they were in no danger of missing the office being open.

"Yet neither your nonna nor Franco Pelagatti remain to tell the tale. And you think that somebody in the family of Franco will know why?"

"Maybe..." Natalie seemed unsure.

"Then what are you hoping to find?"

She looked at him and spoke a single word. "More."

Something in the way she said it grabbed at Pietro's chest, made him think of something he hadn't thought of in a long while—the long-buried part of him that remembered what it meant to search for answers, to crave them no matter how dismal the odds. Though lost girlfriends weren't the same as lost grandmothers and their forgotten friends. Pietro barely knew which one was worse—knowing that answers should have been in reach because the person who owed them was alive and well or knowing that some answers might never be unearthed once taken to the grave.

Pietro thought about this as they made their slow descent into town, finally drawing nearer to Nanca's municipal building, measuring and calculating in his mind. Could the Hall of Records tell Natalie anything of use? If Franco did have a family, would they have heard of Natalie's grandmother, and—if so—how much did they know? What if Franco had a wife and children, and her grandmother had been a first love? What if Natalie not only didn't learn the truth but learned something devastating?

He didn't voice any of these concerns, nor did he attempt to dissuade Natalie from proceeding. With a bit of lead time, he might have looked into this Franco Pelagatti himself. But there hadn't been lead time, and all he could do now was let the chips fall where they may.

"Okay," he said. "Then I will help you."

CHAPTER THIRTEEN

"*Buongiorno*," Natalie began, greeting the clerk with a nod and an apologetic smile—apologetic because Natalie was near certain to botch some phrase. She still had cold feet when it came to using on-the-fly, everyday Italian. But she had painstakingly rehearsed the conversation she anticipated having with this clerk, not wanting a repeat of anything that had happened at the *municipio* the first time.

"I am looking for information on a man named Franco Pelagatti. He died in 2003. When he passed away, he was living here in Nanca."

Pietro and Natalie were seated at a desk inside the office of a clerk. Nanca seemed larger than Zavona and was not only the town where Franco had conducted his final business but an office that dealt with all records for a larger subdivision within Campania.

"Are you requesting a certificate of death?"

The clerk spoke slowly, clearly cognizant of the fact that Natalie was not a native speaker. "He left me money in his will." Natalie relayed the simplified version. "I am from America, but I just arrived in Italy. I would like his former address or anything that would allow me to locate his family."

It was only half of the truth. Natalie would like any information there was to have, from where he had lived to where he had worked to where he had gone to school. There was an astonishing number of

Franco Pelagattis, too many to get anywhere with an internet search working off nothing but a name. But asking for carte blanche would make her sound stalkerish. She would be grateful for something—any small bread crumb—that would serve as a clue.

"Are you a family member?" the clerk asked.

Natalie shook her head.

"Is there any official reason why you need access to this information?"

Natalie felt the rise of tears as she shook her head for a second time.

When Pietro's warm hand touched her arm, gripping it lightly outside the view of the clerk, Natalie lifted her watery gaze to his softened eyes. This time he looked different—much different than that first day with the zoning clerk.

"Natalia...may I speak on your behalf?" he asked in English.

She nodded, willing her tears not to fall, but she would let them flow in rivers back in the privacy of her garage. She hadn't fully appreciated how much she'd pinned her hopes on some official telling her something more. Her internet searches had been so fruitless, she had even considered trying to hire a private investigator. An expense like that definitely wasn't in the budget.

Pietro began speaking in a low and measured tone—calm and persuasive with moments of soft expression. It was pleasant to listen to, no matter how much of it Natalie did or did not comprehend. His accent, in English, was sexy, but nothing held a candle to the way he spoke his native language. Anxiety over current circumstances notwithstanding, she could have listened to it all day.

For reasons she would attempt not to dwell on, Pietro's hand continued to gently cuff the top of her forearm. Her own hand continued to rest upon her leg, and their knees, as they sat next to each other at the desk, were close. When Pietro finished speaking, the woman responded in a tone that was softer than the one she'd used with Natalie. As Pietro had with the other clerk back in Zavona, he was calming the conversation down.

Natalie caught phrases she recognized—ones like "could be her only chance" and "she could not ask her grandmother while she was alive" that alluded to Pietro's pleas for cooperation—that proved his understanding of the deeper meaning of it all. Natalie heard him say *contro le regole* and *per favore*—proof that he was asking for the clerk to bend the rules. He ended with words Natalie didn't understand, punctuated with a chuckle that made the clerk blush.

The clerk finally tore her attention away from Pietro long enough to speak again to Natalie, and she switched to English when she did.

"May I see your papers?" the clerk asked.

Natalie slid over everything she had. The clerk began scanning through it all, rather quickly, then murmured something in Italian under her breath. Natalie's heart raced, waiting for some verdict. The clerk murmured a second time, shuffling through papers more quickly now before looking back at Pietro and saying something that looked serious.

Natalie looked impatiently toward Pietro for help. He didn't look at her, but he did squeeze her arm. Then he asked the clerk a question Natalie comprehended but didn't understand.

"Did you ever go to school with anybody named Franco Pelagatti? Or anybody named Pelagatti?"

It was an odd question, especially since the clerk herself looked to be in her early thirties, about Pietro's age.

"I don't know," murmured the clerk, tapping her computer screen awake with a nudge of her mouse. "Let me think."

Then something miraculous. She began typing, began searching, began looking for Franco Pelagatti on Natalie's behalf.

"I knew the son of a Franco Pelagatti when I was younger," she murmured in Italian. "If I remember correctly, he lived in Rivela, on Via della Spiga at number seventeen. But it is possible that he sold the house in 2005."

Pietro gave her a nod of genuine gratitude and a small smile. "I understand that you cannot give us official information. This would be against the rules."

The clerk nodded, as if to say *you're welcome*. But the words that came out of her mouth in Italian were: "You are correct, sir. I cannot."

When Pietro spoke again to Natalie in English, he was all sly gazes and contented, conspiratorial smiles.

"The clerk says that she is sorry. But she cannot give out confidential information."

• • •

"What did you tell that clerk?"

Natalie practically demanded it the moment they

sat at the café that overlooked the water, which was just down the road from the Hall of Records.

Feigning innocence, Pietro shrugged. "What do you mean?"

"You were flirting, weren't you?"

He chuckled again, that low chuckle. "I only flirt with women who I am interested in."

Natalie had the distinct feeling that she was being flirted with in that moment, or at least being misdirected so that he could shunt off her question.

"Then do you want to tell me why she blushed like a schoolgirl?"

"Blushed?" he repeated, an inquiry about the meaning of the word.

"When a person's cheeks turn pink, like they're wearing makeup."

Pietro smirked in comprehension. "In Italian, *arrosire*. Like *rosso*—the word for red."

Feeling her own cheeks fall prey to the very same charm, Natalie attempted to stay on task. "Come on. I'm serious—what did you say?"

Pietro picked up his glass and swirled his drink around, then set it back on the table without taking a sip, training his gaze on the liquid he didn't drink. His lips still curled upward, but some of the smile drained out of his eyes.

"I reminded her that everybody has a first love and a broken heart they regret. Everyone has something they wish they could make right, and that the day might come when the man who broke her heart will want to make amends. And when that day comes, I hope that he can find her."

Natalie couldn't help but wonder whose heart

Pietro had broken or to count him among the growing number of people who were convinced that her grandmother's story with Franco was that of a first love and a broken heart. The week before, she'd told Ellie the whole sordid tale, including a few details she hadn't had time to relay to Pietro earlier, in the truck.

"What makes you so certain that Franco and my grandmother were in love?"

"I cannot be sure," he admitted. "But great loves are not soon forgotten."

Natalie paused, considering whether to prod into pieces of Pietro's own life—to ask who, for him, came to mind. She forced herself to stay focused on Franco and Gram.

"By the time Franco left your grandmother the money, she had been gone from Italy for more than twenty-five years. Whatever they were to each other, it was important."

Natalie paused again, having a sip of her drink, no longer able to ignore the doubt that was creeping in. Taking a step forward suddenly felt like taking a step back. Knowing definitively now that Franco had a son felt like it changed the game.

"What if his son's like me?" she asked.

"How like you?" Pietro wanted to know.

"Never heard of Gram…doesn't know a thing?"

He spun his glass in his hand a little and nodded neutrally before giving her a soft look. "But what if he knows it all?"

Natalie quieted again. Pietro let her think. She liked that about this moment—being with him was easy and quiet. There was something comforting in just knowing he was there. It was like when they worked together in washing her walls and getting ready for her plaster. Whenever she managed to forget about his sexy—to tune out the hiss and crackle of heat he brought into any space—there was an ease to being with him.

"I want to be careful with this," she decided finally. "If it is what you think it is—what everyone seems to think it is—I don't want to risk tearing apart his family, not if he can't be here to speak for himself."

Pietro looked up from his drink and back over at her. "From you, Natalia, I would have expected nothing less."

When he spoke this time, his voice was deep and thick with affection, with not a hint of mocking about how she loathed risk. In moments like this, it was hard to ignore what she had written off as proof that there was nothing between them. Of course, she felt swoony when she was near him. Italian men were flirty. Of course, she felt blushy. Pietro was ridiculously hot.

But it was starting to feel like more than that, like there were more adjectives to describe how she felt when she was with him. More and more, she felt seen. Understood. Admired. Noticed. More and more, it felt like she was a woman and he was a man and nothing was about pity or plaster, though not one thing she could point to proved that was the case.

"Anyway, I'm sorry," she said. "I don't want to keep you from your errand. Where should we go from here?"

She watched him carefully, because she had a hunch. Her heart flip-flopped when he looked guilty, as if he had just been caught in a lie.

"Ah, yes. I forgot. My errand," he said, looking a bit startled in his response. "I am overdue to see a church."

• • •

"This tile is unbelievable," Natalie whispered to Pietro as they crept into the building, as if speaking at normal volumes would disturb the peace. Unlikely, to the extent that they were alone. The beautiful little chapel was pristinely maintained, a triumph of stained glass and mosaic tile.

"It's called the *chiesa degli amanti*," Pietro said as they made their way past the simple vestibule, into the sanctuary where the real artistry began. Behind the altar, an inlaid cross made to look as if it glowed was surrounded exquisitely by tiles in hues of yellows and golds. Individual scenes were designed in the same tile within the recessed arched walls. Mosaic renditions of the Madonna and child and Christ's resurrection were like nothing she had ever seen.

"You had an errand to run at the chapel for lovers?" Natalie translated its name.

He smiled sheepishly and gave her a little shrug. "I am overdue to visit my friend, Umberto. Plus, you have said you would like to see some of my restorations. This is one."

"*You* restored *this*?"

Pietro put his hands on his hips and stopped,

mid-aisle, casting his gaze upward and around. "Most of this is Umberto's work. He's one of Italy's premier artists in working with tile. Three years ago, it was condemned to be torn down. I helped him to restore this place. I texted him a minute ago, to let him know we were here."

"So what, he lives here now?" Natalie was confused. Didn't artists who did this sort of thing tend to work on commissions? Why was Umberto still around?

She stopped alongside Pietro, and they stood in the middle of the aisle.

"It is where he married his late wife. Umberto is the owner and the caretaker now." Pietro had a sad smile on his face as he told the story.

"Did you know her? When she was alive?"

He shook his head. "No. But I always admired this chapel. When I was young, it was a working church with a small congregation and a priest. It was called *Capella di San Andrea*. I always wanted to be married here."

She arched a questioning eyebrow. A thirty-year-old bachelor talking about his dream wedding wasn't something you heard every day.

"I was engaged once," he said.

"Once?"

She asked the question reflexively. A second later, she regretted it. What if Pietro's fiancée had died, too? It seemed the only logical explanation for why anyone wouldn't go through with marrying him.

"I'm sorry. It's none of my business..." Natalie backpedaled. He interrupted her before she could say any more.

"My wife-to-be, Vittoria, a week before the wedding...she left. She ran away to go be a model in New York."

Natalie mentally dropped her jaw. "I'm sorry."

"I'm not. Vittoria insisted that we marry in a church I didn't like. It means I will one day be married in this church, with my rightful wife."

Natalie didn't know what to say. As she grasped to think of something, Pietro gave a half-playful, half-rueful smile. "Don't pity me, Natalia. I was very young and it was a long time ago. My poor heart has mended."

"Well, I'm hoping to get married in my villa," Natalie announced, wanting to lighten things up.

"You are engaged?" Pietro seemed alarmed.

"No, but when the time comes, I'm not paying for a church. You should know by now, I'm cheap."

He laughed for real then, a belly laugh that broke the tension. By the time he stopped, they had made it all the way down the aisle and stood at the altar. He turned to face her, and whatever she had been about to say stuck in that same place where her voice had caught earlier, when he'd calmed her with his hand on her arm.

"Your villa has a very romantic history," he told her. "Did someone tell you this? Lovers have always owned this villa, even back to its very construction. You must not break the tradition—"

"Ciao, Pietro!" The man who had to be Umberto appeared from nowhere at the top of the aisle and barreled down the center with haste. It might have been just as well. Everything Pietro-related was messing with her head.

Umberto bypassed the standard handshaking and back-swatting Natalie had seen Italian men do and joined Pietro in a hug. They greeted each other in Italian too rapid and colloquial for her to understand. From there, Pietro made his introductions in much slower, much more textbook Italian.

"Natalia, this is my friend Umberto, the artist. Umberto, this is my friend Natalia. She recently moved to Zavona and this is her first time in Nanca."

Natalie and Umberto exchanged greetings and shook hands. She expected Umberto to turn back to Pietro, to continue to catch up with his friend. For some reason, he was having trouble keeping his gaze off Natalie.

Pietro seemed to have noticed. He looked back and forth a few times between Natalie and Umberto before asking a rather neutral question, small talk if Natalie had ever seen it.

"The chapel is not very busy today. Surprising for a Saturday in the summer. Has tourism been slow?"

"So-so…" Umberto trailed off distractedly.

"I am sorry to stare," he said to Natalie in English, then turned to Pietro and spoke rapidly. "*Sembra una donna in un famoso dipinto. La somiglianza è incredibilie.*"

Pietro scrutinized her then as well. Umberto continued to speak, so fast this time that she understood even less. Did she have parsley in her teeth? If so, why hadn't Pietro told her? Hadn't he been gazing down at her, deeply, just moments before.

"Umberto says you look like a woman in a painting, that you resemble her greatly, with your dark skin and curly hair and your very light eyes."

After Pietro said it, his gaze washed over Natalie's face as Umberto continued. She thought she heard the word "Botticelli."

"In the painting Umberto is thinking about, the woman's hair is blowing in the wind, like it is in *The Birth of Venus*," Pietro translated.

"Oh. *Grazie*." Natalie smiled, relieved that she hadn't grown an extra head, and figuring the correct response was "thank you" when someone told you that you looked like a muse.

Umberto kept going in rapid Italian. Pietro translated in quick succession.

"The painting is at a museum in Florence. But it is based on a legend that originated from this region. About a woman who lived in the sea."

"Do you know what painting he's talking about?" Natalie asked.

Pietro shook his head. "And Umberto cannot remember the name of the painting or the artist."

Even as Umberto spoke to Pietro, for help with translation, he stared intermittently at Natalie, wide-eyed.

Twenty minutes later, as they left the church, Pietro was apologetic.

"Umberto is not usually as he was today. He is often quite subdued." Pietro seemed a bit rattled himself. "I wish I knew the painting he spoke of. I'm very curious to see it now."

"What about the legend? Have you ever heard of it?" Natalie had been curious about that, too.

Pietro nodded. "I think I remember a little. But I will ask my nonna. She will remember it well."

CHAPTER FOURTEEN

Hours after Pietro had dropped Natalie off at her darkened villa, he found himself awake in his own darkened home. It wasn't for lack of fatigue. Helping Natalie on top of his daytime projects and his own weekend work had left him exhausted.

Then why am I still up?

At this time of year, Pietro slept with the windows open each night. At this time of evening, he could hear the sounds of the sea, its risen nighttime waters crashing against rocky shores. In the daytime it would be calm again, just as it was on many nights. But on nights when his own mind was restless, rushing waters seemed to echo his speeding thoughts.

The answer is so simple. Is there any other conclusion to draw?

Franco must have been some sort of lover to Natalie's grandmother, Kate. Carrying a torch for a person you hadn't seen in twenty years—enough of a torch to leave them so much money—said it all. Though he couldn't fault Natalie for not wanting to accept it. Natalie was a reasonable person—a practical person. Pietro got the sense that she would have accepted the news had she heard it straight from her grandmother. But wasn't it the betrayal and not the truth that people found they couldn't accept?

Go to sleep, Pietro.

Too many nights, he'd lain in this very bed, restless with thoughts of betrayal, of why *she* had chosen to keep the truth from him. Betrayal was never accidental. It was always a choice. Kate's betrayal was the worst kind. She had taken her secrets to the grave. But if Pietro wanted to ask Vittoria why she had betrayed him, he could just call.

Go to sleep, Pietro.

He didn't want to think about Vittoria. And he certainly didn't want to talk to her. He had drawn his own conclusions about her reasons years before. Though she'd never come to him with an explanation for leaving. But this thing with Natalie, it felt so familiar, it made him ache somehow. Because he knew both sides of the story—the side of the betrayed, but also the side of the person eager to leave a young love—a first love—far behind.

"*Mi arrendo*!" Pietro grumbled loudly, finally throwing his covers off himself with a flourish and announcing to his bedroom his plan to give up on sleep.

Pietro's cottage wasn't much compared to all the grand villas and palazzos and castellos he helped restore. It wasn't even much compared to the rehab properties he'd bought in town. This cottage was the most modest dwelling Pietro had ever lived in. It was an outpost of sorts—a groundskeeper's home on the far end of his family's property. It had been built as a second location where someone in the family could sleep and monitor their property against destructive animals and thieves. It was a throwback to a different time, a time before reasonably priced fencing solutions and video cameras.

When Pietro had been younger, it had been inhabited by Uncle Cristobal, who had never married and eventually left the business, much to his nonna's chagrin. Though Cristobal did well for himself—very well—working in finance in London, he was talked about in the family as a quasi-failure.

This, no doubt, had more to do with his marital status and his decision to leave Italy than it did with any real successes or failures. It didn't matter that they had redone the cottage after his departure, with an update to the kitchen and the bathroom, and a new construction of windows and a patio that overlooked the sea, everyone in the family still called it *casa solitaria di scapolo*—the lonely bachelor house.

And he did feel like a lonely bachelor as he padded across his room, barefoot, shirtless, and wearing only his snug briefs. He saw his way through his living room and into the kitchen by light of the moon. He wasn't particularly thirsty, though he hoped water from the tap might make him calmer, might tell him what exactly—if not surrender to sleep—his mind was meant to do.

I must occupy myself.

It would be more restful to his mind to do something productive rather than to languish in his own thoughts. Only, Pietro didn't feel like doing any of his own work. He didn't feel like drafting plans on his table for the job he was working on or even pulling out the plans for his dream museum. Something drew him, kept drawing him, to helping her.

She did not ask for your help.

Pietro doubted that she ever would. Natalie was a woman who liked to do things by herself, in her own way. With or without her help—even without Fabio having been there to offer her a ride—Natalie would have found her way to the Hall of Records. And, just as she had when he'd met her that first day in the zoning office, she would have dug in and stuck with her questions, even if she was having a hard time with the translation. Natalie was tenacious. He liked that about her.

She was also not from Italy. She'd done well in figuring a few things out on her own, but there was plenty she didn't understand.

I must help her because, in some things, she cannot help herself.

Yes, Pietro convinced himself. That was why. And because a woman alone in Italy—a woman searching for something, relying on the kindness of strangers, could get mixed up with the wrong people.

Yes. Pietro would help Natalie, a woman who needed people in her corner—people who wished the best for her. People who could be trusted. Wanting to help Natalie had nothing to do with how much he smiled when he was near her. It had nothing to do with him having something to look forward to—finally—for the first time in a long time.

• • •

Believing her own lemon pastries far superior to anything that could be found in the *pasticceria*, Nonna liked to order them for sport, just so that she could quietly brag about the fact that hers were better. According to Nonna, Signora Maldotta did not use enough egg in her lemon crostata, used lemons that were too bitter in her *delizie del limone*, and positively ruined her lemon ricotta cake with too much caster sugar.

It was for this reason that Pietro ordered two desserts every time they visited the *pasticceria*—one of whatever dessert he really wanted, plus a non-citrus favorite of his nonna's, something that she never made herself (and therefore could not compare) and might actually like. This, because Nonna would only finish one or two bites of whatever lemon dessert she had insisted on ordering but felt was beneath her.

The same routine that would be repeated now carried out with every visit. After her face soured in disgust and she pushed her plate away, Pietro would insist on sharing some of what he had gotten for himself. They would eat the rest of each of those without incident. Then, left with Nonna's barely eaten original dessert, Pietro would offer to finish a respectable amount so as not to insult the owner of the *pasticceria*.

Not that any of this was a surprise to Signora Maldotta. Nonna was not always subtle about her gripes. The quality of the signora's confections as compared to his nonna's was a long-standing feud between the two women.

"Pietro. Please. I can't." Nonna threw an accusing look at the pastry, as if the confection itself had insulted her. "I have told her many times not to ruin it by using whole almonds rather than blanched almonds. I even whispered this secret into her daughter's ear. Do you think she was thankful?"

She didn't wait for Pietro to answer with a "no."

"She knows that I am right, but she has too much pride to take my advice, though I only want her store to be a success."

Pietro didn't mention that, out of all the businesses in Zavona that weren't struggling, the *pasticceria* was one. She had only to walk by at the busiest hours of the day to see a line out the door. Nonna herself would have been ecstatic if there were enough shoppers in her own store to warrant a line.

"You can't blame her for being jealous, Nonna. It's not her fault that our family grows the best lemons and that she can't impress you, the best baker in town."

"One of the best bakers in all of Campania," she corrected, raising one finger in front of her face to emphasize the point. "I've known how to bake since I was a child, but I, too, had to humble myself to learn the art of baking with lemons."

Pietro made no attempt to hide his smile. "Yes, Nonna, you are quite humble. I have noticed this as well."

She only kept going, too busy trying to make her point to call him out on his sass. "...I did not truly know what it meant to cook with them until I joined this family, until I married your grandfather."

Getting her to talk about the old times was exactly what Pietro wanted. He wanted her to recall things from decades before—to remember what she knew about the legend. Not every day was a good day to ask her to take a walk down memory lane. Some days, reminiscing was all she seemed to want to do. But other days, days when she didn't want to talk about the past, were days that Pietro could imagine caused her some pain. On days like that, she shut up tightly, like a clam.

"Do not understate your talents, Nonna. You are a world-class cook when it comes to seafood. You taught Lucia and me everything about cooking fish. Sometimes, I think you might have taught Lucia a little bit more."

"Lucia is a better apprentice than you," she informed him. "Where you have passion, she has patience. She cooks like a child of the sea."

A child of the sea.

This was how Nonna liked to refer to herself whenever she spoke about her own upbringing, as if she'd been raised as a mermaid in the depths of the gulf. She was not from Zavona but from Rivela. Her father had been a fisherman, and her mother had run the shop, a fishmonger in the town square. Rivela was practically mythical itself—rarely visited by outsiders and rather hidden away. It didn't appear on most maps, though the delicacies it supplied only to the finest restaurants remained critical to the seafood supply chain farther up the coast. It was only because Nonna had grown up there that their family received a special catch every Sunday morning. All those years, and she had managed to maintain ties.

"I was near Rivela yesterday," Pietro mentioned casually. "In Nanca, helping a friend search for something."

He was careful to use the masculine version of "friend" so as not to open himself to a line of questions about his company. He had learned that lesson the hard way before. Rivela was thirty kilometers from Zavona, right below Nanca, where he and

Natalie had been a day earlier. His nonna would know all the old stories from there.

"Did your friend find what he was looking for?" Her tone held intrigue. She had picked up on the mystery in his voice.

"My friend's search led him to an old legend. The one about the woman and the sea. Only, he is not from Campania and never heard of it. I do not remember it well."

When Nonna's lips melted into a smile, Pietro knew with certainty that this would not be one of the days when his grandmother closed up like a clam. This would be a day when she opened up with memories of her previous life.

"The woman and the sea," Nonna repeated with a wistful look in her eye. "It was my grandfather who told this one when I was a child. It was always the men—the fishermen who spent their days and nights out on the water—who claimed to have seen her. Many people believe in her as a ghost. But the fishermen, the ones who lived on the boats, they say she was real."

Even this seemed cryptic. As Pietro had racked his brain the night before for any recollection of the narrative, he hadn't been able to recall any. All he remembered was the cautionary aspects of the tale, that children should not go close to the water for fear of the woman in the sea. That adults should neither venture out at certain hours of day, or out in certain weather, and certainly not alone, for fear of the woman's revenge.

But revenge for what? That was the piece that he could hardly remember—the part about what had embittered the woman, the reason she stalked the seas. Pietro also couldn't remember whether there had ever been any actual incidents that anybody could prove had happened in relation to this phantasm.

"Did you ever see her?" Pietro wanted to know.

It seemed as fair a question as any.

"My papa admitted that he never did..." Nonna trailed off. "But his brother—my uncle—that was another story. There was a sighting when he was young. Not just my uncle himself believing that he saw something. He and some other boys who claimed they saw her, up at the lighthouse point."

"Was this ever documented?" Pietro asked.

His nonna had been staring past him, out toward the street, still looking rather far away until she heard Pietro's question.

"You and your documentation. So official. What is this search? For one of your historian friends?"

It wasn't a bad theory. Given Pietro's line of work, the restoration of so many old buildings, he counted archaeologists, and archivists, and, indeed, historians among his friends.

"Not for a historian friend..." Pietro murmured. "But a friend who is trying to find a piece of art, one related to that legend. Apparently, there is a painting of some local fame. Have you ever heard of anything like that?"

She gave him a strange look. "You do not remember?"

Pietro frowned. "Remember what?"

"There used to be a painting in Salerno. It hung in the *municipio* in town. We used to go there to see your father when you were a child. You liked to look at this painting. This, I remember."

Pietro remembered going to Salerno when he was little, but he certainly didn't remember anything like that. Still, his grandmother's comment tugged at him. If he had liked the painting and Natalie looked like the woman in the painting, could there be some other reason—some deeper reason—why he was drawn to her?

"No, I don't remember," he admitted.

"That's a shame," Nonna said. "These old eyes don't work as well now, but I can still see her in my mind's eye. That painting was beautiful."

CHAPTER FIFTEEN

I need a water delivery service, Natalie grumbled internally as she entered the gates of her villa, dreading the long walk up her gravel drive. Her back and arms were heavy under the weight of bottled water, which she bought by the liter at the market in town. The middle-aged man who always seemed to be there in the mornings after her coffee cart stop had taken to calling her *acquadonna*, which translated roughly as "water woman." She worked so hard each day that she required a fair amount of hydration, and no small quantity for washing up.

Bypassing her front door, which had some sort of notice stuffed in the jamb, Natalie continued walking to the back side. People who missed her often left notes in the door. Either that or they lent or returned items to Natalie using her front step. Among the expats in the program, a fair number of resources were given back or borrowed. It explained why Chris had been so eager to feast his eyes on what tools she might have in her garage.

Those who knew her best knew that her garage was where she lived. Chances were, anything dropped there had been left by Ellie or Chris or even one of her contractors. It recalled things that Gram had always said about the heart of the region and the generosity of the people in the towns. The more people she met, the more she saw why Gram had loved this place.

Natalie's arms thanked her when she dropped her bags on her back steps. She would keep some of them in the kitchen. She also set down her heavy backpack there. She rolled her shoulders and stretched out her arms for a few seconds before starting toward her garage. That's when she saw the paper bag.

Not just a paper bag, she soon discovered. A paper bag with handles and a box inside and a folded note. Actually, two folded notes, the closer she looked. Maybe Chris and Jorge had been by. They had promised her more groceries, but maybe they'd dropped off other supplies. They had offered to help her build a chicken coop.

But this box—whatever was inside it—did not appear to be from Chris and Jorge, as a glance at the first note revealed. The use of her first name said it all.

Dear Natalia,

Please throw away your wireless earphones. They are not safe for a woman who ladders dislike as much as you. This speaker will work with your phone. Please use it for your safety.

Pietro

Natalie was fairly certain that his note had insulted her coordination. She was also fairly certain she didn't care. Pietro had left her another gift. Granted, the gifts he liked to give her usually came from the hardware store. But there was something endearing about all of this.

Natalie was still smiling as she picked up the

second note, which was far less formal than the first. The first had been on real stationery—a note card with lemons that felt a bit surprising. The second note was made of a fine graph paper and folded artistically and with precision. It simply said:

P.S. Why did you not tell me that your garage door was unlocked? This is also unsafe. I am in Tuscany on a client project but will fix it the next time I come.

Reading the next note, even though she was fairly sure that she had been chided a second time, still made her grin like a fool. What it took to wipe the grin off her face was opening the box that contained what he had already told her was a speaker. Not just any speaker. A beautiful speaker. The kind that cost real money. The kind that was practically too nice for a renovation site.

What is Pietro doing?

Natalie was afraid to answer that. Gram had warned her off charming Italian men—men who would pursue her and catcall her and fetishize her darker skin and spiral curls. Mixed-race women in America were a dime a dozen, but nobody here looked like her. In Italy, Natalie was a rarity, someone "exotic."

But was Pietro flirting? It didn't feel like he was. Oozing sexuality, yes. Able to bend space and stop time with his panty-dropping smile? Yes to that as well. But Pietro's charm was universal—not something meant specifically for, or uniquely affecting, her. Natalie had seen toddlers swoon in his presence.

Get ahold of yourself.

Natalie scolded herself not to get carried away. Pietro was just a nice guy—a chivalrous guy with three sisters who pitied her situation. Between her dead grandmother and being all alone up here and having made it clear that she was pretty much born yesterday when it came to rehabbing, he had taken her under his wing. And she suspected there was something—something personal to him—that compelled him to help her on the case with Franco. The truth was, a lot of people were helping her. And the only difference between Pietro's help and anyone else's was how it felt to receive it. Pietro was the only one she had a crush on.

• • •

Ellie had a car and a loose work ethic, neither of which found Natalie complaining. It meant she was always up for a jailbreak or to help Natalie with a ride. She was the only person in the program who seemed to have zero stress about the progress of her restoration.

Much like what had happened to Natalie, Ellie and her ex had applied to the program as a team, during better times. During the months-long application process, the marriage had deteriorated. Ellie had received the acceptance letter to the program a week after her husband moved out, and she'd faced the same decision as Natalie—abandon the idea or go it alone?

Plenty of cash from the settlement explained why Ellie always seemed to have contractors over, and why she never seemed to be doing much of the actual work. And who wanted to get their hands dirty when they had a fabulous wardrobe like hers?

Whereas Natalie spent most of her time looking like Rosie the Riveter, Ellie was on a different fashion plane—a purple-and-blonde-haired bedazzled unicorn in couture. Natalie loved hanging out with her—not just because she was fun and the only other singleton but because she'd set out to reinvent herself. And it was working.

"Take my picture?" Ellie handed Natalie her phone, plucking it up from the cupholder even as she was driving. "It'll look good, right? With the wind in my hair?"

Natalie smirked but did as her friend asked.

Not wanting to be completely upstaged, Natalie had worn an actual dress. It was apropos to their agenda—a leisurely lunch, an hour or two of exploring the town and window shopping, and a recon mission. A drive-by of Franco Pelagotti's old address.

"So what have you been able to find out?" Ellie inquired, even as she multitasked to both drive straight and look cute.

Natalie took shots as she answered.

"They installed my internet yesterday," she reported. "I got in two solid hours of research last night."

Ellie looked impressed...and maybe a bit jealous. "Are you kidding? I've been waiting for an installation appointment for, like, a month."

"Being a commercial enterprise has its privileges. Business installations are a separate department."

Ellie pouted. "Well, that was bloody fast. You just got your electricity in this week."

After Natalie had gotten her work permit, the Fiorellos had her power up and running in four days. It had taken her only three days to get an internet installation appointment with Enel.

"Real-estate records confirmed the house was sold by a Franco Pelagatti two years after the older Franco's death."

"Which means he left the house to a son," Ellie cut in.

"I searched for obituaries based on that—him living in a different town than I knew about before, and the idea that he had a survivor with the same name."

"And?" Ellie was impatient.

Natalie took a shaky breath. "I found a convincing match."

"What did the obit *say*?"

"Franco had a wife. They married in 1967, a year before my grandmother even arrived."

Ellie cringed, just as Natalie had.

"The obituary had his birth date. 1946, which made him five years older than Gram."

"So if the two of them were…" Ellie didn't finish. She didn't need to say it, though. Both of them had done the same math.

"It would have meant my grandmother was having an affair with a married man."

"You know what I'm going to ask next," Ellie prodded. "You said your grandparents met in Italy… but when did they get married? And what year was your mum born?"

By then, Ellie knew Natalie's sad story about her parents. Her mom had died of an overdose when she was four. Paying for rehab when her mom had been alive was one reason Gram had wound up with so little money. Gram trying to save her only child had prompted her to mortgage her house, which she eventually lost.

"1972, I think."

Natalie not growing up with her mother meant that a lot of details were vague. She had always been told her mother had her at twenty-one. If that information was correct, her mother would have been born in that year.

"You *think*?" Ellie challenged.

"I've never had a reason to doubt it. But I've also never had a reason to confirm the math."

"But you have her birth certificate somewhere… right?"

It was filed away neatly with Gram's papers.

"Sure I do. In a cargo ship somewhere over the Atlantic."

"Right, then." Ellie took a minute to absorb this new information. "Then why are we going there now? Why ask questions before you're sure?"

Ellie had a point.

"I still want to look around. The obituary said he was a fisherman. It made it sound like he lived simply. But he left Gram close to fifty thousand dollars. I just want to see what his house is like. What the town is like. The place where he spent his time."

The town of Rivela turned out to be a hidden little gem by the sea, one of the flatter areas Natalie had seen so far on the coast. Collections of homes were low-lying, and much of life within the town still seemed to revolve around the docks. It was a fishing village stuck in time.

The restaurants weren't flashy or riddled with tourists or even particularly large. But most of them were full. Natalie and Ellie were conspicuous as the only English speakers in the place where they had lunch. Menus, and conversations around them, were exclusively in Italian.

Two hours later, they'd eaten and perused the shops in the town, which, to Natalie's delight, had a *gelateria*.

"They could've at least given you a forwarding address for the son," Ellie remarked as she drove carefully up a winding, narrow road that led to Franco's former house. "He's the one we ought to be spying on. For all we know, we just ran into him in one of the shops or passed him in the street."

"They weren't even supposed to give me this address."

Natalie's gaze was glued out the window, as if the neighborhood itself could give clues.

"Well, how'd you get it, then?"

"Pietro helped me." She hadn't mentioned that part yet.

"No." Ellie drew out the word and threw Natalie an incredulous look. "Pietro, the hot architect?"

"He gave me a ride to Nanca."

A sly smile melted on Ellie's glossed lips. "Sounds like he gave you more than a ride."

"Trust me. It's not like that."

"And why not? He wouldn't be helping you like this if it wasn't."

Ellie had popped by once when Pietro was over and caught the two of them laughing together as they washed Natalie's walls. She'd had it in her teeth that Pietro was interested ever since.

"His last girlfriend was a model." Natalie swung her gaze back out the window. It wasn't exactly true. It was the woman from his ten-years-ago annulled marriage, but the point was, he had a type.

"Models are overrated," Ellie countered. "They're built like clothes hangers. I mean, isn't that the point?"

Natalie shook her head, grasping to come up with another protest. "Seriously, I wouldn't read too much into it."

When Ellie narrowed her eyes and smirked in victory, Natalie knew she'd said something wrong. "Good," Ellie concluded. "Then I hope you take your own advice. If you don't read too much into it, maybe you'll let it happen."

It happening with Pietro sounded nice. Too bad making *it* happen was an advanced skill that required a lot more experience with casual sex, and guys in general, experience Natalie was light on for reasons she understood. When you worked two jobs to make ends meet and you were the caregiver for a relative in decline, dating took a back seat.

But there was no need to have the same debate she'd been having with herself for days with Ellie, out loud. Ellie's thoughts on Pietro were liable to confuse her, to give her hope she shouldn't have. So instead of saying that, Natalie scoffed.

"I need to focus on Franco Pelagatti. And remodeling my villa. And furnishing it once it's done. Did I tell you I found the most adorable antique furniture store near the piazza?"

Natalie knew how obvious she was being in changing the subject. She also knew that Ellie was on the brink of furnishing a few of her downstairs rooms. Ellie's restoration had its share of problems, but her place was livable, at least, with parts of it much further along.

"I think I've passed it. But I've never had a look." Ellie narrowed her eyes, aware that she was being misdirected but clearly interested in getting the scoop.

"The coolest old lady runs it. Signora Carlota." Natalie smiled. "She watches soap operas and eats cookies and yells at the TV. She kind of reminds me of my gram. And the things she sells in her store… they're beautiful."

"All period pieces?" Ellie wanted to know.

Whereas Natalie planned on more classic decor, Ellie was doing a mix of classic and modern pieces. They'd geeked out on her design vision one day when they'd hung out at Ellie's house.

Natalie wove her head from side to side. "She's got a good mix. If you go in, you'll find things you like. But be nice to her. I've seen her in action with buyers. She doesn't sell things to people she doesn't like."

"Oh, that is fantastic." Ellie laughed, and Natalie laughed with her.

"See? That's why I came to Italy. To live in a beautiful little town with quirky but lovable people, great weather, and delicious food. Jorge gave me a rundown on the merits of naked beekeeping last week. Between him and Signora Carlota, I'm exceeding my goal."

"Maybe..." Ellie trailed off, giving her a look that told Natalie she hadn't forgotten their earlier conversation, about how Natalie ought to let Pietro in. "But you didn't come to Italy so you could become a dried-up spinster. You came here so you could live."

"Hey. Slow down." Natalie didn't need to make an excuse this time to change the subject. "I think this is the street, Via della Spiga."

Doing as Natalie asked, Ellie slowed the car and made a careful right. They wouldn't want to drive too quickly. Though, as they approached, it was clear there wasn't much to see. The houses on this street were common. They were up a bit from town, on enough of a perch that they would have a nice view of the water from the back. The houses looked lived-in, with their flower boxes outside the windows and front sidewalks and stoops kept clean. And number seventeen...it was just a house.

• • •

"It's just so fast."

Ellie blinked down at her laptop in jealous disbelief, using her touch pad to click around. "This might be the fastest internet in all of Italy."

Natalie smirked. "That's what happens when you own a hotel. It's commercial-grade."

Strategically placed equipment—routers and signal boosters and other things she could barely explain—meant she could now enjoy Wi-Fi in every corner of her property. She even got a signal in the garden and the garage.

"Totally worth it," Ellie breathed, tearing her

eyes away from her screen when the saw started up again. The pair sat at the table in the side yard outside the kitchen.

"I'll bet you could sit here all day," Ellie continued in a murmur. It prompted both women to let their eyes rake over Pietro, who stood by the workhorse. He was engrossed in the task of cutting boards for Natalie just outside her garage.

"Ellie, don't stare!" Natalie whisper-hissed, turning her own gaze away. Not noticing Pietro always took effort. For the past hour, she'd been not noticing the way his muscles flexed whenever he pushed a new board forward on the blade. The man had a way with power tools.

"Oh, he wants you to stare." Ellie swung her gaze back to Natalie, throwing her a conspiratorial smirk. "Why else would he have his shirt off?"

"I don't know. Because it's hot?"

Ellie half snorted. "If it's so hot out, why hasn't he broken a sweat?"

Natalie stole another glance. "I don't know. He's kind of…glistening."

"Glistening with need for you."

Natalie threw her a look. "We've had this conversation. As recently as yesterday."

"Right," Ellie confirmed. "And you're still too stubborn to admit the truth. He does not pity you just because you're alone. I'm alone here, too. And you don't see him helping me…"

Ellie kept coming at her from different angles about why she and Pietro made sense. But Natalie's own doubts made sense, too. What if the only qualities of Natalie's that Pietro found sexy were her appreciation for Byzantine architecture and her encyclopedic knowledge of natural marble? Maybe it was all just geek chemistry—that's what Ellie didn't understand.

Natalie rolled her eyes. "Remind me to make sure Pietro's not here next time I invite you over to use my Wi-Fi."

"Impossible," Ellie murmured distractedly, her eyes still on her screen. "I'm going to be here now, like, every day. Bloody hell, I can stream the BBC News…"

Natalie herself was in the middle of downloading movies off Netflix. The connection may have been fast, but the network itself was spotty. Better to get a few things done while it worked.

"Chris and Jorge are coming later," she mentioned. Functioning home internet was a hot commodity, and she was happy to share with her new friends. "They're doing a virtual meetup on the conscious farming website where they met. You should stay. It'll be a party."

Ellie looked at her watch. She'd been slow to get online given their chatting and gabbing. Her visit was coming up on an hour. "I've got a contractor coming. I can't."

"What is it today?" Natalie wanted to know.

Ellie smirked. "More electrical."

Thirty minutes later, Ellie was gone and Natalie was still online, or rather splitting her attention between random tasks and enjoying the view. If Pietro knew she was looking, he didn't let on. Men who looked like him were likely so used to being ogled, they barely even noticed anymore.

"Were you able to get an appointment at the consulate?"

Natalie must have been engrossed in what she was doing for a minute, as she didn't hear Pietro's approach. By the time she looked up from her computer, he had settled into the chair next to her. He smelled like sawdust and lumber and just a hint of sweat. To her regret, he had replaced his shirt and was now fully clothed.

"I gave up on that an hour ago," she said.

Pietro knew all about the circuitous route she was taking to dig up her mother's records. The cargo ship that carried Gram's papers wasn't due to arrive for at least another month, maybe two. Since she couldn't very well walk into the office of the county clerk back in Illinois, she wanted to see whether she could get help through the US embassy after appearing in person at the consulate in Naples.

She looked over at him at the same time as he leaned in, looking over her shoulder at her screen. It was a gesture she wouldn't have appreciated from anyone else. With him, she didn't mind. She shifted the base of her laptop, angling it so he could see.

"There's a thing I want to do, but the tickets sell out quickly. A new batch goes on sale every day at exactly noon."

"Tickets for what?"

"I'm booking a lemon tour."

Pietro stopped what he was doing. "As in, a tour of lemon groves?"

Natalie smiled dreamily. "Not just a tour of the groves. It's an all-day lemon experience. There's a cooking class, and then everyone sits down to a big meal."

Pietro came closer and stood so close behind her that she could feel the warmth of his body, and she caught a whiff of his scent as he squinted and had a look at the screen.

"There is no need," Pietro proclaimed definitively, then started back toward his work.

"No need to spend the day in a place like this?" Natalie motioned back to the screen and threw him an incredulous look. "I've had this place scoped out for more than a year. I've been waiting until things were more stable with the villa to go. And this—right now—is supposed to be one of the best seasons."

"€250 for a ticket to such a tour? They are robbing you at that price."

Natalie threw Pietro a little scowl. He had seemed in a good-enough mood earlier. Why, all of a sudden, was he trying to steal her joy?

"In America we have a saying—don't rain on my parade."

Natalie liked the way Pietro smiled. It made her want to smile herself. She continued with her stern look instead, not at all wanting to be pushed around.

"I didn't mean that you should not visit any lemon groves. Only that you should not visit these lemon groves. The price is very high. This is not for you. This is a place for tourists."

Natalie had been poised to protest. Then she'd heard his last line. Being called not-a-tourist gave her a thrill.

"I know a local lemon grove," he said. "It's very

close. I can take you. It is considered to be one of the best in the region. There will be no tourists there. It will be like a private tour."

Going to a lemon grove with Pietro did sound appealing. But Natalie had been looking forward to this. She had sighed over the photos on the website a dozen times.

"But what about the cooking class?" Natalie tried not to sound like a petulant child.

"Natalia. When you visit an Italian home, you eat. You will not leave this place without being served something very good."

As usual, Pietro was convincing. But Natalie was also convinced of her original plan. Apart from the sheer indulgence of a freshly prepared Italian meal, she stood to learn something.

"I know it might not be soon, but one day I'll have a kitchen. And guests who don't want burgers and fries and milkshakes for their meals. I have to learn how to cook some local cuisine sooner or later…"

Pietro didn't respond for a minute—just bent his head, lowered his safety glasses over his eyes once more, and turned on the saw. Natalie didn't turn her attention back to her computer. The task of buying tickets at exactly noon could wait. Watching the flex of his forearms—the subtle movement of his muscles just beneath his skin as he pushed the wood forward at measured speed—took precedence now.

A minute later, he stopped his saw. "I believe you will like the lemon grove I can take you to, but I will make you a guarantee—if you do not like it, I will get you this tour." He motioned back to her computer. "The tour you speak of. I will get this tour for you for free."

"You know the farm?"

Pietro nodded. "Yes. I know the owner. He will not charge a tour for one of my friends. Saturday is your day of leisure, no?"

Apart from seeing no real objection to the plan, Natalie saw every reason to find more things to do with Pietro, regardless of what she would or wouldn't admit to Ellie. She nodded acquiescence.

"Good. Then it is settled."

CHAPTER SIXTEEN

Pietro didn't bother with knocking anymore or calling out for her inside. Much better to do his part to ensure that she didn't fall off a ladder. He had also come to enjoy the small surprises that awaited him from catching her unaware. He liked the way she hummed along and danced to her music when she thought she was alone.

Right then, he lingered for a minute, eager to get his fill, especially since he wouldn't get it later. In ten minutes, he would have to turn around. His visit then was a courtesy. On second thought, it was better that she'd missed his texts. Delivering his message in person was his license to be here now.

When her song ended, he said, "I see you're enjoying the speaker."

She jumped a little, then smiled. "Since I'm too clumsy for headphones, you mean?"

Pietro pretended to look hurt. "I don't think you're clumsy. I think you're perfectly elegant when you are flat-footed and standing still on solid ground."

More often, now, when he smiled at her, she didn't look away. It was even better when she smiled back, when she got that playful look in her eye.

"You're early." She crossed her arms. "Or, like, Italian early, which is the same as being on time."

On any other day, he would have teased her back.

"How was your trip?" she continued, un-pocketing her phone and turning down the volume of her music. "You get a lot of good rehabbing done? The job in Lombardy is the one where you're preserving the catacombs, right?"

Natalie was the only woman he'd ever met who asked for details about his restoration projects and actually cared about the answers. She'd been rapt with attention for a full hour as she questioned him about restoring crumbling architecture underground. Pietro had been smiling and animated as he talked about it, in sort of a rapture himself to be able to marvel at the fascinating parts of his own project. It had made him fall just a little bit in love.

"Yes, I was in Lombardy," he replied, but left it at that, not mentioning that he had been there to see an investor, and that he hadn't set foot on that project site. He also didn't mention that a second trip, to Tuscany, was why he had been gone for two days. He doubted venting to her about what he disliked about her program would go over well.

No. He wouldn't get into all of that. He would do what he came there to do, which was just to stop by and deliver his regrets. He had to cancel the work they were meant to do that day.

"Natalia..." he continued. "I apologize. You did not return my messages, so I came to tell you personally. There is something I must do on one of my own properties this morning. Some staging and some minor repairs."

"Oh..." Natalie started tapping around on the screen of her phone. "Sorry, I didn't get your texts. They don't come through when I'm listening to music."

Pietro shook his head. "It is I who should

apologize. The work must be done now. I will miss working with you today."

Today would have been the day he casually proposed another fact-finding expedition about Franco. He already had a plan. He'd also done some asking around about the painting. A call from Caterina about prospective buyers he might actually like visiting tomorrow from out of town had prompted this change of plans.

"Another day, we will plaster. Please decide when. I will make time on any other day."

The spread of supplies on the floor riddled him with guilt. She had gotten the room ready—all the drop cloths and trowels and vats were in the right place. It was to have been their first time to use the special technique to apply the final top layers of plaster. It would have been a productive day.

He waited for her to say something, like that they could reschedule or even words of displeasure if she was frustrated by the change. But she didn't say either of these things.

"Can I help?"

• • •

"I love this place."

Pietro couldn't help but smile at the expression on Natalie's face, at the dreamy look that came over her as she began her slow walk through the cottage. It was the smallest of the four properties that Pietro owned. He had acquired it recently, and, given its size, had been able to restore it quickly. He liked the prompt sense of completion that came with the smaller jobs.

"You like my little *villeta*?" Pietro followed after her, hands on his hips, shadowing Natalie in her observation of the details. It had only five rooms—one for living, two for sleeping, one for cooking, and a palatial bathroom with a deep soaking tub in front of a window that overlooked the sea. He had barely been inside this place since he'd finished it three months earlier. Walking through with her and basking in her admiration felt like a victory lap.

"These arches..." she gushed in clear adulation of the space's most notable feature. The interior walls were all exposed stone, the ceiling painted white with the exception of the natural wooden beams. Pulling the spaces together, and letting one room flow into the next, were segmental arches made out of a light-colored brick that matched the walls' irregular stone.

"In English, you call this 'rustic style,' no?"

Natalie nodded as she walked into the kitchen and ran her fingers over the pale travertine of the island counter, which contrasted with cabinetry of a darker hue below, custom cabinets that were reminiscent of a classic style. The chandeliers that hung down struck the same balance as the design of the rest of the cottage—their glass casing was modern, but the lights within were made to look like candles.

"This is..." She trailed off again and finally stopped walking when the only other place to go was outside, to the terrace that overlooked the sea. "I don't know what this looked like before, but you did an amazing job."

"Now it's time for my least-favorite part," Pietro admitted.

"Which is?"

"Putting the furniture in. Tomorrow, my sister will show the house."

Natalie smiled conspiratorially. "You know I'm really good at that, right? Interior design is kind of my thing."

Pietro stepped in close to her. "No, I did not know that it was *your thing*."

He liked repeating her Americanisms, and he especially liked when she rolled her eyes at him for having a little fun.

"So where is all this furniture?"

He angled his head toward the terrace and cast his gaze outside. "In the truck."

A minute later, they were on the other side of the house, where Rodrigo had parked a trailer of furniture that had been brought out of the back room of his nonna's store. The truck that had hauled it was long gone, leaving the trailer and the furniture itself waiting beneath a tarp. After all the moorings were untied, Natalie counted them to three and they whisked the covering off.

Without ceremony, Pietro began to unload the tightly packed furniture and set it all down on the gravel where the trailer had been parked.

"Wow. These are really nice pieces."

Pietro made a sound of agreement, continuing to unload the trailer.

"I can already see where a few of these could go." Natalie ran her fingers over a wooden sideboard with reverence.

"These are the kinds of things I want for my villa when it's done. I found a store that sells stuff like this in town."

"You did?"

Pietro's back was to Natalie as he busied himself moving a small sitting bench. It meant she couldn't see him smile. Natalie had to be talking about Nonna's store.

"Yeah…this place near Piazza della Republica. The sweetest lady runs it. I drop in and talk to her sometimes." Natalie chuckled. "She even gives me cookies."

Pietro put down the chair and regarded Natalie with surprise. "She gives you cookies? What kind?"

Natalie raised an eyebrow, as though he was asking very strange questions. "I don't know what they're called. They're shaped like little doughnuts, but they taste like lemons. They have this glaze on them that's really good. They're a lot better than the ones at the *pasticceria*…"

"*Zuccherini*," Pietro supplied. He hadn't resumed his unloading of chairs. "Wedding ring cookies."

Pietro could hardly believe it. Natalie knew his nonna. Not only that, Nonna had been giving cookies to her. It tugged at something inside him, unraveling some of the knot in his stomach that worried about his nonna being all alone. Natalia—*his* Natalia—adored his nonna's baking and kept her company.

"Anyway…" Natalie continued, still side-eyeing him a little. "That's where I want to buy some of my furniture when I'm finished renovating my place. That's why I can't blow my budget. The finishing touches…they matter."

"I know the store you speak of. You must negotiate with this woman. She will give you a good price."

Natalie shook her head. "No. I want to pay her fairly."

Pietro smiled and started moving again, ready to take another load off the truck. "Natalia. This is Italy. The first price is not the real price. The fair price comes after the negotiation."

Natalie hadn't exaggerated her skills when it came to staging furniture for the house. She chose pieces, and their placements, with astounding speed. They were fairly opposite to what Pietro would have chosen and how he would have arranged them. Her choices were making the result infinitely better.

Best of all, working side by side got them to talking, the way they did all those days they'd worked together at her house. When he'd texted his regrets about backing out on plastering for the day, this was the part he would have missed.

Their conversation meandered from her love for interior design, to how she had worked her way through college as a house stager, to what her grandmother had been like. Pietro listened and asked questions greedily, certain he would never get tired of hearing her stories.

I cannot stop this.

It was time to face the truth, no matter the excuses he had made, no matter how much he didn't want to be the creep who showed up to help her with her walls only to be a shameless flirt. He was falling for her. And pretending he wasn't was making things worse.

It wasn't as if he brought women gifts every day, even if those gifts were things like high-quality primer and ladders that were safe. He didn't give other women rides to other towns. He didn't offer other women whole days of unpaid labor. And he didn't spend hours on end with anybody only to leave and feel empty, as if he'd wanted more.

"Hey," Natalie said. "Do you have a ladder?"

During his musing, she had left the room. A minute before, Pietro had brought in the final piece. He'd been bringing them in from the outside, but he was blown away by how capable she was with moving them around. She had a system that managed the weight of the pieces and perfectly preserved his floors.

"Yes," Pietro answered. "Do you need me to hang a picture?"

Natalie rolled her eyes.

"Pietro. I know how to use a ladder. Come on. Where is it?"

"You're joking with me, right?"

Natalie crossed her arms. Though she bit her lip against it, the smile beneath gave her away. "You know, I'm starting to get insulted."

Pietro smirked. "Of course I have a ladder. But I wish only to be a gentleman. Tell me, Princess, what can I hang up for you?"

Natalie's eyes widened upon hearing the endearment. Pietro's might have, too. He hadn't intended for that to come out. There were a lot of things he didn't intend to have happen when Natalie was around.

"That." Her voice was softer when she pointed to a wrought-iron he-didn't-know-what.

"Where do you want me to hang this?"

She walked halfway across the room to touch a

bare wall. "I think it would look nice here. Right between the window and the door."

Pietro knew that he was selling this house, hopefully as soon as tomorrow, but he couldn't help the sense of rightness that came over him as he worked with Natalie. Working with her made him feel like he had a partner. It was the one thing he hadn't known how much he craved.

He took off his work gloves and set them down on top of the piece that he'd just moved, gave a little nod, and went in search of the ladder in the cellar. When he emerged a minute later, tools in hand and ladder over his shoulder, she still looked a little dazed.

She had brought in his toolbox and set it on the floor, opening it so he could choose this or that, the set of mounting accessories that would allow the wall sculpture to hang correctly. It was heavy and wouldn't have held anywhere except for a wall that was made of stone. Pietro measured and drilled and measured again.

Finally, it was time to do the actual hanging. He repositioned the ladder. Natalie held the sculpture ready. Once he was in exactly the right place, he looked down and held his hands out to take it. It was heavier than it looked, a bit unwieldy, too. He was just ready to breathe a sigh of relief when he set it down on his hooks, but setting it down the way he did caused the weight to shift too quickly. It was then that he pulled a Natalie, becoming unsteady first on one, then on a second, foot. Too far gone to salvage his balance, Pietro fell.

"Pietro," Natalie said breathily.

How had she ended up with him on the floor? Why was she on top of him right then? Had he somehow grabbed her and pulled her down? More importantly, was she hurt? Had she bumped anything essential on her way down?

"Natalia..." he said hoarsely. "Are you hurt?"

She shook her head. Now that he had established that, he could focus on other things. Like the way every soft, fragrant part of her body pressed upon every hard, needy part of his. Like how easy it would be to do something about it.

"Natalia..." he repeated, hoping she wouldn't break the spell. He would have stopped immediately, would have loosened his protective hold around her and salvaged the moment, if she had given even the tiniest signal it was what she wanted. Only, Natalie seemed as if she didn't want to be released.

He rolled them over until they were on their sides, then kept her rolling until he had deposited her on her back and he hovered over. It was very difficult to kiss a woman properly from beneath.

And then he swept in, tasting lips he had dreamed about for weeks and snaking his arm around her waist to pull her in. It was at once intensely gratifying and not enough. He was glad that her hair was untied right then, better for his fingers to twine their way through her thick strands. He wanted to touch her everywhere.

"Pietro."

He wasn't fully cognizant that his lips had moved to her neck until she spoke his name. Her fingers had found their way beneath his shirt and splayed over his stomach. Their touch was light and just close enough to the waistband of his jeans that he wished intensely for them to dip lower. His tense abdominals, and his breath, both quivered.

His gaze flew up to hers and he prayed that, whatever her plea, it would not be for him to stop. Already, he wanted her mouth again.

"Yes, Princess?" he whispered.

She opened heavy-lidded eyes, focused on him for just a moment, before letting them fall shut once more.

"Again."

CHAPTER SEVENTEEN

I kissed Pietro.

She wrote it out in her chat space to Ellie, stared at it for seconds, and didn't hit Send. Natalie had repeated the same pattern for the past five days. She wanted to tell someone, and Ellie was her best and only girlfriend here. Ellie was also her only friend who was single. Fellow singletons were the only ones who cared about first kisses. Natalie had always wanted someone like Ellie who would jump up and down with her for a good squee when good things happened. But some other part—some bigger part—wanted to keep it to herself.

She knew it was silly—the fear that telling someone would jinx it—that it would be dilutive somehow to share Pietro's amazing kiss. Not just kiss—kiss*es*, every single one a masterpiece, delicious and luxuriously long.

Seriously. Where did he learn to kiss like that?

She had once thought kissing straightforward—formulaic—then she experienced what Pietro could do with his tongue. Natalie was torn between wanting to be jealous of all the practice that had left him with skills like that and wanting to write personal thank-you notes to every woman who had contributed to his technique.

Kissing may have been all they had done, but he made it feel like an event. Anytime their lips came together, time warped and she felt like they kissed for hours. It led her to some strange completion that felt comparable to sex. What Natalie had noticed from their epic make-out sessions was that, when she said his name, he stopped. She was learning to delete it from her vocabulary during those intimate times.

What he rode when he arrived in her driveway that morning made her definitely not want to kiss him. Perhaps the only thing that could have dampened her anticipation of their lemon grove visit was Pietro showing up on his Vespa instead of his truck.

"No," Natalie said after he parked his death trap on wheels, looking sexy as he pulled off his helmet and ran his fingers through his hair. "I do not ride motorcycles," she informed him. Again.

"Ciao, Natalia."

He strode over, snaked an arm behind her back, and looked down into her eyes for a long moment before he bent to press a kiss to her lips. Since they'd entered kissing territory, she was very much enjoying his greetings. His good-night kisses—increasingly lusty—could be even more delicious. She'd reached the point at which she half looked forward to goodbye.

He stepped back and motioned to his bike. "This is not a motorcycle. This is a Vespa. We have had this conversation before. I do not even need a special license to drive this thing."

"And I don't even need a special death wish to want to ride in it."

"This one…it drives very slowly. Some other Vespas can go to higher speeds. This one does not drive faster than eighty kilometers per hour."

Natalie's quick math told her that, in miles per hour, that was about fifty. It still sounded fast to her.

"It doesn't matter anyway. I'm not riding on the back of a"—she stopped herself just short of saying "motorcycle"—"*Vespa* without a helmet."

When Pietro's smile turned into a full-out grin and he motioned back to the bike, she knew instinctively that he had beaten her somehow. The back seat of his Vespa, it seemed, was not empty today. It held a box tied down by a black cargo net, the stretchy kind made of bungee cord.

"Then it is a good thing that I have an extra helmet right here."

Pietro stepped back toward his Vespa and worked to unfasten, then open, the box. Natalie smiled when the first thing she saw was the color pink. She even laughed a little when he pulled it all the way out. It wasn't just a pink helmet; it was sparkly with a deep hue that fit her perfectly. On the back was a gold decal that looked just like a crown.

Pietro bought me a helmet.

Was it wrong that she loved his gifts? They were so practical. So utilitarian. The part of her that wanted to try it on and wondered whether all of her hair could possibly fit under it warred with the part of her that remembered the bike itself and pushed her anxiety to rise.

"You said the place was nearby. Maybe we could just take a taxi."

Pietro placed his own loose helmet down on the seat. "Taxi drivers in Italy are reckless. Our *tassistas*...they drive very fast."

Damn. He had her there. He had her everywhere, in fact. Pietro was beginning to know her too well.

Natalie was so busy formulating another reason

why she shouldn't get on that bike that she didn't realize she was wringing her hands. Only Pietro's warmer hands separating hers stopped them from moving.

"Natalia." His voice was deep, and his playful smile had lost some of its humor. It had melted into something compassionate, something soft. "Natalia," he repeated. "I know that you are afraid."

He kept one of his hands on hers and lifted another to her face, to stroke her jaw before tucking an errant curl behind her ear. "But if you plan to live in Italy and refuse to ever ride on a Vespa, you will lead a long, inconvenient life."

Natalie tried not to smile, even as her stomach jittered. She didn't think she'd ever felt so many different emotions at once. Pietro appealed to her sense of freedom, to her sense of humor, and even to her sense of logic. He knew how to get at her from anywhere.

It didn't help that he was wearing his sexy motorcycle jacket. The smell of leather worked well with the smell of him. The jacket was open, and she brought both of her hands to his lapels. He didn't continue to try to convince her, only stood with quiet patience until she made up her own mind.

"Drive slow, okay?"

He nodded. "I will not let you fall."

• • •

"Are you sure your friend is okay with us just walking around like this? I mean, shouldn't we at least drop by the house and, I don't know, let him know we've arrived?"

Two minutes earlier, Pietro had keyed in a code on the touch pad of the private driveway to let them into the gate. He'd parked the Vespa in the carport, ending a slow, scenic ride that Natalie had actually begun to enjoy after she'd gotten over her initial fear and opened her eyes to take it in.

Now, off Pietro's bike, she didn't know why they were moving so quickly, why they had bypassed the small cottage where Pietro's friend must live, why it felt like they were breaking into the place. Pietro was walking toward a gate that would take them directly into the groves.

"I don't think that will be necessary." Pietro smiled that easy smile of his.

Even from where she stood, Natalie was fascinated by their beauty. Wooden trellises that arched above a wide walkway seemed neatly constructed and naturally rustic all at once. Natalie couldn't see the trunks of the trees, but she saw the upper branches where heavy, ripening lemons dripped down.

The lemons themselves seemed larger than she expected at first glance, though she wanted to have a closer look. She also wanted to inhale a bigger noseful. There was something magnificent about the smell. She wanted badly to enter this supremely magical place.

"But we're allowed to be here, right?" she said. "Your friend does know we're coming..."

Pietro smiled but kept his eyes in front of him, ushering her forward by placing a hand on the small of her back.

"I didn't say the house belongs to a friend of mine. I said I knew the family."

As they walked up to the gate, a plaque with an inscription next to its stone pillar came into view. Natalie read it.

Limoneto Indelicato

But Indelicato was Pietro's last name. Which meant that this farm belonged to someone in Pietro's family.

"You grow lemons?"

He stopped next to the gate and turned his bright green gaze upon her. His eyes, now, were alight with humor. "Not technically, no. The lemons grow themselves. They have been growing on these very trellises for generations."

Natalie rephrased the question to be more precise. "This belongs to your family? This is where you grew up?"

She motioned beyond the gate, toward the first glorious row and the vast expanse of terraced rows beyond. There were dozens of them—up and down from where they stood. Natalie was fairly confident there was no way Pietro could also be running a farm, with everything else he did, unless he never slept or had some sort of clone.

"Yes and yes." The openness returned to his face when he finally dropped the ruse. It certainly explained why he had insisted that she not spend €250 on a tour. She wondered whether his claim to know the other family from the other farm had been true. She also wondered whether the little cottage they had just passed was Pietro's house.

"These groves do belong to my family," he continued. "And I did grow up on this farm."

Natalie allowed her eyes to feast again, to wander over the trellises and the trees, to take them in again with new imaginations of a small Pietro with all of this as his playground as he ran and gallivanted among these trees. It was a far cry from how Natalie had grown up—confined to small apartments and houses, never a wide, safe backyard to call her own. Growing up on a farm like this seemed like a dream.

"What was it like?" She suddenly needed to add more detail to the picture in her mind. "You have siblings, right?"

"Three sisters. All older. All with their own priorities and personalities by the time I came along. We played hide-and-seek and games we had in common for a few years, but I was very young. I spent much time alone."

Natalie didn't want to be nosy, but she was curious as to why. Siblings were the one thing she had always wanted. If she'd had a brother or sister, she had reasoned, she would never have been alone.

"I thought you had a big family..."

"Yes. But it was not easy being the youngest and the only boy."

With practiced ease, he unlatched the gate and it swung open, then he gestured toward the path, an invitation for her to begin walking again.

"To be the youngest person in a big family is to be surrounded by love, but also by people who are too busy for you. With running the farm, and managing the family, and my father managing the town, everybody had their hands full. My sisters liked to help on the farm, to follow my parents, and to help with the business. I was different from my sisters. More thoughtful and artistic. I liked to be in town. I did not like to work."

This last part, Pietro admitted with a sheepish smile. It made Natalie once again imagine him as a boy.

"So you didn't have to work on the farm growing up?"

"Oh, no… Believe me. I did have to work a lot on the farm. I just didn't love it the same as my sisters."

"So what did you do?"

"I fit into the family as best I could, but I knew from a young age that I would not ask to take over the business, even though, as a son, it would have passed along to me."

"Do your sisters run it now?"

"Two of them work full time in the business, yes. The other one, she sells real estate. She's the one who showed the buyers the house we staged."

Natalie thought about this for a moment as they walked up a gentle slope, thought about what it might have been like to be born into something that could be considered a birthright. She had never expected to inherit anything. The inheritance she'd ended up with had been a fluke but still didn't quite seem real. She'd always imagined that, if she'd been born with a legacy to take over, she would've considered it a gift.

"What are you thinking about?" Pietro wanted to know.

Natalie didn't think about how long she had been quiet or whether her expression had taken on that thoughtful look Gram sometimes said she got on her face. These were deep thoughts, the kinds of thoughts she had never shared with anybody. But she wanted to share them with him.

"I grew up without much," Natalie began. "I was always jealous of the kids who had something from the start. I thought it would be a gift not to have to struggle. This is beautiful, but I just can't imagine you as a lemon grower. It's obvious that what you do with architecture and restorations is what you were born to do."

Pietro stopped short and gazed down at her. He stared for a long moment, his eyes washing over her face as his expression registered something intense.

"Nobody has ever said that to me before." He continued to stare down, and she continued to look up into his eyes as he went on. "No matter how much I wanted them to."

Pietro started walking again, and her insides flipped when he took her hand, which seemed barely necessary between her Roman sandals and the easy-grade hill. She dared to let in another imagination, not of small Pietro this time but of a very grown-up Pietro doing very grown-up things to her in the groves.

"Tell me about your lemons, then. Since you grew up here and these are your groves."

Natalie didn't think it was a figment of her imagination that he squeezed her hand a little as they climbed.

He did tell her about them then, and launching into an explanation of their origins in history was far richer than anything she had read on the tour website. For somebody who hadn't wanted to work in the family business, he spoke about these special lemons with knowledge and excitement and a crystal-clear sense of pride.

"Have you ever eaten one?" Pietro asked. "I mean, have you eaten one with the skin on? They are not bitter, like the lemons you eat in the States."

Gram had talked about these lemons. Natalie still remembered her wistful face, the expression that came over her when she reminisced. Her own memories of talking about the *sfusato* lemons was most of why Natalie had been so tied to the notion of a perfect tour. Gram had called eating them a religious experience.

"I tried to eat a lemon once, when I was little." Natalie smiled at the memory. "My grandmother talked about them, told stories about biting right into their skins. She made it sound so delicious that I figured I ought to try."

Pietro laughed. "You ate a eureka lemon?"

"Is that the same thing as an American lemon?"

"Yes, the bitter kind they grow in the States," he confirmed.

"Then yes. And it didn't turn out very well."

Pietro was still laughing. "What happened after you ate it?"

"I think I cried. Bear in mind, I was only about six years old."

Pietro chuckled, his face still lit up. God, he was beautiful when he smiled. "I would have liked to see this."

"Would you mind?" She motioned to the trellis above, which she was a bit short to reach.

Pietro inspected the space above him, as if

searching for the perfect one. One day, Natalie would ask exactly what constituted "perfect." In the meantime, she would take the proffered lemon and savor the much-awaited bite.

"Here. This one."

The lemon that Pietro handed her was neither the largest nor the smallest, but plump. He watched her intently as she bit in. She maintained eye contact with him for only a moment before hers fell shut, surrendering to the intensity of the experience.

The skin was spongy and soft and had the texture of a dense cake. And it did have an expected zest—not so much astringent or bitter as lemons from home, more like perfume. The waxy outer skin wasn't as hard as she had anticipated. The skin of this lemon was more like that of a Granny Smith apple, but with only softness beneath, rather than the crisp hardness of tart apple.

The flesh of this lemon was quite different from what Natalie had expected. Sweeter, yes, but more complex in flavor. It had an acidity to be sure, but it was dimensional, with a true bouquet. It struck her as almost herbaceous—something that hit at the intersection of culinary and floral. This was one of the most interesting and wonderful foods she had ever tasted.

But there was something else about it, something that made her smile for reasons she couldn't explain. Eating this lemon made her happy. She understood now why it was protected by the Italian government, why the outer gates from the street were locked down like Fort Knox. This indelible smile came from a place that she was just beginning to discover.

Within this lemon was pure joy.

"This is the best thing I've ever tasted."

Natalie opened her eyes slowly, as if emerging from a dream. She wondered whether it was customary to just have a bite or two or to eat the whole thing. She half expected that Pietro would be laughing at her again. His lips held the hint of a smile, but the humor didn't reach his eyes. Instead, his eyes held that intensity they sometimes did just before he said the things that gave her chills, the way they did the second before he kissed her.

"You must allow me to bring you lemons."

His voice was rough, and he said it in a way that told her that hadn't been what he meant to say at all—that there was something, maybe many somethings, that he wasn't saying. She cast a nervous glance back down at the lemon in her hand, not knowing how to react. Nothing remotely close to this had ever happened to her. Never this chemistry. Never a guy like Pietro being so interested. None of the men she'd dated—or even met—in Urbana were anything like Pietro. So open. So creative. So complex.

When her eyes flitted back up to him, his hand was extended, palm up, offering to bring her with him.

"Come, I will take you to see the upper part of the grove."

CHAPTER EIGHTEEN

Pietro couldn't remember the last time he had spent hours strolling through the groves, meandering through trellised pathways, visiting production buildings, and stopping in enclaves where benches had been constructed to sit. Showing it all to Natalie reminded him how many stories there were to this place—the bench his grandfather preferred, where he would smoke a pipe in the afternoon and tell stories; the tree that Pietro had fallen asleep under at the tender age of five, which had prompted a search party and worried his mother sick. He also couldn't remember the last time he had held a woman's hand.

But for the need to eat, he could have kept them in the groves all day, through the late afternoon and into night. When Natalie's stomach had growled and he'd noticed she looked a bit thirsty, he'd guided them back. Next time, he might pack them a picnic to eat inside.

"This is luxurious."

Natalie made the proclamation the moment she stepped into his cottage, arms full with her own satchel that she had grabbed off the porch. Pietro held a freshly picked basket of lemons. It was the warmest part of the afternoon and their long stroll, plus the late hour, had earned them a hearty meal.

"You are the first person to use this word to describe my house," he quipped, smiling as he walked toward his kitchen and left her to take it all in. Something in her voice, in her expression, was sincere, though he couldn't imagine why. The cottage was small, comfortable for one person, and quite a bit modern for Pietro's tastes. Its best features were its verandas and the breeze from the sea.

A wide living room was the first room you entered when you walked through the front door. The room spanned the width of the house and was furnished simply, with modern pieces of Scandinavian design that Caterina had chosen when she had fixed the cottage up. An arched door in the center of the room led down a short hall. The door to the sole bedroom was on the left, and a small bathroom was on the right. The bathroom hadn't been part of the original construction. Though, when it had been remodeled, Caterina had added walls.

At the end of the hall, the space opened up to a modern kitchen with a counter island in the middle for preparation, a dining table off to the right, and a stovetop range and ovens behind. Windows that faced the water stretched wide above more countertops and a sink, giving both the cook and any dish washer an idyllic view. But the biggest improvement to the kitchen after the remodel was the addition of doors that opened to the terra-cotta-tiled veranda, which wrapped all the way around the sea-facing side of the house.

Pietro set the basket of lemons next to the sink. Natalie fell in next to where he stood. He snaked an arm around her waist and hoped she would inch closer. He thought she would comment on the view. But she didn't move closer. She reached her hand out in front of her and did the most unexpected thing—Natalie turned on the faucet.

"Clean running water..." She trailed off. "I can't believe I get to help cook a meal with water I don't have to pour from a bottle."

She'd said it jokingly, casually, but he could hear a note of sadness—of struggle—as well. More so than ever, he saw how resilient she'd needed to be. Her strength, her capability, only made him want to take care of her more.

"You have endured much, my Natalia." He pulled her in closer and kissed her temple. "We will make a delicious meal and you may use water from my tap as often as you wish. Perhaps you would like to be the one to rinse the lemons?"

The lemons didn't need rinsing, but Pietro didn't mention this. He would find the colander and give it to her to set inside one half of his deep double sink. She could rinse lemons, and anything else, to her heart's delight.

"So you really know how to cook..." Natalie trailed off, as if disbelieving. At some point on their walk, she had ribbed him about this. How she'd been promised more than just a tour—she'd been promised a cooking lesson and a meal.

"I really know how to cook," he replied laughingly. "Do *you* know how to cook?"

"Of course I know how to cook," she scoffed, though she was smiling.

He faced her and crossed his arms. "I don't believe you."

"I'll show you how to cook American food when my villa is finished and I open my kitchen. Right now, it's your job to teach me a typical Campanian dish."

"Food from Campania is easy. Most Italian food is. The quality of the ingredients and the way the flavors mix matter more than any recipe. Our lunch will be good because the ingredients are fresh."

"What's on the menu?"

He let his hand fall from her shoulder and began moving around the kitchen, picking up items here and there and setting them on the island.

"A Campanian meal would not be a Campanian meal without seafood. We will cook a fish. Very simple—olive oil, white wine, lemon juice, tomatoes, and salt. We will also use the leaves from the lemon tree to place the fish upon while it cooks. This will add much flavor."

Pietro pulled an oven platter from beneath the kitchen island, after he had taken out the other ingredients he had mentioned. The branzino had been purchased that morning at the fish market on the waterfront and was still wrapped in brown paper. The tomatoes he'd grown in the sunshine of his own small garden. They sat on the countertop, still on their vine.

"Have you ever cut open a clam?" he asked next, thinking of his second dish.

"I never even had a fresh clam until I moved here."

"It is very easy. I will show you the technique."

By then, he had pulled the package of clams and a bowl of soaking lemons from the refrigerator.

"What are we making?"

"*Spaghetti alle vongole.* Spaghetti with clams.

Also very simple. It needs only olive oil, parsley, a little bit of wine. But this is very delicious. The flavor from the clam, it does all the work."

By then, she was eyeing the bowl of lemons. "Okay, then what are these for?"

He smiled, thinking already of how good one of his favorite dishes would taste. "*Pasta al limone.* They would not have taught you to cook this on your expensive tour."

Pausing for a moment from pulling out ingredients, he stopped behind her. For a fleeting moment, he let himself wish that their meal was over and that he could have his dessert. He wanted his dessert to be her.

"Why are they soaking?"

Pietro righted his thoughts, because Natalie wanted a cooking lesson. And what Natalie wanted, Natalie got. What Pietro wanted could come second. Though he was beginning to hope—and maybe even to believe—in the commonality of what they wanted. Maybe both of them were hungry for something sweet.

Pietro leaned closer, ensconcing her from behind, speaking into her ear as he set his hands on either side of her on his counter. "I am going to tell you a secret about the authentic way to make this dish. But only if I can trust you."

Lowering his mouth to plant a kiss at the juncture of her neck and her shoulder gave him an ideal view. He was very grateful for the low cut of the blouse she had chosen that day.

"*Cosa ne pensi,* Natalia?"

He had noticed how much she liked it when he

spoke Italian to her and he had started to use easier phrases he knew that she would understand. He had only asked her what she thought about his idea.

"*Sai tenere un segreto?*"

"Can I keep a secret?" she repeated in English, a bit breathless. "Yes. Your secret's safe with me."

"Good." Pietro switched back to English and released her from his embrace, stepping to the side and leaning his hip against the counter, motioning toward the lemons in order to explain. "Then I can tell you that the secret to *pasta al limone* is not to add lemon peel to cooked pasta. It is to use lemon water to cook the pasta itself. I have soaked these lemons overnight in order to give the water the lemon flavor. When we cook the pasta, the flour part of the pasta mixes with the lemon water to make a cream."

"So we don't need to add cream? I mean, that's how I always made cream sauce with pasta in America."

"Sometimes, but not often. Many of the Italian pasta sauces…carbonara, alfredo…do not use milk or other liquids. Only butter and cheese."

Pietro reached into the refrigerator for two final items—a basket full of eggs and a bottle of wine. They would use the same one to cook as to drink.

"I'll wash the lemons, then," Natalie remarked with a contented smile, a smile he loved, because she looked relaxed. He had seen her more relaxed here, in this house, walking among his groves, than he had on any other day. It made him want to have her over more often. And the way she made him feel—the way she made him laugh and forget all of his problems for a while—made him want to do things that he hadn't even thought of since Vittoria.

Pietro considered all of this as he uncorked the wine bottle, found two glasses, and watched her unabashedly. He still stood at the island countertop, but her back was to him now as she stood at the sink. Not for the first time, he thought of what it might be like to draw her. After he'd had a good look, he handed her a glass of wine.

"Oh, I forgot!" she exclaimed the second she laid eyes on it. "I brought you something. It's in my bag."

"You brought *me* something?"

She smirked. "Actually, it was for your friends who were kind enough to let me take a tour of their lemon groves."

He chuckled. "I'm honored that you think I deserve it after my trick."

"Oh, you don't," she joked right back, giving him a little bump with her hip. "But if you can teach me how to drink limoncello, I can teach you how to drink bourbon."

• • •

"Tell the truth. Do you like it?"

Natalie still looked nervous as Pietro took a second pour of his bourbon, which, as it turned out, was actually whiskey. Much like he had given her a primer on limoncello, Natalie had given him a primer on American spirits. It turned out that you could only call American whiskey "bourbon" if it came from Kentucky, just like a whiskey had to come from Scotland in order for you to call it scotch. Every other sort of whiskey from America was, apparently, just called whiskey. Pietro had tried Jack Daniel's and Jim Beam. This one was called Uncle Nearest.

"Yes, I like it," Pietro insisted.

"You're not just being nice?"

He chuckled again. "Natalie. It is very good. Trust me. I enjoy the stronger spirits as well."

Mollified, Natalie finally accepted his answer and sat back a bit easier in her chair. They were outside on his veranda. The remnants of their meal had been cleared away. Now, all that remained in front of them were the small ceramic cups he used to serve his limoncello—he'd opened one of the finer bottles—and two small glasses he'd brought out for the whiskey.

"This limoncello is so good."

Pietro liked the dreamy look of her expression and the way she drew out the letter "o" in the word "so." He had also enjoyed watching her eat. It wasn't unusual for anybody—even Italians—to become enraptured in the food of the Amalfi Coast. But there was something that delighted him specifically and particularly about Natalie's brand of enjoyment.

"One day, I will show you the secret of my family's limoncello."

She couldn't know that these were weighty words. That the secret method of his family was protected and not given easily. Promising to teach Natalie the secrets of his family's limoncello, the business that had been their lifeblood, was not a promise to be taken lightly. But the words had spilled forth from Pietro's mouth naturally, easily, willingly, and maybe even automatically—as if some part deep inside him knew that he wanted to say it.

Between their cooking and the slow savoring of their meal, the sky was getting darker. Talking and laughing quietly, they had watched the sun set. Fullness from the food and buzz from their drink was easing them into the later evening. He watched her for long seconds, a slight smile on her face as she closed her eyes and breathed in the warm breeze, looking joyful and calm and content all at once as she savored this moment. This moment, here, with him.

"Natalia. We must stop drinking."

"But this is so good." She gave a little pout for a second before taking in a small gasp of surprise. "Oh no. Is it because you have to drive? I'm sorry."

She pushed the glass away from herself, looking genuinely repentant. "I shouldn't have pressured you to drink bourbon. I could always call a—"

"Natalia," he interrupted. Whenever he said her name like that, she stopped short. "That is not why."

"Oh." She eyed her glass again, as if she wanted to bring it back toward herself, to pick it up for another swallow, but she didn't dare. The remnants of guilt stuck to her features, though he didn't understand what she had to feel guilty about. He swiveled his legs around to the side of his own chair until he faced hers. In one swift motion, he closed the space between them by dragging her closer, right next to him. The wrought-iron feet of her chair against the stone of his patio made a loud, low-pitched screech.

"We must stop drinking because I want us to be sober for what might come next."

He had leaned in closer to say this, speaking quietly next to her ear, calling on every shred of willpower to keep his nose from tracing her jaw. Noses would lead to lips and lips would lead to tongues and tongues would lead to tasting lower and lower. He wanted all of it too badly—for one thing to lead to another. And he had to be sure she wanted it, too.

"You must tell me, Natalia. If I am mistaken and there is nothing between us. Tell me, and I promise… I will behave myself with you."

It took him saying this out loud and hearing inner Pietro's responding laughter to comprehend the precariousness of his words. It was a sure sign that he had just made a promise he couldn't keep. How would he stay away from her on the off chance that he was wrong? How would he stop making silly excuses to see her every day? When he went over on weekends to help her with her house, how would he stop touching her?

"I don't wanna behave anymore," she whispered, then leaned toward him, tipping her head in the opposite direction, exposing more of her neck. He lowered his head to kiss her jaw, his restraint weakening as he watched her goose bumps rise. Wanting to graze his lips across more of her skin, he used a light touch to sweep her hair off her shoulders. This second pass was more nip than kiss and caused a different reaction—the puckering of her nipples, which stood in relief against the thin fabric of her shirt.

He had barely mumbled half a curse before her hand snaked around to grip the back of his neck at the same time as she turned toward him and tipped her chin up to capture his lips. The fervor in her kiss was all the confirmation he needed.

CHAPTER NINETEEN

Somehow, they ended up in the lemon groves. It was a delicious migration from his patio, to his bed, to his shower, and beyond. Pietro had taken his time, making a slow meal out of Natalie, from the kisses he left in the wake of clothing removed to running his nose the length of her bare skin. His eyes were the greediest, feasting and lingering, never in a rush to get his fill of all that had once been hidden from him.

He'd stopped to make confessions, whisperings of things he'd never said, confirmation of things she'd thought she'd seen in his eyes—things she hadn't allowed herself to hope were true. Drunk in rapture and bursting with undeniable truth, she'd whispered a few of her own.

"It is said, in my family," he began, his voice quiet and deep, "that the lemon groves are where all of the Indelicato children are conceived—that it has been this way for many generations."

They lay atop a thick blanket, Natalie's cheek on his chest and his arm slung down her back to her waist. Stargazing had been the plan. Their hair was still wet from their sexy shower and they remained naked. A second blanket covered them to their waists, but Pietro was her main source of warmth.

"Do you think you were conceived in the groves?" Natalie wondered aloud as her thumb stroked his skin. Pietro's chest was gloriously smooth. He was a triumph of textures, as her own leisurely exploration had revealed, all silky top hair, soft stubble on his chin, and hard muscle beneath skin that felt permanently heated by the sun.

"It is possible." The tips of Pietro's fingers played absently at her hip, tickling her a little. She didn't mind. "There is no privacy in a family like this. Everybody lives in one house – the parents, the grandparents, the sisters and brothers."

"Probably why you moved to the cottage," she murmured.

"For privacy with women?" She felt him smile against her temple. "In my family, they call this the lonely bachelor house. We laugh and say that it is cursed. The true reason why I moved to the cottage was to keep peace in my family. Between my father and me, the main house is not big enough."

Natalie thought of asking for details but was rather enjoying the calm serenity of Pietro's even breathing, his warm body, and the blanket of stars above. She could have slept from relaxation like this. Not just relaxation—contentment, a sense of rightness she hadn't known, a sneaking suspicion that this was joy.

"I don't mind all the privacy we're getting right now," she murmured.

"Yes," he agreed. "This is very nice. But we have much privacy, Natalia. Many moments when we are alone. Many rooms in your villa. Many olive trees on your property that offer the right amount of shade. Many opportunities to do as we would like…"

The suggestion in his voice—the way he lowered it just a little and spoke closer to her ear—always gave her the tingles, and it did now, even after all the attention he'd lavished on her most sensitive parts. Said parts awakened yet again upon hearing his words—a throb between her legs and awareness that she was getting wet.

"Hmm, I've never thought about it," she lied unconvincingly, her voice breathless, even to her own ears.

Pietro brought his finger to tip up her chin. She was hoping for a kiss but was met with his penetrating gaze. "I thought about being with you like this every time we were alone, Natalia. I thought about it every day. And now that we have, it is not enough."

His claim was corroborated as he angled himself to kiss her, depositing her onto her back as he rolled half on top of her for a thorough kiss. His tongue stroked hers, deeply and desperately, in that way she had come to crave. The hard press of his thick length on her thigh proved his cock was awake.

Earlier, he had pleased her with his fingers, tantalized her with his tongue, sent her into fits of ecstasy as he'd sucked her clit, and let her set the pace by putting her on top, gripping her thighs as she'd moved over him, driving into her from underneath. In the shower, he'd whispered filthy things in her ear as he'd stroked into her slowly from behind, her cheek against the tile, the way he had her pinned giving her a thrill.

All of those moments, he had seemed in control, like the orchestrator of her pleasure, swept up in his own handling of things. But now, for reasons she couldn't understand, hours into their marathon of lovemaking, he looked like he was about to be unraveled.

"I lied," she panted when they pulled back from an intense kiss, both breathless and desperate for air. "I thought about it, too. Every day, I've wanted for you to rip that trowel out of my hand, take off your shirt, and get me up against a wall. I've wanted you not to hold back."

He paused for a moment, half on top of her. Even by starlight, his gaze was intense—smoldering as she gave him permission.

He rolled closer then, fully on top of her now, his tip pushing at her sex. She spread her legs a little to invite him, wanting nothing more than for him to slide forward—maybe never having wanted something so much in her life. She nudged herself down a bit, enjoying the slipperiness of his tip at her entrance. She whispered his name, encouraging him to drive home.

"*Merda*," he cursed, pushing into her ever so slightly, then pausing and pulling out. It wasn't until he was off her, until her nipples puckered at the sudden whoosh of cool air and she heard the rip of the foil, that she comprehended. Pietro was getting a condom.

This time, when he returned to her, he pushed in with a single motion. His strokes were harder and faster, infused with a desperation that gave Natalie a sense of power she'd come to crave. Pietro Indelicato, hottest architect in the world, was desperate for more of her. Not only that—his body was magic, the way he moved, how hard he was, how thick and heavy he was for her as he filled her up.

Not that Natalie had ever been part of an all-afternoon-into-the-night lovemaking marathon, but she didn't think it was supposed to feel this good. Now, out in the open air, it was only enhanced by the ocean breeze, its coolness blowing on her neck and across her breasts giving her even more.

By then, she'd learned his tell, learned the way his breathing changed when he was getting close. It only spurred her on. Watching him come was a glorious thing. Hearing his sounds was even better. His escalating moans and soft, sexy grunts pushed her so close, so quickly, her own orgasm took her by surprise.

She might have screamed. She didn't know. All she knew was him pulling her closer, of him slowing inside her, nearly stopping as he emptied and pulsed. All she knew was his arms locked around her and him stroking her hair, kissing her face and her lips even after they were finished. And feeling, perhaps for the first time, that she was complete.

• • •

Natalie smiled through the haze of her sleep, feeling luxurious for some reason, nestled and snug, but also light, as if atop a feather bed. A soothing breeze whispered over her skin, blowing at light sheets that kissed her ankles, sheets that felt silky and smooth.

She didn't want to think too hard about where she was at that moment—didn't want to think too hard about anything at all. Much better to indulge in the glory of whatever this was. She snoozed once. Twice. The room was getting warmer and the sun was now heating her bent arm. Wakefulness now inevitable, Natalie gave her reluctant surrender.

It took only prying her dry eyes open to comprehend her surroundings. She had awakened in Pietro's house. Only, Pietro himself was nowhere to be seen, and judging from the time on the clock on his bedside table, the day was getting long.

Last night...

She and Pietro. In the groves. More than once. And a vague memory of them together again, in his bed. Her body ached but didn't hurt. It felt attended to and worked in the most delicious way. The workout he'd put her through the night before certainly explained why she had slept so long.

The bed had something to do with it, Natalie thought as she closed her eyes again and snuggled back down. She'd been sleeping on that uncomfortable cot for weeks.

It took another ten minutes for Natalie to motivate herself to finally rise, and another few to accept that she had no idea where she might find her clothes, and a full minute to organize the top sheet from Pietro's bed into a makeshift toga. Hearing absolutely nothing from the outer rooms, she was certain that Pietro was gone, which likely meant she had fashioned her garb for her sole benefit. Still, one never knew.

Natalie let out a big yawn as she padded into the kitchen, finding it empty, just as she had thought. Though she did find a striped pastry box in Tiffany blue and white, bearing the logo of Pasticceria Maldotta. On top of the box sat a note.

You looked so peaceful that I could not wake you. I believe these are one of your favorites. There is coffee next to the espresso machine. Please help yourself.

Also, please enjoy my running water and my working kitchen. You may shower and cook as much as you would like.

Natalie bit her lip against a smile she didn't need to conceal, a smile that nobody was there to see.

Shower first, she scolded herself as soon as she had read Pietro's note, though the prospect of coffee sounded good, and whatever the sugared smell was coming from the closed box was even better. But a shower was a shower. And she hadn't had such easy access to one of those in more than two months. Right then, nothing was going to stop her.

• • •

"You smell nice," Ellie reported as she pulled out of the private driveway that led to Pietro's house. She had picked Natalie up just next to the gates. Pietro's place was a few kilometers out of town. Closing her eyes for the first half of the Vespa ride had left Natalie with only a vague sense of where she was.

In order to summon Ellie to pick her up, she'd had to use technology—to drop a pin that Ellie could use on her GPS. Natalie had taken another luxurious shower as she'd waited for Ellie to show up.

"Are you saying I don't usually smell nice?" Natalie joked, still in a fantastic postcoital mood and always happy to see her friend. "You know the bath in my luxury villa has the finest soaps."

"Truthfully?" Ellie played along. "I was enjoying your specific fragrance. Rather masculine but quite nice."

Natalie just giggled, barely able to keep up the ruse.

"So...?" Ellie prodded, drawing out the short word. "How was kissing Pietro?"

Natalie smiled and looked out the window, biting her lip against her smile. "Really, really good."

Even without the impromptu call for pickup, they'd had plans to get together. Or rather, plans to see each other at Chris and Jorge's little farm. Though Natalie's initial hen had long since flown the coop, she'd hung on to the idea of keeping chickens. Today was the day they'd invited Natalie over to show her some of the basics of chicken care. Before committing to being responsible for animals, she wanted to make an informed decision.

It would all be discussed over one of Chris and Jorge's fabulous farm-to-table lunches, which Natalie didn't mind at all. Their business was a sustainable farm that would be the production site for the ingredients for a number of specialty goods. They had built a new barn and were converting the old one into a small manufacturing facility, where they would hire local workers to produce their goods.

They would make goat's milk soaps and beeswax candles; they would can jellies and preserves; they would introduce different methods for curing meats. They had a deal with a distributor that would allow them to export. Their products would appeal mostly to tourists but could be sold in Zavona and the surrounding towns. Before coming to Italy, Jorge had been wildly successful in Argentina as a fair-trade exporter of *yerba maté.*

"Hey, girl." Chris sounded as American as apple pie when he greeted Natalie, a fact she always found refreshing. Still, they'd begun to greet each other the Italian way—with two air kisses. "Long time no see. Where you been hiding? We missed you at the café this week."

She made a tiny, repentant sound to match the look on her face. "I know, I'm sorry. I lost track of time."

What she didn't say was, since she and Pietro had entered the kissing part of their relationship, she'd been a bit swept away. He'd started showing up more often, bringing her the most unlikely hodgepodge of gifts. Just the other day, he'd arrived with a painted glass vase he'd said she might like to use in furnishing her house someday. Only, the vase wasn't empty. It contained beautiful flowers.

"I've been painting more," she tacked on. Technically, this was the truth. A week before, she'd awakened early, from a dead sleep, and found herself inspired. It wasn't until she sat down at an easel that she realized how much she missed it all—from the excitement of a blank canvas to the smell of the paints.

"Tell me you didn't quit with the plaster," Jorge begged, leaning in for a greeting of his own. "If you can't figure it out with your *private lessons*, then there is no hope for us."

Jorge made the words "private lessons" sound the same way he made a lot of other things sound—full of innuendo. By then, every one of the regular crew who showed up at Café Ludo knew that Natalie was getting help. It made her uncomfortable now that she and Pietro had started doing very private things. More so because, however nice it felt, she wasn't sure what it meant.

"She's not talking about her house." Ellie saved Natalie from having to answer, throwing her a little wink. "Natalie's a real painter, like with oils and pastels."

"You never told us that. What do you paint?" Chris wanted to know as he led them around the side of the house to a table that had already been beautifully set.

Chris and Jorge still had a lot of work to do on the house where they lived, but they'd started by getting the farm itself in order. Along with Natalie, they were one of few tenants who would work on the property where they lived. Where Natalie had been staying in her garage, they'd been staying in their barn. When he'd had a lot to drink and was ready to go home, Jorge was entirely too tickled by the American idiom someone had taught him. He liked to tell Chris it was time to head home for a roll in the hay.

"I paint landscapes," Natalie answered easily, taking a seat at the table. "Not much else to paint back home. Illinois has a lot of farmhouses and plains. *One day*, when this is all finished, I'm going to go to Florence to take a painting class with a master artist."

The other three exchanged knowing smiles as they settled down at the table.

"One day," they all chorused back.

The *one day* thing had become a kind of inside joke. It spoke of all the fun things they'd get to do once their projects were complete. On the bad days, it seemed their work would never be done. Natalie's troubles were not unique. They'd all had their share of construction gone wrong, of sticker shock at vendor quotes, of administrative issues and permitting problems.

"How's the inside coming?" Natalie wanted to know. Chris remained standing and poured the wine.

"Expensive," he said bluntly. "We're gonna take a leaf out of your book. Delay some of it till we need it for tourist season. Then do some of it ourselves."

At their lunches at Café Ludo, they did more than compare notes about vendors. They compared and brainstormed strategies as well. Where Natalie had saved money plastering her own walls, her budget was still being siphoned away, given all the surprises. The more unexpected expenses cropped up, the further out she delayed plans to open her pool. If her budget got tight enough, she might have to delay a whole season.

"It's smart," Ellie praised Chris. "The bills are getting ridiculous."

"What is the alternative?" Jorge interjected. "After investing all of this money, to lose our house at the end?"

Natalie thought of all the creative accounting, all the elbow grease, all the sacrifices she'd made to get to this point. She also thought about the sheer luck of her windfall from Franco Pelagatti. She thought about these friends who had helped her since the beginning, and Pietro, who was in her corner and without whom she could never be this far. It was a complex patchwork, all the things that had gotten her there.

Instead of voicing any of that, she just said, "I guess we do what we have to do."

CHAPTER TWENTY

"This thing has life jackets, right?"

Natalie looked down into the space beneath the gangplank that stretched between the dock and Pietro's boat, a seven-and-a-half-foot motor yacht he'd invested in three years before. He'd gotten the idea to take Natalie out when she had revealed—quite astonishingly—that she'd been there for weeks without getting close enough to the ocean to feel the spray of the water.

The extent of her time on the coastline had been to eat and drink with Pietro or any of her small group of friends. Some restaurants were closer to the water than others. Making up his mind to not let another day pass without Natalie having the full experience of what the coast had to offer was his own revelation—it had been months since he'd been out on the water.

"Yes, this thing has life jackets," he repeated in a voice that told her she was being at least a little bit ridiculous. "It also has an experienced sailor who knows where to find all of the very best coves, who has packed us a very nice lunch and planned a very nice time for relaxation."

"It's not too late to relax on land..." Natalie hedged. She looked a bit panicked.

"Very true," Pietro conceded. "But on a private beach, we can do very private things."

Ten minutes later, they were navigating away

from the docks and sailing into the bay. Pietro headed south, into open water. The high-speed ferry that went from Sorrento to Salerno was the largest vessel frequented on these waters. Smaller boats, like Pietro's, could venture to private beaches, the ones that only locals knew.

The one Pietro was set to take her to was just south of Rivela, in Cocenza, the town where her grandmother had lived. Though the military base was no longer in operation, the hulks of abandoned buildings still stood.

"I've been to that village," Natalie commented, loudly enough for her voice to be heard over the sound of the engine and the ocean spray. "Rivela. It looks different from a boat."

Pietro had traveled between Zavona and Rivela by boat a hundred times. It recalled memories of his grandfather, now long gone, ferrying him and his grandmother to this place and that. His nonna still loved the water.

"The legend about the woman in the sea…this is where it came from," Pietro called in response.

He had recounted Nonna's version of the story to Natalie, had inquired casually to a few art-world friends about a Botticelli-esque painting of a woman in the sea, but the reference was just too vague. Despite what Nonna had told him, he had avoided asking his father. If the painting was still in Italy and Pietro could locate it and it really did look like Natalie, he would turn it into a reason to have a getaway together, an excuse to go and see.

Cool air rushing from the speed of the boat contrasted with the warmth of Natalie clinging to his arm as he maneuvered with the wheel. At first, as they'd left the docks, she had clung to him with a bit of lingering fear. Now, she clung to be close.

He slowed his boat as they neared the base to let Natalie have a good look, and to tell her what he knew about the older buildings, about the American military presence and about the operational years of the base. All of it was well before Pietro's time. Yet, it remained in the consciousness of the older people, who liked to reminisce about what Italy had been like after the war. Natalie shared her own recollections of what her grandmother had told her. To the extent that her father had only been stationed there for its decommissioning, she had remembered it as a mostly abandoned place, too.

The contrast was stark between the old buildings—austere and official-looking even years after their useful life—and the pristine beaches at the bottom of the cliffs below. The place where Pietro took Natalie was known only to locals and quite hidden. A trick of the coastline made the line of the beach look smooth from a distance, concealing an inlet navigable only by a small boat, much like the one that Pietro rode them in.

"Who does this place belong to?"

Natalie finally loosened her hold on him, stepping back to spin in a circle as she took in the cove. Pietro imagined what it must be like for her to see it for the first time. It was otherworldly, with its high cliff walls and its narrow passage that opened into a dramatic crescent of a beach of dark-blue waters and black sand. The sand on this part of the beach was softer than some other areas of the coast, another feature that made it special.

Some speculated that this beach had been altered, man-made for the leisure of the American soldiers who had inhabited the base. Rough steps carved out of the cliffside could be followed to the base above. Pietro liked to think that the steps were man-made but that the soft sand was not—that it was simply one of nature's wonders. He knew just where to moor his boat to get it closest to shore. He enjoyed watching Natalia out of her element, thigh-deep in the water as they waded to shore.

Wet clothes were as good an excuse as any to strip them off, to hang them to dry on the branch of a tree, to revel in the heat of the day and to go for a swim. Sex was one area where Natalie didn't let her apprehensions and inhibitions rule, the one area where she surrendered. Watching any woman claim her pleasure was sexy, but Natalie wasn't any woman. It cost her something to let herself go, to give herself permission to fall apart, to give Pietro dominion over her gratification. He had never seen himself as the kind of man to be drunk with the sexual power he held over a woman. But he'd never been more aroused, more unraveled, more crazed with lust than he was when they were perfectly connected, even as he held her in his thrall.

It began as wading, then playing in the cool water as they were warmed by the sun above, swimming out, then standing, then swaying with the gentle waves. By the time they were in up to her shoulders, Pietro could no longer resist the urge to hold her, to kiss her, to lock her in his embrace. Natalie's lips were soft, her fingers on the back of his neck, threaded in his wet hair, insistent. The buoyancy of the water made it easy for her to wrap her legs around his waist. His hands under her thighs and the lightness of the ocean made it so he could have held her there forever. If only her center weren't so distractingly slick.

It didn't take long before his own kisses became more insistent, before he tugged at her lips with his teeth and moved his soft bite down her neck. She had tasted different on the beach—like salt and sea and sand. Now, he could move and ply her body in different ways. He could drive into her at angles and at speeds that were impossible to achieve on land, slow and thorough and deep. Completing their connection with her legs wrapped around his waist was exactly what he did.

Once he was inside, he bent her backward over his forearm, until her shoulders were in the water, her body half floating and her face turned toward the sky. It splayed her out in front of him in an unexpected way, making her look every bit a sea goddess as her breasts with their puckered nipples poked out of the water and her hair floated around her face. It made him clench and ache driving into her, watching his cock slide in and out of her, making him feel like some kind of god.

"So tell me, Natalie Malone..." He said her name in his best American accent, an hour later as they lounged on a beach blanket covered by an enormous towel. "What is your real dream? It cannot be to work so hard. What will you do when your villa is complete?"

They had snacked on the contents of the picnic

basket and remained quite undressed. Pietro was hoping for round two and didn't mind the long intermission. After sex was the best time to ask her things, and Pietro had thought it a playful question until he saw the look on her face.

"I'm not sure," she answered quietly, looking beyond his arm and out toward the horizon. "Most days, I can't see past finding out the truth about Franco and the villa finally being done. I think some part of me didn't think this would ever really happen."

Then she repeated to him a sentiment—the same sentiment she had expressed months earlier when she began to tell him the story of how she had come to own the villa.

"I hadn't planned on doing this alone."

Pietro thought of his past, of what it felt like to be abandoned, of not having been able to see your life beyond a certain point, of having your future pinned on a vision that swiftly disappeared. He also thought of what it had taken to begin to see, not that he had been using much of his own vision lately.

"Sometimes the best things that are waiting for you are over the horizon. And what awaits you is a beautiful surprise."

"Have you met me? I don't like surprises. I like for things to go as planned."

"If things had gone as planned, Natalia, I would not be here on this beach with you."

It was yet another comment he had said half playfully that she took fully to heart. When she didn't speak for minutes, only stared out at the horizon, he didn't push, ready to drop it if it was something she was working through.

"I think maybe my dream is to relax. You know? To feel like I'm not always waiting for the other shoe to drop."

Pietro must have looked confused.

"It's an American saying. It means when you're waiting for something to go wrong. My whole life, a lot of things have. I really want this place, this villa I've invested in and the business I can build with the *pensione*... I just want it to lead to something secure."

"People are what make you secure, Natalia. If you have people around you, nothing can go wrong. You have met people, good people, here. This is why your grandmother never forgot this place, I think. Not just because of its beauty. She wanted to grow old here, to die here, and for you to go on living here in Campania. She wanted you to find your *famiglia.*"

• • •

"This meeting of the Zavona Economic Development Council may now come to order."

As usual, Pietro was eager for the meeting to be over before it had even begun. The agony would be worse given a lengthening list of other things he would rather be doing. When he'd agreed to be on the council, he hadn't been so angry with his father. He hadn't been so exasperated with the state of the program and the other council members. He hadn't had an insatiable girlfriend with needs he was only too happy to tend to. He would rather still be with her now, asleep in bed.

A chorus of greetings was exchanged as Alfonso stalked into the room, walking too quickly as usual, disturbing the otherwise calm chatter of moments before. Pietro often wondered what business seemed to always have Alfonso so rushed. He should have budgeted ample time for at least this.

"First, a serious order of business," Alfonso proclaimed as soon as Signor Schivo announced that they should go through the report. "The town of Cocenza is bankrupt. It can no longer pay its debts." With a heavy brow, Alfonso shifted his gaze all across the table. "In addition to being tragic news for our region, this is bad news for Zavona. It will become more difficult for us to secure funding from the bank."

"We shouldn't be borrowing now anyway." Pietro's remark was automatic, a gut reaction to Alfonso's news.

"On the contrary," Alfonso argued. "This is the exact moment when we should borrow. Before the national bank reassesses the risk. We don't want to run into a need to borrow money only to find that the well is dry."

Pietro scrutinized Alfonso, in honest wonderment of whether there was something severely wrong with his father.

"The national bank would be wise to make it more difficult to secure funds. It is an accurate reflection of challenges faced by our region." Pietro felt for a moment as if he were channeling Natalie. "We should not discuss how to mislead the bank. We should discuss the reasons why Cocenza has gone bankrupt, how we can help them and avoid the same fate."

Alfonso's eyes narrowed. "We can avoid the same fate by having a cash reserve."

But that would mean paying interest on a pot of money that hadn't been put to work. Whatever his father's scheme, it wasn't germane to what business loans were for.

"You do realize that if we made the town profitable, that if we fundamentally fixed what is broken, we would not be relegated to desperate measures?"

Alfonso punctuated his next commands with the hard pulse of his finger on the table each time he said "no more."

"No more of this nonsense about benefactors who never materialize. No more distracting this council from its real business. A cash reserve is real funding that we can put in the bank. No more talk about some benefactor bailing out the town for free. Nobody would give us something for nothing. Being smart and practical is how we will succeed. Most days, you are worse than the *sognatori*."

Pietro sent back just as icy a glare.

"What bothers you more, Papa? That the kinds of people who you tell me don't exist are taking my meetings? Or that you talk and talk until you believe your own lies…and that without me, you are failing to lead this town away from a tragic fate?"

Pietro could see that he had deeply insulted his father and scandalized the other council members. In that moment, he didn't care.

"I have served this region—and this town—for more than twenty-five years, Pitruzzu."

"Yes," Pietro agreed. "And look at where we are."

Alfonso's eyes blazed, and he talked through a

clenched jaw. "You are not one to tell me about empty talk. Every time, you mention these investors. Where are they now? Where are these benefactors of which you speak? These people lining up with their wallets open to make a postcard picture out of this town?"

Pietro stood up. "They are in Tuscany. And Verona. And Alto Adige. Two of them are in Florence. I am paying them visits, and some of them are deciding whether to invest. They are giving me their time and consideration, which is more than I can say about you."

CHAPTER TWENTY-ONE

The apartment suite was coming along, with the plastering complete in the bedroom, the new bathroom put in, and light fixtures installed. The simple iron bed frame had sheer white linens draped down from the canopy; the complete apparatus was shaped like a box.

Natalie had borrowed the modern dresser and bedside tables that matched the modern frame. None of the three was really her style, but minimalist furniture in the guest rooms was part of the plan. The hospitality supply outfit that sold them had leased her a set of demos. If she liked them, she would place a big order when the time to buy furniture for the guest rooms finally came. For two months, she would get to try it out.

"Where are you going?" came a gravelly Italian voice at the same time as strong arms circled her from behind. Pietro liked for her to stay in bed. Natalie didn't mind getting back under the covers after she'd taken in the morning. She loved to have a little outdoor stroll.

The main bedroom suite in the apartment was the room with the very best view. Double doors opened onto a stone veranda as wide as the suite itself. Being close to the top of the hill, Natalie had a cascading view of Zavona itself as it stretched down to the ocean. Looking directly west gave her sunsets and blue water, but she had a wide view of the entire coast. Waking up in her apartment every morning was like waking up in a five-star hotel. Two weeks sleeping there with Pietro, who had been there nearly every night, made their time together feel like a honeymoon.

"Come with me." She looked back at Pietro, who she didn't think would ever stop looking like a work of art splayed out as he liked to be in a tangle of covers.

Before he could answer, she relieved the bed of the blanket they had slept under. Middays were still balmy, owing in part to a warm year. Fall weather meant the mornings were getting cold.

Five minutes later, the two were huddled under said blanket, sharing a single, long-pulled coffee from a glass teacup. An espresso machine for her apartment was Pietro's latest gift, and one of the only appliances in her kitchen, though he'd insisted it was more like a gift to himself.

"I think today might be our last day," Natalie remarked after having a sip and handing the cup back to Pietro. He stood behind her, leaving her ensconced in his arms. At her waist was a thick stone wall. She didn't need to clarify what she was talking about. The milestone was close, and astounding. Only two more rooms—both guest rooms—needed fresh plaster on the walls.

"You've done so well," he praised, and not for the first time, his voice was laced with pride. "You are an expert now with plaster. I could not have done this better myself."

Natalie normally would have come back with something quick and clever, maybe ribbing him for his perfectionism, but she surprised herself by choking up.

"Yeah, because of you," she said simply, afraid that if she said more, she would actually cry, which she really didn't want to be doing at seven o'clock in the morning.

Natalie—being Natalie—had done the math. So many things had cost so much more than she had expected, so many things had gone wrong that she was dangerously close to being over budget. Pietro's tutelage had easily saved her €10,000. Without his help, she would have already run out of money.

"We do not have time to finish today." Pietro said it in his typical way, his voice husky, his tone self-assured and gentle. His warm coffee breath tickled her neck.

"We should've finished yesterday," she pointed out. They had deemed it too nice a day to stay inside and work. It had been unseasonably warm and reminiscent of the summer. They'd taken a picnic lunch to the beach, spent hours there, reading and lounging, kissing and drinking wine.

Getting caught up in Pietro had become a bit too easy. It made for slow-going work. The time Natalie had taken to do her own plaster had saved money, but it had also put her behind. She had fewer than three months to finish the restoration. It wasn't a long time. For as tirelessly as Natalie had been working, she had miles to go to get the villa up to code.

"There is a place I must go. I would like you to come."

But Pietro had already taken her to all manner of places. The past three weeks had been the biggest whirlwind of her life. He'd shown her every town on the Amalfitana, the name for the stretch of highway that runs from Sorrento to Salerno. She'd seen what felt like the entire coast from the back seat of Pietro's Vespa. He'd even started teaching her how to drive.

But it had to stop. Or rather, it had to at least slow down until she finished her repairs. It was getting too easy to get swept up and lose all track of space and time. Just as she was ready to issue an immediate and adamant "no" to whatever scheme he might be concocting, Pietro said the last thing she expected.

"I would like you to meet my family."

"Your family?"

Pietro put the coffee down on the wide part of the stone wall and turned her in his arms until they were facing each other.

"The ones who are new to you, yes. You have already met my nonna."

• • •

"Did you bring me something good?" Carlota whispered to Natalie soon after she arrived, after they were out of earshot of the others. For what had seemed like a solid ten minutes, Natalie was introduced to Pietro's parents and siblings and their kids. All of them were gracious, and welcoming, and with some hints of the charm that came off Pietro in waves. The Indelicato resemblance was striking, with Pietro and Alfonso looking the most alike. It was easy to tell the blood relatives from the marry-ins.

"Your favorite," Natalie whispered.

"I knew you would. I have something for you as well. I made *delizia a limone*. Far superior to Signora Maldotta's. You will see."

Natalie leaned in and lowered her voice. Pietro had told her all about the rivalry. "I can hardly eat her pastries anymore. They're not as good as yours."

She had been mistaken before in thinking she'd experienced his family's estate. The main house was a sight to see, a villa smaller than her own but still grand. This was what she had always hoped dinner would be like at her own villa, people talking and laughing around the table. The scene filled her with joy.

"You must miss your family," Pietro's sister Lucia observed kindly after grace had been said and food was going around. "Will they come and visit you when your project is finished?"

"No family. Just friends. My parents died a long time ago. My grandmother died earlier this year."

Natalie was used to the sorts of responses that came in the wake of such revelations. Parents who had died when she was young meant that she had been given some version of this explanation all her life. She didn't enjoy the pity or the platitudes, but people commiserated out of kindness, and she learned to hear their comments with grace. Carlota patted her arm and offered kind words.

"Then it's a good thing you've found us. We will look after you."

When Natalie swung an astonished glance over to Pietro, he gave her a little wink and a smile, then helped himself to another forkful of potatoes.

"Natalia's grandmother lived in Campania when she was a teenager. This is why she always wanted to return," Pietro explained. "She is searching for information about her grandmother's first love."

This new information turned a few heads. A relative she had met twenty minutes earlier spoke rapidly, asking a question Natalie didn't completely hear.

"My aunt wants to know whether it was her first love or her true love."

Pietro's eyes twinkled as he asked this. It was too close an echo to the conversation they'd had a dozen times over the past month.

"Pietro is not telling the story correctly. My grandfather was her true love. I'm looking for a man who was my grandmother's friend," Natalie said with emphasis, throwing Pietro a playful, indignant glance.

"Natalie is the one who is not telling the story correctly. The man she is looking for left her grandmother money, even though they hadn't spoken in twenty-five years."

Natalie gave him a look. "Pietro left out one fact—my grandmother never mentioned him."

Carlota said something quick, something that rhymed, and slapped her hand on the table to punctuate her phrase. It caused the others to burst into laughter. Pietro chuckled and repeated it slowly.

"*Tra il dire e il fare c'è di mezzo il mare.*" Then he translated. "It means there is an ocean between what we tell others and what we actually do."

Natalie joined in the laughter, feeling at ease with Pietro's family even though there was still much to resolve about her own. This was what family was supposed to be, the kind she had wanted and never dared to dream of. It felt sacred just to be part of this.

As the evening wore on, the serving plates emptied, but the conversation kept flowing. Natalie melted into Pietro's arms, leaning into him as they talked and laughed with his family, their chairs pushed together closely.

"We should walk back before it gets too dark."

She got chills from the low rumble of his voice, her body now hyperaware of his breath on her neck and his arm around her shoulders. His fingertips grazing her arm reminded her of the ecstasy of other light touches. Earlier, they had walked from his cottage through the groves to arrive on this side. Suddenly, she wanted nothing more than the give of soft earth beneath them and the sweetness of lemon in her nose.

"Wouldn't it be rude of us to leave?" Her question was half-hearted. She wanted to make a good impression on his family, and still…when it came to Pietro, she had trouble saying no.

"Start saying your goodbyes. Tell them you must wake up early tomorrow. I will do the same."

With that, he kissed her cheek, moved his arm from her shoulder to the back of her chair, and released her by sitting back a little in his.

By then, the affair had lost some of its cohesion. The table had been abandoned by half. A few people had retreated back to the kitchens. Alfonso and Rodrigo and Matteo had strolled to take in the best view of the ocean from the corner of the lawn. The children had run into the lemon groves. They'd left minutes earlier, but their laughter could still be heard.

Thinking to use the powder room and to find the one person she couldn't leave without speaking to, his nonna, Natalie squeezed his shoulder as she rose from her chair, smiling to herself as she imagined where Carlota might be. She had become progressively entertaining as the night had waxed on, to Natalie's utter amusement. Maybe she had retreated inside to find her way to another nip.

"Did you enjoy dinner?"

The voice of Pietro's mother startled her as it rang out from behind, catching Natalie in the hall.

"Thank you, yes," she answered in Italian. "Everything you served was delicious. And you have a lovely home."

Natalie wished she had something more to say, something intelligent, something that would ingratiate her to Michaela. But being liked by her was something Natalie didn't yet know how to achieve. Michaela had been polite all evening but difficult to read. Halfway to asking where she could find Carlota, in order to say goodbye, Natalie heard Michaela speak before she could get the sentence out.

"You are the first woman Pietro has brought to dinner in a very long time. I was worried about my son. We are very happy to meet you."

With a final gesture and a small nod, her face broke into a smile, the same exuberant smile she had sported when speaking animatedly at dinner, one Michaela had yet to turn toward her. Natalie couldn't help but grin. It wasn't a glowing testimony to Natalie as much as it was a sigh of relief that their son might not die a bachelor after all. Whatever it was, she would take it.

Yet another interruption saved her from having to formulate a response, this time in the form of a ruckus. Urgent shouting could be heard from outside. It was too fast and too frantic and in Italian too advanced for her to understand, but it sent her into a panic nonetheless. It was Pietro's voice.

"*Mamma mia*," Michaela said under her breath, one hand flying to her chest as the other flew down to grip Natalie's arm.

"What happened?" Natalie demanded, her stomach already turning with worry. Heavy footsteps came from behind them, and she looked back toward the kitchen just in time to see Pietro burst through the doorway and into the hall.

"I must go help. There's been a collapse."

CHAPTER TWENTY-TWO

"Show me what's happening down there," Pietro demanded, bracing the hand that didn't hold his phone to the roof of the car. Alfonso had just turned sharply to get them on the road. The location where the collapse had occurred wasn't far—maybe five kilometers—but it could take minutes on tiny, winding roads.

"We think he's in the basement. The collapse was in the entryway. It's messy in here and it's hard to tell what's what." Men shouted in the background, their voices faint and faded compared to Berto's voice on the phone.

"That doesn't tell me enough," Pietro growled. "I need to see."

He pressed the button on his phone to start a video call. They always took an extra moment to connect. Every second that he waited felt like an eternity. His shirt felt hot all of a sudden, and sweat had begun to pool in his armpits and crawl down his neck.

"You do not have to talk to him that way," Alfonso argued from the driver's seat in the same frustrated tone.

"Don't lecture me. It's your fault that we are in this situation."

Alfonso didn't skip a beat when it came to navigating the roads. They had already sped past an astonished-looking Signora, who had shouted in protest at their speed. But Alfonso's face hardened at Pietro's words.

"Pietro? Can you see now?" came Berto's voice.

Pietro ripped his glaring eyes away from the unrepentant face of his father, then held his phone in front of him to get a better look. It was as he expected—a lot of dust and rubble. Still, there were things he could tell by taking in the big picture. Understanding what was still intact would tell the tale.

"Back up," Pietro commanded with a bit less bite. "I want to see the whole room."

On his command, Berto panned out. Now Pietro could see more than just rubble.

"How many men are there?"

"Five so far. The rest, like you, are coming. We have called every able-bodied man in town."

"Form an assembly line," Pietro managed to grit out after swallowing hard to stave off a wave of nausea. The scene brought back memories he had tried hard to forget. The last time he'd been present for a collapse, things had not ended well.

That time, it had been an old monastery in Tuscany. A restoration commissioned by the town. Nothing could've been done to avoid that collapse, which made it all the more tragic. They had managed to dig out an injured worker after more than two days. On the third, the remaining two had lost their lives.

Berto issued instructions, asking two of the men to stop throwing rocks aside, asking them to get into a different formation.

"You need fewer men standing on the rocks," Pietro directed. "And the men who stay on the rocks must transfer the weight of the stones away."

The view through the phone camera went sideways as Berto repeated the sentiment to the men in the room, forgetting the phone's video feed.

"Do you have light?" Pietro demanded.

"Not enough," Berto admitted.

Pietro hadn't thought of swinging by to get his truck. He sent out a swift text to Matteo—who was in a different car with Rodrigo, hot on their heels—telling them to go back and bring Pietro's supplies.

"Tell the Fiorelli brothers to bring them. Then call anybody else, even Aldo."

Pietro tightened his grip on the roof as they made a final, dangerous turn onto the street of the house in question.

"I'm arriving now," Pietro told Berto before he hung up, pocketing his phone with a shaking hand, and unbuckled the seat belt he'd barely remembered to put on. He was already opening his door as his father screeched the car to a stop.

"Pietro, you're here," one of the workers said, never stopping his motion of transferring stones. He was sweating and straining, as if he had been at this for a long time.

"Has anybody been keeping time?" Pietro asked loudly enough for everyone to hear.

Berto was on the phone with someone else, speaking quickly, asking for supplies. Glancing at his watch, he counted thirteen minutes since he'd gotten the call. He wanted to know how long it had been since the collapse itself.

"My son was riding his bicycle and heard the noise," a man chimed in. "He rode home to tell my wife and me. When he told me what happened, I ran over from the next street. It has been around an hour since then."

"How can you be sure that anybody was home?"

"The lights were on inside. Food was cooking in the oven. I could smell it as soon as I came in," the neighbor reported. "This house is owned by foreigners."

He turned to his father, who had just burst in. "Papa, I need you to call Signor Schivo to identify the tenant who lives here. We need to call them. The ringing of their phone will tell us where they are."

Alfonso, seeming shell-shocked, gave Pietro a short, unreadable look before turning and rushing out the door. Pietro turned back toward the disaster, training his attention on what he could do in the moment.

The good news was, with construction like this, large air pockets were likely. Pietro wasn't too worried about whether those trapped beneath could breathe. If they were alive, chances were, they could. But were they? Any number of injuries could have finished them quickly, and another long list could be killing them slowly.

Berto hung up the phone, clearly rattled.

"Thank God you're here, Pietro. Tell us what to do."

He had been assessing, calculating since the moment he came in. "Our goal right now is to find out where they are so we can be smart about where we dig."

To his own ears, Pietro sounded collected and confident. He didn't want to think of what his backup plan might be if listening for cell phones didn't work. The person's phone could have been on a cord, charging somewhere, or crushed.

Alfonso returned with two hard hats, the kind Pietro always kept in his truck. It meant Matteo had arrived. Alfonso thrust one of the hats into Pietro's hand.

"Give it to one of the workers," Pietro said. "I don't want it."

But Alfonso kept pushing until Pietro took it. "Put on the hat. You're still my son."

With that, Alfonso walked forward and gave the other hat to a man Pietro didn't recognize, who seemed in the clearest danger from where he stood on top of the pile.

"Tell me where you need me," Alfonso commanded.

"All I need from you is the phone number," Pietro said.

Alfonso looked ready to protest at the same moment as additional men arrived. The operation became more advanced, with longer assembly lines and men removing rocks and wheelbarrows brought in to help carry the load.

The rock pile was diminishing. Not as much as Pietro would have liked, but there were many men and they worked quickly. The Fiorellos arrived with their lights.

No sooner had Pietro arranged their position than Alfonso burst back into the space, looking far paler than he had looked just moments before.

"I'm sorry… Natalie's friends…the farmer from Texas and his friend from Argentina—" Alfonso cut himself off, then mopped his brow with the handkerchief that had appeared in his hands. "This is their house. I have their telephone numbers."

"Everybody quiet!" Pietro roared every bit of rage at hearing this answer into silencing the room. Then, in a more subdued voice, "We will try to locate them by calling their phones. We have learned that there may be two men buried."

Pietro's gaze followed the last stone that had been plucked off the top of the pile as it made its way from the hands of one man to the next. He followed it as it disappeared out the door. He swung his eyes back toward the pile of rubble. If something happened to Chris and Jorge—if he had to tell Natalie that the council's negligence had killed her friends—he didn't know how he would look at himself in the mirror. And he would never speak to his father again.

"Call them," he ground out through gritted teeth. Alfonso dialed. Pietro moved closer to the rubble, then closed his eyes, wanting to focus only on sound.

"It went directly to voice mail," Alfonso said. "I'll try again."

This was the most difficult part. The moment of listening for survivors and hearing nothing in return. They listened for thirty seconds. A minute. Alfonso called three times more, but no phones rang.

Please, God. Pietro prayed silently for them to have a fighting chance.

Then a ruckus started outside. Someone from just beyond the door. By then, there had been no shortage of men from town who had come to help. Somebody was telling the newcomers to keep it down.

"Please, you must be quiet," the voice from outside implored. "We are trying to locate the owner. It will be easier if we know exactly where he is."

"And I am telling you to move," came an indignant response, louder this time and with an accent that told Pietro the owner was not from Zavona. "I am the owner of this house."

CHAPTER TWENTY-THREE

I'm coming to get you. I'm driving now.

Natalie had sent and received a flurry of texts for the past hour, but this one was the one she had awaited. Pietro had left in haste nearly three hours before. Hasty departure, along with his shouted plea for Lucia to see Natalie home safely, was the last that she had heard from him.

Instead of taking her anywhere, Lucia had ushered her into the kitchen with the other women. The able-bodied men had all gone, and the children had been called back from the lemon groves, as if the dangerous moment warranted collecting and keeping everyone close who they held dear.

Natalie only picked up some of what was said. All the courtesies of speaking slowly for her benefit had been abandoned given the excitement. Conversation flew past her, but it was hard to tell how much of it was facts or speculation. There had been an accident at somebody's house. Among the words that sailed by, she had heard Pietro's and Alfonso's names and mention of the redevelopment program.

Michaela distributed more glasses and filled them this time with something different, something bitter that the women put down in a single swallow, the contents of which Natalie deemed it the wrong moment to find out. Later, in Lucia's car, Natalie wasn't shy about digging to know what was going on.

"What do they know so far?"

"Only that the collapse happened at one of the houses in your program. And that Pietro has warned of this danger. Pietro and my father, they are not speaking because of this."

The more Natalie thought about it, the more she realized how little Pietro spoke about his father. At dinner, things between them had seemed a bit cold.

"Pietro inspected my property. He was very thorough. He knew exactly what to fix. Why did he think that something like this would happen?"

Lucia gave a sad smile.

"You are not like the others. The care Pietro takes with you is unlike the care he takes with anybody else."

The comment was enough to quiet Natalie, and Lucia's answer was enough to satisfy Natalie's curiosity. It might have been all that she knew. At home, she waved goodbye, squinting against Lucia's retreating headlights before turning and walking to her house. The bedroom in her apartment felt empty without Pietro. It was late and he hadn't gotten back yet. If he didn't return that night, it would be the first time she slept in her bedroom alone.

I wonder whose house it is.

Now that Lucia had confirmed it, the thought ran through her head on repeat. The fact that no one had texted her meant the others didn't know. But if she called around to find out what had happened, it might start a panic—might open a Pandora's box she couldn't close.

She didn't have to wait as long as she thought. Soon enough, Pietro could be heard coming down the hall. The part of her that wanted to rush to him warred with the part of her that was terrified of what he might report. And so she sat, frozen and a bit dazed, as she awaited his arrival, her mind wandering to what their night might have been, the two of them naked and content once more beneath the stars.

His footsteps were heavy, coming up fast—it set her heart racing. Urgency in finding her right then couldn't mean anything good.

"Natalia!" His voice would have put Natalie at ease if only he hadn't sounded as frantic as his footsteps.

"Natalia." When he burst in, she finally rose to her feet. He was barely recognizable compared to the Pietro who had left her hours ago at his parents' house. His hair—usually so clean and beautifully tousled—was dusty and wild, as if someone had poured gray talcum powder on his head. Everything from his clothes right down to the hairs on his arms had a sort of dusty look. The one part of him that shined with vibrancy and color and in perfect clarity were his eyes, only she'd never seen them so scared.

She threw herself into his arms unabashedly and squeezed her eyes shut, saying a silent prayer of gratitude that he had come back alive, terrified from the look in his eye that maybe somebody else hadn't.

"I don't want you staying here."

Pietro all but ordered this as his arms encircled her tightly. He held her for long, desperate seconds before pulling back, then pinned her with an intense gaze that seemed meant to drive home his demand.

From there, he began to look around, his eyes

washing over the ceiling and circling the doors.

"Please. Pack your things. You can stay at my house. I will tell you everything. But now we must leave. I will explain everything in the car."

Staring at him for a beat or three, Natalie just blinked.

"Pietro...what happened?" she finally managed to get out.

No sooner did she ask than Pietro began stalking across the room. In her closet, he plucked up one of the suitcases she had emptied just days earlier.

"I will tell you. But please, begin packing your things."

"*Adesso*, Pietro." Natalie put her hands on her hips, insisting he tell her now.

She wasn't sure which surprised her more—that she spoke to him in that tone or that he had given her reason to. Pietro did not seem himself.

"Thank God that they were not at home, but the collapse tonight—it was in their house. They are lucky to be alive. If they hadn't—" Pietro cut himself off. "They went into town for thirty minutes. By the time they got back, their ceiling and their floor was gone."

"Who?"

Pietro was rambling. She doubted he knew he hadn't said. He was clearly traumatized by all of this.

"Who?" she repeated.

Pietro swept his hand across his face. "Your friends. Jorge and Chris."

Natalie's lips went numb and her stomach bottomed out. "I don't understand. Their floor caved in?"

Pietro looked tired. "Their ceiling caved in first. A month ago, they demolished a load-bearing wall. Today, they hung a chandelier that compromised the ceiling. When the ceiling came down, it came down with such force that it punched through to the basement. There is damage on every level. It may not be salvageable."

Oh my gosh.

Natalie could hardly believe what she was hearing. She'd been to that house so often that she could picture every bit.

"Where are they now? I have to call them."

Pietro brought the suitcase over to her bed. Natalie's mind hadn't caught up thoroughly enough to wage any sort of protest, though she might do that in just a minute.

"Tonight, they will stay with a neighbor. Tomorrow, I do not know. Tomorrow, many things will change."

Pietro looked even more exhausted than he had a minute earlier.

"Pietro. Stay here tonight. I know I don't have a shower, but I'll help you wash up. You need rest. We'll talk about it in the morning."

But Pietro didn't stop moving.

"Natalia, please. I cannot allow you to stay here another night until changes are made. I cannot risk what almost happened to Jorge and Chris happening to you. At my home, I can keep you safe."

His voice broke on the last word. When it did, he stepped back from his unzipping. Now, his hands were on his hips and his eyes shone.

"Okay." She conceded for now to what sounded

like a half-baked plan. It sounded like he was asking her to move in for a while. She wouldn't agree to that, but she could at least stay the night.

"I'm exhausted and you are, too. I'll bring a change of clothes. Let's just be thankful that no one got hurt. Everything will be fine."

• • •

It felt especially empty waking up without Pietro, given the way he had held her throughout the night. Her sleep had been more fitful than usual and she'd half awakened several times. Instead of holding her loosely as he usually did, one arm hooking her to his side while the rest of him splayed out in godlike perfection, each time she'd awakened, she had been firmly ensconced—nearly cocooned—in his arms.

Once they'd reached his house, she'd had to talk him down from going back out—something about paying visits to the other tenants as soon as possible. It had taken her tugging him farther into his house and pushing him into his own shower to convince him not to go. She had never seen him so out of sorts. Another first—however desperate he had been to hold her close, however desperate both of them had been to be together, it was the first time they had laid down together and only slept instead of making love.

Everyone's meeting at the café.

The group text meant that people had heard, though Natalie didn't know from whom. She'd given Ellie an update but asked her to keep it under wraps. If anything, it was a courtesy to Chris and

Jorge—who could imagine how they must be feeling?—and it wasn't their business to tell. Others would find out who needed to when it was time.

The next hour found Natalie doing something the old Natalie never would've seen herself do. After dressing, she walked into Pietro's kitchen toward the hook on the wall where he kept his keys. She ate the breakfast pastries he had left her, pressed the button on the machine to expel the coffee, then she went to borrow his Vespa from his garage.

Driving it wasn't nearly as difficult as she'd once made it out to be. It came easier than the first time. No stops or freak-outs. She rode it slow and smooth. People she knew, and people she didn't, waved to her as she took the winding roads, descending carefully into town.

Pulling up in front of Café Ludo barely earned her a glance from anyone at the table. Jorge and Chris sat in their usual spots, surrounded more closely than usual by friends. Chris looked like he hadn't slept all night. Jorge's sorrow was written clearly across his face. Someone's arm slung around him in comfort. The food in front of him sat untouched.

Climbing off Pietro's Vespa did earn Natalie an eyebrow raise from Ellie. Making room, she pushed her own chair back and pulled in a chair from an empty table next to theirs, positioning it for Natalie to sit.

"Guys, I'm so sorry."

She walked over to Chris and Jorge's side of the table and stooped to give each a one-armed hug, then headed to her proffered seat so as not to interrupt what they were saying. Jorge, for once, was quiet, leaving Chris to do all the talking. Chris was early enough in the telling of the story that Natalie surmised they hadn't been there for long.

"We were cooking dinner," Chris resumed explaining in his southern lilt. "I realized we were out of onions; then Jorge realized we were also out of wine. You know nothing in Zavona is open on a Sunday, but I had the roast slow-cooking in the Dutch oven. If there was anything we needed to get, we had time."

Chris shook his head a little and looked to the side, his eyes shining as he blinked. He took a breath before he continued. Jorge's hand came in to cover his biceps.

"So we made sure the oven was low, got in the truck, and headed down the coast to the supermarket in Nanca, the one that's always open."

Chris paused his retelling, his face crumbling a bit in anguish. "At first, Jorge was going to stay and get a little more done. But for some reason, I still don't know why, I convinced him to tag along. The kid who was riding his bike when he heard the collapse…we passed him the next road over, while we were riding out of town."

"Bloody hell," Ellie said under her breath.

"When we got back to our house, it was unbelievable." Jorge took over then and looked up at Natalie. "Pietro was there. He was directing people. There were at least twenty-five men from the town. They all came for the sake of saving our lives."

The table descended into silence.

"You know you can stay at our place," Helmut said. "Sleep there and eat there and go to your place every day, to rebuild."

"And you know, on our downtime, we'll help you clean up," Natalie supplied.

Heads nodded all around.

It didn't seem to appease either of them. It was fitting that nothing would. Natalie was ready to let it lie when the two men exchanged a look.

"That might not be an option." Jorge's face had gone, in an instant, from sad to bitter. Natalie shook her head, confused.

"What does that mean?" Ellie was as blunt as ever.

"It means they're meeting right now. The development council. Not just about what'll happen to us. About the viability of the program in general."

"The viability of the program?" Now Helmut's hackles were up. "What does that mean? The program is underway. It exists."

"With very specific terms," Ellie pointed out. "We still don't fully own our houses. Our provisional deeds give us the right to earn the permanent deed pursuant to certain conditions."

"But *we* didn't do anything," Helmut piped up.

Jorge glared over at him and spat, "Neither did we. What happened to us could've happened to any of you." He looked around the table.

"They can't take our houses away." Chris was adamant. "We have to have the opportunity to fulfill our end of the contract before they can."

Natalie surprised herself by speaking, and when she did, her voice was grim. "That would be the case under American law."

When Ellie caught her eye, she knew they were on the same page, knew they were both too aware of the same flaw.

"But this is not America."

CHAPTER TWENTY-FOUR

"Monday, November twenty-first. I call this emergency meeting of the Economic Development Council to order."

Alfonso spoke grimly from the head of the table. Dark circles appeared under his eyes. He looked every bit as bad as Pietro felt. Pietro's only moments of respite from the past twelve hours had been the time he spent with Natalia in his arms, not sleeping. He had kept her close as he thought too hard, taking in the contours of her face by the light of the moon.

"I second," Signor Schivo put in.

"The meeting is in order," came Signora Sanguigna's voice.

Pietro had yet to speak. When he did, he wasn't sure what might come out. That was what he hated most about all of this. He had already said everything. He had issued countless warnings. There was nothing left for him to say.

"First order of business," his father began, "is the matter of my resignation. My poor decisions have lost whatever privilege I may have once claimed to serve on this committee. I tender my resignation, effective immediately. Obviously, you will have the full support of the office of the mayor. But it is time for me to step away."

With that, Alfonso rose. If Pietro had been speechless a moment earlier, he was doubly so now. The part of him that felt a deep sense of rightness from his father's decision warred with some other sense of wrong. For the first time in a long time, he worried about his father, not the role he had played in all of this but the toll that it might take on him.

"Papa..." The word left his mouth, unbidden. Alfonso had risen to his feet. Pietro found that he had risen as well. Alfonso had already begun to walk toward the door, but he halted for a moment before sharing a long look with his son. Pietro didn't speak again, hardly knowing the exact objection he meant to wage.

"Your first order of business should be to elect a new council foreman. Not because he is my son, Pietro would be an excellent choice. He tried to warn us all."

Pietro remained standing until his father left, still in a bit of a daze over his decision.

"Pietro..." Signora Sanguigna's voice cut into his thoughts, with compassion and urgency all at once.

"I am ready." Pietro's gaze remained on the door his father had just exited.

"Alfonso is correct," Signor Schivo spoke up. "Procedurally speaking, we must have a foreman. Especially today. Official decisions will be made. We will be answerable to entities outside of ourselves."

It was the entities outside of themselves that had Pietro worried. The entities outside of themselves had kept him up all night. Safety violations came with consequences.

Accountabilities went beyond those between the tenants and the council. The town itself had to remain in compliance with guidelines set forth by a regional council. Incidents such as these would create scrutiny. A serious-enough infraction could cause the program to lose its funding. At worst, the regional council could fully enforce its oversight, take over the projects, and revoke Zavona's rights.

"I nominate Pietro," Signor Razzo suggested.

"Second," said everyone else at the same time.

"Please, Pietro," Signora Sanguigna implored. "Say you will accept. What happened last night, we know you had thought it through."

Pietro finally sat down, the exhaustion of the night before catching up to him. Or perhaps he was exhausted at the mere thought of taking this on—now, when it was time to clean up, not when he could have prevented some of this months before.

"We must put in safety controls," Pietro said, for once speaking in a softer voice. So often, in this room, he had needed to fight. "Stringent ones. We must prioritize this above all else. Even one accident is too many."

Natalie's face flashed in Pietro's mind, a vision he didn't welcome—a vision of Natalia, hurt. He didn't know why his imagination played such tricks. He blinked them away, forcing himself to look around the room, to see the reactions to his proposal. Heads nodded all around.

"What will it take?" Signor Razzo asked.

"To mollify the regional council? We'll need immediate inspections. I know some specialists. I'll call my friends. We must do what it takes to get them here, and we must pay for it out of our budget. Work on any property must be halted until such time that structural integrity has been ensured. Each project must get a pass in order for its tenants to be permitted to return."

"The architects should also review not only current structural integrity but also future building plans," Signora Sanguigna remarked. "The collapse that happened yesterday wasn't due to a structural problem with the original building—it was due to modifications. The tenants made alterations to a load-bearing wall."

"This will be critical," Pietro said. "What else?"

He looked around the room at the other council members, not wanting to carry this work alone. Yes, they were looking to him now—finally—for guidance, but every one of them needed to be actively involved.

"We need better standards for vendors. You were right, Pietro," said Signor Razzo. "Some of the tenants cut corners. We need to ensure they use contractors who hold themselves to high standards, even if tenants don't."

Pietro nodded, agreeing with all the suggestions, thinking of Natalie again as he brought up another aspect. "What happens when they run out of money?"

"We must change the requirements for new applicants," Signor Razzo said. "We must require additional funds in the bank, or perhaps a guarantor who can commit to providing more capital."

"That's fine moving forward," Pietro concurred. "What I meant to ask was, what will we do if people already in the program run out of money?"

The room quieted again, another uncomfortable silence. A sweet smell wafting through the window contrasted with the tension in the room. Pietro didn't know what was cooking but remembered how much Natalie loved baked goods. He was tired and not at his best, but still, he resolved to remember to pick her up a box of something tasty that she could enjoy when he got home.

"We must give our tenants more time to complete their projects if we are changing the rules. We must give them opportunities to raise the money. They are in this position through no fault of their own," Signora Sanguigna said.

"This assumes that our tenants will want to continue as part of the program. We have not considered how many might want to back out," reasoned Signor Razzo.

The thought hadn't occurred to Pietro—that some might want to leave. He absolutely could not let that happen with Natalie.

"So we lose some people, maybe. We start over with new tenants with more resources to finish the rehabilitations."

Signor Schivo said it with a casual dismissiveness that Pietro didn't like. It seemed that Signora Sanguigna didn't like it, either.

"But how would we compensate those who came into this in good faith? It is the right thing to do, to look out for the safety of the program participants, but the wrong thing to change the rules like this and expect them to follow."

"It could be achieved." Pietro finally spoke, making eye contact with every single person at the table as the gears in his mind turned. "If we go back to my original idea."

• • •

A dip in the bed roused Pietro from a heavy slumber. After returning from the meeting midmorning, he'd slept hard. He must have slept long, too, judging from the warmth of the day. The more wakeful he became, the more he noticed small details of his circumstances—sheets up to his mid-back and, on the left arm thrown above his pillows, heat from the sun's rays.

Speaking of sunshine…

His right arm hooked around Natalie before he even opened his eyes. She smelled like everything good, like lemons and sugar and hours spent in the sun. Her skin was warm, and she made a little sound that told him she hadn't known he was awake. He could tell already she was wearing entirely too many clothes.

"I borrowed your Vespa," she said. "I had no other way to get to town."

Pietro responded, "I saw."

What he didn't say was how much he wanted more of this—of her driving his Vespa, of her coming home to him, of the two of them in one house.

"Come. Have a nap with me." He squeezed her in tighter. "Last night, you did not get healthy sleep."

"You look like you want to do a little more than sleep," she said just as he opened his eyes.

It wasn't until that moment that Pietro consciously noted his body's reaction. Waking up a little excited was nothing new. The more he breathed her in and the closer her body came to his, the less invested in sleep he became. He blinked down at her, and she tipped her face upward, and he swooped in to capture her mouth.

"You taste like sugar," he murmured.

She smiled against his lips. "Somebody bought me *sfogliatelle*."

"Really? Who was that?"

"The same person who got the coffee ready."

"He sounds like a good person. I think you should make love to him. He is hungry for you."

He pulled her a little closer and felt what he said to her down to his bones. It was true—since the night before, he had felt a sort of desperation.

Searching her eyes for permission, for evidence that she was okay, that—just for that moment—she wasn't broken by everything that had happened, he let out a breath he hadn't known he'd been holding. At the very same moment his name issued from her lips, she lifted her hand, snaking it up his back and bringing her fingers to scratch in his scruff as the heel of her hand gripped his neck.

It was she who kissed him that second time, rolling him halfway onto his back as she leaned into him with vigor. She needed this as much as he did. For just a moment, he reveled in the thrill of her pursuit.

"Pietro."

There it was, his name on a whispery breath that, after everything that had happened, somehow broke him. It was all he needed to flip her so that she was fully on top and he was on his back. It was the angle he needed to disrobe her. In the end, she didn't force him to make the effort. Before he even had her fully on top of him, she had already shimmied up the skirt of the dress she was wearing, bunched it up from where it pooled around her waist, and crossed her arms in front of herself to pull it off.

By the time she threw it across the room, he had already raised himself up and organized her legs so that they folded around his waist. His hand cupped her breast and his lips fixed themselves around her nipple. She let out her first gasp at the same moment as her fingers threaded in his hair. He regretted not having removed his only garment—his boxer briefs—before she'd gotten on top. Right then, they were the only flimsy reason why he wasn't already inside of her.

Remedying that situation would require some acrobatics. Not in the mood to wait, he did another flip, this time to get her underneath. He relieved himself of his underwear so quickly, his cock sprang free. Natalie was already handing him a condom as he came up on his knees. His eyes washed over her, thinking about how he wanted her as he rolled it on. He wanted her as close to him as possible.

Wasting no time, he hovered over her, then coaxed her legs around his waist, exactly as she had been before, then hoisted her from the bed until she straddled his lap, front to front. Heat from her center pressed up in the space between his balls and the base of his cock. Anxious for him, she moved ever so slightly, tantalizing him with her wetness. It only added to his desperation to be inside.

Lifting her a little, then maneuvering himself to her entrance, he relished every inch of his initial slide. This was his favorite part, the way her eyes lolled shut and she melted with relief as she took him into her body, as if he were water and she had thirsted for him.

Yet, it was he who thirsted. He who would have

waited for anything and everything with her for as long as it took until she was ready, until she had worked through her shyness and culture shock and grief, until she made her calculations and decided that Pietro was worth the risk. Only, now that he'd had her, now that he'd acted on his feelings and he'd let her, it felt impossible to put on the brakes.

He kept his eyes open as he moved inside her, working from underneath as she held on to him and enjoyed the ride, her body heaving in ecstasy with his every thrust. She coiled ever tighter, nearly driving him from his own skin with every delicious clench that threatened to rip the pleasure straight out of his body.

Natalie had told him laughingly that he sometimes talked when he was in the throes, exclusively in Italian, mumbled swears that she didn't understand. He didn't know about that, either, only that Natalie was the only woman who had the power to make him forget how to breathe, to make him forget that anything else in the world existed but them.

"Let's do that again later," she whispered, still breathless as they came down, both splayed out on the bed, staring at the ceiling, sated and spent.

She looked over at him to drive her point home. "Like, that exact thing."

Pietro didn't broach the issue he had planned on talking to her about the night before. Now wasn't the time to tell her what he wanted them to be.

"I promise, we will do that exact thing again," he vowed. "But we will not do it tonight. I must fly to Alto Adige."

"To see a client? At a time like this?"

Pietro nodded. “It must be done.”

“All right…” Natalie pouted a little. “We’ll do it again when you get back from your trip.”

“Can you do me a favor?” he asked, praying that she would not fight him on this. “Please continue to stay here at my cottage. I called a friend to recertify the structural integrity of your house. I wish to be very sure. Natalia, I cannot take chances with you.”

CHAPTER TWENTY-FIVE

Natalie arrived at Café Ludo that morning, ready for her coffee. None had been brought to her that morning—or even half made—with Pietro out of town. No pastry box had awaited her on Pietro's kitchen counter, and no company in the shower. Her distress over all of this proved how richly she'd been spoiled.

At least the group had vowed to meet early, before the open meeting that had been called by the EDC, the one that would happen in the early afternoon. Natalie would grab some food with the others and commiserate over their situation, then they'd all walk over to the *municipio* as a group.

"It's a bloodbath," Ellie warned the second Natalie sat down, for once just sitting and watching. Ellie's was usually a prominent voice. Today, more tenants than she had ever seen in one place had congregated at the café in animated—if not heated—conversation.

Ellie leaned closer and lowered her voice. "Well... what did Pietro tell you?" It came out in a bit of a whisper-hiss.

"Not much," Natalie whispered back. "I mean, I think they're trying to figure it out."

The truth was, Pietro hadn't talked much about what was going to happen next. He'd seemed set on keeping her safe but also adamant that she shouldn't worry. He'd told her he was handling things and she would be all right.

"He had to travel for work, so he won't be there today. But he said there would be changes. He didn't say anything about shutting things down, just safety stuff. It sounds like they're already rolling with the reinspections."

"What inspections?" Helmut suddenly wanted to know. It seemed they weren't speaking as quietly as they'd thought.

"They're doing inspections," Natalie said at normal volume now that several pairs of eyes had turned toward her. "A guy was at my place this morning. I dropped by before I came here. I saw he left the report."

"You dropped by your own house?" Helmut asked.

Natalie realized what she had just revealed. "I was staying with Pietro."

Helmut turned to the others at the table. "Has anyone else had an inspection?"

Heads shook all around.

It was the first time something occurred to her. Had Pietro given her special treatment? She was the only one who seemed relaxed.

"I'm sure everyone will be getting their inspections soon," Natalie hedged. Only, she wasn't sure.

"There's a rumor…" Helmut began to catch her up on whatever she had missed. "They're going to dismantle the program."

Natalie's head was already shaking before he even finished getting that thought out. "Why would they do that?"

"Apparently, there's been infighting on the council. People are saying the mayor quit."

"Who's saying that?" Natalie tried to keep her voice even, tried to show neither surprise nor hurt. She didn't like this pressure, of feeling that she ought to be in the know or having to suspect now that maybe she wasn't.

Chris spoke up. "We wanted to talk to him about our case, him being the head of the council. We went to the *municipio*, to his office, and he turned us away."

Why didn't Pietro tell me that his father quit the council?

But even the notion that Alfonso had quit was conjecture. Maybe Alfonso was against continuing the program and the rest of the council had voted him out. Yes, that had to be it. It lined up with Pietro's explanation of the tension between him and his father. Pietro had said they disagreed about how the program should be run, and Natalie knew for a fact how much Pietro cared about continuing with the restorations. Alfonso being against the program might even explain why he'd been a little weird at Pietro's family dinner.

"Maybe him wanting to break up the program is why they got rid of him," Natalie speculated aloud, then repeated something Pietro had told her days earlier. "Cocenza just went bankrupt. Maybe he wants to make some changes that don't line up to the original plan."

"Whether he's on the council or not, he's still the mayor," Greg piped up from the other side of the table. "He still has a lot of power, even if the council voted him out. Maybe he has some sort of executive privilege."

Even Soni, who rarely spoke, had thoughts. "He is a small-town mayor. Not the president of the United States."

From there, the conversation reverted to what it had been when Natalie had sat down at the table. People talking all at once and flinging a lot of opinions. Ellie stayed quiet and sipped her drink.

After a few minutes of listening to the theories, and feeling more than a little unsettled at how quickly a sense of order seemed to have dissolved, Ellie finally spoke again.

"What did I tell you? A bloodbath."

CHAPTER TWENTY-SIX

Pietro remembered Roman's palazzo well. He had been the one to restore it some six years before. He hadn't been back in at least five. Under any other circumstance, he would have relished a slow walk-through, an indulgent victory lap for a well-loved building in gorgeous repair.

This was where Roman actually lived—too much house for a man and his wife and more like a museum. Pietro had always gotten the sense he didn't live there out of vanity, a king in his castle. Apart from restoring the building itself, Roman had painstakingly furnished each room with priceless antiques that were specimens of Italian artistic importance. Pietro had always wished for an occasion to bring his nonna.

"It's good to be back here," he complimented when Roman walked into the room. "You have cared for your palazzo well."

"I try to spend as much time here as I can."

Pietro had been shown to a sitting room that overlooked the gardens. He knew the palazzo well enough to have shown himself. "You know why I have come."

Roman nodded. "For you to travel such a long way, so suddenly, yes. I was very sorry to hear about the collapse."

Just hearing Roman mention it stabbed Pietro with guilt. "I feel partially responsible."

He had not admitted this to anybody, perhaps not even fully to himself. For all the blame he had foisted squarely on his father, he regretted not having insisted on more stringent inspections from the beginning, and not having pushed harder himself.

Pietro returned to his task at hand. There would be plenty of time for wallowing on his return flight. It could work to his advantage if Roman had heard of the incident already. "It seems the news coverage made it as far as Trentino."

"It is being covered outside of Campania, in Tuscany and Emilia-Romagna. I read it in a Venetian paper. The truth is, Pietro, I've been researching Zavona since you brought me your proposal. Trying to get a sense for the place."

And? What do you think?

Pietro had to stop himself from asking. Doing so would make it too easy for Roman to say no. He'd come all this way to make a different case. The last time he'd gone to Roman, the program had been in trouble merely on paper. Now that safety was in question, they were in different territory.

"The stakes are higher now." There was no time to mince words. "Problems with our program could cause us to lose our status with the regional council. Without their affiliation, we lose the support of the national government. We would lose our funding, and the members of our program would lose access to special immigration status. Unless we can prove that the rehabilitations are safe, we will lose everything."

"I understand that they can be salvaged with a substantial-enough investment. And I would like to help. But I do not see how it might work, legally. How could I enter at this moment as a private investor?"

Pietro had spent the entire plane ride thinking this through, and he'd been on the phone with Signor Schivo since he stepped off the flight. They had worked it out as Pietro had walked down the halls of Alto Adige's small airport, and as he had ridden in the car from the airport to the palazzo. Signor Schivo had modified Pietro's ideas to describe what he thought was legal under Italian law. The solution they had reached was astonishingly simple—had been under his nose the entire time.

"The program is for foreign investors who would bring economic growth to the region," Pietro began. "Do you mind if I ask your immigration status?"

Pietro was nearly certain he knew the answer, but now was the time to ask.

"I remain a citizen of Austria," Roman replied, his eyes crinkling at the corners as recognition dawned.

"And—hypothetically—if you were to purchase properties in Zavona—would you have the means to restore each private home with a budget of at least €300 per square meter?"

Roman actually laughed. Pietro knew for a fact that Roman was paying an average of €1,500 per square foot for his own restorations.

"Yes. I think I could manage."

"And could you agree to placing additional funds in escrow to cover any structural remediation costs?"

"Of course." Roman nodded.

"And would you agree to restore each property

according to the standards of our program?"

Roman was smiling now. "Yes, Pietro. Yes."

For however much Pietro's heart raced, and for as shallow as his breathing had become, he wouldn't let himself feel triumphant yet.

"I have spoken to Signor Rodolfo Schivo, the attorney who represents Zavona. Given your foreign status and the fact that you have the means to cover the cost of renovations, it is our belief that you qualify as a standard member of the program."

Roman lowered his brow and narrowed his eyes at the same time as he smiled. "Could it be so simple?"

"Yes and no," Pietro hedged. "You can hire a *geometra* to manage the rehabilitation. There is no explicit requirement that says you must visit the property or to personally conduct the projects. But there is one piece of fine print. As a condition of purchasing each home, you are required to demonstrate an ability to bring permanent jobs to Zavona."

Roman's smile fell a little. This was where things could go badly. Worse than badly—this was where it could all fall apart.

"Pietro, this is a major limitation. I would be willing to invest in the homes and to hire people to have them restored. This is where my experience lies. But starting a business…this is something quite different."

Pietro's fingers itched to reach into his bag. "May I show you something?"

This time, he didn't rely on his tablet to show Roman what he had in mind. This time, he pulled out a double-sealed cylindrical tube that held architectural plans. These were hand-drafted on his own table and were so many years in the working, they predated Pietro's relationship with Roman by years. Pietro had begun this drafting a decade earlier, when he had still been an architecture student—plans for an Italian architecture museum.

He paused for a long moment as he allowed Roman's eyes to wash over his plan, gave him time to comprehend what he was looking at. Roman was no stranger to reading documents such as this. He was easily the most knowledgeable and sophisticated amateur Pietro had ever met. Pietro waited, said nothing, as Roman allowed what Pietro was proposing to sink in. It was a good sign that Roman wasn't shaking his head as he often did—possibly subconsciously—when he was about to tell you he didn't like an idea. After working with Roman for so long, Pietro knew many of his tells.

"I know that opening a museum may not have ever factored into your imagination," Pietro began again when the time was right. "This is something I had always planned to create and to finance myself. In fact, I own the building and have been in the process of restoring it for the past two years. Should you remain interested, this business could be opened in your name."

"A museum..." Roman nodded subtly as he continued to scrutinize the plans. Pietro didn't want to oversell it, but he did want to give Roman assurances of exactly what sort of effort he might have to put forth. No matter how much Pietro, and the town, were willing to do in order to make Roman's relationship to the town and to the project successful,

Roman would be the one to assume all of the risk.

"Here is how it could work," Pietro continued in measured tones. "You would commit to completing the building of the museum, which would begin as a private effort. As long as you open and operate your business for a period of at least three years, you will be in compliance with program requirements. At such time, should you wish to sell it, the town of Zavona agrees to purchase it at fair market value."

Pietro began to pull out his tablet. He had a business plan for the museum—an old one he'd written and not looked at in more than a year. Given the plan that he and Signor Schivo had cooked up, Pietro had dug this up and perused it in the taxi, refreshing his memory as to whether it was in good-enough condition to show Roman.

"I have a business plan for the museum, but it's old," he began to explain as he started to thumb on his tablet. Before he could promise a revision by the next morning or explain that the museum could be profitable, Roman cut him off.

"Pietro," he interrupted.

It wasn't until he stopped talking that Pietro realized how fast he had been speaking, how short of breath he had become. It humbled him to witness his own desperation. He'd been to other potential investors he knew, a month earlier, when circumstances had been more attractive and might have come with fewer strings. But Roman was—and always had been—the best possible investor for this project.

"I accept."

Roman smiled, aware of the multitude of things he was agreeing to and all that it meant. This had become more—so much more—than the financial investment Pietro had in mind all those months ago.

"Thank you, Roman, from the bottom of my heart." And Pietro swore as he had always been prepared to: "I will personally oversee the management of all of your projects. I will get you everything you need so these do not become a burden."

Pietro rose, wanting to be respectful of Roman's time and wanting to speak to Natalie. He couldn't tell her anything official, but he wanted to hear her voice.

"Tell me, Pietro, what is the next step?"

"The attorney for our council will send you some paperwork. Please have it looked over by your own attorney. You have several months to begin work and another expanse of time—now a full year—before you must complete it."

Roman nodded and slid his hands in his pockets. "But what of the purchase price of each property? Will you send me the initial purchase price so that I may transfer funds?"

Pietro smiled. "The math is easy. Each residence costs only €1."

• • •

"Can somebody call the meeting to order?"

Pietro sat in a small, private workspace in the first-class airport lounge for Alitalia at Villafranca. He had ninety minutes before boarding for his flight. It gave him enough time to brief the rest of the development council on how things had gone with Roman.

"I call this meeting to order," came Signor Schivo's familiar voice. Pietro had joined by video meeting. As usual, they sat at the long conference table in the *municipio*. They had placed a single laptop in Pietro's place at the head of the table. It gave him a long and not-very-effective view.

"I second," came the voice of Signora Sanguigna.

"This meeting is in order," Pietro came back quickly, very much conscious of time. "I would like an update on this morning's inspections in just a moment. But first, I will share the news. We have a verbal agreement from Roman Kissinger to invest in any and all properties that we deem to be in need. After my meeting with Roman, I called our liaison with the regional council. They have agreed to be lenient if we can demonstrate that we are working with experienced renovators."

"Pietro, you have saved us." Pietro might have guessed what it cost Signor Razzo to say so. He had always been a close friend of his father.

"The contracts have not been sent and nothing has been signed," Pietro was careful to say. "Let us discuss what this means when the deal goes through."

"We will have to revise the rule specifying that participants are eligible to purchase only one property," Signor Schivo said.

"And revise language specifying that there is a one-to-one relationship between the number of houses he buys and the number of businesses he must create," Pietro concurred.

"We must also change other rules. All applications for structural alterations should go through a preapproval process."

Pietro did not dwell on how many times he had made this recommendation before.

"Pietro…what about the money?"

He answered honestly. "I tend to think most of this is the responsibility of the town. If we are changing the rules in the middle of the game, we owe it to our tenants to give them a chance to win."

"Zavona cannot commit to budgetary assistance," Signora Sanguigna replied in no uncertain terms. "We do not have the funds, and, without knowing what kinds of issues might come up and what kinds of cost estimates might come back, we would be in violation of our own fiduciary duties to agree to a blank check."

Pietro quieted with no answers this time. Both of them were right.

CHAPTER TWENTY-SEVEN

It all felt very…official. A mandatory meeting at the *municipio*. A large, auditorium-style room with a table set up on a stage. Four name tents in front of four chairs split across two tables. A microphone in the middle of each of the two. The dull roar of the tenants in the audience, some huddled in groups while others sat apart, seemed alive with precisely what Natalie had seen at the café—unbridled speculation.

The chatter quieted when a door next to the stage opened and a short line of three people shuffled in. One of the tables held a folded paper tent bearing Pietro's name. Alfonso's absence was notable and left things looking a little thin.

"We all have some responsibility for what has happened," a woman named Signora Sanguigna began after brief introductions were made. "Though none of us wanted an outcome like this.

"We recognize your wish to rehabilitate your properties at prices you can afford," Signora Sanguigna continued. "We also recognize the common practice of undertaking some of the reconstruction tasks upon yourselves. Not all elements of a rehabilitation project must be undertaken by professionals. What we have learned is that some of them should be."

She paused long enough to give the audience a pointed look.

"We apologize for the mistake we made in omitting interim safety checks and more stringent safety standards into our original terms. In order to prevent further danger, these are standards that we must implement now."

Ellie leaned over a bit to whisper into Natalie's ear. "Here it comes."

The part of Natalie that was sweating bullets over what this would mean for her rehab and her anemic budget warred with the part of her that knew this made sense. Because what if Chris and Jorge had been in there after all?

"Beginning tomorrow," Signora Sanguigna continued, "we will conduct comprehensive safety audits of each property. The council will incur this cost, and we have employed certified contractors to do the work. The culmination of these audits will be a set of recommendations. Any recommendation that poses a critical to moderate safety hazard will require immediate remediation by certified contractors in order for your project to remain in good standing."

A collective groan rose up in the crowd. Pietro hadn't mentioned this. It sent question after question flying through Natalie's head. What if they found something she had overlooked? Something that required her to tear down work that had already been done?

"Who will pay for the remediations?" Helmut stood up.

For most tenants, it was the most important question.

A Signor Schivo pulled out the microphone

closest to himself. His English was not as strong as Signora Sanguigna's.

"This requirement is not new. The original contract specifies that all work must take safety into account. Tenants have always been responsible to ensure safe project conditions. It is our duty to enforce."

Signora Sanguigna pulled their shared microphone back toward herself and was quick to add, "Tenants may apply for assistance. However, it is not guaranteed."

"What about time? What if the list of recommendations sets folks back?" Chris had been the next one to stand. Despite the collapse that had just happened in his own home, he brimmed with determination.

"Timing will be altered on a case-by-case basis," Signora Sanguigna remarked.

"You said certified contractors..." Jorge stood up, emotion coloring his voice. "But some of the contractors you certified were garbage. Some of these contractors are why some of us are behind."

Signora Sanguigna covered her microphone and leaned in to confer with Signor Schivo in a quick exchange of words.

"Please report any grievances you have had with our recommended contractors. If we find that they are unsuitable, we will take them off the list."

The next person who asked a question didn't bother to stand up. "What if we run out of money or don't get the assistance?"

The room quieted, in rapt anticipation of the all-important answer that was to come. As Signor

Schivo pulled the microphone back toward him, Natalie held her breath.

"If you cannot rehabilitate your homes safely within the allocated budget and revised time, you will be asked to leave the program."

Pietro needs to be here for this.

Why hadn't he canceled his client meeting on a day like today? There was too much happening, too many questions and threats. And Pietro—the only architect among them—was absent. Yet, his calm credibility might reassure them all.

Natalie reached into her satchel and fished out her phone. One missed call from Pietro. No voicemail message, but there had been a text.

I'm about to get on a plane. I have an inspection to do late in the afternoon but will come over when I'm done.

His text only left Natalie feeling marginally better. She needed more answers—more insights—than it seemed this meeting would realistically provide. She needed him, and she needed him to tell her it would be okay.

She placed her phone back into her bag and turned her attention once again to the front of the room. Things had gotten more contentious.

"Why were members of the program not consulted in the aftermath of Sunday's collapse?"

"What will happen if you kick all of us out? It seems like you're setting all of our projects up for failure."

"The program expectations are too high. What about all the people who already left?"

Questions flew from left and right.

"Please," implored Signorina Sanguigna. "Let us answer these questions one at a time. We have already heard direct concerns from several members of the program. Some of the suggestions do not align with our regulatory reality and our legal circumstances. We are doing everything within the constraints of the law."

"How will you make the program sustainable?" came a voice from behind Natalie.

"We believe this is a good next step. We have changed the language in our bylaws and are in the process of changing our contracts to make safety standards clearer. We have secured an investor to take on the remainder of the properties in the program in Zavona and to perform rehabilitations under more stringent safety terms."

"An investor?" Natalie didn't make the conscious decision to pipe up. Her incredulous question emerged, loud and shocked and unbidden, from her mouth.

Signor Schivo took the microphone again. "Yes. A private investor will take over the remaining properties."

"What does that mean?"

Signorina Sanguigna looked like she wanted to take the microphone back from Signor Schivo, as if she knew that what he was about to say would not be well received.

"The investor will renovate any property that is canceled because of an owner's inability to finish the project."

The air seemed to whoosh out of the room. This was bigger—much bigger—than new rules and safety standards for the existing tenants. This seemed like a huge change—a change designed to push investors like the original tenants out.

"Where is the mayor?" came another voice.

Signorina Sanguigna took back the microphone and attempted to keep moving. "Mayor Alfonso Indelicato resigned from the council yesterday. He believed that new leadership was needed to take the program to its next phase. Pietro Indelicato was elected as our new leader yesterday. He is absent in this critical moment but not away from the business of the council. He is outside of Campania, meeting with our investor now."

• • •

Don't bother.

Natalie sent her return text to Pietro in the privacy of the bathroom stall in the municipal building. The text that had told her that he would come visit her that night. After that meeting, she needed a moment alone. She wouldn't let her tears fall just yet, but she needed a minute of her own privacy. Just one minute to fall apart.

Estimating that Pietro would be somewhere over the middle of the country, midway through his short flight, she didn't expect an answer right away. She didn't want to hear from him at all. And she certainly didn't want him coming over. Rule number one of making amends with Natalie Malone—especially if you were in the wrong—was to give her ample time to cool off.

"Hey. Are you all right? We waited for you."

Ellie parted from the dense gathering of tenants. They still stood in the lobby and congregated near the bottom of the stairs. Everything about Natalie felt heavy—her bag, her feet, and definitely her mind. Worse than the heaviness was the dread of knowing she would be faced with questions that she couldn't answer. Like what Pietro's plan was and whether he really hadn't known.

"Sorry..." Natalie mumbled, all too aware that they were headed back to Café Ludo to regroup. "I'm actually not feeling too well."

Ellie raised a half-skeptical, half-commiserating eyebrow that told Natalie that her friend had her number. "If you're not up to it, maybe you ought to get some rest."

As the others saw Natalie approach, they began to move toward the door, letting her and Ellie bring up the caboose. As the others started down the hill, Natalie waved a quiet goodbye to Ellie and split off.

As if she hadn't had enough of the Economic Development Council that day, Natalie returned home to find a note on her front porch saying that a *geometra* had been by that morning in an attempt to do a safety audit of her building. They asked that she be present in two days' time, at nine a.m. That gave her a day and a half, by herself, to whip this whole place into shape. Natalie had been focused on large steps forward and was certain that a litany of small things in her villa were still unsafe. Had she known that an inspection like this was coming, she might have taken care of those things first.

The tears that came on next had been building within her all morning, had been building within her since she heard about the collapse and that the house belonged to Jorge and Chris, had maybe even been building since she'd fully comprehended that renovating the villa alone had her overwhelmed. Maybe they had been building for more than a year, since she lost Gram and realized that, for the first time in her adult life, there was a feeling she had never planned for, a feeling for which she was wholly unprepared.

But there, as she sat weeping in the heat of the afternoon, bent and limp upon her cool front step, the flood of her own sorrows became less bitter. Her shoulders stopped heaving and the tears that flowed began to change. Soon enough, she no longer tasted the salt of her own disappointment but instead, bitter confirmation of her deepest truth—she was alone.

Alone without Gram.

Yes, that was the most obvious one.

Alone without my friends.

Because, with all of them in the same mess, how could they help one another now? And why would any of them even want to help Natalie? Pietro had become a dubious figure. How could she face them now that she was sleeping with the orchestrator of their predicament?

People who aren't alone have something to fall back on.

Only, Natalie didn't. She'd needed the windfall from Franco and that was almost gone. For the very first time, it felt chillingly real to consider that she might leave with nothing. Before, it had been a threat, one of her dreaded risks that felt real to her only because risk was how she made sense of life. But this felt different. The prospects that she feared right then felt imminent.

Alone without Pietro.

And how was it that this one could hurt the most? Had she really put so much stock in him as this? And how had she given him so much without even noticing? What did you do when you had your heart shattered by someone who had the power to shatter your dreams? What had she been thinking, giving anyone that much power at all?

"Natalia?"

Oh no.

Before she could think any better of it, she raised her face from her hands, her elbows propped up on bent knees. She didn't want to think of how she must look, face splotchy and tear-stained and eyes swollen, a total mess.

"Natalia, what has happened?"

He had come around from the back.

"I told you not to come." Her nose was congested and her voice hoarse, with a croaky quality that made her sound like a frog.

"Natalia, tell me what is wrong."

She knew instantly from his voice that he had no idea what she knew about the investor—that he had no clue that she was crying because of him.

In the seconds since he'd announced himself, he'd been on the approach, from the corner of the front house wall toward where she sat on the steps. He had that look on his face—the one that he got when he was worried, and he was about to pull her into his arms. Later, she would mourn that it was likely the last time she would get to see him make that face. But right now, she needed to stand up—stand up and stop him from whatever he thought he was about to do.

"All these months..."

He stopped short when she stood to her full height. His brow, already furrowed, worried now in a different way.

"All these trips...were all of them to meet investors?"

"Who told you about the investor?"

Answering a question with a question was never a good sign.

"We all know about the investor. Signorina Sanguigna announced it earlier, at the tenant town hall."

Pietro's eyes stayed on Natalie, though his hands came to his hips.

"I'm sorry." He always seemed sincere. "You should not have heard about it like that. It was not yet public information. The deal is not complete."

"So you admit there is an investor..." Natalie repeated back.

Pietro nodded. "Yes. There is a man who will purchase the remaining properties and handle the costs related to their rehabilitation."

"And he'll buy any new open properties in the event that any current projects fail."

"Natalia. It's not a bad thing, like you're making it sound."

"What is it, then?" she practically roared. Natalie couldn't remember the last time she had yelled anything at anybody—couldn't remember the last time she'd felt strong enough to truly raise her voice. But some part of her knew she was fighting now. She was fighting for her life.

"I risked everything to be here. Left everything I knew. Put in every single penny I earned that I could actually afford to keep. I gave up a good job and sacrificed everything in my house for this? For you to convince the council that you ought to hand over the program—and maybe even my house—to an investor, without even consulting me?"

"Natalia..." Pietro continued, taking a cautious step forward.

"You told me you were meeting with a client," she accused.

"Roman is a client. I did not lie to you about that."

"But you weren't meeting with him on business. At least, not your business. You were meeting him on behalf of the town."

It was a question with an easy answer. The fact that Pietro huffed out a sigh, cast his gaze downward, and ran his fingers through his hair told her everything she needed to know.

"You always give me these sayings that your nonna tells you..." Natalie was so angry in that moment that she had to stop and breathe, a deep inhale with her nostrils flared followed by a deep sigh. "Well, you wanna know what Gram always taught me?"

Pietro only stood quietly, waiting for her answer.

"Keeping the truth from someone who would want to know is just the same as lying."

Pietro winced ever so slightly. Natalie caught it in

time to see that it stung. She had meant it to, but saying it hadn't made her feel better.

"Natalia..." he began again. "I did not keep this from you with a plan of keeping it a secret. Everything that happened since the collapse has happened quickly. You can see that you were my first call this afternoon, after my business with the town was done."

She squeezed her eyes shut, willing her tears not to fall. Because Pietro himself had given something away. That discussing an investor and changes to the program was not a first-time thing.

"Please believe me when I tell you it was not like that. After the accident...finding an investor immediately was necessary. An act of desperation. Now that the collapse has happened, we will be under scrutiny. Without proof of viability, the program does not stand a chance."

"What about me? Do I stand a chance?"

Pietro looked absolutely baffled. "Of course you stand a chance. I am helping you, no? Of course I will not let your project fail. What kind of person do you think I am?"

Natalie bit her lip against that answer. Because if Pietro was saying what Natalie thought he was saying—that he somehow had her covered by virtue of his personal help but was in favor of all the other things, it sounded a lot like he was A-OK with hanging her friends out to dry.

"So let me get this straight... You spent months finding an investor to take over the program and figured I didn't need to know about it because you had a plan for how you hiring an investor wouldn't impact me?"

Pietro looked helpless, as if he were disoriented now around exactly what they were talking about. His gaze darted past Natalie, back toward the note from the *geometra* that had been waiting for her on her step.

"You are worried about the inspection? You do not need to worry about the inspection. I am helping you, Natalia. I have always been helping you."

She choked back a sob and looked toward the ocean, unable to look at him as she said the words.

"Not anymore."

CHAPTER TWENTY-EIGHT

Natalie quelled the instinct to curtsy after she swung her heavy front door open. The *geometra* was right on time. A *geometra* was part architect, part inspector, part general contractor—an authority on buildings and renovations all rolled up into one.

Though she knew intellectually that not all Italian architect types would be hot like Pietro, Natalie half expected somebody who reminded her of him. This *geometra* couldn't have been further from such a reminder. He was short and bespectacled, significantly older and with the half-bored, half-exasperated face of a person who had been doing this for a long, long time.

Natalie, by contrast, was dressed in her Sunday best, or at least, the best outfit that had accompanied her from the United States. In three-quarter-length white jeans, a pretty blouse, and a pair of closed-toed espadrilles, she knew she was overdressed. She also knew that, in order to have this inspection go well for her, she would bend over, and far. From what she had heard from those of her friends who had undergone their own inspections between Monday and Thursday, they were coming out with remediation lists a mile long.

"Hello, you must be Signor Ponti," Natalie said in her best Italian. "Please, come in."

He nodded distracted confirmation as he stepped into the front hall, eyes wandering already as he began to look around. He didn't look displeased exactly, but he didn't look pleased, either. He carried a clipboard that was not unlike hers. For the very first time, the sight of one struck fear into her heart.

"Where would you like to start?" she asked politely, thankful that her Italian was so much better than it had been when she arrived.

He had yet to make eye contact with her again after that first moment. He wrote something on his clipboard, even as his eyes swept the ceiling.

"I will find my own way around." He multitasked all the while. "If you could please follow me as I walk through, I will have questions."

Natalie did the only thing that she could do—she followed him quietly, stepping where he stepped and looking where he looked. The exercise took on a surreal quality, as if the tour through her house were both the first and last time. Since her true first time through, so much had changed. She remembered the bird's nests near the check-ins, the water damage on the shelves in the library, the broken tiles on the backsplash in the kitchen, the buckets and buckets of plaster that had been put on the walls. She remembered Aldo Fumigalli and all of his quirks, and the miles of extension cords from the Fiorello brothers, who had lent her their generator for weeks.

"Have you made any structural changes?" he finally asked as they got to a grove of arches where hallways intersected. The area was newly plastered. Pietro himself had inspected the stonework underneath.

Natalie answered honestly. "No."

The man pointed. "This does not look like

original construction. It does not conform to typical design. You will have to find records to see whether the change was registered on the property."

Natalie hated wishing that Pietro was there to correct the *geometra*. Pietro had confirmed the opposite himself and had a lot more expertise than the man who was performing the inspection now. But thinking about Pietro hurt, so she made herself stop.

All in all, his walk-through took a full two hours and involved not just the main villa but also the outer buildings, including the garage and the shed, the well down the hill, the pool and gardens, and even the chicken coop. Twice, she had to return to her garage to find receipts from earlier contractors, verifying that certain work had been done.

He didn't leave until nearly noon, and not before he had taken photos of said receipts and handed her a paper of her own. It wasn't a copy of his report but a printout notifying her that she was expected to appear for a meeting with the council to discuss the results on Monday. As if the experience weren't nerve-racking enough, his departure only narrowly averted disaster. Stepping outside her front door, he nearly tripped over an item that hadn't been there earlier—a basket of lemons. She couldn't think about that right now.

Hey. You guys at Chris and Jorge's?

Natalie was already texting Ellie, even as the *geometra* drove away. She had run herself so ragged, physically and emotionally, in preparation for the inspection that it felt like she couldn't do another thing. What she would have done a week ago was taken the afternoon off, napped in the shade of her garage, or convinced Pietro to play hooky. But right then, she didn't want to be alone.

• • •

"Wow. You're making progress."

Natalie set down her basket of lemons on the front table inside the farmhouse door, then walked onto the middle of the floor of Chris and Jorge's house. You could barely tell that, too recently, it had been a collapsed pile of rubble. The floor wasn't where it had been. For now, it was a series of walking beams and slats set above the basement; you could see through the slats where concrete needed to be poured for pillars to support the floors.

"Yeah, well, $20,000 later," Chris half groused, rising from where he pored over his laptop and papers at the kitchen table, long enough to stand and turn to give Natalie a hug. Through the window, Jorge and Soni were visible in the fields. Their friends' version of helping out involved doing anything that needed to be done on the farm to keep Chris and Jorge free to worry about their house. For the past two days, Natalie herself had helped tend to the chickens and the crops.

"$20,000..." Natalie winced. "Just to clean up the collapse or for everything?" She wasn't sure she wanted to know.

"Just for round one," Chris confirmed. "After we get the load-bearing walls squared away, they need to come in for an inspection to see whether there's anything they missed while our place was a mess."

Natalie's stomach twisted with something she

had to get off her chest. "I feel responsible," she confessed. "You said you got the idea from me to do it yourself. Only, my situation's not like yours. But my DIY wasn't really DIY. I got free help from a professional."

"Uh-uh. Don't talk like that. What happened to us happened because we cut corners. You took time to do things right."

It was Natalie's turn to shake her head. "No, I planned to do it a certain way, only to find that I had completely miscalculated."

"Girl, everyone underestimates renovation projects."

A sting of tears sprang up behind Natalie's eyes. "Not me. I never used to miss things. But this year, I've just been *wrong*."

The second she said it, it resounded as painfully, utterly true. She'd been overconfident about her budget for the rehab. And how well she knew Pietro. Even how well she knew Gram.

"I was wrong about Pietro. I thought he was on our side."

Natalie didn't know what she expected Chris to say to that. She searched for words to say, for the explanation her friends deserved, to tell them she'd been naive, that she hadn't known.

"You should have seen him that night. The night of the collapse. The way he stood right in here and directed things. I saw the look on his face, the way he was before he found out we were alive. I don't know what he did or didn't tell you, but I can't say a bad word about him or the people who showed up for us. They walked into a house that was falling down to save our lives."

She quieted, pondering the message. Was Chris telling her that Pietro was a good person or that people were complex? Anomalies that didn't—and maybe never would—make sense? Chris moving past that cut off her train of thought.

"You never told me how your audit went with the *geometra*."

"Stressful," Natalie admitted. "My place is so big. I just feel like they're gonna find a ton of problems."

Chris gave her a look. "I hope not. Everyone's betting on you for being in the best shape, seeing as how you took precautions. Folks had a good laugh at your expense with all your earthquake proofing and inspections. Trust me. No one's laughing now."

Natalie didn't know how all of it was supposed to make her feel.

"Can I ask you an indiscreet question?"

Chris smirked. "You've met Jorge, right? Shame does not exist in this house."

Natalie sat down at the table. "How are you guys paying for all of this?"

Chris closed his laptop. "Jorge's tapped out. So I bet the farm. Literally."

Natalie's eyes widened. "The farm in Texas?"

"There's a couple guys, told me if I ever wanted to sell, to give 'em a call. So I did. I got a fair price and a cash deal."

"But what about your whole backup plan? Your whole safety net?"

All this time, Natalie had been sure that Chris would be eager to leave—that he would salvage what he could and be out the door. All this time, she'd been jealous of his backup plan.

Chris looked out the window then, toward Jorge and Ellie and all the people in the back, with their tools, as they helped to tend to the farm.

"Tough as this has been, I had to ask myself what I was thinking, holding on to it, thinking I needed something to fall back on. Looking back…sometimes it keeps you from moving forward."

CHAPTER TWENTY-NINE

You need sleep.

Pietro scolded himself silently as a third woman who was definitely not Natalie sauntered by. The first two, at least, had been dark-haired with curls and more or less of Natalie's stature. This last one—for whom Pietro had held his breath in tense anticipation—was not only not Natalie but also looked absolutely nothing like her when she turned around.

If Pietro was honest with himself, he had hoped to run into her in town, had even lingered in places where she liked to go, from Nonna's store, to Café Ludo, to the *pasticceria*. The former hadn't worked out so well, not least of all because Nonna had clearly taken Natalie's side. Thanks to Zavona's lightning-fast rumor mill, Nonna knew plenty about the aftermath of the collapse, of the precarious situations of many people in the program, and of the investor he had arranged, who—overnight—had become one of the largest landholders in the town.

Not Natalie, Pietro whispered to himself, staring unabashedly at the main door from his perch near the top of the stairs on the *municipio*'s second level. Natalie's meeting wouldn't start for another fifteen minutes, but Pietro had been there for twenty already. He'd wanted to see her—to talk to her—before she came in.

Definitely not Natalie.

Yet another dark-haired woman passed through

the *municipio*'s doors, this one holding the hand of a child. Pietro was so desperate to see Natalie, he had no idea how he'd survived this long with them apart. It had only been four days since she'd cast him away, four days since she'd told him not to bother, four days since he'd been forced to face how precarious their relationship was.

No, not precarious. Just undefined.

It was the mantra he used to comfort himself. The notion that things could be different if they just talked. If he could just explain that it hadn't been personal—that he would do everything in his power to make sure no one in the program lost their house, that they all wanted the same things—maybe she would understand.

"Natalia."

That time, he said her name out loud. The figure who had just walked through the door was unmistakably her. He ached to breathe in her aroma, to feather his fingers through her soft curls. And yet, it wasn't her. Not with her slumped shoulders and heavy walk and furrowed brow—not with anguished eyes that made him wonder whether she had slept.

"Natalia," he repeated when she arrived on the second floor, this time loudly enough for her to hear. But when she turned her eyes to him, her features didn't warm. If anything, the moment she cast her gaze upon him had made her seem sad. She looked every bit as shattered as he felt.

"Pietro," she uttered with a tinge of awkwardness he'd never heard from his own name on her lips. He didn't like it at all.

"You look beautiful."

He had decided to say such things to her more often, but he hadn't planned to say so then. And she did look beautiful, even in her low points and her not-so-shining moments.

"Pietro..." She began to shake her head, but he didn't want to give her a chance to brush him off. He needed to talk to her, to straighten out whatever was in her head.

"Natalia. After the hearing. Please come with me somewhere, to talk. Things between us should not be like this. Please. Will you allow me to explain?"

She shook her head, vehemently this time, as if shaking unwelcome thoughts away. "You don't owe me an explanation. Honestly? You don't owe me anything. I only got this far because of you. But you don't have to keep doing for me. And you don't have to bring me lemons anymore."

Pietro's hopes plummeted the moment he understood her words—sank to the bottom of the ocean right along with his heart. Out of all the things he had anticipated that she might say, not a single thing he had imagined would have hurt as much as this. If anything, he had hoped she would understand his continued lemon delivery as a sign.

It was yet another thing he hadn't said clearly. In his family, bringing lemons was a tradition given between husbands and wives. But that wasn't something he could explain right then.

"I have never been obligated to give you anything, Natalia. Everything that I have given has been given freely, as a gift. I like to give you things."

She would know he wasn't just talking about the lemons.

"Well, it's okay. I don't need your help. I can afford to buy my own lemons now."

He took a step closer.

"Natalia. This is not America. This is Italy. It is not about what you can afford. Here, we are neighbors. Here, we trust each other. Here, we give."

Something different came over her face, a fleeting look that mixed repentance and shame. There was her guilt again. He still did not understand it, why she felt so much guilt.

"And I should thank you. You've given me a lot. You've taught me so much about my villa, and about Italian architecture, and about—"

"Signorina Malone?"

The voice of Signora Sanguigna, along with the telltale clipping of her heels, came from twenty feet away. Signor Schivo was in tow, and both walked at a faster-than-usual clip to get to the conference room.

"I am very sorry," Signora Sanguigna repeated. "We did not mean to be late."

"*Di niente*," Natalie replied easily, telling them their tardiness for their meeting was nothing. Only, it didn't feel like nothing. It felt as if Natalie wanted nothing more than to step into the room and get it over with, as if she wanted nothing more than to escape from him.

After Signor Schivo had opened the door, he ushered Signora Sanguigna inside, following her himself and leaving Pietro and Natalie to come in at their own pace.

When Natalie began to step inside, Pietro took his hand and cuffed it around her biceps, not harshly but strongly enough to stop her from moving forward.

"Do not thank me yet, Natalia. I'm not finished helping you."

• • •

In addition to speaking fine English, Signora Sanguigna was adept in the language of remodeling, diplomatic and precise. It was for that reason that she had been chosen as the designated council member to lead the audit recap meetings. She had taken most of these meetings with Signor Schivo. Pietro had insisted upon presiding over Natalie's meeting himself.

It was known by then that he and Natalie were together. Or, at least, had been until she'd told him to stay away. That, too, would also be common knowledge before long. Natalie's cold shoulder made it obvious. Sitting there on the long side of the conference table, alone on her side and facing the three council members who would declare her villa's fate, it was clear that she took no comfort in Pietro's presence.

"Thank you for cooperating with our inspection process," Pietro began after tense pleasantries had been exchanged. "We know this has been an inconvenience and that the events of the past several days have been personally upsetting. This is a certified translation of your inspection report."

Pietro pulled the English-language version out of the folder in front of him and slid it across the table to Natalie.

"Before we review your document," Signora Sanguigna interjected, "we would like to commend you on a beautiful restoration so far. You have repaired your villa in the true spirit of the program. We consider your restoration to be an example of our hopes. Under the normal terms of the contract, you still have more than two months to complete all of your repairs. You will still be afforded that time to make all of the finishing touches. The list of repairs you see in front of you now is considered to be critical. These are safety issues that must be resolved by the deadline."

Pietro took control of the meeting again. "You are fortunate in that your main building is in very good shape structurally…"

Pietro had memorized every inch of her report, which gave him a chance to watch Natalie, to read her body and see her reactions. She was silent but chewed her lip in that way she did when she was nervous. Her breath, and both of her hands, trembled just a little.

"A big issue is plumbing," Pietro continued in a voice that had soothed her during their better times. "Because plumbing that does not function properly constitutes a critical safety issue, we require that it passes inspection by the safety deadline."

It tugged at his heart to watch her face fall.

"We found one more big issue. Your pool and your pool cottage require significant repair. The cottage itself has serious structural damage. The underwater lights inside the pool and lighting around walkways of the entire garden area need to be functional in order to pass."

Natalie winced as if someone had dealt her a blow. Pietro knew that he had. This would be the big wrench in her plans. So would the list of at least fifty minor safety infractions he read aloud after that. He knew every inch of her villa by then, was visualizing exactly what every repair meant, right along with her.

Pietro closed his copy of the inspection report, a simple stack of four papers stapled in the left corner. Task by task, it was an intimidating list. Three months earlier, the *geometra*'s thoroughness would have pleased Pietro immensely. But he saw things differently now that he was with Natalie, saw how the time constraints and forcing her to switch around the order she would do things in was messing up what had been a good strategy.

"How long do I have?" Natalie finally spoke, though her voice had taken on a ragged quality that it hadn't done in the hall. "I've heard that other tenants are getting a month. But I have a much larger property. Has that been taken into consideration?"

By the end of her question, her voice was wobbly. Her eyes had begun to shine. Pietro wanted to stand up and go to her. To cradle her, then look into her lovely eyes and tell her that everything would be okay. He would have done it, if only he had believed that Natalie would accept his comfort.

"We did take that into consideration," Signora Sanguigna replied. "The regional council has dictated that our tenants must fix all safety problems within one month's time. But we will grant you an extension for all of your non–safety related work. The final timing for finishing your entire restoration has shifted by sixty days."

Natalie's eyes did fill with tears then.

"Then I guess I'd better get started." She gave a big sniff and rose abruptly from the table, snatching up her paper. She didn't make eye contact with Pietro as she muttered a half-hearted "*Grazie*" and made to walk out the door.

CHAPTER THIRTY

For the second time in a week, Natalie found herself in the second-floor bathroom of the municipio with her back against the stall door, crying. This time it was more than a few silent tears crawling down her cheeks. This time, it was runny-nosed, tear-flooded sobbing that blowing and cheek-wiping with two fistfuls of toilet paper had done nothing to solve. Each time she tried to pull herself together long enough to at least get back to her villa for a proper ugly cry, Natalie remembered the gravity of her situation.

The pool house. That's what's going to cost me this. That's what's going to cost me my villa.

It was the one repair that she had decided to delay, a fact that she had always deemed her smartest decision. Delaying was the only way she could afford the repairs themselves. Even then, in her moment of despair, she could not deny her own brilliant, original logic. To take on guests in the three months before pool season began and to use that early revenue to complete the remaining improvements to the house.

I can't afford it. And I'm not qualified to do it myself.

Natalie's inclination was always to resort to problem-solving, though this one seemed straightforward. And most of her creative ways to economize had already been exhausted. Which meant that the only solution was to somehow come up with the money.

Impossible. She had exhausted her savings. Getting a job would mean that she had no time to work in the villa. And the fact that there were no jobs around here was why the program existed. She wasn't too proud to ask for credit or an installment pay program, but most of the tenants were in the same boat.

What do I have that I can sell?

Natalie thought of all her worldly and salable possessions, which mainly consisted of new appliances and items of sentimental value—the few pieces of furniture she had shipped to go in her personal apartments; her new industrial refrigerator and dishwasher and range; Gram's wedding china if it survived the cargo ship and if she got extremely desperate.

Maybe Carlota would consign it for me.

But thoughts of Carlota led to thoughts of Pietro, which led to thoughts of how much harder this would be now that she had turned her nose up at his help. The part of her that had never so desperately needed help in her whole life regretted what it meant that she no longer had Pietro's. The part of her that had needed him to be the man she had thought he was was grateful that she wouldn't have to see him, wouldn't have to keep reliving the hurt.

Yes. She would see what she could sell, just as soon as she figured out how dire her situation was. Because she had a decision to make. If there was one thing Natalie knew how to do better than anyone else, it was run the numbers. And there was a growing possibility that they simply wouldn't work.

Cold, hard logic dictated that it might be better to get out of the house now, to walk away with the $12,000 that she had left and go back to the States. It was enough for a plane ticket, for reverse ship cargo fare for her most prized possessions, for a month or two worth of decent food and basic utilities, and for the first month, last month, and security deposit on a small apartment.

Because if she didn't walk away—if she put every last cent into the rehab—and they didn't let her keep it in the end, she would have just given away hundreds of hours of free labor and tens of thousands of dollars in materials used for repairs. The only thing of value Natalie had now—and she didn't even really own it—was the villa itself.

• • •

"I come bearing cheap wine!"

Natalie announced herself with a holler as she walked into Ellie's kitchen. She hadn't bothered to knock on the door, having long since learned that Ellie's place was a vortex for sound. It wasn't large, but cavernous enough that finding Ellie might require a bit of hunting. Natalie had half expected to find her outside with a book and a cocktail, as she often was by this hour of the afternoon. Ellie's typical workday was short.

"Out here!" came Ellie's voice from what sounded like far away but could have been a bit closer based on the way sound carried.

She put the wine on the kitchen counter and her

bag on a chair, and followed Ellie's voice. It turned out to be coming through the screen of the open back door, which meant that Ellie was in the garden.

"Wow. You're doing actual work." Natalie's astonished observation came at the same instant Ellie asked, "How did it go?"

Ellie wore honest-to-goodness work clothes—albeit stylish ones—and appeared to be digging a trench with a shovel. Said trench was a straight line from her roof drain pipe that currently emptied out onto a small, sloped-stone platform.

"Seems that I've got to pipe some of my drainage farther away from the house in order to be up to code." A bit breathless, she stopped what she was doing for a second and leaned a little on her shovel.

"It could have been better. I need your advice. I honestly don't know whether all the repairs they're asking for are doable."

Since her good cry in the bathroom, Natalie had put on her thinking cap, which effectively turned off the emotional part of her brain. She had gone home to her laptop and gotten her spreadsheet out. But, in seeking perspective, she had lost perspective. Maybe she wanted it so badly, she was only telling herself it could work.

"Spit it out, then," Ellie insisted as she went back to her digging, motioning to the patio table in a prompt for Natalie to sit down.

Natalie launched into her story, which included a lot more than Ellie had asked for on the grievances front, maintaining that the council's expectation was still too high a bar.

"It's total shite," Ellie groused unabashedly. "I

don't know how they expect all of us to make the same kinds of repairs at the same time when there are only a handful of contractors in town."

Natalie tended to agree. Not for the first time, she thought of how slow going it was for Pietro and his flips. Some of Pietro's projects had gone on for years.

"So what do you think?" Natalie asked the only question that mattered. "I really don't think I have the money."

Did she want platitudes or the cold hard truth? Ellie was the kind of friend who was capable of dispensing either. She wiped her brow with the back of her arm.

"Your project isn't a complete disaster. The things on your list are things you were already planning to do. Your only problem is, you have to pay for them now rather than later."

"I need to be open for a few months before I can afford the pool repairs. That's the reality. I'm just not budgeted for this."

Ellie stopped long enough to give her a sympathetic look.

"You don't need to actually get the pool open. All that painting and cleaning and sterilizing and filling can wait. You just need to have a safety cover installed and do the electrical."

"I don't even know a pool guy." Natalie didn't mention that, even without painting and cleaning and filling, she still couldn't afford the repair.

"Shouldn't Pietro have someone he can refer you to?"

The news she hadn't looked forward to sharing had been bound to come up.

"Pietro and I aren't together."

Ellie looked offended, as if the idea of Pietro and Natalie not being together somehow disgusted her. "Why would you break up with him?"

"First of all, thank you for assuming that I'm the one who did the breaking..." Once word got around, most people would think that it was her, and not Pietro, who had been dumped. Then, the hard truth. "We broke up because he lied. All those times he told me he was going on business trips, he was really courting investors."

"So all of this was planned? Not the collapse, obviously, but..." Ellie cut herself off. "I'm sorry, I don't understand."

Even without full comprehension, she was starting to look upset. Natalie's next words hurt her to say out loud, even though she'd been saying them to herself every waking hour of every day since she'd found out the truth.

"All this time, I thought Pietro was fighting his father in the name of saving the program. But he's been meeting with investors for months. Pietro never wanted to save it. This is how he always wanted it to end. And now he got what he wanted."

• • •

The journey from Ellie's place was a rather long walk, twenty minutes, but Natalie didn't mind. All that awaited her at home was a modest dinner and a long sleep. A little exercise never hurt anybody, and she could stand to sober up from the wine. Ellie was in no shape to drive, and taxis were a frivolity

Natalie couldn't afford.

She also had jitters and feelings to work off. She was mentally exhausted, but she wanted to tire herself out, like mothers did with toddlers. Heavy thoughts made it that much harder to sleep at night. Best-case scenario, she would wash up with a warm washcloth and one of her fragrant soaps, would double-bag a cup of chamomile tea, and fall asleep the second her head hit the pillow. Best-case scenario, she would get through the rest of the night, through her dreams, and through waking up alone without pitiful thoughts about missing Pietro.

I'm not finished helping you.

What could that possibly mean? That he would show up on nights and weekends, just as he had at the beginning? Even after she had warded him away? Did he even think what he had done was wrong? Had he somehow compartmentalized that hurting the program meant hurting her? The lemons had seemed like a peace offering, a gesture toward making amends. But she didn't think that amends were possible. If there was one thing the Franco Pelagatti mess had taught her, it was this—half-truths and omissions were just as bad as lies.

It was another hard truth, another kernel that had come from the self-reflection of her solitude. She might have been mad at Pietro. But she was really mad at Gram.

And how am I supposed to deal with that?

At least Pietro she could tell off. If she wanted to, she could ask why he did it. She could show him—was already showing him—the hurt he had caused. Gram hadn't owed Natalie all of her stories or all of her secrets. Gram hadn't known anything about the inheritance. But if there was a person, some unfinished business, that had to do with Gram's reasons for wanting to return to Italy, hadn't Natalie had the right to know?

You don't have time for this.

There was enough feeling sorry for herself—enough feeling sorry for all of them—to occupy her thoughts and break her concentration. But when all this was over in thirty short days, after she sprinted to the finish line and put everything into pulling this off…when all this was over, succeed or fail…only then would she let loose her frustrations and let fall her tears.

By the time she walked through the gates of the villa, the sky had darkened past dusk, the light not long from completely fading. Had the sky been ten minutes darker, she would have missed the note stuck in the crack of her door. She hated the way her heart flip-flopped from wishing the note was from Pietro, then hated herself even more for diverting from her trek to the back entrance to pluck it off the door.

He could have just texted, she thought bitterly to herself, though she hadn't been answering those.

The closer she drew to the door, the better the paper came into view. It wasn't one of his. What had been dropped by the door was an envelope with her name typewritten on front. Inside was a receipt—more like a claim ticket. Her cargo ship had finally arrived.

CHAPTER THIRTY-ONE

"Ciao, Nero."

"Ciao, Pietro. I did not expect to see you today. Are you here for an inspection?"

If he had gone there and not encountered the Fiorellos, that would certainly have been his excuse. As a member of the development council, he had a right to drop by for an unannounced visit to any of the properties and to enter the grounds and the buildings, with consent.

Today, he had received the consent of Natalie's friend Ellie, though she hadn't looked happy with him. It was hard to tell whether she was hostile to Pietro personally or whether it was generalized hostility directed toward what he represented.

In his new role, he was the embodiment of the program, the most hated man in Zavona at the moment, as far as the tenants were concerned. Signora Sanguigna's decision to announce the partnership with Roman had served only to worsen already tense relations between the council and the tenants.

"Not really," Pietro said honestly. "Though, it looks like it's coming along. Have you been able to remain on schedule?"

Nero laughed. "What schedule? We are working every day. Six clients right now, and those are just the ones in the program."

"And somehow, I knew that I would find you, and not Nico, here. Somehow, I knew that you would be helping Eleonora."

Nero stopped what he was doing for a second time. This time he rose to his feet, looking around with paranoia, as if to see whether she stood somewhere in the shadows, listening. "What do you mean by saying this?" He didn't look defensive, only suspicious.

"Only that you and I are the same. That we each have our hands in the dough. And that, if you didn't, you wouldn't be here, helping Eleonora."

Nero crossed his arms in front of his chest but didn't bother to deny it.

"You must also know by now that Natalie is not speaking to me. And that I am not currently in a position to help her as you are helping Eleonora. Not openly."

"What now, then?" Fiorello wanted to know.

"You know what I wish to know. Tell me how she is doing. Are her electrical repairs on track? How is her mood?"

Nero looked around again, worried, perhaps, that Ellie would overhear them talking. He lowered his voice.

"Nico and I are helping her. She needs only minor repairs inside her home. Those fixes are easy, a bit picky if you ask me. But the gardens and the pool…" Fiorello shook his head. "The wiring needs to be replaced, and these are specialized parts. The overhead lights on the pathways are simple to fix, but she needs ground lighting or light posts, and outdoor fixtures are more expensive. She is going through the same thing as many other tenants in the program. More work, but not more money."

Pietro nodded. "Anything else?"

"She is very busy, running errands, taking the bus. Some of what she needs is in Nanca and Eleonora is no longer available to drive her. The steering wheel is on the wrong side for Natalie, so she cannot borrow Eleonora's car."

It was troubling to hear of Natalie's hardships, but Pietro was grateful to know at least this.

"We have known each other for a long time, have we not?" Pietro asked Nero, who nodded. "Then you know that I am an honorable man."

Nero nodded again.

"I need you to do something for me. In confidence."

"What is it?"

"I need you to tell me when Natalia is in trouble if it ever seems as if she's in over her head with the rehabilitation."

Nero smiled. "She has been in up to her neck since day one. She will be in over her head until the rehabilitation is finished. This is why we have always helped her. Why we referred her to you. A house that big? All by herself? She has needed support from the beginning."

"She will not accept my help right now," Pietro continued, with a lowered voice. "She is a very proud woman and angry with me for reasons I deserve. I ask only that you do what you would want a friend to do for you, for the woman you love. I ask that you keep an eye out for her. And to let me know what I can do."

"What you can do?"

"Yes. Anything she needs. I will make sure she gets it."

• • •

Pietro was dead tired. The kind of tired that made the idea of falling asleep before the sun set seem like a possibility. The kind of tired that the two espressos he had drunk an hour before managed to cut through. The kind of tired that made him ready to set aside—even if only for a few hours—every last one of his responsibilities. As the gates closed behind his car and he slowed his speed to pull into his driveway, he made a deal with himself—the next time he yawned, he would take it as a sign to go to bed.

"*Merda.*"

Pietro cursed out loud as he made his controlled descent, his truck headed for the carport in between the cottage and the groves. He was too irritable, too exhausted, to react well. His father sat on the bench in front of the carport, his back to Pietro as he looked out at the water, feet stretched in front of him and arms crossed.

Pietro took a moment longer than he strictly needed to turn his engine off and prepare. He had expected Alfonso to arrive on his doorstep sooner or later, though he had hoped for later. He didn't want to do this right now. Between bringing Roman on board, watching over Natalie, managing the workload of the council, and managing his own clients, Pietro was barely getting four hours of sleep every night.

"Papa."

His father rose from the bench, turned to face

Pietro, then stuffed his hands in his pockets. It was a testament to how much distance had grown between them.

"Pietro. You are a busy man."

He kept his mouth shut. A natural—and honest—response would have been to say that he *had* been very busy. That with the program in crisis, there had been much to do.

"It is a surprise to see you on this side of the farm," he remarked instead.

"You haven't been to the house or to my office," Alfonso replied. "It seems that, if I want to see you, I should find you myself."

Pietro half smirked. "Was it you who wanted to see me or Mama who insisted?"

His father did not smile. "Your mother is very worried. She believes that we will never reconcile."

The hint of Pietro's smile faded quickly. He did not like to cause his mother distress.

"Some days, I believe the same."

If he wanted them to be men, he wouldn't shield his father from his thoughts.

"We are both too hardheaded," his father agreed.

"Is that what you think? That we are here because neither one of us likes to give in?"

Alfonso smiled. "Pitruzzu. It has always been like this. With you insisting things be one way and me insisting that things be another. This time, we have let our stubbornness go for too long. Your mother is right. We are family."

"Family? Yes," Pietro conceded. "But we are not the same."

A hardness came over Alfonso's features, one

that Pietro had seen before. It was masked by his politician's veneer, his perpetual amusement. "To this day, it still insults you to be compared to me, the mayor and his embarrassed son."

Pietro let out a sigh, his spirit still exhausted but his body on high alert, hackles up as Alfonso dug in. Even after all that had happened, Alfonso's humility—his regret—hadn't lasted. It always came back to him and his pride.

"You've learned nothing," Pietro said simply, turning to walk into his house, where he hoped to collapse on his bed and sleep for hours. Going more rounds with his father would only make him restless—get him more spun up.

"You've learned nothing," Alfonso repeated, "says the boy who never allowed himself to be taught, who never respected my advice, who treated me like I had nothing to offer and he nothing to learn."

"Never respected your advice?" Now it was Pietro's turn to repeat. "You talk to me about respect in the same sentence that you call me a boy?"

Alfonso finally quieted.

"Pitruzzu, you call me, in business meetings, as if I were six years old."

"It is a term of endearment—" Alfonso protested, but Pietro cut him off.

"It is by design. But what kind of father would do that? What kind of person needs to so constantly diminish his thirty-year-old son?"

Alfonso quieted again.

"And not just any thirty-year-old son, a son who is one of the best in his field, a son who is respected for what he does throughout Italy and beyond. You condescend to me constantly. And you cry when you feel that I have not done enough to respect you. But the one who lacks respect here isn't me, Papa. It hasn't been for a long time. The one who fails to show it now is you."

It took Pietro getting through his soliloquy, took him finally stringing together disjointed pieces that had lived separately in his mind for him to see how much it was all true. All this time, Pietro had waited for his father to treat him as if he were worthy, to finally say it out loud. All this time, it was Alfonso who hadn't been—who still wasn't—worthy of him.

"Pitruz—" Alfonso cut himself off. "Pietro," he began again. "You forget that I know what it means to work outside the family business. Both of us gave up our birthrights to walk our own paths. I only wanted you to follow me so that you could learn from my mistakes. Out of all my children, it is you who I worry about. I teach you because I want you to be practical."

"Practical?" Pietro shouted. "You dare to call me impractical when I predicted the collapse? You dare to call me unstable when I have built enough wealth to buy and restore these properties? You dare to call me a bachelor after your actions endangered the woman I love? Natalia is in danger of failing. If she is forced to leave—if I am forced to lose her—it will be because of you."

Pietro stood there long enough to let his words sink in, to bore into his father with the most hateful look Pietro had ever given. He hadn't ever felt so against his father as he did in that moment. When enough was enough, he turned his back once more and continued to retreat toward his cottage.

"It wasn't your mother who told me to come and make amends," Alfonso called, his voice breaking on the words. Pietro halted but didn't turn around. "I came on my own, to apologize. I never wanted things to be like this."

Pietro didn't mention that his father hadn't actually said he was sorry. That he hadn't apologized for anything. Alluding to the intention of an apology was the most that Pietro was likely to get.

"Tell me, Pietro. What can I do? How can I make things right with you and with everyone I've harmed?"

Pietro thought of Natalie then and all her friends.

"Don't just sit there. You're the mayor. Use your influence. Now is not the time to wallow. It's the time to help."

CHAPTER THIRTY-TWO

It was three full days before Natalie had a chance to organize delivery of her belongings from the docks, for her to get the logistics straight to have them brought from Positano. It was a storage cube—one small enough to fit in the flatbed of a pickup. Pietro had offered weeks ago to drive her, but she wouldn't take him up on it now. They felt faraway, the simpler times of anticipating the shipment, of hours spent on meandering roads, driving with windows open to cool breezes as they headed up the coast.

Prioritizing the hiring of contractors over claiming possession of her things had been more déjà vu, the walking of strangers through her house catapulting her back to more memories of early days. It should have felt gratifying, to know she'd crossed a threshold that placed her further from the beginning than the end. The downside was, she had a month to achieve the impossible. The upside was, if she pulled it off, she would be spectacularly far ahead. Hurtling to the finish line should have felt good.

But not much felt good right then—not the promise of going through Gram's things, of re-scrutinizing her letters and papers and albums, of making progress on hunting down Franco. She wouldn't have time for that sort of thing at all. Instead of going through her belongings with love and with care, maybe even shedding a few tears of grief and remembrance, she would rake through like a scavenger, seeing what few remaining valuables—heirlooms, really—she could sell.

"Be honest," she instructed Ellie, hours later, over coffee. It seemed to be the only thing she drank anymore. With all the repairs, her days and nights had gotten long. She had spent all morning triaging the contents of her cube. Everything had arrived in one piece, in the condition in which she'd packed it. But the space it took up was different. It all looked tiny against the backdrop of her grand villa.

"Define honest." Ellie made a slow walk across the floor to observe the collection of three dozen different items, from china to a jewelry box to art.

Natalie motioned to the collection before her. "Do you think any of this is actually worth anything?"

Ellie seemed to choose her words carefully. "The question you ought to be asking yourself is, what are they worth to you?"

Natalie must have looked ready to protest, given how quickly Ellie put up her hands.

"What I mean is, you need to know the price you would accept for something without feeling like you gave it away." Ellie picked up a china teacup. "Would you sell this for one euro?"

"Never."

"All right. Would you sell it for ten euros?"

Natalie shook her head.

"Twenty?"

At that number, Natalie wove her head from side to side in a gesture of indecision.

"What about these?"

Natalie stepped closer to Ellie, who had come

across the paintings. Natalie had unrolled canvas after canvas and secured the corners with stones.

"She bought these years ago, when she lived in Campania, and kept them ever since. We said, when we moved here, that we'd hang them in the guest rooms."

"They're quite good..." Ellie trailed off, possibly code for, *They might actually be worth something.*

"See that one?" Natalie pointed to one of a noticeably different hue than the others, which had been tucked away and stored for years. "That's the only one we ever hung in our house."

"I recognize some of the views on the landscapes," Ellie mused. "The coastline has really changed. And the other ones, of people, and the lighthouse...I can't place the locations, but they're really beautiful."

"So you think I should try to sell these?"

Ellie had a sip of her coffee. "I think you should know your price. And I think you shouldn't judge yourself for what you let go. Nothing you do now could disappoint your gran; you know that, right? The only thing that would disappoint her is you not fighting for this. You've worked too hard just getting here to lose it now."

• • •

It seemed wrong to stop visiting Carlota just because she and Pietro were on the outs. For all Natalie knew, his grandmother hadn't heard anything about their fight. That was why, just like she did every week before meeting the other expats at the café, she headed to the furniture store to see her friend.

Sure, if Carlota really had her ear to the ground, as Pietro always insisted she did, it was possible she would take one look at Natalie and run her out of the store. Pietro was clearly her favorite, her piccolo. For all Natalie knew, Pietro had already gone to Carlota with his own sad story of their rift, of how he had tried to reconcile with her and she had rebuffed him.

"Ciao, Signora Carlota." Natalie announced herself as she entered the store.

"Natalia?" a faint voice came from the back. "Finally, you have paid me a visit."

Natalie heard her voice before she heard or saw Carlota shuffling forth from the back. Natalie considered it not a bad sign when Carlota fixed her with a pitying look.

"I'm sorry, Miss Carlota, it has been a very busy week. This is the first time I've been in town."

"Yes. All of the dreamers are busy after the collapse. And your friends, are they okay?"

Natalie's own heart grew heavy at their mention. "Honestly? No."

Carlota shared a sorrowful look with her, and the two women stood in silence for a long moment until Carlota motioned her farther into the store, toward the back where there were two chairs.

"Did you bring me your special American spirit?" Carlota wanted to know.

Natalia gave an infectious smile and patted her bag. "For you? I filled up the flask."

"Did I ever tell you about my husband? Pietro's grandfather?"

Natalie shook her head.

She bit the bottom of her lip, rocked back in her

chair, and brought her hand to her chest. "*Ostia*! That man was good-looking. Tall like Pietro with the same bright green eyes. The way he looked at me sometimes…the way he held me, made me dough in his hands. I still remember how it felt to be under his gaze."

Carlota nodded to punctuate her statement, giving Natalie a knowing look. And Natalie did know. She knew what it was like to feel like that. Instead of confessing to how much she missed Pietro, she gave a nod of understanding.

"For all of his beauty," Carlota continued, tapping her forehead with her finger, "he did very stupid things. Not all the time, but enough. What we go through as women dealing with these men…" She shook her head and rocked back in her chair once more. "Nobody knows."

That Carlota was commiserating with her made Natalie wonder whether she should confess the trouble she was having with Pietro. On one hand, Carlota was Pietro's nonna, his own confidante and friend. On the other hand, she and Carlota were both women. Carlota knew Pietro, and Natalie could use some advice.

"Men aren't perfect, are they?" Natalie asked mildly, not wanting to put Carlota on the spot. If Carlota wished to say nothing more, she would leave it at that. To her abject surprise, Carlota chuffed out a laugh.

"Ha! Not perfect! These men. They do not think. Did Pietro tell you the name of the cottage where he lives?"

Natalie nodded, but Carlota told her anyway.

"It is called the lonely bachelor house. Years ago, it was this cottage where I sent my husband when he had done something stupid."

Natalie smiled. "In America, we call it the doghouse."

"I like that." Carlota laughed. "Women will need lonely bachelor houses and doghouses and all of the different houses until the end of time. The men will make sure of this."

Natalie tried to smile even through her worry about the complexity of her own predicament. Yes, Pietro had steered clear of ever mentioning things he should have told her. But what they were to each other and how it had all started…it put her in an odd position in relation to her friends.

How could she explain all the flavors of her guilt? About having been helped by Pietro and about not knowing? How could she explain that she had never done this before—never, ever been in love with a guy—and knew nothing about fighting or reconciling? How could she explain that the only way to deal with it was to *not* deal with it, since the singular task of saving her house had left her overwhelmed?

"I will tell you, now, something my grandmother always said to me," Carlota continued when Natalie didn't speak. "My grandmother had a very serious voice. She would say, *senza moglie a lato, l'uomo non e beato*."

Carlota affected a bit of an accent. Natalie understood the phrase—without a wife by his side, a man cannot be blessed.

"It means a man needs a woman to find his own

way," Carlota continued. "The important thing, Natalia, is that a wife does not lose her own way in helping her husband find his. Do not fear the doghouse. Let it give you room to think."

• • •

Natalie couldn't be sure whether Carlota was telling her to rethink her relationship with Pietro or to take her sweet time in forgiving him. Either way, she left the store feeling better. Carlota had served her *zuccherini*, the cookies she liked best, and had made extra this time, telling Natalie to share with her friends.

Lunch at Café Ludo that day was an abbreviated affair. The few who came seemed tired and stressed. They came not only for lunch but also to lend and trade and broker deals. With less time for finding and ordering parts and equipment and less money for buying them, tenants borrowed and gave and lent a litany of things.

Ellie wore work clothes for the second time in a row and spent nearly the whole time on her phone, begging a roofer from Nanca to start her project that week. Even she seemed to be running out of options and money. Her inspection had been after Natalie's, which meant her thirty days ended a bit later. Only her electrical work seemed to be going well.

Natalie had steeled herself for questions and comments about Pietro, about the council, about the investor, and about this mess. Her plan, if asked, was to insist that she was focused on her rehab. To her relief, nobody asked. And so it happened that

Natalie made her way home midafternoon with a full stomach she would need for the hours of work ahead.

Instead of walking onto her property the front way, Natalie took the service road from the back, which would deposit her right next to her garage. She had agreed to leave it unlocked for Soni and Greg. They needed to rebuild some cabinetry in the upstairs of their home in town. She had told them they could come by whenever to take her saw. If she hadn't gone in to unlock the door, to locate her saw and put it front and center where they could locate it easily, she wouldn't have seen the Vespa.

Only, it wasn't her Vespa. It was…beautiful. It was cleaned up and restored. The paint that had once been the orange she hadn't cared much for had been refinished in a flattering champagne color that matched her pink helmet's gold crown. Said helmet hung on one of the handlebars by a strap, and the keys were on the seat. The thing hadn't run before, but she would bet it did now. All week, it had taken her longer than she could afford to run errands, to pick up little things she needed to stay on track. How could he have known?

CHAPTER THIRTY-THREE

The truth was, it would've been difficult for Pietro to help Natalie as much as he wanted, even if she had allowed him to try. Being the head of the council at a time like this came with responsibilities. The scrutiny of the collapse had made the council answerable to a small handful of regional and national authorities. Over the span of a week, Pietro had been to what seemed like every corner of Italy, answering tough questions for stern-faced officials in tense meetings.

He had also flown out to see Roman again. Pietro wanted to keep him happy. That meant making sure he understood the contracts, facilitating the onboarding process, and bending over backward to make sure Roman had to put in as little personal effort as possible to make this happen. He was a benefactor and a busy man, a *sognatori* only in name.

Pietro had just settled in his seat on the Alitalia flight that would take him from Trentino to Positano, had been ready to obey the attendant's request that passengers turn off their phones. He'd been ready to lean his temple against the bank of his window seat and be asleep before the plane took off. Just as he was thumbing the screen toggle to switch it into airplane mode, a text came in.

Not a text. A photo. And not from her.

Pietro still held his breath with every twitch of

his phone, hoping against hope that it would be her. He had never truly known the agony of being on the outs with a woman.

Pietro perked up when the photo turned out to be a photo of her backyard, forwarded to him by Nero. As he was zooming in to figure out what he was supposed to be looking at, a text arrived.

We finished the safety lighting in the garden. On Thursday we will start in on the pool.

Pietro tapped back onto the picture and looked closer. Sure enough, the new fixtures were what he had missed. Pole lighting around the perimeter and ground lighting along the paths. It wouldn't look complete until the landscaping was done, until a mason repaired the stonework on the pathway, until the fountain, and the rest of the area, was cleaned up. But even this small change made the gardens look better, especially the elegant pole lights that aligned to the villa's architectural style.

Thank you, friend. I know this will ease Natalia's mind, Pietro replied, feeling his gratitude was worth more than his praise for beautiful work.

What would ease Natalie's mind is if we could get her the special recessed pool light she needs. You are still in Alto Adige, no?

For now, yes. Pietro was already getting a sense for where this was going.

There is a pool supply store there that carries this light. It would save us a week in processing and shipping if you could go pick it up. From Campania, no one has it in stock for three hundred miles.

"I'm very sorry..." Pietro apologized to the

person sitting on the aisle next to him, the person who he had just brushed past fewer than five minutes earlier to take his seat.

"Sir?" the attendant asked upon seeing him go the wrong way.

"I'm very sorry," Pietro repeated. "But I have to get off the plane."

• • •

Four days later, Pietro was rushing through security at Fiumicino, the international airport in Rome. It was the third time he'd been in an airport that week. He'd secured the special part for Natalie's pool, but journeying to the store that sold it had caused him to miss the last flight back to Naples, forcing an overnight stay in an airport hotel.

No sooner had he arrived back in Zavona than he received an awaited call from the head of the National Council for the Arts, an old friend whose endorsement the museum project could really use. He was lucky to get the meeting on such short notice. Said meeting, however, would have to take place at his friend's office in Florence, which found Pietro back on a plane that very same night.

The trip had been worth it. Pietro had made his case for why Zavona—and his palazzo—was the ideal location for a regionally and nationally important museum. Showing support at her level would cut red tape and attract some of the right resources to the project. With so many new projects financed by Roman, they could start as soon as there was a team.

Pietro had been close—so close—to flying back home after Florence, then he got a call from a different friend, someone who did what Pietro did with specialty restorations, only on the general-contracting side. He was the perfect fit for the museum job but difficult to book. Because Andrea's company was busy, it behooved Pietro to move sooner rather than later to have Andrea on board.

"You have ten minutes, sir. You're out of time to check your bag," the woman at the Alitalia counter informed Pietro. He had been so busy traveling from A to B to C that he hadn't booked a flight. So many things had gone off schedule this past week, he surrendered to taking the next available. Pietro handed over his credit card for the seat he had booked in first class.

I'll be asleep before it even takes off, Pietro thought to himself as he hustled through security and made his swift way to the gate. An attendant announced the final group for boarding as soon as he arrived. This time, he hadn't been able to get a seat on the window like he preferred.

One of the last people to get on the plane, he was quick to stow his bag in the overhead compartment, then settle down into his seat. He politely declined the flight attendant's swift offer of a drink before takeoff, insisting that he planned to sleep the entire time. Seconds after he closed his eyes, a voice he thought that he would never hear again broke through his consciousness.

"Pietro? Is that you?"

He briefly considered faking sleep. Knowing Vittoria, she would persist. He pried his eyes open with trepidation. Vittoria looked different. Older. More expensive. Better. And definitely not for him.

"Pietro," she said again, her glossed lips melting into a smile. "I can't believe it's you."

"Vittoria. How long has it been?" he asked, as if his past hadn't been on his mind lately.

"Too long." Her face took on a sorrowful look.

A silence fell between them, or rather, a weight. Would Vittoria make small talk when the betrayal had been so big?

"I thought you would be married by now." Her voice was light—joking—but her eyes told a different story. Vittoria cared, after all this time. The only question was, why?

"What makes you think I'm not?"

She pointed to his hand, then to her own ring finger. "No ring. Unless you are unhappily married?" she asked.

He shook his head. "I do not cheat. That has not changed."

"I was certain that you would be living in that big house on the hill with children everywhere. That they would grow up in the lemon groves."

Her smile was wistful as she issued this speculation.

"Did this fantasy make you feel better?"

He asked it without venom. But still, her smile faded. "Yes. I suppose it did."

The flight attendant interrupted them then, apologizing for her reach as she leaned over to clear Vittoria's preflight drink. Next to the iceless glass with only squeezed lime remaining in the bottom were two empty mini bottles of vodka.

"What did you imagine that I did all of these years?" she wondered aloud a minute later. The flight attendants had begun their takeoff spiel.

Pietro looked over and smiled sadly. "I made it a point not to imagine. I didn't ask about you, or search for you, or follow your career. I did what I could to move on."

She quieted for a moment. "I was going to come to see you. I have business in Naples this week. I was going to come to Zavona. Did you know that I haven't been back once?"

Pietro shook his head. "I didn't know."

"I didn't just leave you, Pietro. I left everyone. My family. My friends. Everything and everyone I'd ever known."

The one question that Pietro had obsessed over, had raged over, had wept over, and had ached to know, he didn't care about anymore.

"It looks like running into me here has saved you a trip. Tell me. What were you going to say?"

She sighed and looked down at her fingers. "That I know I broke your heart when I left."

By then, the plane was being backed up out of the gate.

"It wasn't the leaving. It was the lack of explanation."

She quieted again, and Pietro wondered whether the conversation was over. They had gone long enough without seeing or speaking to each other, maybe this was all that was necessary, more so for her than for him, it seemed.

"Why did you never marry, Pietro?"

He thought about this.

"I was always too busy fighting for the things I believe in. Both of us always were. I think us against the world is why we were together. We fought for our families' blessing to be together at a time when just leaving their houses was as far ahead as we could see. Then once we got to that house on the top of that hill, we saw the rest of the world."

Pietro had never explained their marriage to himself that way. The true ring in his own heart proved it true. Tears pooled in Vittoria's eyes, not so much tender as anguished. It made Pietro suspect that she was still caught up in the fight.

"I have met the woman I would like to marry," Pietro announced next. "With her, I am ready to leave behind the bitterness—to taste the sweetness of life."

CHAPTER THIRTY-FOUR

Selling a painting in Italy was harder than it should have been for a culture that prided itself on art. Natalie had called fifteen galleries in Campania. None was interested in the collection, despite a rather flattering set of high-resolution digital shots. Since Natalie wasn't the artist exhibiting original work, most declined to even take a look. She had finally received interest from just one gallery, in Naples.

She'd ridden there and back that morning, the cylindrical container that contained the canvases strapped crosswise around her front. If she didn't get a call back soon, she would resort to taking it to a dealer. Only, dealers were notorious for playing games, for lowballing prices and spinning stories to convince sellers that their paintings were worth less than they were. Not wanting to drag out the process with the gallery, she had lied and said she had another offer on the painting. With such a claim, the gallery owner had promised to call or text her within twenty-four hours.

Back in town, she had errands to run. A trip to the bank to take out money. The roofer had agreed to a discount if she paid in cash. A trip to the *municipio* for yet another permit. Food, so she could eat. After returning from Naples, she'd stopped home and dropped off the Vespa.

Sure. The only reason why she'd even been able

to make it to Naples on her own, and on such short notice given the gallery owner's availability, was because of how easy it was for her to hop on her bike. But nobody needed to think about that. She also didn't need to think about how another basket of lemons had awaited her on her front step when she'd returned.

She was busy *not* thinking about him as she descended into town, taking the long way to the bank by heading to the square. It seemed as good a time as any for a coffee. She missed her *caffè con panna*—her whipped cream over espresso. She'd visited the kiosk less frequently since Pietro had bought her an espresso machine of her own.

Pietro.

Natalie stopped short on the cobblestone street on the edge of the piazza when she laid eyes on the man himself. For a split second, it seemed likely that her intense thoughts of him had conjured him into existence. But if that were true, he would have appeared days earlier. And because she couldn't let the half of herself that longed to run into his arms win over everything else she was feeling, she let the other half take hold.

His stroll was leisurely—Italian speed as he made his way to Carlota's, no doubt. It irritated her right then that he could be so casual while, without even seeing or speaking to her, he'd gotten her more spun up.

On the surface, he was just helping, just trying to get back into her good graces. But he was also meddling and going against her wishes that he give her space. Only in order to chastise him, not out of any desperation to see him, would she say something now.

"You're distracting me."

The accusatory words came out hotly, with a bit of breathlessness thrown in. She'd had to jog a bit to catch him on the other side of the square. If she'd let him get too far too quickly, they would be doing this too close to Carlota's store.

"Natalia."

She had clearly caught him by surprise, which made his unfiltered response even sweeter. The smile that came over his face when he set eyes on her was so hopeful, and so relieved, that it nearly broke her resolve.

"You're distracting me," she repeated.

They had both stopped their walks and stood on the end of Carlota's street, just past the corner of the square. She shifted her bags farther up her fingers. They had slipped a bit on her run.

"These look heavy. Please let me carry them for you." He didn't ask for further permission to pluck the bags out of her hands.

God, he smells good.

She'd noticed this a second earlier, but his step into her space made her notice it twice.

"These are too heavy to carry back to your villa," he continued. "I will give you a ride. My Vespa is just on the other side of the square."

The bags were fully in his hands, but Pietro didn't step back. His adoring smile returned as he fixed her with his bright green eyes.

Today they're the color of moss, she observed, already getting pulled in. Maybe she should have texted after all. Not being around him may have been agony, but it also made her less susceptible to his charm.

Focus.

"Don't change the subject." With her hands free of bags, she could put one on her hip and use the other to point at him accusingly. "You heard what I said. You need to quit it, with all your lemons and your letters and your supplies."

But Pietro didn't look repentant. He looked thoroughly amused. "So I am distracting you. With lemons."

Natalie narrowed her eyes and hissed out a "yes," not at all liking how stupid he was making this sound.

"I thought you liked my lemons," he protested, his voice lowering in a way that told her they were hardly talking about lemons at all.

Focus, Natalie.

"Your lemons aren't the point. All the things you're sending me are. A case of commercial-grade smoke detectors, lights for my pool, a *Vespa*?"

"These have helped you, no? That was my intention. To help you finish on time."

"Except I can't accept help like this. With you pulling strings to get me everything while my friends are barely getting by. I want to succeed. But not because I'm sleeping with the head of the Economic Development Council. Not like this."

"Ah, I see…"

And, in that moment, it was clear that he really did see something he hadn't. It was also clear that talk of their relationship had hit a nerve, not that there was much to speak of in that department.

"Does this conflict of interest mean we can begin

sleeping together again? Because I miss you, Natalia. I miss you very much."

It would have been easy then to take a cheap shot at his wording, to call him a pig and slap him in the face and ask him how he could bring up sex at a moment like this. But it would have been too cheap a shot. Pietro was most definitely not just talking about sex.

He leaned in even farther. "Tell me, Natalia, what I must do to return to your favor. Without you, I fear that my heart cannot survive."

The sincerity in his voice—his desperation—confirmed something she had barely let herself consider, something that had been messing with her even more these past days. It was all caught up in Franco and the notion of lost Italian loves and secrets kept by Gram. It was all caught up in parallels and paradoxes and the prospects of her leaving—the prospects of her having to leave—a man she was increasingly certain she loved.

I miss you, too, Pietro.

Only, the words wouldn't come out. Because the one thing her own heart couldn't survive was giving even more of it away. In every literal and figurative sense of the word, Natalie barely had anything left. Giving away even this small truth…it felt like it could leave her with nothing.

"Butt out," she finally said, her voice in a whisper. "I don't want your help. Not like this. You have to let me do it on my own. Promise me that."

Pietro didn't look like he wanted to promise her anything. Yet, he answered with a single word. "Okay."

• • •

Natalie had two flavors of fixes to her renovations at this point. First, the kind that required unspecialized resources and hours to take on the tasks that even mildly trained people could do—installing smoke detectors and replacing every single plug with safety outlets; hanging signage and maps that told guests what to do in case of an emergency. Technically, these were things Natalie could do herself. Only, the villa was so large, it was a substantial effort to replicate individual safety measures in every room.

The second flavor had to do with fixes that had to be, unequivocally, managed by professionals. This set was dictated by scheduling and money.

Natalie was in a catch-22. If she didn't book contractors and get them on the schedule, she would miss out on booking them on time. But did she have any business booking a vendor she couldn't pay? Natalie still didn't know where she would get the extra money. Her remaining budget was for the plumber and roofer she had so desperately needed all along and who she had managed to book on timing that would allow them to finish the work within the thirty days. The problem was the extra vendors she hadn't counted on. The general contractor who she had inquired with to rebuild the pool cottage and take care of safety walking issues in the garden had quoted her $4,500.

There were other things—little things. A secure cap for her well. The relocation of her brand-new chicken coop, which had yet to house chickens but that needed to be situated no closer than ninety meters from the main house. Unable to think too hard about hired contractors she couldn't yet afford, for fear of complete overwhelm, she focused on rallying the troops.

Hey? Are you free today? I could use a bit of help.

Ellie still had mostly contractors working on her flip. It meant she might be free. Even a few hours lending a hand would help.

Sorry. Can't come over now. Waiting for the plumber. Ellie's text was punctuated with a sad-faced emoji.

No worries. I know how that is, Natalie fired back even as the last of her hopes for more help that day were shot.

She'd gotten similar messages over the past two days. Chris and Jorge would be busy with concrete—the pouring in of pillars they'd needed in the first place in order to avoid the collapse. Helmut and Julia had run into some of the same issues as she had with parts and pieces and had needed to make a three-hour drive to pick up some supplies.

What did you think was going to happen? That all this help would last?

She thought it to herself as she picked up a bucket. On some level, she had believed in the all-hands-on-deck vibe of the past few weeks as each tenant helped the others. But the closer they got to their final inspection dates, it was every man for himself.

Natalie was putting her work gloves on when her phone buzzed again. Believing it to be Ellie, she took her gloves back off and prayed that Ellie had sustained a change of heart. But the text wasn't from Ellie. It was from an unfamiliar number, the owner of which identified herself.

This is Amalia from Galeria Napolitana. We can offer you $7,500 for your painting.

CHAPTER THIRTY-FIVE

This time, Roman had come to Campania, set foot for the first time in Zavona; been welcomed for lunch in the big villa, his parents' home next to their groves. After lunch, Pietro took him a meandering route on their slow walk to his palazzo, which would serve as a museum that they had yet to name.

Pietro had been so eager to sell Roman on the program and on the idea of a museum that he hadn't thought of how earnestly he might fall in love with Zavona for the same reasons why Pietro was in love with the place himself. To an untrained eye, Zavona was barely distinguishable from any of the other two dozen towns on the Amalfi Coast. But to people who could envision how it could look following key restorations, it had potential.

The potential to ship in salvaged Corinthian columns with a comparable, cross-hatched style was the topic under discussion. The current ones seemed beyond repair. Or, if not beyond repair, ridiculously expensive. Pietro's job, in light of all that Roman was doing, was to help economize and to support the market for precious artifacts, which ought to have been a win-win.

"This is a good solution, is it not?" Roman asked with a small smile.

Petro tried to look equally enthusiastic.

"Then why do you look like I just stole your lunch?"

Embarrassed, Pietro shook his head. "I apologize. You must know that the last thing I would ever want to seem is ungrateful."

"Not ungrateful," Roman countered with an easy smile. "But if there is something more, something I do not know about yet, now would be the time."

"No, no, nothing like that." Pietro doubted that one day he would be a multimillionaire, but he did envy Roman his ease, that carefree air enjoyed only by the superrich. "Women problems," Pietro confessed.

Roman let out an easy chuckle. "What did you do to the girl?"

Petro was a little offended. "What makes you think it was me?"

Roman chuckled again. "Pietro. I am a hotelier. I see the cycle, from sin to apology, from apology to sin. I am also a married man. You should know as I know how much smarter, how much more savage they are than us."

"I wouldn't use the word 'savage' to describe your wife." Roman and Paola seemed perfectly and genuinely happy, not like so many of the other couples Pietro had observed through his work over the years.

"Make no mistake. Paola can best me any day, not only because she is smarter, because I am hopelessly in love with her."

Just as I am hopelessly in love with Natalia.

"The first time you messed up..." Pietro began haltingly. "What did you do to make things right?"

"All of the wrong things. I was every bit as unimaginative as the men who come to my hotel, trying to make up for whatever they did with candlelit dinners and champagne and flowers. It took me years to understand how to make up for my mistakes."

"Gifts are a mistake?" This logic went against nearly everything Pietro had ever been told, and observed, about women.

Roman leaned in a little, as if he were about to impart a guarded secret. "Gifts are designed to appeal to her sense of grace. You are betting that if she sees that you are truly sorry—truly repentant—that she will forgive you. But the way back into a woman's heart is to appeal to her sense of fear."

Even without understanding, some part of Pietro knew that he had hungered for this advice. He had missed out, somehow, on someone explaining this. If things hadn't always been so complicated, the person who might have explained things like this could have been his father.

"Please, say more." Pietro leaned in, needing to understand.

"This woman of yours is afraid of something. She cannot let go of whatever crime you committed until she no longer carries her fear. The fear that your actions caused. Flowers and candy are nice, but they cannot compete with her reptilian brain. Women cannot see their way to truly forgive us when we make them too insecure."

Pietro considered this, remembered Natalie's own words.

I'm always waiting for the other shoe to drop.

I want this life to lead to something secure.

Have you met me? I don't like surprises.

Pietro felt like the biggest idiot in the world. It wasn't just that he'd steered far clear of talking about his real plans for the program. He'd withheld the whole truth from a woman who only felt safe when she knew exactly what to expect. A woman already out of her comfort zone from taking the biggest risk in her life. A woman who had only needed one thing—for him to be steady.

"What if her fears are killing her?"

In that one question held Pietro's own fear—that Natalie's thirst for control was the source of her unhappiness, that it could drive her to the point of obsession if indulged. His wish for her was that she would keep letting go.

Only, she trusted you and you messed it up.

"The deeper the fear, the larger the response needed to counteract it. Do something that turns the way she thinks, and the lies that she tells herself, upside down."

Pietro waited until he saw Roman off that night, after he had put him in a car to Naples, before leaving the palazzo and getting in his own car, Roman's advice about Natalie still fresh in his mind. The problem with all of it was, it was complicated. Pietro was certain that the thing he had promised to do—to stop with his help and his preferential treatment—was exactly the thing he needed to double down on to assuage her fears.

It went back to his initial instinct—Natalie needed to be held, to be taken care of, and not because she was incapable or weak. Sometimes, it was the strongest people—the ones who had been through the most—who needed people around them to lighten their load and make things okay.

If Pietro obeyed her wishes, he would be able to say he had respected her boundaries. But he would have to watch her lose an unwinnable game. The program had been set up so badly. Even if she hated him afterward, he could not stand by and allow her to fail.

It's worth the risk.

Even if she never spoke to him again, she had come too far, worked too hard to lose her villa. Even if it failed the inspection, he would launch an appeal. Even if he had to sell everything he owned and buy it for her himself, Pietro would. Even if he had to see her in town every day for the rest of his life, brushed aside by her cold shoulder, it would be worth it if he had given Natalie her dream.

CHAPTER THIRTY-SIX

Something about the hue of the light that morning reminded her of that first day. Some chill coursing through her body left her feeling just as exposed, though no hen had intruded upon her sleeping space this time around. Maybe it had been the lightness of her slumber, the way she could never get a good, deep sleep if something heart-racing was to happen at dawn. That first day, she hadn't slept long and her sleep had been shallow, too.

But that first day's jitters had been something else—pent-up excitement steeped with fatigue, anticipation of the giddy variety, the kind that held the promise of something much-awaited and something good. Based on how things were going, today held something dreaded—a ticking clock that had just over thirty hours. The inspector would come through tomorrow morning.

Today's the last day. And there's no way in hell I can finish.

There was so much of everything left to do, Natalie hardly knew where to start—hardly knew which list items, if left incomplete, would give her inspection the best chance for a pass. Should she go all-hands-on-deck for the biggest safety threats and hope that some of the smaller infractions would be overlooked? Would resolving as many individual issues as possible earn her more favor? Would they accept the fixes if she couldn't prove that all of it was certified work? Would the inspector know how far she'd come in a month? Would they even care?

Finché c'è vita c'è speranza, she thought to herself.

Then she had to laugh. Not a funny laugh. An ironic, bittersweet, I-might-be-going-crazy laugh, for scolding herself. Because only now—now that she was inches away from being run out of the country on a rail—had she finally begun to think in Italian. *As long as there is life, there is hope.*

Hoisting herself from bed, Natalie was deliberate in getting dressed. She put on her favorite cutoff jeans, her favorite V-neck T-shirt, and her favorite pair of Chucks. She had even saved her favorite bandanna. She was briefly entertaining the idea of descending to town—sacrificing forty minutes of work to enjoy her favorite cup of coffee—when her thoughts were interrupted by the sound of an old, loud engine and the toot of a horn.

By the time she whipped the door open, Chris had already parked the truck, climbed out of the driver's seat, and was in the process of slamming the door. Jorge wasn't his only companion. Jorge also wasn't in the passenger seat. He was busy climbing out of the flatbed where, evidently, he'd bumped along with Helmut and Ellie. But the front seat wasn't empty—climbing out right then was Julia, Helmut's very pregnant wife who, owing to said pregnancy, Natalie hadn't met on many occasions.

"What are all of you doing here?"

For a moment, panic gripped her as the threat of bad news—of another tragedy—entered her mind. Ellie was as stylish as ever but with a different look.

She wore khakis and leather ankle boots and a cute, plaid button-up shirt.

"What do you think? We're here to help."

Ellie answered the question at the same moment as Jorge helped her down. Helmut jumped down and rushed around the side, taking the bag in Julia's hand and throwing it over his own shoulder. She walked quickly, though it was clear it took a bit of effort.

"But—" Natalie sputtered. "You guys should be working on your own houses. How can you possibly have time to help me?" She looked at Chris and Jorge in a bit of a panic. "Your inspection is on Friday."

"Friday is five days from now," Jorge replied with an indignant eyebrow arch. "This means you can help us from Tuesday to Thursday. So really, we are getting the better end of the deal."

Chris just gave her a shrug and a look that said, *He's not wrong*, before putting in his own two cents. "Come on, Nat. You've been helping us all along. You were right there, the same day they let us back into our place, hauling rubble and moving rocks. Now we're in it with you."

"I'm great at painting," Julia chimed in.

Natalie gave a hard blink. "I can't let you work. You're, like, a hundred months pregnant."

"Which is why you have to let me help," she reasoned. "I need something to get things going. This baby needs to hurry it up."

"We wanted to help you last week, but Pietro said he knew we needed to work on our own projects. He said he would call when you needed us and that he had a plan." Helmut looked up at the main building. "Is it complete? Do you no longer need help?"

But Natalie's gaze was too busy flying to Ellie's. "Seriously? Did you know about this?"

"I found out about it yesterday. And I was sworn to secrecy. Under duress."

Natalie shook her head, not understanding. "Sworn to secrecy by who?"

Then Ellie did something Natalie had never—not once—seen her do. She blushed. "Nero. We're kind of dating."

"She does not look finished," Jorge observed before Natalie had a chance to be surprised. He jutted his chin toward the garden. "You still did not have the pool house fixed?"

"There's a lot of stuff that's not done," Natalie muttered in absent, quick response, then refocused on her shock. "I'm sorry…*Pietro* put you up to this? I told him to help other people finish their own projects. I told him to stop focusing on mine."

"Natalie," Ellie said in that half-soft, half-sharp way of hers. "Do you want to pass inspection or not?"

The answer to the question stole Natalie's breath so quickly, all she could do was nod, to try to breathe and wait until at least the respectable hour of noon to cry.

"Well, that's why we're here." Ellie's voice was kinder now. "I know you're a proud woman. But come on, we're your friends."

Chris's arm came around her, but the weight was still on her chest. There was something more she had to get past, something she'd been grappling with all week. The three words she couldn't ever once in life remember herself saying. But she whispered them out now, looking around the tiny circle, with tears brimming in her eyes and a rapid, breathless nod.

"I need help."

Chris squeezed her shoulder and Julia gave a little rub to her arm. Ellie gave her a wink. "I got you, girl."

"Have breakfast," Helmut said with a bit of command. "As you're eating, you can tell us where to start."

Natalie gave a sniff and nodded at the same time she let Chris begin to usher her to a seat at the table. Then another horn blared from around the back of the building toward the driveway. That's when the trucks showed up.

• • •

Natalie managed to make it into the garage with all of her composure, all smiles until the moment she slipped inside, slumped back against the door, and, for three long seconds, held her breath. She'd barely held it together as the caravan of cars and trucks had meandered down her drive. She'd barely held it together when Pietro had coaxed her out of her speechless astonishment long enough to meet and help direct the professional crew of twenty. And she absolutely couldn't hold it together now.

By the time she took in a shuddering gasp, tears streaked down her face, which felt every bit as hot as her hands. She wrung her fingers as she let her head fall back against the wall, let herself sob out every hit of emotion she'd pent up.

He came.

Even after how she had treated him, even as pride and betrayal had driven her to refuse his help, Pietro had come to her aid with every resource she needed to get the job done. With every contractor in a fifty-kilometer radius tied up on jobs with other *sognatore*, Pietro had brought crews from places beyond. Natalie's was one of the first houses that would be subject to the safety inspection, but Pietro hadn't just called in the crews for her. He'd contracted them to come to Zavona and help all of the tenants. They had come and would stay for days.

How? she wondered. How was he paying for all of this? How many favors had he called in? It was obvious that he'd brought a serious team—a team that had worked with him on prior restorations and artisans uniquely suited to some of the work needed for her house—a stonemason for her steps and even a restorationist for her fresco.

How? she asked herself again. Somehow, he'd helped her without defying her, without breaking any of her rules. He'd broken down the one defense that had been her justification for keeping her distance. He hadn't forgotten anyone or left her friends behind. Pietro had a plan for taking care of them all.

Natalie jumped a little and turned her back when she realized the door was opening. Wiping at her face, she worked to compose herself. The din of activity outside filled the space for seconds, rendering it quite loud. Not quickly enough, the door closed again, leaving Natalie not alone. Her companion was inside.

"Natalia."

In just one word, Pietro's voice said so much. When she didn't answer, he sighed. "Please tell me what you need."

For the first time in Natalie's life, she didn't know.

"You've taken care of everything," she whispered.

Pietro shook his head. "No. It is you who did everything for many months. Those who are here now will help you only on this final day."

Natalie hardly knew what to say to that. The bustle happening right then, outside her garage, with fifty people on her property, was hard to measure. Beyond the professional contracting crew, Pietro's family had shown up. Like, his whole family, including nieces and nephews. Even Carlota, who should have been at the store, was laying out baked goods and asking for bourbon last time Natalie checked.

"It was us." Natalie's voice was still a whisper. If she thought of all the elbow grease that had gone into the villa, it hadn't been just her; it had been both of them. "I can't go inside without seeing you everywhere. In every arch and on every wall. I can't even make myself coffee without—" She cut herself off, not knowing where she was going.

"Natalia. If you will allow me, I will apologize."

She gave a little nod. It felt like all that she was capable of doing. It opened the door for Pietro to go on.

"I knew many things about you," he began. "And in spite of knowing those things, I did not give you what you needed. I am sorry for betraying your trust. Please know that it was not malicious. It is something I am ashamed of, something I have not spoken of as a result—the difficult relationship between my father and me."

"I forgive you," she blurted, knowing more than ever that she had forgiven him a long time ago but still not knowing how to reconnect. She hadn't been able to see past this moment—past this final hour and her impending inspection. It occurred to Natalie with some alarm that she had no idea what she might be doing twenty-four hours from now. Packing to go home? Rejoicing? She still couldn't see past those things.

But there was one thing Natalie could see past, one thing that she'd barely let herself think until then—more days spent with Pietro. She could picture time with him more clearly than she could picture the *pensione* thriving and full of guests. Sure, she had spent time with Pietro before, but she could picture situations she had never been in with him—them living together at the *pensione*, in the apartment suite, children running through its halls and around the grounds, swimming in the pool, and the two of them in old age.

"Do not forgive me out of guilt," Pietro warned at the exact moment Natalie was waiting for him to accept her offer greedily and lean in for a kiss.

Natalie shook her head. "I don't want to feel guilty anymore…or inadequate, or afraid."

She took a step toward him, ready to hope out loud for something she had never dared to with anyone before. "I just want to be happy. With you."

CHAPTER THIRTY-SEVEN

Work on Natalie's house turned out to be a marathon of tasks that lasted well into the night and the next morning. Even small tasks, fixes that looked minor on paper, took time when you were handling a property that had more than thirty rooms. There were also things that helpers had taken on that weren't part of the inspection. Less-skilled workers cleaned the moss off the stone on the fountain, even though its inner workings were up to code and operational. Pietro's own nephews chipped away at mowing the lawn.

Then there were the helpers helping the helpers, the ones passing around food and water and tidying up as the main crew worked, the ones who went back and forth to town when reinforcements were needed. Two-thirds of the helpers—the amateurs and the older people—headed out by eight or nine at night, leaving the work needed to pass inspection mostly done. The ones who stayed were the younger people and the professionals.

Pietro had a checklist identical to Natalie's. When he wasn't needed to lend an extra hand, he made rounds, walking through each item on the list as if he were the inspector, making sure every item was well executed and addressing any flaws. The final touches had come together. He saw no way they would not pass.

Just before sunrise, he was shaking the last hand

of the last man on the last construction crew. He'd offered up the house on the hill as a place for them to crash. He had decided to offer all of his unsold houses as lodging for crew as they built up the museum. It was the least he could do, given Roman's generosity.

Pietro made his way back into the house and toward the kitchen to survey who and what was left. His intention was to find Natalie and coax her to go to bed for a few hours, or at least to agree to rest.

"Please. Allow me to do this for you. I think that you should sit."

Pietro stood in the doorway but didn't announce himself, leaning far enough inside that he could see Alfonso and Natalie talking. Or rather, Alfonso pulling the box that held the commercial-grade smoke detector out of Natalie's hands.

Natalie looked like she wanted to protest. She also looked exhausted. Pietro did not want her on a ladder right then, was grateful that—for once—his father seemed to be talking sense.

"You will drink lemon water while I install this," Alfonso commanded gently, setting the smoke detector down on the counter after Natalie let it go. He motioned to a chair, indicating that she should sit down. "Please allow me to fix your water."

"Thank you."

Natalie stifled a yawn as she sat down. Alfonso got to work, washing his hands, then crossing toward the basket of lemons. His nonna had brought her own basket when she'd come earlier that day, had made lemonade and lemon water outside, right at Natalie's outdoor table. The lemons his father would use had been brought over that morning by Pietro.

"Did Pietro ever tell you"—Alfonso began haltingly, pulling a cutting board off an open rack, reaching to a block to get a knife—"the origin of this tradition?"

"Drinking lemon water?" she asked.

Alfonso shook his head. "The men of our family bringing lemons to the women they love. In our family, to bring a woman lemons is as good as a declaration."

When Natalie quieted, Pietro thought to step in. Natalie had enough on her plate without having to explain their relationship to Alfonso. And whatever they had approached earlier that day, in her garage, it was new.

"I'm not used to people giving me things."

It was the first time she had said what Pietro had figured out along the way, the same thing he knew had made her cry in the garage. For Natalie, accepting gifts—even small gifts—was hard.

"Italian men like to treat their wives like princesses." Alfonso was on to slicing now. "Whatever she wants, she gets. You must allow Pietro to give you things. If you do not, he will believe that he has failed."

Alfonso said nothing as Natalie thought. He located a pitcher and filled it halfway with water, added thin slices of whole lemon, and began to stir. Done properly, the ritual of stirring lasted at least a minute. It was followed by more water—just as Alfonso had taught Pietro the ritual himself when Pietro was a boy.

"This is the origin of our tradition. We give

lemons to the woman we love every day because we have seen these lemons give life. We give these lemons to the woman we love because they help her to live longer. And the practice of picking these lemons reminds us to cherish her every day."

"Do you pick lemons for Michaela every day?" Natalie wanted to know, suddenly seeming a bit more alert.

Alfonso nodded. "Yes. Of course."

She seemed to think about this. Her face drew in concentration, so much so that Pietro refused to interrupt.

"What did she do when you first brought lemons to her?"

Alfonso chuckled. "She did not understand our tradition. She did not come from a lemon-growing family or from Campania. She believed that I gave her lemons because I expected her to cook."

Pietro had never heard this story from Alfonso, stories of how he had wooed his mother. Or not, judging from that story.

"How did you start to understand each other?"

Alfonso smiled. "That's easy. We felt to our bones that we were right for one another. This made everything easy. We knew that we had our entire lives to figure things out."

EPILOGUE

"It needs a name."

Natalie sat at her desk in the room they had turned into a front office, the villa's primary administrative space. Their apartment was a no-work zone. In its completed form, it had the same luxurious feeling they had tried to infuse into all of the guest rooms—the grandest suite in the hotel.

"What needs a name?" Pietro asked.

"The *pensione*."

"The *pensione* already has a name. Pensione Benone."

Natalie rolled her eyes. "That was the old owner's name. Don't you think it should have a name that we pick out? A name that's all our own?"

Pietro smiled slyly. "We could always call it Pensione Indelicato."

He had quipped about similar ideas for the better part of a month, the notion that, perhaps, they would soon be married. He had done more than allude to it one night in the lemon groves after they had made love under the stars. He'd said that he wasn't in a rush, because of how they were both tethered now to their village by the sea, that he would ask her to marry him the moment he was sure that she was sure, that she was ready to say yes.

"Indelicato means 'indelicate'..." Natalie trailed off. "No offense, but I don't want to give the wrong impression."

Pietro arched an indignant eyebrow and pretended to be insulted. "And yet my family makes a very delicate limoncello that is celebrated across all of Italy."

"I didn't say you were indelicate—just that your name is."

"All right…" Pietro turned in his drafting chair, facing her squarely now, ready to take the task more seriously. "How about Pensione Malone?"

Natalie thought about this. Gram's last name had also been Malone, which would make it a bit of a tribute.

Having received its final permits meant the *pensione* was finally able to receive guests. Natalie had done a dry run by hosting all her friends and much of Pietro's family two weeks before. She had been at the beginning of what she figured would be a long day, writing descriptions, listing out amenities, and uploading the professional photos that had been taken of the hotel. Creating a listing profile for all of the major booking sites, and having the listing go live, was the final step.

"I kind of want to name it an idea," Natalie admitted to Pietro.

And she wanted it to be perfect. What one word, infused with meaning, could be used to describe this place? What single word encompassed everything she had wished for sight unseen, everything she had made it into now, and everything it was going to be?

She startled at the sound of the doorbell, an electronic one that Pietro had installed the previous week. It rang in only two places—the administrative office, where they sat right then, and the apartment suite.

Natalie swung her gaze to the video console mounted next to the door. As prescribed, it had turned itself on and now displayed a video feed of a man. He was middle-aged and well-dressed for a Tuesday afternoon. He waited patiently at the door.

"Were you expecting anybody?"

Pietro shook his head.

"No one we know would ring the doorbell," Natalie murmured aloud.

She couldn't decipher Pietro's smile, the mix of warmth and excitement that came over his features then.

"Maybe it's your first guest. People in town talk. They will tell visitors about your *pensione*. Tourists frequently become so charmed by Zavona, they will ask at the shops and in the cafés a good place to stay. Many wanderers have found their way, as if by destiny, to this *pensione*."

Natalie felt a small thrill at the notion. She had dreams of what it would be like to host her first real guest, to welcome them to the home she was so proud of, to provide them with a lovely stay.

"Come, Natalia." Pietro rose from his chair and strode the short distance to where Natalie sat, holding out his hand for her to take and pulling her out of her seat. "Do not keep the man waiting."

Natalie took Pietro's cue. He walked behind her as they left the office but kept a bit of a distance, giving her this experience, letting this moment—whatever it might be—belong to her.

"Ciao," Natalie greeted as she swung open the

door. "How can I help you?" she asked in Italian. Since Pietro had moved in, they had followed an Italian-only rule. She was fluent enough to speak it exclusively, though she still had a lot to learn. With the renovations complete, she'd even begun taking an intermediate Italian class in Nanca.

"Natalia Malone?" the man asked in full Italian pronunciation.

"Yes, I'm Natalia," she responded.

More people outside of Pietro had begun using the local spelling of her name.

"I have dreamed of this moment for many years."

Natalie just blinked, mostly because she didn't know how to say, "Um…you have?" yet in Italian. She settled for, "Really?"

The man was older than her by at least twenty years. His hair grayed only a little at the temple, which put him in his fifties, perhaps. Though, with Italian men, age could be difficult to tell. There was something bohemian about him—something that gave him a youthfulness—that caused Natalie to believe he could be quite a bit older than he appeared.

"My name is Franco Pelagatti."

Natalie was grateful that her hand remained on the door. If it hadn't, she might have fallen against it for support.

"You are the granddaughter of Caterina Clearwater," he continued, speaking more slowly—more carefully—to pronounce Gram's maiden name.

"I've been looking for you for more than a year," Natalie managed to breathe.

He smiled sadly. "I've been looking for you for

more than twenty. Or rather, for your grandmother. Is she here with you, in Italy?"

Natalie's thoughts turned sad, and she just shook her head. By then, Pietro had fallen in behind her, brought his hand up to her shoulder.

"She passed away last year," Pietro explained.

"Ah. I see," said Franco. "I'm very sorry to hear that. My father was very fond of her. We searched for your grandmother after my father died. Not being able to carry out one of my father's final wishes has always been one of my biggest regrets. This is why I am so grateful to have found you now."

"How did you find Natalia?" Pietro asked when it was clear that Natalie was nowhere close to finding her voice.

"By tracking down the person who sold my father's painting."

• • •

Three minutes later, Natalie had invited Franco into the villa, escorted him through the living room to the loggia, and sat him down at one of the sunnier tables outside. The air was brisk and somewhat breezy. In the few minutes it took Pietro to go to the kitchens and bring out coffee and biscotti to serve their guest, Natalie had treaded carefully in explaining that Gram had always wanted to return to Campania and that Natalie had searched for Franco when she arrived.

"Tell me everything, please." She could barely contain her anticipation or her fear. Nothing she had found among her grandmother's things proved definitively that she and the elder Franco hadn't had a fling. Still, there was the question of what the younger Franco knew. And now, apparently, there was something to do with the painting she'd sold. All of it baffled her.

"My father was a fisherman," Franco began simply. "Rivela is a fishing town. It is fifteen kilometers farther down the coast."

They were sitting outside, and Franco vaguely motioned to the water.

"Your father was a painter?"

"Yes." Franco nodded. "Much to my mother's chagrin. Painting was not an activity that she encouraged. She believed in his duty to dedicate himself to a fisherman's life. In Rivela, this is a very strong culture, to accept what you have inherited and to continue in the very proud tradition of the village."

"So the paintings my grandmother brought back to America with her...the ones that I sold...he painted those before he dedicated his life to fishing?"

Franco shook his head. "He painted those after he had already bought his fishing boat, during the very early years when he was married to my mother. When I was born, he stopped."

"Did my grandmother know your mother?" Natalie asked, thinking it a far less rude question than to ask directly whether her teenage grandmother had been some sort of mistress.

"My mother knew about your grandmother, yes."

Well, that was vague.

Pietro leaned forward. "Natalia's grandmother was a teenager, a student living on the military base, when your father was in his twenties, a fisherman. How is it that your father and Caterina knew each other?"

Franco put down his coffee and blinked at both of them, wide-eyed. "Do you mean that you do not know?"

Natalie trembled, no longer sure she truly wanted to. Whatever this was, it didn't sound good. "All I know is that your father left my grandmother money. And that she never mentioned him once. And that maybe there's a reason why she never did. Maybe whatever happened between them gave her reason to be ashamed."

"*Ostia...*" Franco breathed. "Since you sold the painting, I assumed you knew. My father was a celebrated artist, though he did not sell work until late in his life. This is why he instructed that money be sent to Caterina. For his most successful painting...she was his muse."

"His most successful painting..." Pietro narrowed his eyes and threw Natalie a suspicious look.

"*The Woman in the Sea*," Franco said with pride. "It's on display in Rome, at the National Gallery of Modern Art. It relates to an old legend about a ghost." He looked at Pietro. "If your grandmother grew up in Rivela, I assure you, this is a legend that she knows."

"His muse?" Natalie could barely get a sentence out.

Franco looked at Natalie and smiled. "Yes. One day, as he sat on the cliffs by Cocenza, a place where he secretly went to paint, he saw your grandmother walking. Her hair was blowing in the wind. The vision struck him, because it was much like a vision that he had seen as a boy. Even on his deathbed, he swore that he had seen the woman in the sea. Your grandmother reminded him so much of this that he begged to be allowed to paint her. The two of you look very much alike."

Pietro looked at Natalie, waiting for her to react. It seemed she couldn't speak.

"It explains how they met." Pietro spoke for her. "But it doesn't explain the money."

Two pairs of eyes looked back to Franco.

"It only happens in the movies that paintings take a short period of time to compose. Great paintings can take weeks or months. Many artists who paint models pay them money, but my father had nothing. Week after week, they met each other in Cocenza, on the same cliffs. And week after week, my father paid her in the only currency he could. He paid Caterina in paintings."

"Then the money he left her…" Natalie trailed off, still trying to let all of it sink in.

"He sold *The Woman in the Sea* for a good amount, just one year before his death. He believed that your grandmother deserved half, that what he paid her all those years ago was not enough."

Pietro frowned and rooted around in his pocket. Natalie was surprised to see him pull out his phone. "If Franco Pelagatti was a famous painter, why didn't we find anything about that when we searched for it online?"

"My father could not sign his name to his own work. My mother did not approve. Even when he sold *The Woman in the Sea*, he did not correct his pseudonym—Condi. Only five of my father's paintings were ever discovered. The art world took notice when a sixth painting appeared. Though, I regret to inform you, you were not paid a fair price."

A speechless Natalie thought of the $7,500, which had seemed like a fortune at the time. But this… Natalie still couldn't wrap her head around it. This was beyond her wildest dreams.

"Not just six." Natalie's voice sounded hoarse and scratchy to her own ears. "Fourteen."

Franco's eyes went wide. "You have more of my father's paintings?"

She nodded slowly. "All of them. I still have eight more."

"If you would ever honor me by showing them to me, I would like to see them."

When Franco choked up, Natalie did, too.

She stood up. "Come on. I'll take you now. One of them is right here, just in the library."

Natalie led the way back inside.

"If I may be so bold as to offer unsolicited advice," Franco offered as he walked in behind Natalie. "I would advise you to be very careful with these paintings and to take precautions that perhaps you think you do not need. These days, young people are very casual with their belongings. But please. Have these paintings insured."

ACKNOWLEDGMENTS

The first time I visited Italy was on a trip with my mother—a long tour of Europe that began in Rome. I was twenty years old, living in Paris at the time. She was coming from the U.S. and I flew down to meet her at Fiumicino. So began the adventure we never stopped talking about.

This book wouldn't have been the same without her influence. Like Natalie's grandmother, she was a lover of Italian architecture and art who spent years studying its beauty and culture from afar. I will never forget the joy and awe and satisfaction on her face as we experienced Italy together—how she knew all the grand buildings, celebrated paintings, and important places before ever stepping foot on Italian soil.

My mother was also like Natalie. She never let go her dreams. She never wrote herself off. She liked to walk and wander and explore. Zavona is a fictional town but, if my mother were ever to visit, she, too, would have availed herself of the *pasticceria* and befriended Nonna through visits to her antiques shop.

The other people who deserve credit for this book are the people who keep me sane and who give me the space to write. To my real-life romance hero, Mr. Blades, thank you for holding down the fort when I needed to go into my writing cave. Thanks to my assistant, Ed, for keeping me on track.

Weekly talks and Sunday brunches with the Struggle Bus Crew kept me motivated and full of good ideas, as did three-margarita lunches at Sailor Jack's with my author besties. Endless thanks to the very best plotting partner, Eva Moore, and to all the friends who helped me get unstuck at Pickford House and Central Valley retreats.

And, of course, this project would not have happened without my amazing agent, Julie Gwinn, who matched me with Liz Pelletier and the top-notch team at Entangled. Liz, Lydia, Riki, and Jessica: thank you for believing in my work and making key decisions conversations. I feel supported, seen and heard. Having the right team in my corner has made all the difference.

It Takes a Villa is a heartwarming story of love, family, and community set in a charming Italian seaside town. However, the story includes elements that might not be suitable for some readers. Scenes depicting the collapse of a building and the search-and-rescue efforts that follow are included in the novel. Readers who may be sensitive to these, please take note.

Get swept away by another Italian romance from USA Today *bestselling author Kilby Blades.*

Turn the page to start reading for FREE!

CHAPTER ONE

The thrill of checking her mailbox when she got home was second only to the rush of excitement Zuri felt every day when she left work. Sweeping aside her thick curls and extricating herself from her employee ID lanyard was like taking off a yoke. Each afternoon, she tucked it into the pocket of her satchel before bursting onto the busy San Francisco sidewalk, foregoing a leg on MUNI in favor of a single train home and a longer walk to BART. On the platform, and then again on the train, she liked to crack open a book and read happily as the train moved her beneath the city and whisked her across the bay.

Her mailbox was of the small Oakland apartment variety. It held only letters, but the post office wasn't far. Zuri never minded finding one of the orange slips the color of baby aspirin telling her to go pick up a package. She liked to buy from the local shops—mostly paper products and gardening supplies—but specialty items, she ordered from afar.

A sense of calm always overtook her when she opened the wrought-iron gates of home, an old Victorian that was taller than it was wide. Unlike its brightly-painted contemporaries, it felt retro. It had a brown shingled exterior, green trim on the windows, and a quaint front porch.

Walking carefully from the gate to the door was always a necessity. The patterned brick pathway was in bad repair. The building was what some would consider to be run down. Zuri thought it had great, old bones that just needed a little TLC. Its lack of updating was why it came at such an attractive price.

"Zuri! I hoped that was you."

Zuri's hand left her mailbox key suspended when she heard her friend, Nichole. It wasn't uncommon for her to peer out of her own apartment door when she heard a lower door slam. In the space between was a tiny anteroom that housed three mailboxes. The converted house was owned by Mark and Jacob, who lived on the ground floor.

"Oh, hey Nic!"

Zuri took her hand off of her mailbox key and took a step backward, craning her neck to look up. Nichole peered over the second-floor bannister, then began to descend. It was a sign Zuri was in for a longer conversation. Nichole's long braids swished as she skipped down the hardwood stairs in socked feet and stopped on the bottom step.

"First, be happy for me." Nichole's natural pattern of speech was to issue commands. She had the rare ability to do it without making it sound bossy. Out of all the neighbors Zuri had during her six years in the building, Nichole was her favorite. Zuri raised her eyebrows expectantly, waiting for Nichole to spill.

"I got accepted! The Cordon Bleu. The nine-month intensive in France."

Zuri grinned in shared excitement. "I expect you to bring me back Omar Sy and a beret."

"I'll bring you back more than that if you do me a big, pain-in-the-ass favor."

Zuri raised an eyebrow.

"Will you take care of my plot in the garden?"

Nichole gave Zuri a look that was both pleading and triumphant. It was no secret, Zuri had longed for more land. Both of them were lucky to have gotten spots in the Grand Lake Community Garden. Zuri couldn't blame Nichole for not wanting to give it up.

Zuri pretended to think. "So that adds up to, like, three berets."

Nichole smirked. "When I'm a Michelin Star chef, I'll serve you free dinner for life."

"They'll let you keep your plot even if you give up your address?"

She smiled triumphantly. "Mark and Jacob are letting me sublet. So, it'll still be my lease."

Zuri shook her head and put all her energy into being happy for her friend. Nichole didn't need to see all the other emotions her news was dredging up.

"Seriously. Congratulations."

Nichole gave one final, excited squeal before hopping back upstairs. Whatever she had on the stove smelled savory and divine. Zuri smiled after her friend as she retreated, her lips quivering against a smile that longed to fade.

Nichole was the third person who had lived on the second floor since Zuri had lived in the building. She was also the third person to leave in pursuit of a big adventure. It was getting harder not to feel left behind. Phoebe, the aspiring veterinarian, had joined the Peace Corps and been sent off to Burundi. Robin, the artisan ice cream maker, had moved to Switzerland to run a goat farm. Even Mark and

Jacob had trotted off to Ireland one summer, taking six weeks away to track down Mark's family roots.

Zuri, too, might have dreamed herself away from this place if she'd only had time for dreaming. But dreams required rest, the luxurious sort of sleep that imagined what could be. She was focused on more essential things, like paying off student loan debt and being able to afford to eat. In addition to supporting herself, she sent money to her mother.

When she turned back to her mailbox, her key still jutted out, the others on the ring swinging where they hung. Zuri refocused on what might be waiting: a note from her pen pal, or—more likely—the latest newsletter from her favorite paper maker, Emporio. She had the sort of tall, old mailbox that forced letters to be set upright. At a single glance, she could predict what awaited her. She gasped in delight at the sight of the envelope that was too short to be a bill.

It has to be from Alessandro.

Knowing how long a letter could take to travel from Italy to the U.S., Zuri loved that it had arrived with astounding speed. She'd been afraid that running the letters through an intermediary would slow things down. Emporio managed the exchange and oversaw the sanitizing of personal data. Given all the predators and creeps she'd seen at Hookupz, Zuri liked the idea of security controls.

Huh. That's odd.

The envelope felt light and that the paper seemed cheap, nothing like what Alessandro had sent in his initial letter. Participation in the pen pal program came with a subscription to Emporio's finest stationery club. But maybe he'd used a different product. Light weight air mail paper used to be a thing.

THIS MAIL ORIGINATED FROM AN INMATE AT SAN QUENTIN STATE PRISON

Taking in the stamped-on words on the front of the envelope halted Zuri's thoughts, a visceral reaction to the intrusion taking hold. The letter on the cheap paper wasn't from Alessandro. It was from the only other person in the world who wasn't allowed to have her address. This letter was from her dad.

CHAPTER TWO

"Sandro."

Niccolo spoke his brother's name as he happened upon him on the verandah. Alessandro thumbed his phone screen and looked relaxed. His ears were pink at the tips from the crisp mid-autumn and he was typically overdressed—as always, a bit too fashionable for the forest.

Nico himself had wandered outdoors, steaming mug of *cioccolata calda* in his hands, intent on enjoying the fresh air and the changing colors of the trees. It was a ritual he performed daily—though his drink changed with the season—upon his return home from the mills.

"Ciao, Nico."

Alessandro rose from his seat, giving Nico time to set down his cup. The men came together for their customary cheek kiss and embrace. Alessandro's visit was not unwelcome, only unannounced. Nico living on their ancestral estate meant that anyone who had once lived there was entitled to call it home. At the moment, it was only Nico who inhabited the *cascina*—so grand that it looked more like a small castle than a large farmhouse—close to their paper mills but miles from the center of town and deep within their forest.

"Do you want a hot chocolate?"

Nico gestured to his own steaming cup. Alessandro needed no invitation to raid the kitchen.

But lately, he'd acted like a bit of a guest. Nico couldn't tell whether this had simply stopped feeling like home to Alessandro or whether tension around Nico's divorce had wrenched some new formality into their space.

"No, thanks. I just had a coffee."

Alessandro pocketed his phone and sat back down, angling his chair toward the table and away from the rolling hills below. The brothers sat facing one another after Nico did the same. Nico lifted his cup to take a satisfying sip. This was his favorite time of day—a time when the sun had burnt off the thick layer of morning mist that sometimes lingered well into afternoon. The forest was beautiful at any hour but he enjoyed moments when the vista was this clear.

"How are things?" Nico asked, as if the two hadn't spoken the day before.

"Marlena had her baby."

Marlena was Alessandro's assistant now. She had worked for Nico before they changed everything about the way they ran the company. These days, Nico rarely ventured to Salerno to assume his rightful position in the executive office. These days, he relegated himself to the foreman's office at the mills.

"Boy or girl?"

"A boy. Franco," Alessandro replied.

Of course. Franco was Marlena's husband. Nico himself had been named after his own late father. Such was the honor of the firstborn son.

"I'll have a gift sent over," Nico concluded.

"It would be more polite to take it over yourself. I'm sure they would love to see you."

Nico was sure the only people the sleep-deprived parents of a newborn would love to see were Nonnas and Poppas and aunties and uncles who would relieve them when they needed a rest. He was also sure that wasn't why his brother had suggested he deliver the gift. Alessandro was worried about him—had attempted for weeks to coax Nico to venture anywhere other than the mills.

Nico had his reasons for staying in—reasons Alessandro knew well. He would sooner hide away for a year than indulge the paparazzi. Nico shrugged noncommittally, neither confirming or denying his plan. Alessandro knew better than to push.

"The pen pal program is going well," Alessandro mentioned. More news of the world.

Nico's ears perked up. "Of course it was."

The opportunity had been obvious. Correction. The opportunity had been obvious to Nico, who—along with thousands of dedicated customers—understood the sublime joy of the handwritten note.

"I signed up for the program myself." Alessandro stopped long enough to give a little laugh. "But writing the letters has been tricky. My English is not good."

Nico smiled against his cup as he finished taking a sip. Alessandro wasn't strong on written communications. He would sooner pick up the phone and talk or send a flurry of texts than he would write an email.

"Why did you even sign up?"

"Bianca thought it would be a good idea for the CEO of the company to participate in the program, that it would make for a good media piece. We need the good press right now."

Nico bit his tongue against words he'd said before, about his brother's tendency to make promises he couldn't keep. He had also learned to keep his mouth shut about Alessandro's habit of leaning into the optics. Nico cared only about the way things were. Sandro cared how they looked.

"What did you think was going to happen?" Nico quizzed. "That Bianca would take care of writing the letters too?"

Alessandro's sheepish look proved that he had. His voice was petulant when he replied. "I thought she would find somebody to help."

Nico smirked.

"You know how difficult she can be," Alessandro complained. "She reminded me that she is not my assistant, though she ought to rethink her position. Technically, I am her boss."

"What about your actual assistant?" Nico questioned next. "The one who is filling in for Marlena?"

"Elena's English is worse than mine. She has never spent time abroad."

It wasn't any strike against her that she'd chosen not to leave such a beautiful place. Campania was idyllic. Plenty of Italian people studied English at some point, but few spoke or wrote the language as well as Nico did. The apprenticeship he had completed in England in his late teens had rendered him functionally fluent.

"But, you know, Nico, you like to write letters..." Alessandro trailed off, his voice heavy with suggestion. "And you ought to have contact with someone if you refuse to leave the house."

Nico didn't point out that he left the house daily, to go to the mills.

"How long would I have to do it for?"

Nico knew nothing of the mechanics of the program. He had handed it off as an undeveloped idea.

"Just one year. Eleven more months at this point. If penpals wish to be in direct contact after that, Emporio gets out of the middle."

Nico shot off a questioning look. "Why would we be in the middle?"

"To protect us from liability."

Nico didn't like the way his brother answered by rote.

"We did background checks. Held an application process. Participants signed contracts agreeing to the rules."

"Let me guess." Nico frowned. "This was Bianca's idea."

Alessandro threw Nico a sharp look. "This is what we hired her for. Salvatore was like family, but it is because of him that we are so exposed. Bianca represents a change that Emporio needs."

The way things had ended with Salvatore still left a bad taste in Nico's mouth. They had forced early retirement upon their General Counsel of twenty years. It had come as a result of Nico's divorce, and a claim to the business his ex was suing for. It was loophole Salvatore should have insulated them against.

Threat of losing part of the company led to the hiring of Bianca, a bulldog attorney and a colleague who Nico despised. Bianca was cold and ruthless, but charismatic. She'd become increasingly adept at coaxing Alessandro to her side.

"OK." Nico acquiesced. "I will write your letters."

Alessandro seemed pleased. "I'll send you the first one I received. I have already written a reply. All you have to do is translate."

Nico watched Alessandro rise from his seat, ready to leave now that he'd gotten what he wanted. He was almost to the door when Nico thought of the perfect thing.

"I will graciously give you an opportunity to return the favor,"Nico called out to his brother's back. Alessandro turned around with a smirk, clearly sensing mischief.

"What is this favor, brother?"

"I will write your penpal letters if you keep Bianca off my back."

• • •

Elena had emailed the letters as digital attachments that Nico didn't bother to open. Why, when you couldn't tell anything about a person from that kind of rendition? Looking at the scan of a paper letter was like looking at a picture of a picture. In theory, it was the same thing. But only in theory. If Nico was going to write to this person, he needed the originals.

Now that he went to headquarters less, his correspondence was driven to his estate by courier, an extension of interoffice mail. He had gotten back to Elena that morning with a request for the original to be sent up. It was the only way for Nico to know. Now, he sat at his massive desk on the second floor of the *cascina*. What had once been a library now served as his personal office space. Light flooded through the tall, arched window, next to which he had placed his desk. It had the best view in the house of the forest hills below.

130 gram paper. Interesting.

120 grams was standard weight. The 130 gram paper was from their special line. Nico picked up and began to inspect the envelope with the precision of a forensic investigator, turning the item in his hand. He liked that she had written her return address on the back instead of crowding the front with both.

Zuri Robinson

Her handwriting was uniquely beautiful. Cursive script was a lost art. Nico had heard they no longer taught it in American schools. He couldn't guess at the origins of her name, but learning it gave him a thrill. There was something magical about corresponding with people from miles away—something magical in knowing that the planes and trains and trucks and ships that delivered notes between people separated lives that were worlds apart.

The stock that she had chosen was from their Amalfi line. It was one of Nico's personal favorites. It wasn't a top seller, but none of the long form letter paper was. Emporio's bread and butter were notecards of the thank you variety, and custom engraved pieces for personal desks. The paper that Zuri had written on was paper for the serious enthusiast.

When he pulled out the letter, he was able to confirm what the thickness and weight alone had already told him: that three pages were contained within. He had forgotten the simple delight of sustained correspondence—of writing to someone for pleasure. He could only hope to find the same in the heart of the person within.

Dear Alessandro,

It's a pleasure to be in contact. Thank you for writing the first letter. I hope you'll excuse any missteps as we write to each other in the coming year. I've never had a penpal, though, even as I write that sentence, I realize that it's not completely true.

My grandmother was my first penpal. She and I wrote letters when I was young. She wasn't very good with phone or email and she lived far away. Writing to each other was the way we stayed in touch. She always wrote on beautiful paper, which made me want to do the same. I was nine or ten when I walked into my first stationery store.

Ever since then, I have loved shopping for paper, and collecting paper, and writing letters, and sending cards. The people at my post office know me by name. But it's been ten years since my grandma died, and I didn't realize how much I missed writing letters until Emporio posted about the program. Have you ever had a penpal? What were they like?

You asked me where I'm from. I forgot that our personal information is anonymous. I was born and raised in California. Have you ever been?

Thanks for telling me you're from Italy. I've never been there, but I know all about the canals in Venice and the art in Florence and the Colosseum in Rome. Do you live near any of those places? The food in Italy is supposed to be delicious no matter where you go.

I'd like to visit for that reason alone. My neighbor

is a chef who cooks much better than me, but I love to cook, too. Most of my food tastes good because my produce is so fresh. I have a little garden plot that I'm very proud of. How about you?

Until Next Time,

Zuri

The "Z" in her signature was a grand affair, with the stem of the final stroke extending far to the right. It seemed to cradle and organize the remaining three letters of her name. Purple ink wasn't a color Nico would have thought of, but the shade of plum she chose contrasted beautifully with the paper.

The second envelope in the folder was Alessandro's response, the one that only needed translation. Curious, Nico unfolded the single sheet and began to read.

Dear Zuri,

You sound like an interesting person. I like vegetables, too. I have never grown them myself, but I like to eat them at restaurants.

California must be hot. Do you know how to surf? I tried once, and was very good at it. What sports do you play? Living in California, you must be very fit, and probably blonde.

To answer your question, I live in a region of Italy called Campania. Perhaps you have heard of Naples? This is Campania's largest city. I live in a smaller city and I was born in a very small town. In Campania, we are famous for growing lemons that taste very good though I do not grow them myself. You must like citrus too, living in California…(ha-ha). Have you ever met any movie stars?

You asked about my job. I'm the CEO of

Emporio, the paper company which is running this program. Thank you for being a loyal customer.

Alessandro

Nico didn't bother to read this one a second time. It was not a letter he was willing to send. It read like it was written by an eight-year-old. Nico had never seen a single composition jam in so many stereotypes about a place. Alessandro seemed to think that California was teeming with overheated amateur athletes who snacked on oranges whenever they weren't cooling off in the surf.

Alessandro's idea to come out and tell Zuri he was the CEO of Emporio also didn't sound very bright. Didn't that defeat the purpose of anonymity? It would skew things for her to know. People acted differently, the closer they got to power. Nico would not be including anything that identified him as heir to one of Southern Italy's most notable fortunes. And he certainly would not be thanking her for being a loyal customer.

Nico pulled a third envelope out of the parcel Elena had sent. It held the most practical of things: a stack of clean letterhead and envelopes monogrammed with Alessandro's initials. This would be Nico's blank slate—his clean palette for writing something much, much better than his brother had. He rose from his desk, thinking already of which fountain pen he would use. Today—this morning—he would write Zuri her reply.

• • •

Falling in love wasn't part of the fake marriage ruse in this new small-town romantic comedy.

accidentally PERFECT

MARISSA CLARKE

Workaholic Lillian Mahoney has given *everything* to her job. The hugely popular lifestyle show she helped create monopolizes her time, energy, creativity, and anything remotely resembling a life. But all it takes is the show's womanizing, egomaniac star throwing a massive hissy on live TV to utterly implode Lillian's career in a New York minute.

Now Lillian's hiding out in the gorgeous and completely unknown seaside village of Blink, Maine. Out of gas. A stolen wallet. A broken heel. And worse, she's somehow managed to completely piss off the town's resident hunk, Caleb Wright. She'll show that hot, grumpy single father *exactly* what she's made of.

But Blink isn't quite what Lillian expects—and neither is Caleb...or his feisty teen daughter she can't help but love. And while her entire life and career are in shreds, Lillian might just discover what happens when she gives her bad first impression a second chance...

From the bestselling author of the Angel Falls series, two enemies say "I do" in the first irresistible book about Blossom Glen.

the SWEETHEART DEAL

MIRANDA LIASSON

Pastry chef Tessa Montgomery knows what everyone in the teeny town of Blossom Glen says about her. *Spinster. Ice Queen. Such a shame.* It's enough to make a woman bake her troubles away, dreaming of Parisian delicacies while she makes bread at her mother's struggling boulangerie. That is until Tessa's mortal enemy deliciously handsome (if arrogant) chef Leo Castorini, who owns the restaurant next door—proposes a business plan…to get married.

Leo knows that the Castorinis and the Montgomerys hate each other, but a marriage might just force these stubborn families to work together and blend their businesses for success. The deal is simple: Tessa and Leo marry, live together for six months, and then go their separate ways. Easy peasy.

It's a sweetheart deal where everyone gets what they want—until feelings between the faux newlyweds start seriously complicating the mix. Have they discovered the perfect recipe for success…or is disaster on the way?

Secret crushes, stolen kisses, and a scandalous confession set the course of this clever new rom-com from USA Today *bestselling author Tawna Fenkse.*

Nurse Nyla Franklin knows three things to be true. Taking care of others brings more joy than a basket full of kittens. A triple-fudge sundae can cure just about anything. And no good ever comes from keeping a secret... So when her best friend spills his biggest one ever, Nyla knows she's not just holding a secret. She's holding a ticking time bomb.

Mr. Always Does the Right Thing Leo Sayre knows three things to be true. Piloting smokejumpers over burning forests is the best job in the world. His best friend Nyla is the smartest, funniest, and okay, sexiest woman ever. And pain meds are apparently his truth serum. Now his post-surgery confession has everything flipped upside down and turned inside out... including his relationship with Nyla.

Secrets have a way of piling up, and it's just a matter of time before someone lights a match. Because while the truth can set you free, it can also burn completely out of control...

AMARA
an imprint of Entangled Publishing LLC